THE ROYAL GAUNTLET

GAME OF GODS BOOK 3

NICOLE SANCHEZ

First paperback edition May 2023

Edited by Tashya Wilson and Amanda Iles

Cover Art by Karen Dimmick / ArcaneCovers.com

Header and Page Break art by Leigh Cover Designs

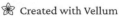

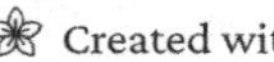 Created with Vellum

For the dreamers and doers – don't be afraid to write your own happily ever after

Author's Note

As an author, it is important to me that all my readers to feel safe when reading my books. Some elements of this story may be upsetting to some readers. If you're not interested in learning more, please feel free to turn the page. If you have concerns, please see the list below:

Pregnancy, miscarriage (past), cutting as part of a ritual which could be triggering for self harm. Please protect your mental health..

If you need further clarity or are concerned about an unmentioned trigger, please feel free to email me at author.nicolesanchez@gmail.com

"I just want to talk."

I can't help it. I scoff at my mother-in-law. Choosing to have a conversation in a dark cavern of the Underworld doesn't exactly scream friendly chat, especially not after luring me here under false pretenses.

Octavia frowns at my reaction. It's the delicate droop of the corners of her mouth that draws the inappropriate laugh from my own. Once I start, I can't stop.

She crosses her arms and taps her finger against her bicep in time with her foot. I've had the rug pulled out from under me many times in the past twenty-four hours, but having my mother-in-law pose as my lady's maid wasn't even a consideration for my bingo card.

And then I'm doubled over as the laughs keep coming and tears are leaking down my face. If I keep laughing like this, I might pee myself too.

"I'm sorry," I manage to wheeze out, and my dog-guardian, Dave, glances between the two of us.

"Really, Daphne," Octavia scolds.

"I'm okay," I assure her before another fit of giggles starts. I straighten up, wiping my eyes. "I'm just—you *really* are a monster-in-law. This is where you're going to have a little villain's monologue and make demands of me." My giggles stop abruptly. "But you forget, Octavia, this is *my* realm. You're just a guest here."

My hands reach forward, and I appear to pull on nothingness, but then pieces of plants, roots and the like, emerge from the ceiling and the ground, extending toward Octavia.

"That's what you think, but you're always going to be a little girl playing in my sandbox."

Octavia's retaliation is swift. With a squeeze of her fist, she cuts off my air. I release the hold on my roots and try to force my fingers between the invisible ones that are severely restricting my oxygen supply. There is no getting between them.

Dave must sense my distress, because I can hear him barking like mad, but the sound is getting farther and farther away until everything goes horrifyingly dark.

I'M startled awake by a cool hand on my cheek and for a moment, I think it's Essos. But then the memory of the morning comes rushing in and I flinch back. It's not Essos. It's Octavia.

The last twenty-four hours have been a whirlwind, and being face-to-face with my mother-in-law might be the straw that breaks the proverbial camel's back.

"Welcome back to the land of the living, Phoenix Queen."

From my vantage point on the ground, I glance around the cavern. I can feel a soreness through my body from when I landed on the damp ground. "I think this is still the realm of the dead," I point out. Dave is beside me, having placed himself between me and the

Goddess Supreme. I don't know when I last saw her in the flesh, but seeing her now can't be good news.

"Are you capable of being compliant for once in your life? My *gods* you've been a thorn in my side ever since you agreed to go to dinner with Essos."

I sit up slowly, aware of how woozy I feel. I hope she didn't deprive me of oxygen for long, but still, my hand brushes my abdomen. Essos was right—I need to worry about more than just myself now.

"As Goddess of Spring, thorns come with the territory," I point out, which earns me a dry look. Despite my assault, the six-foot-tall goddess looks unruffled. My dog, however, looks like he's ready to tear her limb from limb despite whatever role she might have played in his creation.

"If you would stop being so fucking dramatic, you would know that I was coming to *help*. After all, you have a few problems to solve, such as the gates to the Underworld being slammed shut and the veil between the realms being ripped open."

I want to scoff again—the idea that the gates to the Underworld are closed is absurd—but it offers an explanation as to why it feels so empty down here, even though souls have surely passed during the time since Posey revealed herself as the source of our problems.

We knew that Posey did *something* to the souls of the dead. I thought it was as simple as collecting them and sending them back to the mortal realm, but clearly, it's more. My hand goes to the cut on my neck where she nicked me with the God Killer blade. She cut Essos too, when she snatched the scepter from him. Was that intentional? Did she do something to seal the gates of the Underworld so no souls can enter?

I have to hear how Octavia thinks she can help. I get to my feet, bolstered by Dave gluing himself to me. "You have my attention, Octavia. Don't waste it, because once Essos arrives, there will be no hearing you out."

"Might I point out that *you* were the one wasting time? Instead of being my ally, now you have to be my pawn." She smooths her hands over the front of her white dress, and a bolt of unease makes my hair stand on end.

"I am no one's pawn, Octavia."

She looks me over, blue eyes critical. "From what I've seen, that's all you are. A pawn between my sons. A pawn for a Fate. I want you to bring back my son. I'm asking you nicely. I've already taken the necessary steps to ensure he has a body to return to."

"That doesn't feel like a 'nicely' sort of request. That feels like a demand." A cool sweat is breaking out on my skin. I taste bile in the back of my throat at just the *idea* of resurrecting the God of War and Suffering. I don't care that he's her son. I don't care that he's my husband's brother. I don't care why she wants me to bring him back.

Galen murdered me, and for the first time in ages, I'm free of the threat he posed to me. I'm free of my fear of him. Bringing Galen back is not an option.

"It was going to be a nice request, but then you struck first."

I open my mouth to further press the argument, but the ground trembles beneath my feet. Octavia meets my gaze and blanches. She must sense it too.

My husband is coming.

My husband is coming, and I don't know who he's going to be madder at—me, or his mother. I didn't set out to upset him. Okay, maybe that's a *little* bit of a lie. But I'm pregnant, not some liability to be locked away until the threat has passed.

The ground shakes again, and Octavia looks at me, a flash of fear in her eyes. She is the Goddess Supreme and can create life on a whim, but my husband can bring destruction and ruin. It's why he's always kept a tether on his power. He knows it could be catastrophic, but causing destruction is not who he is as a god.

"I want you to bring back my son. If you want any hope of defeating Posey, you're going to need his help. You're going to need *my* help. Don't say no out of spite. I can be your ally or your enemy. The choice is yours."

Then she's gone, leaving me to wonder just how much truth there is to her claims. My calm façade cracks, and I bury my head in my hands, choking back a sob. That's how Essos finds me, his anger crackling in the air around him.

I lift my watery gaze to him, and after he thoroughly surveys the cavern around me for a threat, he advances on me, features softening.

"Daphne, what is it?"

The anger I expected to find isn't there, just concern. I'm sure once we're past the initial confirmation that I'm fine, his ire will find its way to me, but right now, my whole body is trembling.

Essos gathers me into his arms and smooths my hair until I settle down. Just having him in my breathing space calms me enough to meet his eye.

"It was your mother," I tell him with a gasp.

Essos nods. "I know." I stiffen in his arms and pull back to really look at him. "Her perfume. It's always been cloying. It's part of why I hate roses. Are you hurt?"

I shake my head, finding my strength again. "I did this." I gesture around us at the cracks and rocks.

There's a hint of pride in the smile Essos gives me. "What did she want?"

"Something that is *never* going to happen."

Essos tucks me into his side and teleports us home.

Essos gets me nestled into bed, and I feel a little like a child, but I haven't stopped shaking. He tugs the comforter up to my chest and summons a mug of hot chocolate for me. Waffles, my cat from when I was a mortal, decides to get in on the action and curls up in my lap.

"I would appreciate an explanation," Essos demands softly, tension stiffening his shoulders even as he sits on my side of our bed, one thumb idly rubbing my arm.

"Miranda told me that Celestina might still be alive. But I don't think there ever was a Miranda. I think she was always your mother."

He nods like this makes sense. "And who is Celestina?" It's a valid question, but it makes me sink into my pillows, weighed down by all the things we haven't been able to share.

"She's a reporter for the *Solarem Sun* that I leaked information to about how Galen was handling the Trials."

"We hate the *Solarem Sun*, so I'm a touch confused *why* you would do that." There is a curtness to his voice that I don't love, and I turn in on myself. When he sees my reaction, he shakes his head. "I'm sorry. I don't mean to be short, but my wife and child were in danger *again* right after I almost lost you both. You're avoiding explaining what happened because you know I'm angry about you leaving the house after we discussed you staying here."

This jolts a different sort of response from me, and I nearly shove him off the bed. "*We* did not discuss it. *You* decided that I was going to be your pliant little queen and incubate our child while you went out and did the man's work of defeating the woman who has been gunning for us for a truly embarrassing amount of time. You know exactly who you married, and I'm not going to change."

It's a far cry from the stark realization I came to earlier, that if Octavia wanted to, she could have killed our child before they breathed. If I want to ensure that this baby has a future, then I have to fight for it myself.

"What did my mother want?" Essos demands through clenched teeth, ignoring the issue at hand.

"She wants us to bring Galen back. Claims that she and Galen will both help us if we do." The fight winks out of me when I give voice to the idea that it's even something we could do. Finn has taken care to hide the god-killing dagger after being the one to pull it from Galen's body. Without it, Octavia can't bring back her favorite child. It was always a possibility that we would need Galen; that's why the dagger containing his soul was placed somewhere safe, so we had him on ice. I just never expected the time would come so soon.

"No," Essos says. "This is not up for negotiation."

"He was your brother," I point out. I don't know why I say it. Guilt, I think, for having been the one to come between the siblings. I didn't do anything wrong, didn't instigate Galen's infatuation, but he was fixated on me all the same.

"He ceased being my brother the moment he pursued my wife against her will. Daphne, I'm not going to agree to bring Galen back unless it's an absolute last resort."

"Octavia said she'll help us if we do it. What if we need her?"

Essos shakes his head and tries to settle me back into bed by gently pushing my shoulder so I have to relax into the pillows. I allow it. In truth, I want the bed to swallow me whole, only to spit me out once we've defeated Posey.

"We won't need her. I won't let us rely on her goodwill—she's too capricious. This is all so new. We need time to come up with a plan to take Posey down. My mother is just looking to get in your head. Don't let her."

"I just...I need a *break*, Essos. I've died, gone through the Calling, and been dealing with the Trials. All I want is to be able to lie down and *sleep*."

Essos climbs into bed and pulls me toward him, dislodging Waffles. The cat glares at both of us and hops off to make himself at home on the lounge in front of the window.

"I'm making this suggestion as your concerned partner, not as a father-to-be trying to restrict you. Let me handle what is going on with the realms for a little while. If something dire happens, I'll loop you in, but you said it yourself—you're tired. I'm sure we can find something for you to do. Gods, we both know Cat is going to need help adjusting."

I let him hook his body around mine, creating a comforting cocoon in the form of arms and legs. "Do we tell Xavier and the others about Octavia's offer?"

Essos's body goes stiff, but then he seems to consciously relax himself as he tugs me tighter. "No one needs to know."

"Are you certain?" I ask, sitting up. Essos is beside me on the bed, and he squeezes my hand. My shirt is pulled up and away from my stomach as a midwife checks me over. Her soft hands still frame my belly. I miss the modern technology of the mortal realm that would have let me see and hear the baby. There's knowing, and then there is *knowing*. I want that hard evidence.

"As certain as I can be. I would estimate conception sometime after the Calling ended. You're around seventeen weeks." The healer's wording is careful but pointed. She wants Essos to know that I got pregnant after he left, while I was putting on the best performance of my life.

I pull down my shirt, knocking her hands aside. "If you're trying to insinuate that this child is not my husband's, save your breath." I move out of Essos's grip and get off the bed to push past this woman. A carpet of greenery follows in my wake, energy and righteous anger crackling through my veins.

I move to the large bay windows and cross my arms. I can feel how my stomach protrudes, like I've had too many tacos and chips on dollar-taco night.

Essos comes up behind me and places a hand on my shoulder. It's silent solidarity, and I reward him by reaching a hand up to his.

"I didn't mean to insinuate anything," the woman tries to hedge, but the way she glances at Essos tells me all I need to know. She thinks my husband is a cuckold.

"Thank you. That will be all," Essos commands. His voice is firm and dismissive even while being the height of politeness.

When I hear the door close, I turn to him. "This child is–"

"I know, love. You don't have to defend yourself to me." His rich blue eyes soften me like butter left out too long.

"No, I'm just going to have to explain myself to the realms. Why did I think the Trials were a good idea?" I pace away from him, cutting across the floor toward the paper Essos was reading this morning. He's been trying to shield me from the vitriol spewing in my direction. I went from being a beloved queen welcomed back from the dead with open arms the night of the Calling Ball to...to this cloistered pariah.

Essos scoops up the paper and throws it onto the chaise lounge by the window. Today's headline wonders when the Underworld will reopen to our employees. We're being accused of keeping people from their livelihoods; meanwhile, we're just trying to get a full grip on what went wrong and what we need to fix.

It hasn't even been a week since Posey turned our world upside down. In an effort to keep tensions low, I've let Essos be the one to venture out, whether to the Underworld itself or to check on his brother Xavier, King of the Gods, who is staying in our apartment in Solarem. Meanwhile, I've had Sybil help me back into the Underworld banking systems, which I'd been locked out of during the Trials.

I've sat at home, biding my time, reviewing numbers while Essos has been out investigating. It worked out somewhat because, after the stress of my almost-wedding to Galen, my body wanted me to sleep forever, but now I'm feeling clearheaded and ready to face the world.

Our biggest struggle to date is that as each soul passes from life, it comes to the Underworld only to boomerang back to the mortal realm. Nothing Essos has tried works to keep the souls inside, and his continued insistence that I not get involved is only making things worse.

At Cat's request, I've given her the space she wants to try to digest this new revelation that she too is a goddess reborn, only, unlike me, she's been subjected to centuries of reincarnations.

It's left me with precious little to do other than my husband and relearning everything I thought I knew.

I glance at the paper on the chaise, trying to see what is frustrating Essos. In the paper, Posey is featured with a quote listing all the ways in which Essos and I have managed to fail. The length of her comment lends itself more to an op-ed than just her "simple" opinion on the matter. Looking at the paper sends a flash of fury through me. There is too much wrong to even figure out where to start to fix things.

Just as abruptly as the conflict with Posey started, life went quiet. The papers have been relentless in their coverage of me, going as far as blaming me for the death of *Solarem Times* reporter Celestina, who was actually killed by Galen. Posey has conveniently thrown her own crimes at my feet, and the people of Solarem just...believe her, because I also spent the past few months being torn apart by the media. Something I wouldn't be surprised to find out that Posey orchestrated.

She broke the veil between Solarem and the mortal world during what was supposed to be my wedding to Galen, exposing the realm of the gods to the mortals. To add insult to injury, she also unleashed the zombie apocalypse on the mortals.

And that was just Tuesday.

"You thought the Trials were a good idea because you wanted to buy time to get rid of Galen. You did it because your focus was on surviving, and I'm so glad that it was." Essos retreats to sit on the bed.

"Es—"

"Am I supposed to be *sorry*? Am I supposed to be sorry that he's dead, and that I have not only you, but a child on the way?"

I stop where I am, across the room from him, and turn. "Maybe a little? I did all of this. I royally fucked everything up. We should be able to celebrate our child without worrying about everyone whispering that you've been had."

Essos flashes me a wicked grin as he jumps to his feet and comes to me. "My love, this only makes it clear to everyone that you've been had, again and again and *again*." He whispers that last word against my throat before kissing my skin.

Did I say his words make me feel like butter left out too long? I meant he makes me feel like butter left in the sun, melted and bubbling with need that, unless fulfilled, might burn away to nothing. My lips crash against his, full of wanton desire.

It's been like this since he's been home, my hormones making me insatiable at all hours of the night and day. His hand cups the back of my head, angling my neck so he can better kiss me, deepening it until I reach between his legs. His arm winds around my waist, and he pulls me close. I can't get any closer to him until he's inside me, and that's what I want.

I walk him backward to the bed. I haven't said as much, but I've taken to wearing only dresses and skirts so I can have him whenever I want. When we reach the mattress, I shove him back—maybe a little too hard, because the headboard hits the wall.

Essos raises a brow at me. "Still trying to temper your strength?"

I scowl at the little lift to his lips that shows his amusement. "You will hush, sir, if you want to be inside me in the next few minutes." I lift my skirts so I can straddle him. He pulls me down and assaults my lips with renewed fervor. He wasn't lying when he said he was going to make up for lost time. Whenever he's in the house, he's never far from my side.

Essos has just begun to peel off my shirt when there's a knock on the door. We barely break apart, breathing heavily, as we listen to see if someone is still there. The knock comes again, and I groan, grinding against Essos, needing the friction between my legs. A small moan escapes me, the pressure alone making stars burst behind my closed eyelids.

"Someone better be dead or dying," Essos growls, his hands finding my hips and lifting me off him. I step back and follow him to the door, the threat of violence for being interrupted clouding around us.

"I truly am sorry," Sybil starts once we've opened the door to them. They can see the look of us, utterly disheveled with swollen lips. "Rafferty is here for you."

"Right," Essos looks at me, his blue eyes full of yearning. "We did summon him."

"We did. *Last* week." I move to shove past Sybil, but Essos gently grabs my wrist and pulls me back. His fingertips graze my skin as he fixes my skirt, extra diligent over the taco-night swell in my abdomen. His gaze lingers, along with his hands, before he reaches up and sweeps his thumb under my lower lip.

When it became clear that to regain all my memories I'd need to have them unlocked, we decided to seek out the elusive God of Memory. Better to be fighting with every weapon in my arsenal than constantly wondering who I'm even talking to. I don't know how Rafferty is able to do it, but he's able to mask his location. Once I actually *remembered* that I wanted to talk to him, I was able to discuss with others how he can make us forget things, like where he is and how to reach him.

"Probably for the best we don't greet him looking like two teenagers caught necking," Essos says.

"Then you should do something about that." My eyes flick to where his cock is straining against his suit pants. "I'm afraid that even in your pants, it might poke my eye out." When I meet his eyes again, his pupils are blown, and I think he might fuck me against the door frame even with a Fate standing right there.

To my disappointment, he does not. "Gods, I missed you." He turns to Sybil. "Isn't being my assistant, I don't know...beneath you?"

"My Lord—" they start.

"Feels too formal," I interrupt, leading the way out of our bedroom.

"You say that about every title, love," Essos points out.

"My Lord." There is an edge to their words this time. "Until there is a reasonable plan for how to proceed and for what to do about my sister, I think it best that I keep doing what I do best."

"Hiding?" I say, stalling at the top of the stairs.

Finally, Sybil looks affronted.

"Daphne," Essos scolds.

"No, I'm allowed to be angry. Their sister ruined my life. Posey put all the pawns and pieces into play to take out a queen. I'm allowed to be angry that she went unchecked for so long. I'm allowed to be angry that somehow one was stronger than two. I'm allowed my righteous anger. Let me have my righteous anger, because I don't know what I'll do if the anger leaves me. Except I do know—I will fall apart, Essos. I will not be able to stand on two feet. I will not be able to look you in the face or look at myself in the mirror. I *murdered* your brother." My hands clench and unclench at my sides, feeling like they're coated in his blood once again.

There is nothing I can do to stop the tears that well in my eyes, and that just makes me angrier. I've done a lot for the sake of survival, but I've *never* killed, not until now, and it's so wrong. There are moments when I think I still see blood on my hands. It was one thing to talk about killing Galen in the abstract, but another thing entirely to watch the life leave his eyes.

We've discussed Essos's feeling that Galen was no longer his brother and Octavia no longer his mother, but guilt sits heavily on my shoulders. I've fractured him from his family.

With a hand on my belly, Essos reminds me that we're a family too. "Love—"

"Don't console me—don't even look at me, Essos. I swear to the gods, I will turn the next person who tries to console me into a fucking weed."

"No consolation here." He turns to his former righthand person turned Fate in disguise. "Call me whatever you want, Sybil. I just want to get us closer to resolving everything. The sooner we do that, I believe the saying is, 'Happy wife, happy life?'"

"I believe the saying is your wife wants a taco from that taco stand in Santa Monica that is probably overrun by zombies, because as far as everything goes, we are batting zero against Posey."

"Is your metaphor chess or baseball? I want to make sure I'm not mixing my analogies."

I give Essos a withering glare.

When we finally get down the stairs, Rafferty is standing in the foyer, talking with Luminara.

The Goddess of Harmony has been a ghost since the almost-wedding, and I've been thankful for it. I still don't trust her entirely, as she was the couples therapist for Galen and me. Every action Luminara took felt like it did more harm than good. Her only saving grace is that Sybil loves her and insists that she had the best intentions. For now, she's not a succulent, if only as a favor to the Fate. I'll give her a chance to explain herself once I find a spare bit of patience.

For being the God of Memory, there is nothing memorable about Rafferty. His brown hair is shorn so close to the scalp that I'm not even positive of the color, and his brown eyes offer nothing distinguishing about him. He is a perfectly average man who blends into every crowd.

"Rafferty." I infuse my greeting with as much lightness and positivity as I can.

He bows to Essos and barely spares a glance for me. "Your Majesty. Goddess. I was surprised to receive your invitation."

Essos bristles at the show of disrespect, but I only smile. Luminara sees the smile and shrinks back. "It wasn't an invitation, Rafferty, it was a summons and, in my home, you will show me the respect I am due." I clasp my hands in front of me. Dave, Shadow, and Spot circle the god, giving the impression they're looking for an excuse to sink their fangs into him. Spot in particular gets up close and personal while sniffing Rafferty.

"Oh? I wasn't aware that a king's kept mistress was due any special greeting. Those sorts of details are hazy. As far as recent memory serves, King Essos has no bride. Rumor has it his top pick at the Calling chose his brother."

Plants. Once I get my tacos, I'm turning *everyone* into fucking plants.

Before I can do something I'll regret, I take a deep, calming breath through my nose. We called him here for help. He could use his powers to make Essos and I forget each other—not that I think the others would stand for that.

"That is *enough*," Essos barks, shadows bleeding into the edges of the room. "She is my consort and my wife, and you will treat her as my equal."

Rafferty looks smug and it makes me want to beat him with something large, heavy, and dull for a very long time.

Luminara clears her throat, and I cut my gaze to her. "Actually, Your Majesties, Rafferty is correct. You two need to be wed again for Daphne to receive her full honorifics. They were afforded to her during the Trials mostly out of confusion, and because of your absence, sir, but it was not rightly done."

I grab Essos's forearm and dig in my nails. His suit jacket was left behind in our room, so I'm sure to draw blood.

Essos closes his hand over mine and gently pries it off. He slides our fingers together and gives me a reassuring squeeze. "I don't much care. We can deal with whatever trivial nonsense is required to fix this later."

"That would be a wedding," Rafferty says with a grin before reaching out and pressing two fingers to my forehead.

My knees go weak, and I fall for what feels like eternity.

. . .

"What do you mean, it's not that simple?" Essos snaps, jumping up from his seat beside me. Titus is leaning against the fireplace, sipping his scotch.

I want to reach for Essos, pull him back down on the couch, but he's already across the room in front of his father.

We're in the home of the God and Goddess Supreme, discussing Essos's proposal. I understand that we're not in a position that lends itself to romanticism and whimsy, so we have to get permission to get married. It's a formality that means little to us both. Essos and I know that we love each other, that we have what it takes to rule the Underworld, but we still need Titus and Octavia to confirm that we're allowed to wed.

I uncross and then recross my ankles the other way, leaning forward so I can hear all the ways in which I'm not good enough for Essos.

"I mean what I said. You're to be a king. You can't marry just anyone." Titus chuckles to himself, clearly amused by having his eldest son grovel before him. "You need someone who knows when she's outmatched, and your little flower girl is trying to punch above her weight class."

"Don't *speak about Daphne that way, Father. Xavier is to be a king as well, and yet he married Posey practically the day he met her." Essos glances back at me, an apology brimming in his eyes. We expected some opposition, but not an outright refusal.*

"What do you need of me?" I ask, straightening my back so it's a mirror of Octavia's. She's been suspiciously silent. I know that between the God and Goddess Supreme, if you want anything done, it has to go through her.

"You don't need to do anything. There won't be any hoops for you to jump through. We have been through and done enough." Essos leaves his father's side and sits down beside me, taking my hand. He's talking about Ellie, the wood nymph he cheated on me with. I've forgiven him for it, and we've spent the last year and a half working past the trust issues that still come up. Ellie's not our only issue, though. Another is how furious Galen was when Essos and I got back together. He punched Essos in the face then disappeared for months.

"She's caused enough strife in this family, don't you think?" Octavia drawls before taking a sip from her wine glass. She uncrosses her long, thin

legs and stands up, smoothing her perfect pencil skirt down even though it’s devoid of any wrinkles.

“She’s caused so much more good,*” Essos says. “She is everything to me, and if you plan on denying us this for your petty reasons, then I don’t want to be king. I don’t want the Underworld—let Galen have it.”*

My head snaps toward Essos. I stare at him, dumbfounded.

Essos has put his all into making a plan for the Underworld, one that he’s proud of and that he hopes will not only make his father proud but will also be good for the souls shepherded into it. Countless nights, I was woken up by him turning on a light to note an idea he had. He slaved over his strategy, and it doesn’t feel right for him to sacrifice it all for me.

“No,” I say, squeezing Essos’s hand. Octavia tilts her head in my direction as if curious to see what I will say. Her ponytail dips. “I won’t let you give this up. You have worked too hard, done everything that has been asked of you, and more. You can’t just give up your kingdom to Galen.”

“You *are everything that I need. I don’t need to be a king or treated like a prince. I just need you.” Essos cups my face before kissing me with his all-consuming power. I dissolve into stardust and ash in that kiss, my whole world beginning and ending with him.*

Titus clears his throat, and it finally prompts us to separate.

As he looks at me, Essos’s gaze is soft, but when he turns to face his father, it hardens into something cold and desolate. Perhaps all of Titus’s chickens have come home to roost. You can’t spend your time alienating your child and expect them to always bend to your whims.

“If she wants to be a queen, she has to prove herself worthy. I think the Trials would be a lovely way to do it.”

“Father...”

“Stop.” I turn to Essos and take his hands in mine, giving them a gentle squeeze. Petals tickle along our fingers, and he relents, nodding and trusting me. “I’ll do it. I’ll do whatever it takes to prove to them that we’re meant to be.”

. . .

I BLINK my eyes open to see Essos hovering over me. His expression wavers between concern and anger, but for the moment I am his focus.

"Are you all right, love?" he whispers, brushing tendrils of hair from my face.

I had forgotten my own Trials entirely. Was that why the idea came so easily to me the night of the Calling Ball?

"I'm fine." Essos helps me sit up so I can better glare at Rafferty. "What was that?" I demand, standing on uneasy feet.

"Your memory. Thousands of years are enough for anyone to start losing bits and pieces—unsurprising for someone your age."

Rafferty did more than just bring that one memory to the forefront. I'm better able to sift through other memories, namely of the Trials I went through. They were not only physical challenges but also ones that required me to show my wit and cunning. One trial involved my ability to properly set a table, only I wasn't given all the correct silverware. Each trial was more humiliating than the last, but I completed them all until I stood before my future mother-in-law and father-in-law, victorious. I held my head high, ready for whatever bullshit they'd throw my way next.

Luminara comes to the other side of me to support me, and for once, I don't push her away. I feel uneasy and shaky, like my blood sugar has bottomed out. And maybe it has. Maybe this can be easily remedied with a taco.

"I thought I was clear about the respect that was to be shown to my *wife.*" Essos practically bares his teeth as he advances on Rafferty.

Rafferty's edges start to get a little fuzzy, and I worry that I might be on the verge of passing out again, but Luminara's sharp intake of breath tells me she's seeing what I am.

Slowly, Rafferty fades. First his legs and arms and then his torso. He looks like he's choking, like his lungs have disappeared from his chest, and his head and face grow faint until all of Rafferty reappears suddenly. He's gasping for air, falling to his knees before us. He holds his hand before his face, his eyes widening as he realizes he's missing the two fingers he pressed to my forehead.

As the God of the Dead, Essos is gifted with the ability to unmake a soul, but he used it only once in the early days of our ruling as we struggled to find our footing. Essos said he would never use it again, having hated the feeling that came with it. He said it felt like he'd bathed in oil, like the Fates demanded balance. Never in a million years would I have thought this power could be used against another god.

"It was just a reminder of what she went through to marry you the first time." Rafferty's voice is choked.

As much as I want to see him suffer for being such a miserable god, we did call him here for a reason. "Enough. I don't need any reminders. We called you here for help, not for theatrics." I try to imbue my words with the strength that I feel failing me. We still need him, and I hope that Essos hasn't scared him off. "I need you to give me my memories back—all the ones you blocked for Posey."

Rafferty looks away, a faint stain on his cheeks. "I didn't do that," he mumbles.

"I'm sorry?" Essos demands, stepping close to the other god. "I don't believe I heard you."

"I didn't do it." Rafferty meets Essos's eye with defiance.

"Explain." I cross my arms.

"What are you two not understanding? Posey blocked your memories. I had nothing to do with it."

"How were you able to show me the memory from my Trials?"

"I am the God of Memory." He says it simply, like that should explain this incongruity.

"I'm still waiting for you to explain why you can't help me, and frankly, I'm getting tired of not having an answer."

"I am the God of Memory. I can access memories and block them, and I can erase them entirely. What Posey did to you was a bastardization of my power, which means that I cannot remove the block she set in place for you. That's what happens when someone tangles with powers that are not their own."

"So, how did you do what you just did, and how was Posey able to use your powers?" Essos asks.

Rafferty snorts, then looks sheepish. "I can do it because I know that the memory exists. I pulled it from where it was hidden in Daphne's mind. I don't know all her memories, so I can't mine them all."

I shift and press harder against Essos, needing his strength. I never thought that my memories would stay gone. There was always the chance I would get them back. I had counted on that, to a certain extent. I feel bereft, thinking of all the things that I'll never know are gone. Memories of heartbreak and loss, but also good ones, with Helene and Kai and Finn. Sweet moments with Essos.

"How have I been getting them back now?"

"Like I said, what Posey did was a sorry excuse for what I usually do. What do you know of Posey the Fate?"

Nothing. We know nothing of Posey the Fate, or even much about the role the Fates play. They used to be this entity we believed in, but after Galen's Trials, we discovered that Posey had cloaked all three Fates and made it so no one remembered they were actual people we interacted with. During my failed wedding to Galen, Sybil and Estelle were revealed as their true selves—Fates.

Essos and I share a look and shake our heads, expecting Rafferty to continue, but it's Luminara who steps forward and speaks.

"The sisters three, one to spin, one to measure, and one to cut. It was Sybil who would spin, Estelle who would measure their lives, and Posey who would cut the thread of life."

Rafferty looks at us expectantly. "Right, *Queen* Posey, because that's what she still is, unlike someone else." Essos growls at Rafferty when he says this. "The queen hated the tedium of cutting and cutting, so she tried her hand at her sisters' roles like she was Goldilocks, practicing each of their powers bit by bit, such as Sybil's ability to provide a blank slate to each soul, including those meant for reincarnation. That was never meant to be her power. It got corrupted when she used it."

"Corrupted." The word tastes foul as I say it.

"Yes. That's probably why your memories were so easily manipulated and why you've been able to tap into them a little at a time. From the rumors I've heard, the night you chose your 'husband's'—" Rafferty uses finger quotes here, and I want to break every last one of his digits "—brother, you received a rush of memories during the ball, my guess because Posey wanted you to get something, just enough of a taste to torment you further. It's been a trickle since. Like I said, though, that's not supposed to be within her power. I can't explain it, other than to say that maybe there is something to the fairytales and true love's kiss. But I'm sorry, kids, I can't help you. If that's all..." He turns toward the door.

He's just pulling it open when it slams shut, vines wrapping around the knobs to hold it fast.

"We're not through. Follow me."

3

I enter the library alone first, as I insisted I must, and pull the doors closed behind me. My last glimpse is of Essos, leaning against the wall with his arms crossed, trying to look nonchalant as he watches me shut him out.

"You could have let him in. I don't bite," Cat calls from a window bench. I can barely see her through the stacks and stacks of books that surround her.

"I know. I wanted to see you first. Am I allowed to want some one-on-one time with my bestie?"

Her green eyes flick up to me as I approach her. I drop into the seat across from her, trying to bury the memory of Galen and me in these exact same seats as he spun a web of lies and deceit that led me away from my husband.

"No, because you're not alone." She's wearing a gauzy red dress with a high chiffon neck. I can't place what's different about her—maybe her cheekbones are a little sharper, her eyes a little brighter. She has a more ethereal look.

"Rafferty is here to help you," I tell Cat as gently as I can.

Cat snaps the heavy tome in her hands shut and finally looks up at me. I can see the streaks of energy from her magic etched along the floor around her. She's still adjusting, still trying to figure out what she can do and how it works. When I got my magic back, using it was a matter of flexing old muscles. I was in touch with the parts of myself that summoned flowers, that brought them to life and killed them. I knew each thing that was unique to me, but magic is all new to Cat, and she doesn't have any of that.

"Is that why he's here?" Her sarcasm might actually burn me.

"Cat, I just want what's best—"

"If you finish that sentence, Daphne, I swear I don't know that I'll be able to control what I do." Tears brim in her eyes. My scrutiny must prove too much for her, because she pushes out of her seat and walks toward a broken vase.

"How can I help you?"

"You can leave me alone."

"That's not happening, so pick a different option. I left you alone plenty over the last few days, and it's gotten us both nowhere." I get up and stand beside her at the table. The vase was ugly, probably a gift shoved in here to be forgotten. I've tried to give her space to navigate becoming a goddess. I didn't want to, but it was the only thing she asked me for, so who was I to refuse?

Standing in this room now, I'm realizing that I did the wrong thing. I should have pushed to stay involved more. She didn't need space; she needed a friend. She pushed back when I demanded space; now it's time to repay the favor.

"I broke your vase."

"I didn't like it anyway," I tell her with a halfhearted shrug.

"*Stop!*" she shouts. A small concussive force sends me sliding backward, and several books fall from their perches. I probably would have been fine, but that same force overturns a chair, and I fall backward over it, landing hard on my ass.

Cat's eyes are squeezed shut, and her whole body tenses. She doesn't open her eyes until Essos throws the doors open and rushes toward me. I hold up a hand and stop him and get up myself. I have to show Cat that I'm fine, that everything will be okay.

"Stop what, Cat? Caring? Because I won't. Nothing has changed between us," I reassure her, walking back to where she stands.

She's terrified, and I think she might actually be shaking. "It changes *everything*. Is Catalina still my name?" She shrinks away from me when I reach for her.

I hold up my hands, showing her I won't touch her. "Did it change anything for you when you found out I was the Goddess of Spring? Did it change anything for you when you found out Essos was my husband?"

"I just hurt you. I can't control this. I'm going to go all Elsa on you and freeze your heart. Did I hurt the baby?" she asks in a panic.

"No, Cat. We're both fine. My ass is going to be sore, but I'm less worried about that than I am about you. I asked Rafferty to come here to help you. I heard you screaming the other night."

"I was in a bomb shelter in London. It caved in around me, and I couldn't *breathe*, and my body was on fire." Cat lets herself drop, but I rush forward and catch her, both of us collapsing onto the floor. This time I have the foresight to summon a pillow to cushion our fall.

My back is to Essos, and I don't look at him. I know he's just as pained as I am at what Cat is going through. There's nothing we can do to help her through this. I smooth her hair as she cries, her body shaking.

Essos moves around us and drops onto a chair, running a hand through his hair. We share a look, so much communicated between us. Posey was soft on me in comparison to what she put Cat through. My soul was trapped in a gem until she decided enough time had passed. I don't know what metric she used or why she waited so long. Was it to ensure that Essos didn't kill Galen on the spot? Was it her way of flexing her power over us? I was stuck in that stone for over a thousand years, but Cat never had a chance to become the goddess she was meant to be. Her soul was plucked from Fate's tapestry and sent to the mortal realm. Cat lived and died over and over during the millennia I had to fall in love with Essos, wed him, and die myself.

"What do you want from me?" Rafferty asks. I don't turn to face him, only glancing at my husband for his answer.

"We want you to help her, whatever that looks like. Burying the memories of her past lives or helping her accept them or muting them, or whatever it takes. She's suffering."

Hearing Essos's impassioned plea, I want to squeeze his hand, but I settle for hugging Cat to me instead.

"Stop talking about me like I'm not right here," Cat orders, disentangling herself from me. She stands and faces Rafferty, then offers me a hand up. Her gaze is critical of him, and I enjoy watching him squirm. He's known the rest of us for millennia. Cat is an unknown entity. New blood in an incestuous pool of sharing lovers. It's like six degrees of Kevin Bacon, only it's three degrees of former partners.

"What do you want? Do you even know?" Rafferty sasses, and I want to throttle him.

"I know that you are clearly overcompensating for something with that shitty attitude. Does being the God of Memory mean that you alter memories to make yourself seem better in bed than you really are? Or better yet, maybe you just make your lovers forget? Because if so, I'd like to bring you up on charges for abuse of power."

Watching Rafferty turn red is worth every second of frustration this morning. "If you're not interested in my help..." he huffs, turning on his heel.

"Quit being a baby," I order with a sigh. All the energy and anger that was keeping me upright has fled my body, and I am just so tired. I make to sit beside Essos, but he pulls me onto his lap instead, like we're young again with no care about PDA and not the king and queen of a realm. Well, he's the king of a realm, and I'm his...what? Mistress?

"I did not come here to be ordered about and injured by some cuckold and his whore," Rafferty snaps, turning his attention back to

Essos and me. Clearly, losing two fingers a few minutes ago had no impact on him.

"Perhaps you'll listen to me, then," a voice booms from the second floor of the library. I don't turn, because I can picture Xavier with his shirtsleeves rolled up, bracing his hands on the banister so he's looking down on us, just the way he likes it.

Essos slides me off his lap and stands up. As if the tired pregnant woman is going to be the only one sitting down. I get up and stand beside my friend. Cat hasn't outright rejected Xavier, but she's made it clear to me by staying here that she would much rather not face him or deal with anything that has to do with him.

Just to be a showoff, Xavier floats down to us on a dark little cloud. I want to take his dramatic flair and shove it up his ass.

"If you don't have tacos, I'm going to have to ask you to leave." I cross my arms and jut out my hip.

"Do I look like a delivery boy?" Xavier asks, leveling me with a glare.

"No, you look like a bad guest who showed up at someone else's house without food."

Beside me, Cat shrinks back a little, placing herself closer to me and Essos, and Xavier sees it.

Hurt flashes on his face, but he's never been one to let emotion get the better of him, so he buries it, pointing at Rafferty. "Why isn't he speaking?"

"Because I removed his tongue," Essos offers darkly, glaring at the insolent god. He slips his hands into his pockets, rocking back on his heels.

"You did what, brother?" Xavier turns to him.

Essos was never the vengeful type. He was more likely to settle a fight than to start one and was the last to get involved when something came to blows.

"I removed his tongue. I warned him of the consequences of treating my wife poorly, and he insisted on being disrespectful.

Without a tongue, he cannot be disrespectful. I fail to see the problem."

"The problem is, if you want him to effectively help Catalina, he needs to have a conversation with her and for that, he needs his tongue," Xavier argues.

Rafferty, meanwhile, looks like he's turning purple with rage.

"I disagree. He did a fine job of using his powers without words when he got here," I point out. It's childish, but I stick out my tongue at him. I think Rafferty might turn another color at my insult.

"He also seems to be under the impression that Daphne is not my wife and will need to complete the Trials *again* in order to wed me. Dear brother, I told him he must be mistaken."

"For once, Essos, can the world not revolve around you?" Xavier snaps.

"Oh, that's rich, X, coming from the god whose wife started an uprising because you were incapable of keeping it in your pants." Essos stands up straighter. He's no doubt annoyed that he has to defend himself in his own home. *I'm* annoyed he has to defend himself in his own home. At the same time, this brotherly bickering does give me a feeling of normalcy. I can pretend things aren't too dire if they're able to argue like this.

"You boys can take it out and measure later," Cat interjects. "If my opinion counts for anything, which, given the way you're all talking about me, it doesn't, I don't want anyone messing with my head."

Rafferty keeps gesturing at his mouth, and with a petulant shake of his head, Essos returns his tongue.

"Might I, the God of Memory, provide my input?" Rafferty asks.

"No!" the four of us say in unison, essentially blocking him out of the conversation.

"I hate all of you," he grouses before dropping into the window seat.

"Get in line," I snap. Then I turn to Cat and take her hands. "This is entirely your decision. I will support you if you want to discuss options with Rafferty, and I will super support you if you want to kick him out of my house. For what it's worth, I think you should talk to him. I don't know if facing your past lives will help or if it will only hurt. I don't know if you want to just lock those memories away. But you should know what you *can* choose, and you should know none of us will look down on you for that choice."

"But who am I really? I'm Olivia Romonova, I'm Agnes Ceruli, I'm Sinead O'Brien, I'm Temperance Booth—I'm hundreds of lives, with parents and siblings, and I don't even know who *I* am anymore. What if I just make everything worse?" she whispers.

"You are Catalina Mason. You are my best friend. You are who you want to be." I squeeze her hands, hoping I'm getting through to her.

"What *is* going to be worse is if you're unable to control your powers and you hurt Daphne or someone else. You won't be able to live with yourself. Your emotions are tied to your powers—I imagine that's why I woke up surrounded by rose petals." Xavier is trying to spark something in her, but Cat retreats further.

"Sorry, Xav, that was me. I just can't control these pregnancy dreams." I flip my hair over my shoulder with a wink. "Goddess of Spring and all that."

Essos startles. "I'm sorry, did you just say you were dreaming of my brother?"

"Not only him," I reassure Essos. I'm teasing them both. The dream I had was less about sex and more about turning people who pissed me off into topiaries. I guess Xavier made the cut.

"I don't know which scenario is more troubling," Essos muses mostly to himself while pinching the bridge of his nose.

"We're getting off track," Xavier snaps, though I see a touch of pink on his cheeks. Is the Casanova king embarrassed by the idea of me having sex dreams about him? "You should at least hear your options from Rafferty."

"Will it make you go away?" Cat asks Xavier.

He's so unprepared for that response that he doesn't mask the hurt. It's gone in a flash, but Cat must have seen it because she looks away from him.

"If that's what you want, then yes."

"Fine." Cat faces Rafferty, freezing Xavier out. "Hi, Rafferty. My memory is broken. Can you fix it?"

"Let's see if I can." He glances at the rest of us. "You should leave us, and have lunch sent up. Something vegan. I abhor meat."

I narrow my eyes at him but flash the coziest smile I can. "Of course. I'll have food sent to the library."

"And when you're done talking with Catalina, we will have a discussion about what you can actually do for my *wife*."

"I can try a few things. No promises they'll work." Rafferty reaches for my head again.

I flinch away. He said what Posey did was corrupted, and until I talk to my husband about options, I'm not going to just let Rafferty dig around in my mind.

"I swear, Rafferty, if you touch my fucking wife again without her permission, I will shove you in a small box and drop you into the bottom of the Deep, and no one will remember that the God of Memory even exists."

There is stunned silence in the room as we all look at Essos. He's so calm, like he offered Rafferty tea instead of threatening him with torture. Only the fire blazing in his eyes betrays his anger. It is so wrong, but my pussy throbs with need for him after such a possessive and protective claim. When Essos's gaze flicks to mine, that angry fire morphs into something more...something intimate just for me, his wife, and it turns my insides molten.

Rafferty lowers his hands, clenching them into fists. I think he might shit himself. "Understood." His voice is quiet and almost robotic.

Essos ushers Xavier and me from the room so Rafferty can make himself useful. I close the doors behind us quietly, hoping that he can bring Cat some peace of mind.

"I'll go to the kitchens and make myself useful." Xavier doesn't even bother waiting for a response before he stomps away like a child.

Once he's clear of the hallway, Essos backs me against the wall. "Do I have to prove to my wife that I'm the only one who should be in her dreams?" he growls, possessive and needy.

My heart is nearly bursting from my chest with love and appreciation for this man who keeps putting me first.

"You'll have to catch me if you want to try," I challenge before taking off toward his office.

Essos holds my naked body to him. He, of course, caught me. It took nothing for him to corner me in his office and hike up my dress so he could enter me. Not that I put up much of a fight. I was practically panting for him with my legs spread on his desk when he strolled in like he *knew* I was going to be right where he wanted me. It wasn't so much a cornering as it was taking what I had on offer. That was only round one. Round two brought us to the same couch where we used to spend many an afternoon making love.

"We need to go to the mortal realm," I say. Essos idly strokes along my spine as I lie on top of him. I want to burrow closer to him, but there is no closer, so I just kiss his bare chest. We're tangled together on the couch, and I couldn't be happier with his arms around me.

It's rude of me to use sex against my husband to soften him up, but I'll do what I have to at this point to get him to let me out. We had our honeymoon phase, and while it was nice of Posey to give us this time to regroup and figure out how to handle everything, she won't be still for much longer. This media blackout from the mortal realm because of the zombies makes me feel itchy.

"No."

No explanation, no elaboration. If the tone of his voice is any indication, he's unwilling to even consider it. Instead, Essos idly strokes my upper arm.

"That's it? No discussion?"

"That's it. No discussion."

I press my chin to his chest so I can study his face. His dark hair is mussed, falling into his eyes and giving him a roguish look. Despite the external pressures on us, he still smiles more now than he did during the whole of the Calling.

"I disagree with you and your assessment. During our coronation, we took a vow to serve the souls of mortals in their afterlife. Their afterlife is now in the mortal realm. So, I'll leave you with a choice—work with me, or step back and let me do what I need to do."

Essos shifts so he can meet my gaze straight on. "Did you not learn your lesson when my mother lured you into a cave under false pretenses? What about when she choked you? You may be immortal, but the life inside you isn't yet. Never mind that there's still a weapon floating around out there that can kill you."

"That same weapon can kill you, and yet you don't see me telling you to stay home and knit like a good wifey." I try to push away from him, but he holds me tightly.

"I'm the King of Death. Nothing can take me from you."

"You're the King of *the* Dead, and my point still stands. Anything you can do, I can do too."

"My decision remains the same. I don't want you going to the mortal realm."

I open my mouth, but I can tell from the mulish set of his lips that there will be no moving him.

"Yes, *Daddy*," I say sarcastically, which earns me a swat on the ass.

"Don't do that, Daphne. Don't minimize my feelings about your safety with sarcasm. If you're going to be pissed, be pissed, but I love you, and I'm going to be an asshole. You can either act like a brat about it or listen to me for fucking once."

This time when I push off his chest, he lets me go. I turn my back to him as I look around for my clothes, because if I don't, I will say something that will upset us both, and neither of us needs that.

"I love you too, Essos, but we are gods, and above that, we are King and Queen of the Underworld. It is our job to serve the realm." I look over my shoulder at my husband as he lies there, sculpted and watching me with this inscrutable look. One arm is slung behind his head while the other rests on his stomach.

"I'm not saying we should shirk our responsibilities, but we've been at the forefront of this conflict long enough. I have been shadow-ruling Solarem for too long. Let Xavier do something for once."

I grab my top and pull it on. "You don't mean that. This is your fear talking."

"The fuck I don't mean it." Essos sits up quickly and cups my face. "Me being a king made you a target for Posey. I'm not looking to repeat that experience ever again."

I slip out of Essos's grip and stand. "I was dead for a thousand years. I wasn't resurrected to be held captive in this house like a doll. I want to start living again."

Essos runs his hands down his face, then he rises and pulls on his pants. "Am I not enough?"

The vulnerability in his voice plays on my every weakness. His back is turned to me now, and he's pretending to look for his shirt, which is thrown over the back of the couch right in front of him.

I wrap my arms around his middle and rest my cheek against his spine. "You are the thing that keeps my heart beating. You are more than enough. You are my everything, and that's why I can't let you do something that's not true to you. Your decision is being made from a place of fear when it needs to be made from a place of strength."

Essos gives a derisive snort but covers my hands with his,

entwining our fingers so we're connected. "What if my father was wrong, and I never should have been king?"

"What if you had let that chariot maim me? There is no point in worrying about what-ifs. The life we have is this one—the one in which you are an *amazing* king who loves and protects your people as best you can. We were caught off guard by Posey, but now we know better, and we won't let it happen again." I kiss his back then rub my nose along his spine. "Your father was only wrong in underestimating Posey, just like we all were. The best decision he made was picking you to be king. You've been there to help people during some of the most traumatic parts of their lives. You've been there to catch Xavier when he needed help. Never doubt yourself."

"What if I can't do this?" His words are barely more than a whisper.

"Do what?" I release him so I can move around him to look him in the face.

"Be a father."

I can't help it. I smile as I reach up to touch his cheek. "You can, and you will. You don't have a choice."

Essos's gaze shifts from me to my barely-there swell. "There seems to be a lot of that going around. But this—you, our baby—will always be a choice I make. I will choose you both every day."

He brushes his lips against my forehead before folding me against his chest.

Essos might think our conversation is over, but it's not.

Far from it.

I gaze around our dining room at the gods and goddesses assembling before me. Xavier is trying to make the meeting we've organized sound more important by calling it a war council, but really, it's just an informational gathering for those who were not so quick to buy what Posey is selling. It took time to get twenty gods to agree to meet, but as I look around, I see that there are at least two dozen here. I'm lucky my dining room and table can expand to fit everyone.

Posey continues to play the injured spouse. Xavier might be staying at our apartment in Solarem, but he won't step foot into the city. She recently put out a bounty on him, saying she wants to question him about his involvement in removing the veil between the realms. The veil is still broken, something the two Fates on our side are looking into. It's another reason I want to go to the human realm—I want to see firsthand the damage that is being wrought.

Meanwhile, Xavier is lucky the doorman to our building has his loyalties straight and forewarned him of Posey's bounty. Ever since,

Luca has made sure to deliver whatever Xavier might need to the door. That is, when Xavier actually spends time there. For the most part, he spends his days here, trying to not crowd Cat while also keeping an eye on her.

In front of me on the table are platters of food, none of them with tacos. I scowl.

Essos pushes a plate of fruit toward me.

"You could fix this so easily," I hiss while we wait for everyone to settle down. To be fair, I could also fix it, but since starting my second trimester, any time I try to change food, it seems the baby has their own idea about what they want. I've tried on more than one occasion to fulfill a craving only to find that this little pomegranate has tastes that align with their father's. I'll never forget the betrayal of bacon turned celery.

"You're right, I could, but I won't." He tilts his head toward me, all adorable-like.

"And why not?"

"Because you should be eating veggies and fruits."

"Essos, I love you, but if you keep withholding tacos because I should be eating better, I promise the next time you want to put your—"

"I'm calling this meeting to order!" Xavier booms.

I narrow my eyes at Essos, and he just flashes me a grin, squeezing my knee under the table.

Around us, conversations quiet.

Kai and Helene arrive late, stepping in from outside. Dion and Finn drop into the room at the last minute as well, slipping into chairs across the table. We've been scattered, trying to play defense. Finn, Dion, Helene, and Kai have been attempting to drum up support from their friends and acquaintances. We're behind the eight ball on all of it, and the bad press about me from the Trials has made it that much harder to get people on our side. I think those four are the only reason anyone agreed to come today. Posey had the benefit of pre-planning everything, so now we're stuck in a reactionary mode. I can only hope that after this meeting, the tide turns.

"There is much to discuss," Estelle begins. Her ivory skin has an ethereal glow that wasn't there before, betraying her as other, even among our people. She holds out a hand to Zara, who gives her a folder. My friend who felt so useless during the Trials finally has crucial work to keep her busy. She's made herself Sybil and Estelle's assistant.

"I'm sorry, but aren't you the cook?"

I look for the god who asked and struggle to place a name. I feel awkward, staring so hard at his dark skin and slicked-back hair. He looks like a model, and he knows how handsome he is in his tuxedo. He spins in his seat, looking around the room to see if anyone objects. When he catches me staring, he gives me a small nod of acknowledgement.

"Mohsin, God of Dancers. You once got drunk and challenged him to a dance-off for your crown," Essos whispers. His breath is so close, it sends warmth spreading through my veins.

"I'm guessing that didn't end well?" I snicker, ignoring the chatter that started up at Mohsin's question.

"He was a gentleman and let you keep your crown." Essos grins at me before kissing my shoulder. He nods toward the equally ethereal woman beside Moshin, her long, dark hair swept into a messy ponytail and a smudge of flour on her cheek that's a shock against her brown skin. Even from here she smells faintly of chai and vanilla. "His twin sister, Saima. Goddess of Baked Goods. She was always my go-to when I was groveling."

"So, will you be asking her to ply me with treats to get you out of trouble this time?" I whisper, and the man has the audacity to feign shock that he's in trouble.

"I've got nothing to be sorry for."

The conversation around us distracts me from our tiff.

"I don't see why being a cook would exclude her from being a

Fate." Zara's voice is stronger than I've heard it in a long time. She glares at anyone who dares meet her eye in challenge.

"That's because you're a mortal. This would be like finding out that your Jesus guy was a short-order cook at some dive bar in Arizona," someone else calls out. I turn toward the voice but don't catch who it was. It may not even be someone I recognize.

My inability to remember everyone's faces drives another stake into my heart. Whether she intended it or not, it's yet one more way that Posey has managed to fuck me over. I know that when I stop and let myself examine Rafferty's implication that I may never get my memories back fully, I'll be devastated. That's why I can't think too hard about it. That emotion won't serve me.

"The press is calling them False Fates. From the *Solarem Sun* to the *Solarem Times*, no one believes that they're the Fates, and I don't know why you expect us to," Pyrus, Goddess of Fire, says from their spot beside the fireplace. At least that's one face I recognize. It's round with flames dancing in their irises, giving a luminous look to their dark-olive skin. Their blonde hair is shorn close to the scalp, but I can see little sparks when they run their hand over it.

Essos stands. "I hear your concerns about Estelle and Sybil. You're confused and frustrated—we all are. That's why we called everyone here to discuss what happened, so you will have the facts and we can quit fighting amongst ourselves and focus on the broader issue, which is Posey."

"Another Fate?" a blonde woman asks. Her pale skin has more of a tan to it, and when she twists around in her chair, looking at everyone, I catch a glimpse of brown eyes that snag for entirely too long on my husband. I place my hand over his where it rests on the table and give it a squeeze.

Estelle steps forward. "Our sister did this not only to you, but to us. We have been working with Gisella to see what information has been scrubbed from the history books. Posey shielded our existence, our memories, and made us forget who we were. This was not trivial magic. This was huge, the kind of magic used when she tore down the veil between worlds and when she started the zombie apocalypse in the mortal realms."

"So says you," the blonde pipes up again.

I look at her more closely, leaning an elbow on the table. Something about her isn't sitting right with me, and I don't know if it's because I should remember her or because she's irritating me by being adversarial.

"So says us," I respond.

Essos tenses as all attention turns to me.

"Why should we believe the Traitor Queen?"

Essos takes my hand and pulls me to my feet beside him. I'm uncertain as he takes a deep breath before trying to convince these people. "I like to think most people in this room respect me. I believe I've earned your respect over the years as a fair ruler, and I've handled your funds well." He pauses for a beat, waiting for anyone to voice their objection. "Right, well, there's no easy way to say this. We lied to you all."

My husband and his flair for the dramatic. Around the room, people start to whisper. Xavier's eyes narrow at me as if he's asking where the fuck Essos is going with this, but I have no idea what to say.

"We lied about what happened to my queen many years ago. The God of War and Suffering *murdered* Daphne in our home, and rather than explain to you that there was a weapon capable of murdering gods, we chose to hide that. We told you a lie—that Daphne wanted to experience being mortal, and during that time, she was killed."

He doesn't look at me. Instead, he stares at the far wall, his eyes going distant. I can see it, the way my death must have broken him. There's a grim set to his mouth until I squeeze his hand again. Essos finally meets my eye, giving me a quick, small smile. It's all I can do to return the gesture. We can do this together.

"Galen stabbed a dagger through my heart," I say, picking up for him. I glance around the room, meeting people's eyes. "When I returned as part of the Calling, I had no memory of this. I had no idea what I was doing. Galen preyed upon that confusion and naivety. He took advantage of the fact that I didn't know who I was, and he built a narrative that made my husband—that made Essos—the villain."

"He picked the wrong fight," Helene interjects. "Galen and Essos are both my brothers. You know that I have no cause to lead you astray. What they speak now is the truth."

"A convenient truth, after lying to us. Sure, we're totally going to trust you all now." It's the blonde again, and the look she gives me tells me that I'm missing something. She's surveying me and finding me lacking. It makes me want to curl my hands over my stomach protectively, but I'm wearing a loose-fitting shirt to hide my pregnancy. It's the last thing I want to be questioned about.

"From what we're hearing, you're not even actually married anymore. You tried to assert the claim you were still wed during the Trials, and instead, the Underworld was ransacked and we were all robbed blind while you played eenie, meenie, miney, mo between brothers."

I twist to see if I can pinpoint who said that, but I can't find them. If I could, I would silence them.

"What is it going to take to convince you?" I ask, bracing my hands on the table to look at the blonde. More than one of the gods lets their eyes dip to my cleavage. Essos rests his hand on my shoulders.

"Let's see the proof. Call Rafferty in here. He can show us your memory of that so-called murder." She's so calm when she says it, when she tells me to relive the worst day of my life.

My stomach flips, nearly letting loose all the food I've eaten today. Like I didn't already have to live through it the first time, and again when Galen showed me that Essos was on the other end of that blade, and *again* when I remembered it for real. Living through it once was more than enough.

"Absolutely not," Essos hisses, staring her down, hand still on my shoulder. The room feels a touch darker, a touch colder.

"Why not?" She's on her feet now, leaning on the table the way I am. She's looking at my husband, with...desire?

I straighten up. "Because I refuse to let my last moments be replayed for your entertainment."

"I'm just saying. Your husband hardly seemed broken up about your so-called death. He certainly wasn't broken up about it while he was moaning my name."

There is a dramatic *Ooooh* from someone, and when I glance over, I see my first lover, Cassius, the God of Vanity, sitting with a bowl of popcorn.

Somehow, I'm not surprised.

I bite my tongue so hard I taste blood, but I stare down this minor goddess who thinks she can walk into my house and claim my husband. "You should be careful of the accusations you throw around. The last woman who claimed my husband loved her lost her mouth. Make no mistake, the crown rests on *my* head. It is my bed he shares. Consider yourself a consolation prize, not good enough to be his wife. Not good enough to even be his mistress while I was dead. And by the way, green clashes with that awful dye job. It doesn't suit you in the least."

I watch as her skin turns more and more green, and I turn the green a deeper shade, knowing that it will linger longer. She's confused at first by my insult, and then she looks at her hands. That's when I remember where I know her from. She was another assistant on Essos's office floor, and friends with Ellie. If I'm remembering right, her name was Lucky—so unoriginal for the Goddess of Luck. I can't help it; I push on, infusing the green deeper in her skin, smirking as it climbs up her arms. It's temporary, the color change, lasting just long enough for my point to be made.

"Not so Lucky after all?" I ask, dropping back into my seat and then taking a savage bite of a stalk of celery. It doesn't have the same impact another food might have, but it gives a satisfyingly threatening crunch.

I hold the stare down until she looks away first. Part of me wishes she would have kept going so it would distract me from the burning feeling in my chest. Lucky looks like she wants to place a hex on me, but Essos leans forward, leveling her with a look, one that warns her not to push it.

Apparently, my husband has some other secrets he needs to tell me tonight.

Noticeably absent from the meeting is any talk of the mortal realm. No one seems to give a single shit about the zombies that rise and roam there every day. Zara tries to bring it up but is shut down when Lucky presses Essos about how finances in Solarem are strained.

Zara meets my gaze from across the room, a fire burning in her eyes that makes me remember why she makes a formidable enemy.

The gods' reluctance to even talk about the mortal realm reinforces the necessity of a visit. The media tends toward hysteria in Solarem about both realms, so the only way to know what's happening is to experience it firsthand.

We spend hours talking in circles, rehashing the same bullshit. Galen was bad. Posey is the one doing all this. No, she's not trying to do anything good; she's trying to consolidate her absolute power. We don't trust her, and we don't think anyone else should either.

I'm not sure we manage to change more than a handful of minds, but after the showdown between Lucky and me, no one presses me to detail my death.

When everyone gets listless, Xavier calls the meeting to an end and people depart, leaving the usual suspects behind. I've eaten my weight in fruit over the course of the meeting just so I didn't turn anyone into a tree. I lean back in my seat and rest my feet on the vacant seat beside me, rubbing my hand over my stomach, watching Essos and Xavier argue.

"The baby?" Finn asks, dropping into the seat beside me.

"No, the food baby."

He chortles and leans around me so he's hugging me from behind to touch my stomach. "You know Lucky was just posturing, right?" Finn whispers in my ear.

Essos must feel my gaze on him, because he looks over at us and flashes me a smile. It turns my insides into melty marshmallow goo. Now I'm not just full of food, but love, because as much as I am annoyed at having the possibility of another woman Essos slept with flaunted in my face, I know Essos loves me.

I'm not about to believe Lucky just because she made the claim, but the truth is, I missed over one thousand years of memories and events and conversations. As much as Essos wants to, there is no way for him to tell me about all of it.

"I'd like to hear that from him, thank you." I cover Finn's hand with my own.

"I'm sure he will tell you that, but–"

"Then you need to butt out. It's bad enough that I had to be reminded several times today that we're not actually married anymore. I really, *really* want to go to my room, throw myself down on the bed, and cry like a Disney Princess, but I can't." My emotions start to choke me, and if I do keep going, I *will* cry. Not only does the pregnancy mean my safety is paramount, but it also means my hormones can have my emotions turning on a single thought.

"That's right, you can't, because you're a queen, and better yet, this is your castle."

"Damn straight," Dion says, approaching us.

I lower my feet and get up to greet him. "Do you even know what you're agreeing with?" I ask as he folds me into a tight hug.

"With you, it doesn't matter." Dion winks at me, and Helene and Kai take advantage of Essos's argument with Xavier to come over too. Kai's hug is like it always is, big and all-consuming, and he lifts me off my feet. I owe so much to this mountain of a man who did everything he could to support me, including train me, while Essos was unable to be here himself.

"Can everyone stop manhandling my wife?" Essos asks, hastening over, completely cutting Xavier off. My protective husband pulls me into his side, slinging an easy arm around me.

"You're acting like she's the first pregnant goddess ever," Xavier scolds, following him. Essos gives him a withering look that Xavier actually shrinks away from.

"You've had her all to yourself since everything went to shit." Helene slides her arms over my shoulders for a sideways hug because Essos won't let me go. "You told us all to stay away, and we did, so now let us enjoy your baby momma."

"She is a lot more than my baby momma, and I resent that. She needed rest."

"*She* is standing right here, and what do you mean, you told everyone to stay away?" I turn to face Essos slowly. He doesn't even look apologetic, just lifts his chin.

Our conversation about my trying to rest had nothing to do with keeping people from me.

"You went through a lot. I thought it was best that there was less traffic in the house and you had time to relax and not worry about much. Is it a bad thing that I wanted you all to myself?"

At Essos's response, Finn and Dion shrink away from us.

I think I might actually see red when I turn on him. "You thought it *best*?" My eyelid might twitch off from the anger coursing through my body, hot and ugly. Our conversations are apparently caught in a loop, because we've talked about this—that I'm not made of glass, that he agrees he won't hold me back—and then Essos sidelines me anyway.

"Yes. You're pregnant. You almost died several times. Galen almost stabbed you. Posey held a dagger to your neck and to your womb. Your best friend died in your arms. My father was murdered in front of you. Shall I keep going, or is going back over the twenty-four hours before I made that decision enough?"

"Oh, yes, Essos, tell me all the ways that my life has been threatened and how only you, a man, can protect me."

Everyone left in the room starts to back away from us.

"I think that was sarcasm, but in the event you were serious... Posey quite possibly still wants you dead for whatever perceived slight you have committed. I am not going to risk your life, I'm not going to let you risk our child's life, over your pride."

I laugh in his face, poking him in the chest. It drives him back a step, and I keep going. "*My* pride. You're worried about my pride? Essos, love, when in our lives has ordering me around *ever* been a good idea? When has it ever gotten you what you wanted? You think that because I'm pregnant, I should become this thing that is less than who I am, and if that isn't prideful of *you,* I don't know what is!"

Essos grips my cheeks. "Daphne, I don't want you to be any less than you are, but please, for one minute, see things through my eyes. *Please.* I held you as you bled out. I had to watch you choose Galen, knowing what he did to you, knowing you had none of that knowledge yourself when you made that call. I had to hear about him hurting you and touching you and kissing you. I had to hear, secondhand, about him trying to take liberties with *my wife.* I had to do all of this while I was powerless to stop anything. I was in a situation where my hands were tied and yes, in the grand scheme of our lives, that was a drop in the bucket, but it isn't something I can shrug off and pretend didn't happen. I can't pretend that I don't want to wrap you in a protective bubble until this is over and resolved. I would do it in a heartbeat, and maybe you would be angry with me and hate me for it, but it would be worth it if it meant you were safe."

I can't look away from how shredded Essos looks as he tells me this. And damned if it doesn't hurt me too, to think of all the ways he's been broken when it comes to me. But I had to live those things, and I'm not backing down, not now, because this sort of trauma isn't going to heal itself over time.

Essos runs his thumbs over my cheeks as he holds me, trying to soothe the hurt, but it doesn't matter. I am hurt by this, even if his motives do make sense.

"I love you, Essos, and I get what you're concerned about, I do, but I have had no autonomy for almost the last year. I am figuring out what my life looks like in the midst of constant calamity. Being pregnant does not make me less. It does not mean that I am weak. It just means I have more to fight for. Don't assume that I'm going to brazenly jump into danger because I'm back. I understand better than most just how fragile life is. I get what it means to die. I understand what it is to lose. I'm not willing to lose again, and that means not losing the support of the people I need and love in my life. You can't isolate me from our friends and family because you think I need to rest. I'm your wife, not someone who's incapable of making my own decisions."

I stretch up and kiss Essos, because despite my fury at him for trying to control the situation, he means everything to me, and I can understand, once I look past my rage, why he did what he did. But I'm still angry about it. I needed him during those two weeks, but I know that when he wasn't by my side, he was meeting with Xavier or Kai.

I'm wondering how much of the last few weeks was actually quiet and how much turmoil he hid from me. It's like we just jumped back five spaces, and I hate how insecure that makes me feel. He is the thing I should feel the most secure about, but how can I do that if he doesn't trust me?

"As atrociously cute as you two are, can we get back to dealing with my ex-wife?" Xavier asks imperiously.

"When did you find time to divorce her?" I ask, stepping away from Essos to grab a chip off the table. I think I've earned some junk food, especially if it's just the one.

Halfway to my mouth, it turns into a carrot. This is a step too far, and the anger that's been simmering becomes an overflowing boil. I turn to my husband and chuck the carrot at him. Mid-flight, it turns into a leaf and drops harmlessly to the floor. Clearly, we still have a lot to work on.

"That wasn't me," he says defensively, holding up his hands.

"Why waste my money on a divorce when killing her will work

just as well?" Xavier's tone is flippant, but he purses his lips as if upset by the idea of killing Posey.

"Because you would need one of the God Killer blades." I don't mention that Posey also has the scepter, and who knows what she can do with those two things combined? Other than jump-start the apocalypse. It's her possession of the scepter that makes me uneasy. With it, she can control the souls of the dead, *my* people.

"Which we do have," Essos reminds me. When he meets my eye, I can't stop the shiver that runs down my spine. It's hard not to shiver when that dagger holds the one thing that Octavia wants. It's why she lured me into the cavern under false pretenses.

I can pretend that I lost track of it in the aftermath of the almost-wedding, but I didn't. The dagger I used to stab Galen in the heart is still here, and the thought gives me goosebumps. I have to remind myself that his soul is trapped in that gem, unable to hurt me again. Knowing that Octavia is looking for it through me, Essos hid it so I have plausible deniability as to its whereabouts if I run into her again.

I look down at my hands, which feel sticky, like they're coated in something. For a heartbeat, they're red the way they were the night I killed Galen, but then I blink, and there's nothing there. They're clean.

Essos folds me against his body, and even though I'm mad at him, I let him, because I need this physical comfort.

"You mean we didn't drop it into the ocean like the old lady at the end of that movie?" I ask wistfully.

"No, and even if you had, I could have gotten it easily," Kai volunteers.

"It's somewhere safe," Essos answers vaguely.

"Safe," I repeat, not entirely convinced.

"He's never going to hurt you again. I promise." Essos's voice is gruff when he swears this to me, and I know my husband isn't one to break his promises.

Only, I'm not sure this is a promise he can keep.

"I hate to be the killer of moods, especially since I am one," Cassius says, jumping into the conversation. Moments like this make me wonder what I ever saw in him while we were together. I thought we were down to just the core group, but evidently, Cassius chose to linger. A quick look around confirms our cohort is now alone.

"You are a what? Pain in the ass?" Finn asks, then looks around the room for laughs. There are only eyerolls.

"I am a mood," Cassius clarifies, looking affronted as he pulls out a comb to smooth his hair back like it's the 1950s and he's waiting for Olivia Newton-John to sing backup.

"A bad one," I mutter, but then give him a fake smile. "Now that we've cleared that up, can you elaborate on how you're killing the mood, aside from these IQ-lowering comments?"

"Come on, Daphy, you loved it when I got low." He gives me a salacious wink before running his tongue over his lips, and I shudder. What I saw in Cassius is a mystery.

"Make your point," Essos growls, pulling me against him. His fingers dig into my hips. It's been a long time since he's been possessive like this, and I'm not hating it.

"Right. So, since I pay attention and I know things, like that you're from California originally—you and your sorority sisters. Be honest, did you ever make out with one of them? Maybe that kitty Cat? You can tell me. I swear it will be a secret." He has the audacity to wink.

It's Xavier who growls this time at the mention of Cat.

"Your fetishization of women loving women is gross," Helene tells him blandly. "Who invited him? Seriously?"

"Your twin brother, sweetheart. But if you would all stop picking on me, you will get to hear what I know."

"Do you want a formal embossed invitation, Cassius? Gods you're being extra annoying today," Helene snaps.

The room falls silent, and we all stare at Cassius. Thankfully, he gets bored after a few seconds and puts us out of our misery. "There has been extra activity in California. In addition to zombies being drawn in that direction, there's been a cluster of rather strong earthquakes."

California sits on a fault line, so that's not unusual, but I don't expect Posey to play fair. She could be causing both issues. I chew on my lip, thinking it over. Everyone is sharing looks, wondering about the significance of this.

"I did hear she was working with the God of Disasters. They felt that their initiatives weren't taken seriously enough by Xavier," Dion interjects, rubbing his boyfriend's back.

"That's because they had stupid fucking ideas. Like sinking whole countries. Who thinks *that's* ever a good idea?"

"Hadeon, apparently," Finn says with a laugh. "Of course, they would think that. They live for chaos."

Essos shakes his head, "No, Finn, *you* live for chaos. Hadeon lives for destruction."

"It doesn't matter," I snap, stepping out of Essos's grip so I can advance on Cassius. "How did you find all this out?"

Cassius smiles at me and mimics one of Essos's moves. He cups my cheek and smooths his thumb over it. I flinch back and out of his grip. Cassius laughs. Talk about living for chaos.

"In all seriousness, your girlie Zara was talking about how much she hated the media blackout caused by the zombie apocalypse, so I popped into the mortal realm to check on things, because I'm nice like that. She gave me your address and her parents' address and Cat's family's address, and the address of some chick named Tiffany. It's a hotbed of zombies in those areas, except for where that Tiffany girl is. Her boyfriend's got some sort of survivalist cabin in the mountains, so as long as Hadeon doesn't break off the state of California with a massive series of earthquakes, she should be fine. But mortals are much too fragile for my liking."

I turn my back on Cassius to look at my husband, fear threading its way through every last drop of common sense I have. The idea of having zombies clustering around my family's home, around Cat's and Zara's families' homes... It's unacceptable.

Essos shakes his head, mouthing the word *No* to me.

He's not wrong to do so, that last piece of common sense whispers to me. I am pregnant. *I* am protected, but until our child is born and breathes their first breath, they don't have my immortality.

But then fear reaches that corner of my mind, and I know I'll do what needs to be done to protect my family—all of them.

I TELL Kai to meet me outside in twenty minutes because I want to brush up on my training, but first, I need to grab Cat. On my way back to the library I find Zara and drag her along too. Going to the mortal world is going to be a group effort, which means we all need to be prepared. When I break into the library, I find that Rafferty is gone and Cat seems eager to hit something. It's not a trial to convince her to come train with me.

"Everything go well with Rafferty?" I ask cautiously as we walk toward the training pitch.

Cat hums for a moment, like she's looking for the right words. "Well enough. I asked him to just block the memories of my past lives, and I already feel lighter."

I jump on that and slide my arm in with hers. "Lighter already? We like feeling lighter." She nods her agreement before slipping back into her shell. I can feel that there is something else on her mind, but I don't want to push her too hard. "Anything else to add? I know Rafferty isn't the most palatable of all the gods."

"He was, whatever. You know? To his credit, he did help and showed me some easier power basics, like how to tap into my abilities intentionally."

"That's great!" I say with too much enthusiasm for even me. Zara shoots me a look over Cat's head and I just shrug.

The training pitch only has Kai warming up with a staff until my husband steps forward out of the shadows to watch.

Kai glances up at Essos before focusing on me. "You should take it easier on him."

I scoff. "I should take it easier on *him?* He's the one who is ready to lock me up and throw away the key."

"Did you know that someone tried to have a cursed object delivered to you?"

I hesitate and glance at Essos, who has his arms crossed, his face blank.

"Yeah, I didn't think so," Kai continues. "It was lipstick, something so innocuous, but if you had put it on it would have sealed your mouth shut. Yes, Daphne, you *should* take it easier on him."

Another thing Essos didn't tell me, but it casts a whole new light on his behavior.

Essos tracks every movement we make from warming up to progressing from one-on-one to two-on-one up to three-on-one. To get us to work together, it's three-on-one as Cat, Zara, and I take on the hulking god. Kai is brutally efficient, blocking blows and striking against us, trying to drive us back. As he turns, his elbow glances off my cheek, but I shake it off.

"Enough," Essos calls from the sidelines, where he's been watching reluctantly, allowing me to prove to him and to myself that I'm still capable. He's changed from his usual suit into something better suited for working out. A black T-shirt clings to his body, outlining his abs. The shorts he has on hang tantalizingly low, showing off not just the top trim of his boxers, but the start of his Adonis belt and that line of hair from his belly button that disappears into his shorts. My heart skips a beat and then starts again, seeming to chant, *mine, mine, mine.* It's a struggle not to fling myself at him.

His hands on my chin are soft as he tilts my head and studies where the blow connected, and I want to roll my eyes. But I know this comes from a place of love, so I hold back instead.

"You'll live," he reassures Essos, and I hate the smile that spreads over my lips before I remind myself that I'm supposed to be a little pissed at him.

"Sure I don't have to lose the face?" I tease, and he relaxes infinitesimally. "I'm really okay. It was just my cheek."

"Love, there is no 'just' when it comes to any harm you endure."

"I'm no longer the fragile flower of Spring. I'm stronger now, more resilient. You need to accept that. You don't need to shelter me from the storm. I am the storm."

Essos's reaction is unexpected. His mouth crashes over mine, and he hauls me against him in a kiss that is devastating to my anger at him. My knees go weak as my desire rises. He catches me, holding me firmly against him, never breaking the kiss, and scoops one leg under those traitorous knees to lift me.

He takes two steps away from our friends before I feel that familiar drop in my stomach as we move through space and time. I don't stop kissing him, needing him more and more with each passing moment.

We don't stop kissing until he lays me on our bed. He takes his time looking me over, long enough that I'm squirming under his gaze. It morphs from being watchful and full of promise to desperate. He climbs onto the bed, looking away from me. I get the feeling that whatever he wants to say will be too difficult if he's looking at me.

"I know that you're not fragile and that you're strong, Daphne," Essos says quietly. I turn to face him, curling an arm under my head. "I feel as though I'm beating a dead horse at this point, but the thought of losing you sends me into a panic. My head feels too light, sounds are too loud, and I think I might pass out."

"Why didn't you tell me people are making threats against me?" I ask point-blank.

He turns on his side, resting his hand on my hip before scooting closer to me so our bodies are touching again. I try not to squirm as his finger draws invisible patterns on my hip, tickling me.

"Because I didn't want to stress you out. Because stress is bad for our baby, and I want you focused on growing them."

"You can't say I'm not a fragile flower and then proceed to lock me up in a tower and throw away the key because I'm pregnant. That's not you, Essos. Are you doing it because of what happened with Galen at the ball? Do you not trust me?" I hate the sensation of tears pricking the back of my eyes.

"Of *course,* I trust you, love. I'm being a prick because of everything I've already said. We're going to war with Posey. She killed my *father* without a thought. She stripped the souls from the Underworld and caused a zombie apocalypse in the mortal realm. I don't doubt that she would harm you again."

"And the threats that aren't from Posey?" I trace a finger along Essos's side.

"No one is getting near you."

"So, there *are* other threats. Tell me, Essos. I can't defend myself if I don't know about them."

Essos grits his teeth but doesn't look away. "You want to know about the people who say the Traitor Queen should have stayed dead? The people who say I am unfit to rule for choosing you? Who still support Galen and want your head for killing him? That's not even the ugliest of the things they want to do to you."

My insides drop away as fear seeps in. Essos doesn't have to spell any more out. I know what men like to do to women who are more powerful than them, how they like to make sure the woman feels smaller and inferior so she knows her place. I think about being subjected to that. The feel of Galen's body over mine when he assaulted me after the second Trial. I still haven't told Essos the whole of it, in part fearing that he'll give in to his desire to lock me away, regardless of the repercussions.

My hand stops moving, but his don't. He captures my face and rolls us so that his body is covering mine once again. "That look right there? That flash of fear? That stomach-swooping concern that something *might* happen to you that you just felt? That's what I feel *every time* I see one of these threats. I've lived too long without you."

I wrap an arm around him and pull him tighter to me. He still doesn't transfer his full weight to me, but he does relax just a little. When I release him, he rolls back onto his side to face me.

"How about this? Maybe *talk* to me," I say. "Tell me what's going on. I do need to know that people want me dead. I need to be on alert. I can't go frolicking through the flowers and then come across an enchanted spinning wheel and prick my finger on it if I don't know such a curse exists. We got really good at communicating after everything that happened with Ellie, so I don't know what's going on here."

"Is 'I'm a coward' a good answer?"

"No. You also owe me an explanation about Lucky's comment."

Essos winces. "I hoped you hadn't caught that."

"I did. Now fess up. This confession also better involve tacos."

"How about I taco-bout my love for you instead?"

I glare at him, and he only smirks.

"I'm sorry, love. It's hard to take that look seriously when you look good enough to eat." He sighs and looks away from me, his face hardening as if he's girding himself to tell me something I won't want to hear. "No. I didn't sleep with Lucky, but I was at a party where she was coming on to me. I was trashed and can't remember much past that, but I do know that Finn took me home that night. I asked him about it, and he swore up and down that he didn't let me out of his sight."

I can't help the slightly strangled sound that comes out of my throat. It's not as bad as I thought, but how many other women pursued him?

I don't want to know because, at the end of the day, it doesn't matter.

Essos seems to sense that I have more on my mind, because he continues. "The only sober focus I had was you. I was petitioning the Council daily for your return and was being turned down, and Posey finally told me that if I kept pushing, then she would never release you. I was at my lowest, although that's not an excuse. I wish I could tell you you're never going to face other women with similar claims, but I can't."

I disentangle myself from his grip, and his hands tighten for just a second before he releases me.

"I need a shower," I tell him. It's a credit to Essos how well he can read me. He knows I need my space. Not because of him and his actions, but because the idea of someone taking advantage of him while he was drunk is making my blood boil, and if I say anything past the clenching of my teeth, I might level a forest.

While the water warms, I focus on my breathing. It's only as I'm rinsing my hair that it occurs to me that Essos might see my silence as anger directed at him for being with someone else while I was dead.

When I finally emerge from my shower, I'm tying the knot

around my robe when I see a tray on the counter with five perfect tacos.

I look to my husband, who is sitting in our bed, a book open on his lap. There's a wary look on his face, and I want to kiss it away. The covers are pulled up around him like some sort of makeshift armor, and I wonder if his confession has left him feeling vulnerable.

"I love you," I tell Essos as I pull off my robe. "I'm not upset with you. I'm upset that you were put in that position. Whatever happened or didn't happen while I was dead doesn't change anything for me."

He's sitting up in bed, eyes glued to my every move. I want to jump him, but I grab a taco instead, leaving him with a full view of my bare body.

"I know," he says, eyes on my lips even as I chew. "How is it that you can make eating a taco look like porn?"

"It's probably my naked body," I tease, digging into my second taco.

"No, it's all you, my love. You're tempting me to get between you and your next taco." He throws off the sheets and climbs out of bed. His impressive erection creates a tent in his boxers, and he comes closer but doesn't stop me as I grab the third one. He cages me in from behind while rubbing my small bump. "I can't wait to watch this grow."

"Get me some more tacos, and it's going to grow faster than you expect." I lean against him, dropping my head back on his shoulder as his hands move up to fondle my breasts. "I'm taking Cat and Zara to the mortal realm tomorrow, and you can either come with me or stay home, but there is no third option."

"You are *not* taking this off," Essos tells me as he slides me into a brown vest with sheer sleeves. It's hardly the height of fashion, but I can feel magic pulsing off it.

"What does it do?" I ask as he zips me into it. His hands coast around my sides as he checks the fit.

"Tink made it to repel anything that could harm you."

I search my memory for a Tink and hate that I come up blank.

Essos must catch the look on my face because sympathy flashes across his own features. It's all over the softness in his eyes and the small downturn of his lips. "Tink is the God of Craftsmen."

This jogs something, and I snap and point at Essos. "He made those weird rollerblade-type things, and you broke your elbow playing on them when Kai clotheslined you."

I'm sitting on a blanket in the grass while Kai, Essos, and Tink stand on a paved path. Essos hasn't looked over at where Helene and I are drinking with Dion and another woman. My fiancé's hair is windblown and he hasn't even strapped on these odd shoes yet. I can't help but laugh as he gestures for Tink to hand them over.

Tink is a tall man—almost a full head taller than Essos—and while he's brought us to the park to show off his latest invention, his gaze keeps floating back in our direction...no, not our direction, the direction of the woman sitting beside me whose bare legs go on forever.

"I wouldn't do it," I call in warning, and Helene snickers.

"He's going to do it," Dion hedges, refilling our glasses.

Kai glances at Helene, who shakes her head, and the giant sticks out his lower lip in a pout.

Tink helps to strap his inventions to the bottom of Essos's shoes. Essos looks psyched as he kicks off with one foot then leans into the motion, the power in the gadgets propelling him forward. He does a few loops before Kai throws his arm in Essos's way. The action is so unexpected that he has no time to brace, and he winds up flat on his back.

We all jump up and rush forward. Essos is laughing while cradling his arm. "I would have given them to you if you just asked.*"*

"I did ask. Four laps ago!"

I scowl. "It was only two laps, Kai."

"Looks like I still have some kinks to work out," Tink says, stripping the skate-like things off Essos's feet.

"I think I broke my arm."

"Let me look," a seductive female voice says as she moves to kneel beside me. Callista, Galen's new girlfriend, takes Essos's arm as gently as she can. The mile-long legs belonged to her. Tink invited her along, trying to be a good friend, and insisted we get to know her. She didn't suggest inviting her boyfriend, so we didn't offer.

I move to Essos's other side and give him a brief upside-down kiss. "Don't scare me like that," I scold.

"My love, I'm immortal. I'll heal eventually."

"You'll heal even sooner than eventually, since you have me here," Callie tells him with a grin. "You did break it, but I'll have you fixed up in no time."

"In no time—you hear that, Daphne? Nothing to worry about. You're not getting rid of me that easily."

"Despite what my brute of a husband might try." Helene bumps Kai with her shoulder.

"I didn't mean to. How was I supposed to know the shoes would propel him into the ground once his feet were in the air?"

"I think the problem is more why *his feet were pointed the wrong way. My invention works as intended; it just can't account for people being clotheslined," Tink grumbles.*

"Good as new, Essos." Callie lets him go, and he flexes his arm.

"Until the next thing."

"Keep tinkering," I joke, and Tink gives me a flat look that eventually teases into a smile.

"Where is Tink these days?" I ask, poking at the material of the vest.

"He's...otherwise occupied, but I..." Essos looks away from me.

I grab his face and turn him to look at me. "You what?"

He blows out a breath before meeting my gaze. "I had him make you a few impenetrable garments. We're going to the mortal realm, where there are actual zombies. I'm not going to bring you there to be an extra on the set of *The Walking Dead*. What do you even want from the mortals?"

"I want to see what damage is being done. I want to see how we can help. Cat wants to go and see her family. I want to see mine."

"Oh, Daphne. Your parents are safe. I moved them from the Underworld the night of the Calling Ball."

Embarrassed to admit I wasn't even thinking about those parents—my biological ones—I blush. "I meant Phil and Melinda. They're the closest thing I had to parents when I was a mortal."

Now Essos is blushing. "Of course. Will Zara be joining us as well?"

"Yes."

"Right. We should get this over with before I change my mind."

WHEN I WALK into the dining room, Cat is stuffing a croissant in her mouth. Xavier is standing close to her like they might have actually been talking before I entered. His stormy blue eyes flick to me and my husband, who is right on my heels.

They are not alone, not by a longshot, and I shouldn't be surprised that our friends have rallied around us to make this journey. Zara is with Helene, while Kai, Dion, and Finn study the weapons on the table. Most surprising is Cassius, who is also surveying the weapons. He selects a small dagger and hurls it in my direction. Halfway to me I form it into a rose, and it drops to the ground.

"Try that again, and I'll make it so you can never look in a mirror again," Essos tells him with deadly calm.

"Why? Going to fuck my face up that badly?" Cassius challenges. "Relax. I was just testing her reflexes. We need to know if, as a born-again goddess, she's more vulnerable or less."

Xavier watches the exchange with interest, a smirk tugging at his lips.

"No, fuckface, I'll make it so you're unable to see your reflection, always wondering if there's something stuck in your teeth. I wonder if that will make the God of Vanity wither away..."

Cassius straightens from where he was leaning against the table. "You couldn't possibly do that."

"I'm a child of the God and Goddess Supreme. My siblings and I all have untold powers. Is that something you really want to test?"

The room around us is silent as they stare each other down. Perhaps working with my ex is a little more than Essos can bear.

"Enough. If we're going to do this, we should go now," Xavier says. He reaches for Cat but seems to think better of it, placing his hand in his pocket to try to cover up the move. Cat bites her lip and looks around at the group. I can watch the internal struggle play out on her face. After yesterday, I expect her to come with Essos and me, but instead, she steps into Xavier's arms. Surprise lights on his face, and his arms fold around her quickly, like he won't let this chance pass him by.

"Aren't we going to talk about our plan?" I ask, looking up at Essos, and he shakes his head.

"No, because if we talk about this, I'm going to change my mind. I'm trying to remain a man of my word, but you're making it exceedingly difficult."

"We spoke last night," Finn tells me with a playful grin. "After someone went to sleep. We're going to divide and conquer. Half to Cat's family and the other half to Zara's. Daph and Essos to her parents."

"Absolutely not." I make myself a little breakfast sandwich, heaping eggs on top of a sausage patty and an English muffin. "In every horror movie, whenever anything goes wrong, it's because they decided to separate. I'm not interested in one of you turning into the red shirt of this operation. We stay together, all of us. Pick where we start, but being apart is not an option." I inject as much finality into my tone as I can before taking a savage bite of my food.

"We'll start at Zara's house then," Helene says.

"Maybe we should call Bria?" Kai suggests, and affable Dion glares.

"No," he says with as much vehemence as I did.

Finn's cheeks turn pink as he looks at his boyfriend.

"Why not?" Cassius asks. His tone says everything—he's trying to stir the pot. "The Goddess of the Hunt would be pretty handy to have hanging around, since we can't have the God of War with us."

At the reminder of Galen, I step back, but Essos's hand on my shoulder keeps me in this moment and not in any of the torturous ones with Galen.

"Because we can't trust her. You're lucky we're trusting *you*," Dion snaps.

"Why *are* we trusting him?" Cat glances around at the group, then at Cassius with a healthy amount of suspicion. "I know I'm new to this intrigue, but I don't know you from Adam." Cat sees danger lurking in all corners. She doesn't know yet that Cassius is exactly what you expect from the God of Vanity. Sensing we're not quite ready to leave, she steps out of Xavier's grip. He immediately reacts to her absence by shoving his hands back in his pockets.

"I'm the one who tried to help your dear, sweet Phoenix Queen. Even when it meant risking my life. So, excuse you. What have *you* done for her? Besides boink her brother-in-law and be a general weakness, that is. I saw the pretty necklace Posey gave you. Where *is* your newest accessory?"

Xavier grabs Cassius by the throat and shoves him against the wall. "Why don't we see how *you* like wearing a collar?" Sparks thread around the hand Xavier is using to hold Cassius to the wall. "I don't care if Catalina speaks to you first—you are to *never* speak to her, say her name, or even look at her, or I will find the God Killer blade and carve up your pretty, pretty face."

Cat looks at me, her green eyes wide and owlish. There is a faint flush to her cheeks, making me think that she might actually be turned on by this show of dominance. I know I might be too.

"Well, that's settled," Helene interrupts, clapping her hands. "Both of my brothers are being led by their dicks right now. But we still don't have a *plan*."

"We'll go to my house first. I just want to look. I don't want to interrupt their lives any more than necessary," Zara says, cutting the tension much more effectively than Helene.

Xavier releases Cassius, leaving a ring of lighting around the other god's throat before he calls it back.

"I'll go with Finn," Cat says breathlessly, stepping away from Xavier. Her lower lip is in her teeth as she rounds the table to my friend.

"Zara's, then Cat's. Then I want you all to come back to the house," I tell them.

"What about your parents?" Essos asks, his thumb brushing my chin before he licks off whatever food was there. Whether it's because I'm a messy eater or Xavier's response left food falling out of my mouth, I don't know.

"You and I can go there after. I don't want to overwhelm them," I tell him quietly.

"All due respect, Daph, you need back-up too. At least let Kai and I come with you. The rest of these fools can come back to the house and do whatever," Helene offers. "You were, after all, the one that didn't want the group to break up."

"I am *not* a fool," Cat snaps, humming with power.

"She didn't mean you, Cat," Kai says.

"As much as I hate it when my husband speaks for me, he's right. I did mean the menfolk are being foolish. Namely, Cassius, for thinking that he can remotely measure up to Xavier. But that's neither here nor there. Until you accept help getting control of your powers, you're a liability, and Zara is still mortal."

"I can measure up. I'm probably bigger than Xavier, too," Cassius mumbles under his breath.

"*Am* I mortal, though?" Zara asks innocently.

"You're as mortal as you can be. There's not exactly precedence for a mortal existing outside the Underworld for long periods of time." Dion's tone has a hard edge to it, and I think he's still affected from the mention of Bria's name.

I wonder what went wrong with them the three of them.

"What about prior Callings?" Cat asks. "Were they even real?"

"Your Calling was very, *very* real," Essos tells her, gripping the back of my neck. He squeezes it, and I turn to look at him. Just from staring into his eyes, I can tell he's getting lost in those years that he participated in the Callings and I wasn't by his side. "But it was just as much of a farce. I usually welcomed the girls in the Callings and let them be until someone told me I had to do something about them, and then I sent them to their afterlives. I knew Daphne wasn't there, and I wasn't interested in getting to know anyone else. There was only ever her."

"Does anyone know how Posey is driving the zombies closer to our families?" Zara asks. She hugs her arms to her chest, doubt written all over her face.

"It's probably something as simple as the scent of meat, or whatever the zombies want. She's creating something that's drawing them closer," Dion supplies.

I glance into the solid blue of Essos's eyes. "It's got the be the scepter."

Essos nods. "Probably. With the scepter and the dagger, it may not matter that she doesn't have an affinity for the dead. Being a Fate means that her powers aren't as specific as the rest of ours are."

"We really need to get both those things back from her," Finn points out, as if we all weren't aware of the obvious.

"I might have some thoughts on that," Cassius suggests, winking at me. I can only imagine what that wink is suggesting. No, I don't need to imagine—I know, because I know that banging a Fate just went to the top of his to-do list.

I give Essos a warm smile that only grows when he presses his forehead against mine. "We should get this show on the road," I gently prod. I can't think about what Posey's doing with those souls right now, what she can do with them. If she can use the scepter to control the souls, what else can she use it for?

"Autobots, roll out," Finn says before he loops his arm around Cat's shoulders and vanishes.

We congregate on the street in front of Zara's parents' home. I'm surprised to find that the suburban neighborhood seems vacant. I expected zombies would be roaming around aimlessly, but I don't hear any eerie moans, nor do I see any shambling corpses.

I wonder if Cassius's intel was wrong.

The street does look like what I'd expect from the set of *The Walking Dead*. Bloodstains mar the ground, and cars are parked to block off the street on one end with makeshift fencing on the other.

It takes a moment, but the scent of rotting flesh finally hits me, and I can't help it—I turn and puke on Cassius's feet. Sheepishly, I wipe my mouth, giving him an apologetic look.

Essos rubs my back gently then faces Zara. "We can play this one of two ways. We can cloak ourselves and go into your home and check on your family, or we can announce to them that we're here."

I don't think Zara has taken a single breath since we landed. She's staring up at her home with tears welling in her big, dark eyes. Essos scans the area around us as I approach Zara and place one hand on her shoulder.

Zara looks at me, then at the rest of our friends, who are ready to support her in any way they can. "I just want to look inside. Helene, will you go with me?"

Helene's eyebrows lift, but she nods. "Let's do this, kid." She holds out a hand to Zara, who takes it without hesitation.

I can't just stand here and wait for Zara and Helene to return, so I start to walk down the block.

Essos is practically fused to my hip, walking in tandem with me, shortening his stride to match mine. "Where do you think you're going?" he asks tersely.

I stop walking and face him. "I'm going to walk around and see what I can see about what's happening."

"No."

I take a deep breath in through my nose and try to envision that I'm in a garden, and that I'm at peace and not in a post-apocalyptic wasteland.

"Essos..."

"I'll walk with her," Finn volunteers. He steps forward and loops his arm with mine. "You know I won't let anything happen to her. I'm the fastest god alive, and I proved it to all of Solarem."

I can appreciate the effort he's putting in to reduce the tension between me and Essos, even as I see the muscle in Essos's jaw tick. It's a tradeoff I'm willing to accept. I love my husband, but he's suffocating me with his need to protect me.

"Fine," Essos grits out. I feel his stare on my back as Finn and I continue down the block.

The sun is starting to rise, and it's not unlike the morning my mortal life was cut short. Except, when I look into the sky, nestled in the clouds are the spires of Solarem.

"You have to give him a break, Daphne," Finn says.

"Essos can handle his own battles, thank you very much," I point out sourly.

At the edge of the street where the cars are parked to block out the zombies, I finally see mortals. There are five of them that seem to be on patrol. Two sit atop pickup trucks so they can look at the zombies milling about while the other three congregate and share–if the smell is to be trusted–a joint.

"Do you see a safe spot we can view the zombies from?" I ask. "I'm not interested in finding out if zombie gods are a thing, but I'd like to get a better read on the situation."

"Yeah, I'm going to have to pass on that. Your husband will disembowel me and feed my entrails to your dogs. Which I'm sure they would enjoy very much, but I would not."

"Besides, why get any closer to the danger when you're already close as can be?"

At the sound of the female voice, Finn and I both whirl around to find Posey standing there. She gives me a wicked grin with all teeth.

"Posey," Finn greets, sliding his hands into his pockets with a practiced air of relaxation.

"Finn, you're not necessary for this conversation, so I suggest you keep your gaze averted while I speak with Daphne, woman-to-woman."

"Posey, you're crazier than I thought if you think for one *second* that I'm going to take my eyes off you."

"If you think I'm the bad guy you've all dreamed me up to be, then why haven't you tried to kill me yet? Oh, that's right. I have a God Killer blade *and* the Scepter of the Dead, and you're too busy waiting for Xavier to finish scratching his balls to come up with a way to face me. So many clever things I can do with *all those souls* because your husband wanted to save your life instead of those he vowed to protect." Posey giggles. "Oops! I'm sorry, *not* your husband. Your lover."

"What do you want, Posey?" I ask through gritted teeth. I glance at the mortals, then in the direction of Essos and the others.

A blade appears in her hands. "We're glamoured, just like Zara and Helene are in Zara's house. As far as your friends are concerned, you two are standing here watching the sun rise as the mortals you swore to protect eat each other in the streets. Are you having fun yet, Daphne?"

"I wouldn't call this fun, no."

"You never did have a sense of humor." Posey sounds bored. She's wearing a bright yellow sundress and doesn't have a hair out of place. She looks almost friendly, only there's nothing to hide the gleam of insanity in her gaze.

"Are you here to indulge in another villain's monologue, show off just how wrong we are about your plans, and make us second-guess ourselves left and right?" Finn edges himself between Posey and me.

She must see exactly what he's up to, because she *laughs*. "Fates," she giggles to herself. "I guess I can't really use that curse, since you now know we're actually talking about *me*. No, I have a one-time limited offer for Daphne. She can avoid any more bloodshed."

"How?" I ask. Whatever she says, I'm not going to like it, nor am I going to agree to it, but I feel like I need to at least hear her offer. I can use it as a metric for just how out of her mind she is.

"How, she asks," Posey says, speaking to Finn. She turns her focus on me. "Step up and be a queen, but be *my* queen. You've seen just as much bullshit with this family as I have. You've seen the utter lack of respect toward women, and more than that, how the very heads of the family—the God and Goddess Supreme—shirked their *responsibility,* not only to the citizens of Solarem but also to the mortal realm you pretend to love so much. How can you stand here and look around at what the ruling families have wrought and not be *angry*? I know the vicious monster you keep chained in your dark heart. I know that you want recompense for all they have done."

She walks in a circle, waving the dagger around as she talks with her hands. Finn keeps himself between us, never letting there be space for her to lunge at me.

It's unhelpful to point out to her that *she* is the one that did this, but I can't help myself.

"If you want to put the blame at Octavia and Titus and their children's feet, fine, but you can't do that without taking blame too. *You* raised the dead. *You* pulled down the veil. Essos did everything right—he jumped through every hoop you tossed his way to get me back, and he did it while also running the Underworld."

"Your Essos wasn't as innocent as you like to think he was. He might play the weeping widower well, but he fell right back into Ellie's bed the second time just as quickly as he did the first time I put her in his path. He's weak. He will always be weak. But you...you have *power*, real, raw power that comes from being more than just a concubine to a king."

"You would know, wouldn't you?" I ask, my tone haughty.

This seems to be the thing that spurns her into action, because she lunges for me then. Finn intercepts her, and the thought that he could be damaged for my recklessness stills my heart.

Posey swings the blade with menace but manages only to slice a gash down his forearm. "I rescind my offer, you stupid bitch. I think this time, I'll carve Essos's heart out in front of you and make you watch as I eat it." She turns her back, showing us just what she thinks of us as a threat.

To my utter horror, she uses her power to force the cars acting as a blockade apart. Several undead heads swivel toward the sound.

I turn toward Posey, already calling forth my vines. I have no way of holding on to a Fate, or even thinking that my powers are strong enough to do so. Finn didn't attempt it, but I'm going to try, and if we can grab her now, we'll just...figure it out.

My vines don't even break through the ground before she simply vanishes. Her shield over us must be gone as well, because now not only can Essos see us again, but the zombies have scented Finn's blood.

There is a zombie hoard headed right for us.

"I did *not* sign up for this shit," Finn mutters in disbelief.

I throw up my vines, ensnaring several zombies, but they fall forward and rip their bodies apart to crawl toward us. When I was a mortal, I knew I didn't have a shot at surviving the zombie apocalypse. The only way I could have done so was if someone else tripped and fell, letting me get away.

"Daphne!" Essos calls. My name echoes, and I can see people looking out their windows to see who would be stupid enough to shout.

Finn and I back up slowly. We can transport ourselves out of here, no problem, but the barrier protecting the mortals is gone, and I'm not leaving without fixing this situation as best I can.

Essos is by my side before I know it. He takes in Finn's bleeding arm before his gaze sweeps me for any sign of injury.

"I'm fine, but these mortals won't be," I tell him.

"We should be able to send the souls back to the Underworld."

"We can't."

He looks at me, backing up and dragging me with him, one eye on the forms lurching in front of us. Xavier pulls lightning down from the sky and fries a zombie that was getting too close for comfort.

"Not how I imaged my immortality ending, I'll be honest," Cat says, her voice shaking.

"It's not going to end," Xavier growls. He turns to his brother. "Do something about the dead."

Essos gives Xavier a disparaging glare before turning his gaze to me. "Why can't we send them to the Underworld?"

"Okay, *I* can't. I don't remember how." I blink at him, hoping my terror isn't obvious on my face, but I know Essos is seeing right through me. He slides his hand into mine.

"We'll do it together," he assures me.

"Together."

I let the contact of our grip ground me even as we both keeping backing away from the incoming forces. Then, Essos reaches out for my power like he's reaching into my chest for my very essence. Embracing the sensation, I open my well of power to him and let it flow through our connection. Mimicking each move he makes, I hold up my hand the same way he does.

Together, we send a welcoming wave toward the souls, encouraging them to use us as a gateway to the Underworld.

The zombie closest to the front barely stumbles in its quest for us.

Nothing happens. I cast a look at Essos, catching sight of the wrinkle in his brow. He takes a deep breath and, through the tether between us, I feel him gathering his strength and mine.

We try again.

And again.

And again.

"Maybe, it's me?" I ask, withdrawing from him. This failure touches on one of my greatest fears—that everyone is right, and Essos and I aren't actually married.

I can feel his reluctance as he pulls his power away, but he doesn't release my hand until I take it back.

This time, when Essos pushes his will forward on the zombies in front of us, I can see the thread of his power wavering in the air, but when he draws the power back, the zombies keep walking.

"Whatever you're trying is *not* working," Cassius whines. I glance in his direction and see that he is positioned at the back of the pack. Spineless prick.

"I hate to agree, Essos," Xavier says, using his power to physically drive the zombies back a few steps.

"Clearly, the reason there *are* zombies isn't resolved, so maybe we should clear *that* up," Cat suggests.

"That is *not* clear," Dion says, and I can hear panic threading through everyone's voices. We'll be safe, but Zara's family and the other mortals here won't be.

I put a hand on Essos's shoulder. We both know what he has to do. Destruction of the bodies isn't stopping the zombies, which means that we have to follow Cat's logic and take away the thing that is animating them—their very souls.

"I know," Essos whispers.

I keep my hand on him, funneling not my power this time, but my love, because I know my husband. I know who he is at the core of his being, and destroying these souls is going to chip off a piece of him I'm not sure he's prepared to give up.

Essos shakes out his arms before I feel him drop into his magic. The chomping decayed faces are getting closer and closer, but Essos won't be rushed.

He brings his hands together in a firm *clap*. The zombies cease their movement and for one heartbreaking moment, I'm afraid it didn't work. But then the zombies in our immediate vicinity drop to the ground. With nothing to hold their bodies upright anymore, they fall. It's going to be up to the mortals here to rebury or burn their friends and family, unless we do something to start making up for all the ways the gods have interfered for the worse.

Agony blazes over Essos's face for a heartbeat before he throws his mask of indifference into place. My heart breaks for him and for the souls that were just destroyed, and the force of that loss renders me weak.

I don't know what I'm doing. I can't be a good queen when I can't protect the people who are most deserving of my protection. Who do I think I am?

I want to voice these insecurities to my husband. I want to hear him reassure me that we're doing the right thing in the long run, but I'm not sure I believe that any longer.

One look at Essos, and I know that I'm not the one who needs reassuring. The crease in his brow is etched into his skin, and the frown lines around his mouth seem permanent.

Zara storms out of her house. "What the hell just happened?"

"That's an excellent question," Xavier says. It's a testament to how shaken Cat is that when he draws her into his side with a firm arm, she doesn't fight him. She holds on to him like he's her lifeline in this storm.

"Perhaps it's a question that we can answer back at Essos and Daphne's home?" Dion suggests. He's holding Finn's arm, trying to stem the bleeding.

"No. I still haven't seen my parents," Cat tells Xavier, desperately looking up at him.

"You're also not leaving without giving these people some sort of protection. You gods and how you play with mortals... you bring all this devastation, and you don't care!" Zara shouts at us.

I look up and down the street. The mortals are still watching us from their homes. In hindsight, maybe we should have glamoured our appearance, but we weren't prepared to face down Posey today. There's no hope of going back under the radar.

"We will," Kai promises. "Helene and I will stay behind and create a safer barrier, clean this up. Nothing and no one intending harm will be able to enter." It sounds better than the blockade of cars on the roads with who knows what else around them.

"I'll come back here to ensure it has the power of the King of Gods," Xavier offers before turning to Dion. "Take Finn home. It would seem that Daphne and Essos have some research to do as to why the dead aren't staying in the Underworld."

"We know why," I say softly, the memory of my conversation with Octavia coming forward. I had forgotten that my conversation didn't only have to do with Galen. She *told* me that the gates to the Underworld were closed. I just didn't understand at the time what she meant, but now I do. Now I get it, and things are so much worse.

Essos grabs my hand. "We can discuss this later," he murmurs just to me.

I should go with Essos, but I feel like I still need to be here with Cat and I still need to check on my own parents. "I'll go with Cat, if it's all the same," I say, torn between my best friend and my husband.

"It's not all the same, Daph." Cat's tone is harsh, but she softens her voice to deliver the blow. "You need to go home with Essos and fix this. I don't mean to be a bitch about it, but honestly, look at the world. You wanted to come here and see all the things that are wrong in the mortal realm? This is it. People are being reanimated because something is keeping them out of *your* Underworld." Cat's face is warm with sympathy even as she rightfully scolds me.

Essos pulls his hand from mine, drawing my attention to him. "We'll come back for your parents another time. They're all right. We need to figure this out." Essos rubs my back, and I can feel what he's not saying—he needs to find a solution because doing what he just did came at a great personal cost. One that he would pay again to keep our friends and families safe, but I don't want him to be in that position ever again.

"I love you, but I have Xavier and Zara with me. Be the badass we both know you are and fix this." Cat pulls me into a hug.

"I'll stay with Cat," Zara confirms.

"Fine," I agree. I pull back and step into the safety of Essos's arms.

"Everyone knows what they're doing, right?" Xavier looks at each of us. "Dion and Finn are going back to the house. Helene and Kai are staying here to fortify the mortals' boundary and wipe their memories. You shouldn't need Rafferty, but if it is a problem, contact me. Daphne and Essos will figure out what's wrong with the Underworld, and Cassius will escort Zara along with Cat and I to see Cat's family. Unless you have a different location in mind, Zara?"

My heart swells with pride at Xavier for taking command. In fact, most of us have our eyebrows raised in surprise.

"I'll stay with Cat," Zara confirms, gripping Cat's hand.

"Right. Then let's stop wasting time and get our jobs done."

Essos teleports us into a room in the Solarem library that we've been given access to for just this purpose. It's private and alerts Gisella that we've arrived without other people seeing us.

I grab a trashcan and hurl.

"I'll see if Gisella will make a one-time exception for food. I'm pretty sure you've thrown up all of breakfast at this point." Essos holds my hair with one hand while the other rubs my back.

"I will not, but you're welcome to eat in *here* while I gather your reading materials."

At the gentle voice of Solarem's premier librarian, I peer over my shoulder. She's leaning against the doorframe, barring entrance to anyone who might consider investigating.

"Of course. Thank you, Gisella," Essos says.

A glass of water and a glass of ginger fizz appear on the lone table in the windowless room.

"What literature are you looking for today?"

Another wave of nausea rocks me, leaving Essos in charge of

answering. "We're seeking information about the creation of the Underworld."

"I presume you don't mean your layers of the Afterlife?"

"You would presume correctly. I want information dating back to the first souls to ever be sent there, and I want information regarding its formation."

"Much of what you're seeking will be contained in books about the God and Goddess Supreme, and we do not have many of those here. Your family home likely has most of them."

I lift my head to look at Essos, then glance at Gisella. "I take it you don't mean our home—you mean Essos's childhood home?"

His childhood home, if you can even call it that, is the one that Xavier and Posey lived in together. That is, until she held a coup and kicked him out. Feeling just a little better, I sink into the large comfy reading chair in the corner.

"That would be correct. You can also ask Sybil or Estelle if either of them can answer your questions."

I rub my stomach as I sip the ginger drink. Another great source of information would be the Goddess Supreme herself, but she's made it clear she'll help for one reason and one reason only, so she's not an option. Thinking of her brings the conversation Essos and I have to have regarding the gates to the forefront of my mind.

Essos's head snaps in my direction, like he's gone down the same thought path as me. A plate of plain toast and a bowl of smashed avocado appear in front of me, and my husband sets to making me avocado toast. He could have just conjured it that way, but I think he likes being able to take care of me and needs something to keep his hands busy.

"We appreciate your assistance, Gisella," Essos says, effectively dismissing her. She takes the hint and slips from the room.

I enjoy the silence briefly, thinking about Posey and all that she had to say in Zara's hometown.

"You know why the dead won't stay in the Underworld?" Essos asks, drawing my attention back to him.

"Yeah, actually I forgot about it, but your mom told me while we were in that cavern. She said that the gates to the Underworld were closed."

"Closed," Essos echoes to himself quietly.

"Closed. I would assumed it was more like they were open, and the souls were free to leave."

Essos has stopped what he's doing as he goes over the information in his mind. I can see his eyes darting back and forth like he's reading a book. "This gives us a great jumping-off point. Now we know where to start in these books."

I hum my confirmation before letting my mind wander back to where it was before thoughts of his mother came up. "Do you ever think Posey created a self-fulfilling prophecy? Or really, the opposite?"

Essos finishes preparing the food before dropping into his own chair, the full weight of his attention on me. "Explain, my love."

"Like, she did all this, made us puppets meant to dance to her tune so she could be the biggest baddie on the block, only, the prince she manipulated into marrying her rejected her every time he could. They never seemed well-suited, but it all happened so fast, we just went with it. Xavier was never faithful and never wanted any of the responsibility of being King of the Gods. It got me wondering how much our lives—our *destinies*—happen because of the Fates or fate itself. Posey made comments about choosing the wrong brother, and I just wonder... If she had chosen you, would we have found our way to one another at some point anyway?"

"Of course, we would have. You're my whole heart. There is only ever you."

I cup his cheek with one hand. "You're sweet. Truly. But what I mean is, what if she did to us what she did to Cat and Xavier?"

"She didn't, and maybe that's been part of their problem. Posey was never meant to be with Xavier. He was supposed to be with Cat. Posey might be a Fate, but she isn't an absolute power. We still have a level of free will. If we didn't, I doubt there's anything I could have done to not wind up with her, if that's what she wanted. Which I guess brings us back to your earlier point."

"That's correct," I agree, munching gladly as my stomach settles.

"I don't know if we have any way of knowing, but I for one am very proud of Xavier for taking charge just now."

I set my plate aside and interlock my fingers with Essos's. "Are you okay?"

His lips tug down at the corners. "No. I'm not okay about what I did. I don't ever want to be in a situation where I have to do that again." He stares into the distance. "I could feel each soul. Their thoughts, their dreams, who they wanted to be. But the worst part was that they knew to an extent what was happening. They knew that they were hurting people, and they had no way of stopping it. They wanted their torture to end, but I just...it feels wrong to have taken everything from them so thoroughly. We need a plan for after we fix the Underworld and bring these broken souls back where they belong, because they know what's happening, and they'll remember, and that's not fair to any of them."

I release his hand and climb onto his lap. He welcomes me and buries his head in the crook of my neck.

"Maybe we can do something once we get the souls back to the underworld, like how Helene and Kai are wiping the memories of the humans who saw us today. I know it's easy for them to do it to mortals on such a small scale, but souls are different. I would think once they're part of the Underworld, their minds are not as easy to manipulate the way mortals are." It's a general suggestion, and I'm not sure where I'm going with it.

"We would need to come up with a broader-scale distribution system then going house-to-house. That would take too long. There'll be too many souls affected."

I'm looking around like the secrets might be held within the corners of this small closet of a room, but then my eyes snag on the ginger fizz sitting next to the water.

"What if we had a way to distribute the memory alteration that wasn't door-to-door?"

"How?" Essos asks, gripping my chin so I face him.

"We could spell water or a potion of some kind."

"On that grand a scale, we'll probably need Rafferty," Essos mutters darkly.

Gisella enters the room with a cart of books. "You two need to take these and go," she snaps.

"What? Why?" I ask, sliding off Essos's lap.

"I don't know what's changed, but Posey has supporters going into establishments and homes, forcing people and shopkeepers to swear fealty to her. Anyone caught with a white lily is being imprisoned. You need to leave, and you need to leave *now*."

"Would she really imprison you and your scholars?" Essos asks through clenched teeth.

"She can do anything she wants, Essos. So please, heed my warning, and *leave*."

Essos and I make quick work of gathering all the books she pulled for us.

"Will you be all right?" he asks, slotting one last tome in my grip before reaching for the librarian's upper arm.

She gives him a small smile. "I appreciate your concern, and I'll be fine. But if you linger, you won't be."

Not needing to be told again, Essos and I transport home.

It's the last useful thing I do, because no sooner have I gotten home then I pass out, Essos catching me just before I hit the ground.

SOMETHING cool and wet presses against my forehead.

"There she is," Essos whispers fondly. "How are you feeling?"

"Like I've been trampled to death. What happened?"

Essos gives me a thin smile. "You passed out. Sybil and Estelle as well as a healer have all been by to check on you and the baby, to give me peace of mind that all the jumping around we've done hasn't been harmful to either of you."

My hands go to my stomach. "That never even occurred to me." My heart is caught in my throat.

"You're both okay. They did suggest that you should limit how much transporting you do over great distances in a short period of time. Have a minimum of an hour between farther jumps. And now I'm not the only one benching you. The healer said you shouldn't transport again, even on the estate, for at least a week. I promise we'll go see your parents."

"That's right," Sybil says, walking in with Estelle on their heels. "Your baby's magic is still settling. You have to give them a chance to come into it before you bounce around like that again."

"How much is he paying you to say this?" I ask suspiciously. Gingerly, I sit up, and Essos tosses the wet cloth in the general direction of our bathroom. "If you had time to get a healer and for Estelle to whip up some food, how long was I out?"

"Two hours," Essos grinds out.

I cover his hand with mine only to have to pull my hand back so Estelle can place a tray of plain toast and crackers on my lap.

"Bed rest for the remainder of the day," Sybil tells me, their tone serious.

"Understood." I take a bite off a corner of the toast. "But bedrest means I can still do research. Give me books."

"No. For starters, Gisella will burn your garden down if you get crumbs in her books." I flinch back like Essos has slapped me. "Yes, that's exactly what it will be like with her if you do that, so eat first. Second...for fuck's sake, Daphne, I had to carry my unconscious wife upstairs. You can take a rest today. Please."

"Not your wife," I point out, trying to get some sort of reaction other than overprotective hen.

All it earns me is a glare.

"You *are* my wife, and were you not on bedrest, I would show you just what that means."

My cheeks flush and I squirm, wishing he could show me just what he means. "I guess you'll have to give me a lesson tomorrow."

He grimaces more than he grins. "Tomorrow."

Cat and Zara come to me immediately after their return from the mortal realm. They settle in different parts of my room, Zara on the chaise overlooking the ocean and Cat on the bed beside me. Essos makes his excuses to give us some privacy.

I close the tome on my lap a little harder than I intend, wincing as the sound echoes in the room.

"My family is just peachy. They're being tormented by the zombie apocalypse you failed to stop, but thanks for asking." Zara follows her statement up with a glare before looking back out the window.

"I want to hear it all. I want to know what's happening."

"I talked to my family," Cat says, and I jackknife up in bed.

"How did *that* go?" I ask.

"About as well as you'd expect. A lot of shock, a lot of tears. Xavier was surprisingly good with helping me explain it to them, but I don't think anything could have prepared them for me saying I'm a goddess."

"I'm glad I didn't talk to mine," Zara says softly. She gets off the chair and crosses to cuddle in bed with Cat and me. "It would have been too hard to leave them again. They seemed like they were moving on, and I don't want to disrupt that. Well, moving on outside the all the drama of the end of the world."

Helene saunters into the room, looking filthy and worse for wear.

"Where the hell was my invitation?" she demands, jumping onto the bed. I wince, not at the expectation of the impact, but at just how filthy she is. However, before she lands, she's sparkly clean, the scent of sunscreen and a fresh ocean breeze wafting off her white workout clothes.

"We just got back ourselves and came to see why Daphne was lounging about in bed." Cat directs this comment at me, waiting for an answer, but Helene beats her to it.

"She's on bedrest for the next week. Apparently, the little one can't handle all the transportation, and she had some light bleeding."

"*What*?" I demand, the walls of the room shaking. My three friends look around nervously.

"You...didn't *know*?" Helene asks, her mouth staying open. There is a furious flash in her eyes.

Luckily, I don't have to wait too long, because my helicopter husband steps into the room, looking for any threat that might have caused the walls to shake. "What happened?"

"You." I can't hide the hurt from my voice. "I was bleeding?"

Essos closes his beautiful blue eyes. "Can I have a moment alone with my wife?"

All three heads turn toward me, looking for confirmation that I'm okay with this. I give a small nod.

"You have one minute to explain yourself," I tell him once they've left the room.

"I didn't notice it until after I placed you on the bed and saw the blood on my arm, and I panicked. The healer told me that everything was fine, but bedrest and transporting should be severely limited over large distances, like to the mortal realm and back. You should be fine around the house. *Should* being the operative word."

"Why didn't you tell *me* that? Enough with the secrets, Essos. You had an excuse to hide things from me during the Calling. During the Trials, it made sense that I didn't have the full picture. But I think you've gotten so used to bearing the burden alone that you've forgotten that you need to share everything with me. *Have* to share. It's not optional. I am your partner. I am your wife."

"You are my queen."

"Then fucking act like it." Essos flinches back at my angry tone and I'm immediately repentant. "I'm sorry. I'm *sorry*. I'm just so *frustrated* with you right now. I'm frustrated with our circumstances. I want to be able to enjoy my pregnancy and not be afraid for my life."

"I want that too. I want to be able to dote on you and give you foot massages and stroll the streets of Solarem and take you to visit your parents if you want. This is not how I envisioned any of this, but this is the hand we've been dealt. The healer assured me that there is nothing wrong and that the baby is healthy and strong. We're going to take a break and focus on researching the Underworld."

I clench my teeth, hating the tears that spring to my eyes.

Essos sits on the edge of the bed and takes my hand with one of his while the other strokes my cheek. "We will be okay. All of us. And then after, when this is all said and done, we will enjoy the hell out of the next pregnancy and the next pregnancy and the next pregnancy."

"Just how many times are you thinking of knocking me up?"

"I am going to put a baby in you as often as you let me. I love how you glow and how cranky you are right now."

I swat at him. "No more secrets, Essos. I mean it. We do this together, even if it means I have to do it from this bed."

"I swear it." He presses a kiss to my forehead.

"You better not be crossing your fingers." He gives me a smile but shakes his head. "Good, now send in my friends so I can figure out how to better fix this mess we're in."

"As you wish, my queen."

He gets up and opens the door for Cat and Zara to come back in. The door closes behind them, and on the other side, I hear the muffled sounds of Helene reading Essos the riot act.

"Are you okay?" Cat inquires, gingerly sitting on the bed.

"Yes. Essos assured me that we're both okay, but I'm more worried about both of you and what happened today."

"My family is hunkered down in their house and were surprised to find that they now have a generator and a second fully-stocked fridge that never seems to empty, thanks to Helene. They're all a little traumatized, but I don't think there's a mortal alive who isn't."

"I know. Essos and I were discussing what the best plan of action is going to be once we get those souls back."

"Why don't you have Rafferty do for them what he did for me? Block the memories?"

I bite my lower lip. "It's a thought, something I could get behind, but we would need a large-scale way to implement it, and we would need Rafferty's cooperation."

"He seems like a tool, no offense. I get why you needed to call him to help me, but he seems distinctly unhelpful otherwise."

"He is. Rafferty likes to collect favors."

Zara is thumbing through the stack of books on my nightstand. "Honestly, you can figure that all out later. Right now, you need to get the zombies back in the Underworld. I'm not going to be happy if your inability to get a handle on it is the reason my family dies."

"Then let's get to work," Cat says, holding her hand out for a book.

We spend hours poring over every page and paragraph, trying to make sense of how the God and Goddess Supreme created the realms, but there are gaps in the story. Along with Octavia and Titus, there are mentions of the God of the Sun—Lairus—and the Goddess of the Moon—Esmaray—but for all we know, the four of them had a giant orgy and it was their orgasm that created everything.

Once that thought occurs to me, I slam the book shut. "I can't do this anymore. We need to know from Octavia how it happened, and asking her is out of the question. Titus is dead, so he's not an option. All of this is just *hopeless*." I fall back onto my pillows.

"Since when are you a defeatist?" Zara snaps her own book closed. "What happened to the chick who never backed down, who was always willing to fight for what mattered? Who went toe-to-toe with the God of War and *won*. I know Essos has been treating you like his poor little woman, but that's not who you are. So, get the fuck over yourself, and let's fix this!"

Her words reach something inside me—something I know to be true and that I'm afraid of, but she's right. This isn't about me and my problems. This is about the greater good, and I'm embarrassed by how much that fact seems to have escaped me in the middle of all my *woe is me* bullshit.

"Can we ask this Esmaray or Lairus?" Cat suggests, tapping on her book, which pictures Esmaray in all her midnight glory reaching her hand toward Lairus, who is reaching toward her with his palm outstretched. Staged between their hands are two balls, one radiant as the sun, the other more shaded, representing the moon.

"No. They haven't been seen since before I emerged as a goddess. Some think they've taken an eternal slumber or even returned to what they were meant to be—the sun and the moon, no longer personifications, but the things themselves." I rub my temples as say this. Naturally, nothing can be easy.

"Can we, like, summon them?" Zara suggests as Cat flips a page.

"They're not demons. They could be stardust at this point."

Zara pinches her lower lip between two fingers. "What about Octavia?"

"Watch it. She's like Beetlejuice. Say her name three times and she'll appear and never go away," I warn.

"But we want that. We want her to answer questions and tell us how to fix this." Zara's trying to reason with me, but she doesn't know Octavia like I do.

"She's a leech. Once she's here, she burrows in and never lets go.

She won't help, anyway." Since Essos and I never told anyone about her proposition, I can't justify to them why I know that.

"Got it," Cat interjects before Zara says something else. "Mother-in-law problems. What can we do then?"

"Keep researching and hope we're able to turn something up. Did you find out anything from your family about the visibility of Solarem now that the veil between the worlds is down?"

"So, since there's this whole focus on the zombies, the mortals haven't really been paying attention to the fact that Solarem is out there. Maybe we can find a way to fix both the zombies and the veil?" Cat suggests hopefully.

"I heard my dad say they're talking about trying to fire missiles at the floating island." Zara's tone is unreasonably calm for what she's telling me.

I nearly jump out of bed. "Seriously? And you're only mentioning this now?"

"Stay, drama queen. Helene told Kai, and they're handling it. Not every problem is on your shoulders to solve."

"Dave!" I call, ignoring Zara. Like the good boy he is, Dave appears immediately, sitting at my bedside and waiting for a command. He's been patrolling the Underworld, looking for anything that might be amiss now that his master is home with me. "Get Essos."

The dog gives a woof of acknowledgement before he blinks out of the room. It's a tense three minutes before Essos appears.

He bursts into the room like he's expecting it to be on fire. "What's wrong?"

"Missiles?" I ask, my voice sounding as distressed as I feel.

"You've heard." He relaxes a little, and I grab the nearest thing I can, a pillow, and hurl it at him.

"Secrets, Essos! We had this conversation not even two hours ago."

"Yes, *Daphne*, and in that time, I've been told that the world powers are trying to decide *who* among them is going to launch the missiles. I only just found out how we plan to address it on our end. There is no secret conspiracy by me to keep it from you, because I didn't know about it. While you were unconscious, I stayed by your side. I will own up to my mistakes, but this is not one of them."

Chagrined, I relax. "I'm sorry for making that assumption."

Essos leans against the door and gives me a half-smile. "It was reasonable. I haven't exactly been the most forthcoming."

"But now I *have* to go back to the mortal realm. My adoptive father—he's in Congress. Maybe I can appeal to him, and we can sort something out."

"Oh, I like that idea," Essos says dryly.

"Really?" I perk up, not expecting him to be so open to the idea.

"No, not really. My love, we just talked about how you need to stay in bed."

"I have to stay in bed for the rest of the day. And I'm not supposed to transport a ton all at once. That's what I heard Sybil say. That just means we need to stay at my parents' house for longer than an hour."

"You are absolutely insufferable, woman, do you know that?" Essos drops his head back against the door, his eyes closing. I know him well enough to know he's plotting it in his mind right now. What it could mean if we did this. "I doubt–"

"That they're going to take the word of some junior congressman about this? Yeah, I know, but maybe it can buy us some time. I have no idea what will happen if they try to bomb Solarem, do you?"

His eyes fly open and meet mine with grim determination. I doubt their weapons could reach us, but we have no way of knowing for certain. The gods and goddesses who live in Solarem may survive an attack, but our population consists of much more than that. We have nymphs and dryads and harpies. We have gryphons and creatures and a community. The more I think about what we stand to lose, the more my panic spirals outward. The plants in our room start to wither and die while the flames in the fireplace wink out.

"Daphne." Cat says my name with warning in it.

"Yes, yes, I know. I just... I can't control it. So many could die, and that's not even counting what kind of repercussions or blowback there could be on the mortal world. It would be a tragedy."

"We're not going to let it happen," Essos promises.

"Xavier and I will go with you to see your parents," Cat says. "That way, Xavier can be the liaison to the mortal realm. Your parents know me. I think it will help convince them. But we'll do it next week. Essos is right: you need to stay on bedrest and protect your child."

I'm still hyperventilating, but Cat takes one of my hands and Essos takes the other, placing it on his chest so I can feel his heartbeat.

"Breathe with me, my love. One, two, three, in. Hold it. Hold it. Okay, now out, three, two, one." We repeat this a few times, Essos coaching me through breathing until the lightheadedness passes and I'm feeling better.

That night, however, I don't sleep.

I'm too angry. Too scared. Letting Essos keep me in the dark for as long as he did was the wrong move, and I allowed it. I should have pushed back more, insisted that I stay involved, because the monsters in the dark were certainly not content to wait. Everyone else was making plans, and I squandered that time.

Now we have to play catchup.

Take two of going to the mortal realm has a much smaller traveling party. This time there are only four of us. Finn walks over to us in the dining room, his forearm bandaged and a pout on his lips at being left out. It's been a week, and he should be healed. I'm not surprised, though. He was cut with the same type of weapon that left a scar on the God Supreme. The same type of weapon that killed me.

"You can't heal it?" I lament, taking his hand so I can probe at it with my own magic.

"Nope. The God Killer blade takes and takes. It's impervious to magic. It's fine; people dig scars," Finn teases with a wink.

"Who exactly are you trying to catch with that sexy scar?" Dion asks, but there's not as much amusement in his tone as his words suggest. What happened scared him. I can't say I blame him; it scared me too.

"I guess I have all the dick I could ever want." Finn turns to his boyfriend and kisses his neck.

"That's what I thought." Dion gives a responding kiss to Finn's brow.

"Stop. You're disgustingly cute, and I can't afford to throw up again," I warn.

"You going to be okay?" Finn asks, cupping my cheeks.

I nod. "Yes, but I don't recall other goddesses having this problem."

"They didn't," Sybil says, approaching us with a tome in their arms. "I have my theories about *why* you're having this trouble, but it's just that, a theory."

"We're all ears," Xavier says, appearing in my dining room with the rest of us.

Sybil looks at him, then back to me. "You're an anomaly. You and Cat are both goddesses who have lived in mortal bodies. I think it puts you at a higher risk of mortal-related weaknesses because your ovaries are just that—mortal. Over time, your power might saturate your eggs, but right now it hasn't."

Cat frowns. "This baby is goddess-blessed. No natural harm will come to this child." The tone of voice that Cat's using would scare me if it weren't for the good of my child. She reaches toward my abdomen, and there's a small spark as her hand connects. Cat blinks rapidly, like she's trying to get something out of her eyes. "Sorry. I don't know where that came from."

Sybil gives her a smile. "You just bestowed a blessing on the baby."

"Congratulations and thank you," I tell her, sliding my hand into hers. There are tears in my eyes, knowing she's done something huge for my child even if she doesn't yet know it.

"You could have added in no harm at all, but we'll take what we can get," Essos says, trying to lighten the mood.

All attention is on Cat, and she squirms under the scrutiny.

Xavier takes the hint. "Perhaps we should stop dawdling and get this show on the road before the wicked witch of Solarem appears and ruins everything."

"Yes, let's," Essos agrees, wrapping me in his arms.

I close my eyes, trying to welcome the weightlessness, but I hate it all the same. At least this time when we land, I'm able to keep my food down.

I don't know what I expected to feel when I saw the place that I once called home, but this tidal wave of grief was not it. Essos holds me close as I mourn the life that could have been if Daphne Hale were just a mortal girl with mortal needs and desires. I mourn all the ways that Posey's intervention fucked things up.

The street is quiet, and there's no stench of death. It smells the way I remember, of freshly mowed grass and daisies. It smells like home.

"After what happened at Zara's house, Kai and I went to each of your homes to provide a protective charm for a square mile around it. It's not a lot of space, but we needed to do something," Xavier tells me.

Essos cups the back of my neck and pulls my face to his chest as my tears start to fall. Three cold noses press against my legs, licking my knees just south of where my skirt falls. I was nervous when I met the mortal parents who created me, but nothing compares to having to face the mortal parents who had the biggest hand in raising me. They did everything right by me, and I was still a brat to them

"Whenever you're ready," Essos murmurs into my hair before kissing the crown of my head as my tears slow.

The truth is, I don't know that I ever will be ready to face my parents, either set. But Solarem needs me, the Underworld needs me, and I'm going to put on my big goddess panties and get this done, because I've done enough sitting around. It's time to act.

"You need to be ready to catch my mom," I tell Essos as I extricate myself from him. Dave, Shadow, and Spot keep circling our legs. I didn't call them to be with us, so I can only guess that Essos did. "She's a fainter."

"Noted."

He lets me lead the way to my front door. Cat and Xavier fall into step behind us, with the dogs gladly staying by our sides. Shadow, of course, lingers next to Cat.

I'm not sure what the etiquette here is, but I knock on the door. And wait.

It feels like an hour before someone opens the door but, in reality, it's more like fifteen seconds. I wasn't ready to face my dad. I never treated him the way I should have. I was always sure to keep myself just a little reserved with them, and it was so wrong of me.

"Daphne?" he whispers, disbelief in his voice. He looks older. He was already balding, a sharp widow's peak eating away at his hairline, but it looks so much more dramatic now, and there are more lines on his face than before.

We all dressed down. I didn't want to overwhelm my parents with crowns and titles, so I'm wearing a plain light-blue T-shirt with a black skirt that shows just a hint of bump. In hindsight, I should have gone with something looser. My hair is free in curls, just the way he would remember me looking. Essos stands beside me in worn jeans and a dark-blue shirt that hugs the planes of his muscular chest. He couldn't leave all formality behind and has a sports coat on over it. Xavier is dressed in a matching outfit, only he's got on a grey shirt, and Cat is wearing low-rise jeans and a white blouse.

I feel like I've done this all wrong, and I don't know what to say.

"Hi, Dad." The words come out like a whisper.

"Hey, Phil," Cat greets with a broad grin.

"I don't understand," my dad says, looking at all of us. "You died. You died months ago, and we buried you. We had a memorial service for you. We spent countless days grieving you."

"Can we come in? I can explain everything, sort of." I am a goddess, but I feel like a teenager who has to explain to her father why she was sneaking out to see a boy on a school night.

"I don't understand," he repeats, but after a second he steps back and lets us in. "Your mother is going to have a heart attack."

The dogs lead the way, sniffing around. Dave must catch the

scent of Waffles, because he lets out a plaintive little cry from the back of his throat as he looks around for his friend.

"He's not here, Dave," I tell him, scratching behind his ears.

"Who's there, Phil?" I hear my mom call.

I slide my hand into Essos's and squeeze. My heart wants to crawl out of my throat. I had no idea I was missing my parents so much.

"You should come here, Melinda, and don't freak out. I might be having a sensory hallucination." He still sounds wary.

"Catch her," I whisper to Essos, and he nods.

Melinda Hale emerges from a room upstairs while putting earrings in under her black bob. Her eyes find me right away. Essos immediately transports to her side, catching her as she slumps.

"Oh, we've got another one," Cat warns, as my dad's eyes roll back into his head and he passes out too. Xavier catches him, thankfully. We set them both on the couch and wait for them to come to.

"So, this is where you grew up?" Xavier asks, looking at the photos on the fireplace mantle.

"Sort of. I was nine when I was placed with Phil and Melinda. My birth parents died shortly after I was born, and I was raised by my grandma till I was five, and then in a few foster homes before I landed here. I didn't call them Mom and Dad till I was fifteen, and even then, I would call them Phil and Melinda sometimes just to, I don't know, distance myself from them? I think in a way I was always waiting for that other shoe to drop, but they never gave up on me. Frustrating as it was at the time, I know they loved me."

Essos rubs my back. "Do you need anything? A ginger fizz or water?"

"A ginger fizz." The words are barely out of my mouth before he's handing me one.

Cat drops into the chair she usually occupied when she would visit. "Phil and Melinda were super chill, but I think they got caught up in trying to respect Daph's boundaries. Like, they wanted her to love them as much as they loved her, but they knew that pushing it on her was the wrong thing to do and would only drive her away, so they matched her emotional distance. I think that further drove home to Daphne that she was right to feel like they loved the idea of a daughter more than they loved Daphne as their daughter."

I glare at Cat. "I'm sorry, I don't remember you taking psych classes."

She sticks her tongue out at me. "It's a basic human condition. Anyone who spent more than an hour with the three of you together could see it."

I harrumph and drop onto the loveseat. Essos pulls my legs onto his lap so he can reach my feet. He starts to massage my arches, and I moan at how good it feels.

That, of course, is when Phil jerks awake and stands up. When he sees me sitting there, he blinks rapidly. "Not a dream."

"Nope, not a dream," I assure him, my voice cracking. Him thinking it was a dream that I came home makes me wonder how many times that dream has haunted him since my mortal death. I brush the tears away quickly. "Do you want to wait for Mom to wake up for me to explain?"

My dad reaches out and tugs me to my feet so he can hug me, squeezing me tightly. "I don't understand. You're here, you're in my arms, and I missed you, kid."

That's when I feel his tears on my neck, and I can't stop my own, which spring forth in answer. While we're embracing, my mom starts to stir.

"What is going on?" she cries, getting shakily to her feet. She looks good, but I can see the bags under her eyes.

"Just, enjoy it, hun," my dad tells her, opening his arms to welcome her into the hug. It feels so reminiscent of when I met my birth parents that I start crying all over again.

"I'm sorry. I never meant to hurt you," I tell them.

"I was going to say something like, of course you didn't mean to die, but are you dead? Are you a zombie? I don't understand," my dad presses when we finally break apart.

"I am a goddess, and so is Cat."

"I know, sweetie," my dad says, smoothing his hand down the side of my face to cup my cheek. "I always told you how amazing you are."

"No, I am *literally* a goddess. The Goddess of Spring, to be exact." I turn toward the poor Ficus tree in the corner that my mother has killed and I've resurrected more times than I can count. It's looking worse for wear, clearly neglected while I've been gone, but not enough for anyone to just get rid of it. With a thought, I rejuvenate it, breathing life back into the limbs until it's standing tall again.

"Maybe we have carbon monoxide poisoning?" my mom asks my dad. "Or, I think cyanide comes with hallucinations?"

"Daphne is being serious. Would I lie to you, too?" Cat asks, stepping forward.

They look at her like they're seeing her for the first time.

"Considering you died too, yes. I think your hallucination would lie," Mom says.

"I don't know if joint hallucinations are a thing, though." My dad looks down at his wife.

"Then who are those guys?" Cat questions, gesturing to Xavier and Essos.

"Hot hallucinations," my mom guesses with a shrug.

"Eww, that's my husband." I wrinkle my nose even as Essos walks over and presses a kiss to my forehead. "I also don't think you can touch hallucinations."

Dave barks, agreeing with me, and my parents notice the three pit bulls for the first time.

"I'm sounding like a broken record, but hear me out," my dad starts. "I don't understand."

"Okay, I'm the Goddess of Spring..."

"What does that make Cat?" my mom interrupts.

"Goddess of Motherhood and Fertility," Cat supplies with a smile.

"And the hunks?" Mom asks.

"I am Xavier, King of the Gods, and this is my brother, Essos, God of the Dead."

Essos scowls and furrows his brow. "I am *also* King of the Underworld. Why do you have to reduce me to less than you in front of my new in-laws?"

"Because you *are* less than me, brother," Xavier says dismissively.

Essos stands up straighter. "I am the older brother here."

"Guys," I interrupt. "Focus. We're here for Solarem, so maybe play nice?"

"What is a Solarem?" my dad asks, his gaze pinging between the two gods.

My mother still looks skeptical. "If you're kings, where are your crowns?"

Both men conjure their crowns. It's been a long time since I've seen Xavier in one, but the gold band with skyscrapers blended to look like spires all around the circlet does seem very King of the Gods-ish. Essos's looks every bit like it belongs to the God of the Dead, with skulls and bones crossing on it.

The weight of a crown settles on my own head, and I frown at Essos. He gives a small lift to one shoulder, the only indication that he's acknowledging my displeasure.

"Wait, are you a queen?" my mom asks, turning to face me. She looks at the crown on my head, and then she's looking at me in a whole new light. She surveys my body...and her gaze snags around my midsection.

"Yes, but it's a very long story," I warn. "One I'm not sure we have time for."

"Oh, I think finding out our daughter is a goddess is something we can make time for," my dad hedges.

"A goddess and *pregnant*," my mom points out, challenging me to contradict her.

"I, well, yes, I am pregnant." I look to Essos for help, and he seems just as unsure as I am.

He slides an arm around my shoulders. "We're excited to expand our family?" His voice lifts up at the end like it's a question, which it isn't, but I understand. I also feel uncertain of how to handle this turn of the conversation.

"And really, congratulations to everyone involved," Xavier starts. "I'm excited to welcome a new niece or nephew, but–"

"Nibling," Cat interjects.

Xavier's head whips in her direction. "What?"

"If you want the gender-neutral term for niece or nephew, it's nibling."

Xavier narrows his eyes. "Of course, I'm excited to welcome my new *nibling*, but all that is hard to do when your government wants to bomb our home. So, we are here, pleading with you, Daphne's parents, to stop it from happening."

There's a crack of thunder, and all of us jump except for Xavier. I narrow my eyes at him for the unnecessary flex.

My dad clears his throat. "Right, I can see where you're coming from, oh great one, but I don't know how common it is for people to come back from the dead in your world," my dad says, and I know Xavier probably enjoyed being called a great one way too much. "But it's not all that common here. So, excuse me for taking the time to swallow the enormous, horse-tranquilizer-size pill that my daughter is still alive, and not *just* alive, but married and pregnant. Oh right, and a goddess. Does that sum it up?"

"Pretty well, yes," Cat confirms.

Dad blows out a calming breath and smooths his hand down his chest where his tie would usually be. "Great. It seems you're all very eager to get down to business, so we can move to my office to see what it is I can do for you."

"Oh, *hell* no," my mother snaps. "No, you can have this discussion in front of me, right where we are now. I will go to the kitchen and grab some snacks. You—" she nods at me "—need some folic acid, so let's see what I have for you. But don't make this a matter of the men handling something the women can't."

"Of course, Melinda. I don't know what I was thinking." My dad gestures for us all to sit. "So, how can I help?"

"We need you to encourage the President to not bomb Solarem," I say, my voice near pleading.

"I take it that's the floating city in the sky?"

"The very one," I confirm, grateful that Essos and Xavier are letting me take the lead on this.

"There are going to be a *lot* of questions, mostly how do I know you don't mean us any harm? How are we going to negotiate with you? Where did you come from? How long have you been there? I mean, that's just what I can think of off the top of my head. I can assure you that there are going to be a lot more once you get to the global stage."

"We've been here longer than humans have existed. My parents created humans and are the reason you exist. As soon as we can drop the veil between our worlds again, it will be like we were never here."

So much for being glad that Xavier was letting me take over. I suppose I should let him drive this negotiation if he's going to be the main contact between the two realms. But though Xavier is many things, a diplomat is not one of them.

"What Xavier means to say," Cat interjects, "is that we understand that this is not going to be an overnight fix, and we would be happy to work with you to try to resolve this conflict as peacefully as possible. We don't need any Independence Day nonsense."

"I understand that, and the last thing I want to do is bomb your... island? Homes? I don't even know what to call it, but I also don't even know where to start with this."

"Can't you call your president? Tell him to stand down." Xavier makes this sound so simple.

Dave hops up on the couch beside me and Essos. When my mom comes in, she scowls but still gives him a treat I know she saves for the neighborhood dogs when she goes for walks.

My dad laughs at Xavier's suggestion. "Can your people just call you up and demand you do something?"

Xavier looks at me, completely dismissing my father. "I thought you said he was in your government and could help."

"He is and he can, and you can stop talking about me like I'm not in the room with you. I can make some calls, but I can't promise anything. It's not as simple as you make it sound," my dad tries to reason.

I knew this was going to be hard, but I didn't expect it to be *this* hard. I should have expected it, though. It's no secret that government is, at its core, slow.

"Dad," I say, and he looks at me, frustration seeping out of him. "Xavier has offered to be a liaison between our two realms. A king is coming to you to try to keep his people safe. There has to be someone you can call or talk to try to make this work. There is a lot wrong in Solarem, and we're trying to fix it."

"This wouldn't have anything to do with all the zombies, would it?" my mom asks from where she's perched on the arm of the couch.

"It has everything to do with the zombies," Essos confirms. "And the veil between the worlds being lifted. We're working closely with the rest of the royal family to fix the situation and make both worlds safe, so my child—our child—can be born with nothing to fear." Essos's plea has me reaching for his hand and squeezing it.

"Will we get to meet them? The little one, I mean?" my dad asks, and I give him a smile.

"I would love that. For them to know both sets of grandparents," I tell him, and damn it, my mother must be using some sort of new air freshener, because my eyes are watering again.

"Both sets?" Dad asks.

"Both. I got to meet my birth parents."

"They're safe from everything that's going on, and well cared for," Essos assures me, assures us all.

My dad nods. "I'll make some calls, but first, tell me everything."

So, I do. We spend several hours filling in my parents on what has happened, from the Calling to the truth about my existence as a goddess. We spare no detail, so they have the complete picture.

And when it comes time to leave, I find my heart breaking all over again.

After hugging my parents, I get on my knees before Spot. "I have a very important job for you, boy. I need you to keep them safe, and I need you to come get Xavier when my dad has a message to convey."

Spot gets up and turns in a circle before sitting back down. I scratch behind his ears.

"Does he eat anything special?" my mom asks. I can already see her putting together a list in her mind of what she needs for him.

"He prefers human souls, the fresher the better," Xavier says.

"He's kidding," Cat rushes to explain before my mom passes out again. "They eat normal dog food and love bacon."

Essos gives me a look, censure in his eyes. "I wonder where they picked up their love of bacon?"

"Truly a mystery," I agree. I hug my parents again. "This isn't goodbye, I promise."

I hate that it took dying for me to realize that loving Phil and Melinda didn't mean I didn't love my birth parents any less. Love is not a pie with a finite amount for any one person; it grows larger with each person you take into it. Someday, I'll express that to them, but for now, this will have to do. It might make visitation strange, but I'm glad that our child will have not one, but two sets of grandparents who will love them beyond measure.

I just hope that my father is able to convince the President to come to the table.

I'm sitting outside, enjoying the sun after visiting my parents, when Helene appears at the foot of my lounge chair. I have another book in my hands, and I'm hoping it contains something about the Underworld that I don't already know.

"You're in my sun," I tell her, glancing in her direction. The look on her face has me shutting my book and setting it to the side. "What is it?"

"Where is Essos?" She seems truly shaken for the first time in her life. There was horror when her father was killed, but underneath that was anger. Right now, she just looks terrified.

I shouldn't be surprised when Finn and Dion appear beside her. Finn looks at Helene and then to me, and I mark how pale they are too.

"Did you tell her yet?" Finn asks Helene.

"Tell me what?"

"No, I just got here."

"Where is Essos?" Dion echoes the question.

I push to my feet, terror rising in me. At first, I walk slowly and wonder if something happened to him... Is he not where I think he is?

And then I'm running, sprinting through the halls of my home to his office, where he told me he would be outlining a plan with Xavier.

The office door is closed, and I shove it open, then come to a stop when I see him standing in the middle of the room with Xavier, a drink in each of their hands.

"What's wrong?" Essos demands, but now I'm just confused.

I turn to look at Helene and Finn and Dion, waiting for an explanation.

Finn doesn't say anything, but he nods toward the mirror hung over the fireplace. It changes from a mirror to a live report from the Solarem news. Even the newscaster looks pale.

"What is happening?" I demand, fear of the unknown trying to crawl out of my chest.

"In case you're just tuning in," the reporter says, their voice trembling, "Queen Posey has laid out strict curfew times. Anyone caught outside those times is subject to punishment." This isn't as bad as I thought it could be and I start to relax in Essos's arms until the reporter continues. "Anyone caught spying for King—sorry, for *Xavier*—is similarly subject to punishment. At the behest of the queen, we will replay the punishment bestowed on Cassius, God of Vanity."

The picture changes to Posey, standing on a stage set just outside her home. Cassius is on his knees in front of her, his hands tied behind his back. Posey's hands are fisted in his hair, tugging hard. He doesn't look particularly worried or repentant, but I can see the God Killer weapon in her hand, and then she brings it down on his neck, slowing down her strike so she's forced to saw the weapon through his neck.

I can't watch. I look away, curling into Essos's chest. When I try to close my eyes, I see the agony on Cassius's face, and while I harbor no romantic feelings for, this doesn't make sense; it isn't right.

His screams echo through the stunned silence of the room. Only the sound of Cassius and the dagger cutting through his skin can be heard until Essos's voice booms out, silencing the report. "Enough!"

"Oh my gods," Xavier murmurs.

Try as I might to hold in the tears, I can't. And once they erupt, there is no stopping them.

Essos pulls me with him as he sits on the couch and gathers me close. My hands feel filthy, like I've got more than just Galen's blood on them—I've got Cassius's too.

"Why was Cassius there?" I ask through hiccupping sobs. I may not have a deep fondness for him, but I also don't want him to die, and certainly not is such a manner.

"We may never know," Essos whispers to me, rocking me gently.

"He was gathering intel," Xavier says. His back is to us as he fills glasses from Essos's decanter, one for each of us. Even I get one.

"I'm waiting for you to elaborate, brother," Helene says sharply. She knocks her drink before holding it out to Xavier to refill. I hold my glass, staring into it like it can foretell the secrets that Xavier holds.

"After our showdown with Posey at Zara's house, Cassius came to me with a plan. He's expressed interest in sharing Posey's bed in the past and thought maybe he could use that as a way to get insider information." Xavier pauses, hanging his head, his shoulders slumping with defeat. "The idea was that he would get close to Posey and find out where the scepter and dagger are being kept."

When he doesn't elaborate, Finn prods him. "Well, did he at least find out?"

"I don't *know*. We were supposed to meet up in another week. He needed time to ingratiate himself with her. We have a drop point that we agreed on in Solarem. I don't know if it's safe to go to now. I don't know if it's compromised, or if he even made it there." Xavier pinches the bridge of his nose. Cassius's death is hitting him harder than I expected, but I suppose this is the first time that someone has died as a direct result of his call.

"We have to check at the very least, right? What if the intel there is good?" Finn says, desperation clinging to his voice as he runs his hands through his hair.

"Yes," I agree, still unable to grapple with the idea that Cassius is dead. Based on what Posey said, there won't be any reincarnation for him, since the stone is full of souls. Even if it wasn't, I'm under the impression that the blade needs to stay in the body long enough for the soul to transfer to the stone. "All those souls. We have to do something."

"No," Essos refutes. "At the very least, not you. Never you. Hate me all you want—if there is a chance the location is compromised, you're not going."

It's the first time I agree with him without complaint. "Okay, fine, but *someone* needs to go."

"I will," Xavier volunteers. "I put Cassius in this position. I'll be the one to see if his death was in vain."

"You won't go alone. I'll go with you," Finn volunteers, idly scratching at his bandaged arm.

"She can't keep doing this. Who's going to be next?" My words come out choked, because it's not Cassius I'm seeing beheaded. It's Essos, it's Helene, it's Xavier, and I can't bear to lose anyone.

"If she has her way, all of us." Anger threads through Finn's voice.

I want to turn to him and comfort him, but I can't even comfort myself.

"I *will* go alone. We *will* stop her. I know we'll find a way," Xavier assures us, but there is uncertainty in his voice. "With any luck, Cassius's dying act will save us all."

If determination was enough, we would have it in spades, but Posey seems one step ahead of us no matter what we do.

"I WANT TO GO TO SOLAREM," I announce over breakfast the next day.

Essos's head whips to me, and even Cat and Zara seem uncertain. After what Posey pulled the day before with Cassius, everyone retreated to their corners to regroup. Xavier is at our apartment in Solarem. He was spending all of his days here plotting and planning while retreating to the city to spend his nights alone. After watching the news of Cassius's death, he left to go back to the apartment, and we haven't heard from him since. I'm glad to see him stepping up and taking responsibility, but I hate to think of him taking the weight of this onto his shoulders alone.

"Why?" Essos asks, settling back in his seat. Before him are the same three newspapers I'm reading, two from Solarem and one from the mortal realms. I see a flash of a photo of Cassius as Essos turns a page. We're still waiting to hear back from my dad in the mortal world to see if he was able to get in touch with the President. I need to feel like I'm doing something at this point.

"Because I want to confront Posey for being the liar that she is. We must still have supporters there. It's impossible that she's got everyone wrapped so tightly around her finger."

"No."

"No?"

"No. Not after yesterday. You saw the news. She practically put a bounty on anyone on our team. Even Finn doesn't want to go into Solarem. The only reason he's not staying here is that Dion doesn't want to leave Lux, and Lux refuses to be driven from her home by Posey, even if it's not in the literal sense."

It makes sense that Dion wouldn't want to leave his mom, but at this point, he needs to convince her to go. It's no secret that Dion is Team Xavier. I'm honestly surprised that Dion hasn't convinced Lux to leave Solarem, seeing as she's the mother of Xavier's son.

Cat and Zara get up and slink into the backyard. My gaze tracks their every step, and I wait until the door is closed before responding.

"The news yesterday is exactly *why* we have to do something. She *murdered* Cassius in front of everyone. She beheaded him like she's the fucking Queen of Hearts. If we don't show our faces, no one will ever stand up to her. The people need hope."

"I said *no*, Daphne. Someone can go and give them hope, but it won't be you. What if we're surrounded by people who support her? What if we run into people who want to hurt you? You and I both know there are things worse than death. I won't endanger you."

I have to clench my hands until my nails are digging into my palms hard enough to break the skin. "We're going to have to agree to disagree on this, Essos. I will not tolerate being treated like we're not equal partners. You went through something incredibly traumatic, but my sympathy can go only so far if you continue to refuse to treat me with the same understanding that I *also* went through something traumatic."

I shove up to my feet, not caring when the chair tips over behind me. Something in Essos's eyes shutters at the reminder that he wasn't the only one irrevocably damaged by Galen's and Posey's actions. Knowing we both need to cool down, I leave the room and go looking for my friends.

Cat and Zara are sitting in the backyard by the pool. Finn is across the pool, trying to coach Cat in something. His arm is still bandaged and wrapped tight with gauze.

"Be the baseball. See the baseball. Envision how a baseball feels. Close your eyes if you have to. It will start to come naturally and easily with practice," Finn instructs. He's as casual as can be in swim trunks and sunglasses, but he's completely focused on Cat.

"Is a baseball really the easiest thing you could have her create?" I ask, stepping into the sun. I'm wearing a loose, flowy, floral gown with chiffon sleeves and panels all around the skirt.

"It seemed easy enough." Finn rises to greet me with a kiss on the cheek. "I heard that Mom and Dad are fighting again?" There's an underlying tremor to his voice, and he still looks pale, like yesterday shook the very core of him. I can't say I blame him. Even after our confrontation with Posey a few days ago, it seems like she's coming more unglued.

"Stay out of it, Finn," I warn. I hate the idea of people knowing all about my marital discord.

"I'm just—"

"Not staying out of it, apparently," I interrupt.

"Daphne, I had to watch him suffer for an ungodly amount of time without you. Of *course,* I'm going to defend my best friend to his wife."

"Not his wife. Just his pregnant mistress."

Finn gives me a look that says he's very much over my attitude. "You need to stop that right now. Don't demean yourself because you're mad at him, or whatever it is you're trying to do. He loves you, and he's being an idiot about it. Pretty sure he was an idiot about it when he first realized that he loved you too. Correct me if I'm wrong, but wasn't there a moment where he tried to show off just how cool he was by shutting down a restaurant just for you, and you dressed him down because of the loss of wages for the workers who weren't getting tips that night?"

I remember the night; I couldn't forget it, even with the memory block. Essos said it was the catalyst to realizing just how in love he was with me, and it was the last time he tried to be a show-off. He admitted years later that he'd taken advice from Xavier because he wanted to impress me, but I never fell in love with Essos the Prince. I fell in love with the Essos who saved me from being trampled to death. I fell in love with the man who was sweet and tender with me. I fell in love with the man who would move mountains for me.

"Are you ready to go?" Essos calls, stepping outside. He's changed from the casual clothes he was wearing at the table into the menacing King of the Dead. His suit is sharp, with a silk black panel along his lapel. On his head rests a crown that he never wears, a circlet that matches my onyx tiara. The dark metal of his has obsidian and diamonds encrusted in it, a perfect twin to mine, which is in his hands.

Finn looks smug as I stand.

"I guess I am."

"I'll keep working with Cat on her powers. You two have fun." I hate Finn's tone, and my response is that of a mature, graceful queen. I stick out my tongue at him.

Essos chuckles at this as I reach his side. Gently, he places the crown on my head. I move my hair so it folds and tucks itself around the crown into braids, tendrils framing my face. I leave my current mint green dress in place instead of matching Essos. Today, I'm not Queen of the Dead. Today, I'm the Goddess of Spring, a reminder to the people why they loved us.

I step into Essos's space, and he welcomes me with wide arms. Nestled into his side, the feeling of weightlessness descends on me, forcing my eyes shut. Even when we're at odds, the scent of him soothes me.

It takes everything I have to keep my breakfast inside me when we finally stop.

"We're here," Essos whispers in my ear once our feet are on solid ground.

Here turns out to be on the balcony of our apartment, which is accessible only to us. We learned the hard way that letting people other than the two of us drop into the apartment proper could spell disaster. Since Xavier has been staying here, I imagine Essos has given him the access he needs to get in.

"Daphne, I'm trying," Essos says, reaching for my hand. I give it a firm squeeze. I'm capable of understanding where he's coming from while still being pissed about how he's treating me. But taking me here now shows that he really is trying, and it's not just words.

"I know. I'm trying too. I just don't want to be made to feel inferior. I don't want to feel helpless. I was helpless for the last few months. I'm going to be helpless once our child is born and I can't protect them the way I can now. I need to feel strong *now*."

"You are strong." His words make my heart yearn to be joined with his. Now he just needs to show me he means what he says. Essos cups my face. "How can I do that?"

"Trust me. Trust that I want this—" I rub my hand over my stomach "—just as badly. I'm not going to fuck it up."

I tilt my head back and stretch up to plant a tender kiss on Essos's lips, which he responds to with fervent desire, pressing against me until my hands are fisted in his lapels, drawing him closer. His tongue, the feel of his hard body against mine, and the growing hardness between his legs remind me of one of the last times we were here together.

We break apart, gasping for air, and I don't let him go. Essos keeps holding me, but his blue eyes are sparkling with mischief, no doubt remembering the same moments I am. Heat rises to my cheeks, and I turn and step inside our apartment.

This whole pregnant libido thing is out of control, but what I find inside helps to douse my desire.

Xavier is sitting on the couch with a towel covering his bare chest and a box of tissues beside him. In one glance, I see more of my brother-in-law than I have ever cared to see, but I can understand why the women of Solarem are always throwing themselves at him, and it's not only because he's king. His hand is jerking along the length of him, and he's already started to come when we walk in.

"What the fuck?" he screams and fumbles with the tissue box as if unsure of what to do because he has cum squirting onto his chest, but his need to finish keeps his hand pumping. I choke back my laugh as he unhands his balls and pulls down the towel.

"What the *fuck*?" Essos echoes, his hands covering my eyes and turning my face into his chest, only I was already turning in the opposite direction, so I get another eyeful of Xavier. Thankfully Essos also turns his body so his back is to Xavier. I, however, lose the ability to stand because my silent laughter has finally erupted.

"Why are you here?" Xavier sounds frantic, and in all the years I have known him, I have never heard him sound like that.

"Better question: why are you jerking off on my *couch*?" Essos demands.

"Because it's more comfortable," Xavier whines.

"I'll be in our bedroom," I manage to choke out between laughs.

"Stop laughing!" Xavier orders, but it's too hard to take him seriously while he has a towel over his crotch.

Once we're safely ensconced in our room, Essos pinches the

bridge of his nose and closes his eyes for a second before they fly back open.

"It's burned into my retinas. I can never close my eyes again," Essos cries, cringing. It sends me into another fit of giggles. "I'm so glad that you're amused," he deadpans.

"I'm going to try to pretend that I'm sorry, but that was..." I double over again in a fit of laughter. I'm laughing so hard, tears are leaking out of my eyes.

"You think it's funny that my brother was jerking off on *our* couch?" Essos catches me around the waist and tickles me as he lifts me off the ground and lays me onto our bed.

He follows me, his mouth going to the most ticklish spot on my neck. I squeal with laughter as he kisses the hollow of my neck. His crown falls off his head as his hands stop tickling and start roaming along my side and up to my breasts.

"Essos," I giggle, pushing on him lightly.

He rolls off immediately but stays within striking distance. "The only thing that will get the image of my brother's cock out of my mind is to see you naked and under me." He nips at my neck, and I turn my head so he has better access to me.

"Not now. Not while he's still cleaning up his mess in there."

Essos flops on his back. "And now I have the image of my own brother covered in his seed in my mind. My love, why are you torturing me?"

"Maybe because when you lock me back in my tower, I'm going to be stuck with that visual too." As soon as I say it, my stomach drops out. I don't want to fight with him anymore. "I'm sorry. I don't know why I said that."

Essos sits up and reaches to pull me to face him, and I let him. "You said that because you're hurt. Throw whatever you've got at me. I'm not going anywhere."

I reward him for his words with a small kiss, a graze of my lips against his while I reach for his crown and set it back on his head.

"I love you," I promise him as I get back to my feet.

"I never deserved you. Not the first time I somehow convinced you to love me, and not now."

"Essos, that's the crux of the issue. You *do* deserve me. You do deserve love. You have it in your head that you don't deserve a great love, and apparently thousands of years of me loving you didn't convince you."

"It did, but it felt like losing you was some sort of cosmic balance righting itself. It felt like I never should have had you to begin with, and that I was lucky to have had you for the time that I did." His fingertips dig into my sides. I'm standing between his legs, and I hate the hurt in his eyes. I hate that he's not just saying this but really believes himself unworthy. He believes that my love is not something that should have ever been given to him.

If I see her again, I'm going to punch Octavia in the face, not only for raising a psychopath in her youngest son, but for making Essos feel like this. I also wish I could bring Titus back from the dead just to kill him again.

Essos's head drops forward, resting against my sternum as he hugs me to him. There is still so much trauma that neither of us has resolved.

I hug Essos, pressing his head against me. His arms come around me, tugging me closer until I perch on his lap. It's going to take us some time to get back to who we were before Galen did the damage that he did.

A pounding on our door startles us both. Essos doesn't hesitate, moving gracefully to stand and place me behind him. It takes me a heartbeat realize where we are, causing my body to shudder. In the space of that heartbeat, I thought it was Galen here for retribution, but then I remember he's dead. I did that.

It's just Xavier.

There is a slight release to Essos's posture before he turns to face me. His cheeks have pinkened, like he's embarrassed that his first reaction was to protect me. I can't blame him; my first instinct was responding to a threat too. It's a reminder of the reason we're here, of the danger that comes with Posey running roughshod over the whole city.

I step around him, sliding my hand into his, and open the door to find Xavier, whose cheeks are still red. Good. He deserves to be embarrassed for jerking off on *my* couch.

"Why are you here?" Xavier asks, following me into my kitchen.

"That's a good question," I hedge, furrowing my brow. "You seem to have everything in hand." I can't stop my smirk.

"That's right. Get it out," Xavier snarls.

"Nope, you already did, and all over my nice towel too," I point out, grabbing myself a glass of water. I didn't realize how badly I needed some levity. Every day since I met with Rafferty has dealt another blow. I wish I could go back to the easy time immediately after the failed wedding, when things were just regular-hard as we tried to figure out what was wrong, and not this fucked-up situation where we don't know who could die tomorrow. The image of the slash on Finn's arm comes to mind, and I have to shake it away.

"You could have at least used the tissues," Essos points out.

Lightning crackles off Xavier's finger.

"Not in the house," I order. I want to plop on the couch, but I settle in my old reading chair instead. I'm going to need a whole new living room set.

"I think that applies to more than just magic," my husband adds. His cackle doesn't help the situation.

"Seriously, why are you two here?" Xavier asks again. Essos perches at the foot of my chair while Xavier sits at the table.

"I've come to bargain." I give a small shrug of my shoulder.

"With whom?"

"I thought that was obvious. I want to force your wife's hand and make her give up all of this. I want to find out how to get her out of our lives."

"*Ex*-wife," Xavier corrects.

"Wait, I'm sorry, that's your grand plan?" Essos interrupts. "You walked into breakfast like you had this idea or some way that we could solve this."

"I do—it's called reason. I'm hoping that if Posey sees that the people will not be easily cowed by her, that we will not be pushed around, maybe she'll second guess *her* plan long enough that we can parlay with her."

"I think you've seen too many *Pirates* movies. You cannot parlay with her. You are not Jack Sparrow. You're not going to walk into the room with a crazy person and walk out ahead," Essos says through clenched teeth.

"I do not think I'm Jack Sparrow. I think that it's one route we haven't tried, because honestly, we haven't tried anything other than sitting on our asses. You told me to sit back while the menfolk handled things, and it's gotten us nowhere."

"And you're just going to let her do this?" Xavier scoffs, addressing my husband and not me. "After putting her on lockdown? After all your talk last night of how you should have trusted your instincts to keep her in the house after the whole zombie thing?"

Essos snorts at his brother. "You're funny if you think I *let* my wife do anything. I was reacting emotionally last night, and I was wrong."

"So, she's got you by the balls. *Again*."

The room gets darker, shadows crowding in around us. I sit up in my chair and put a hand on Essos's arm. The room is suffocating as the darkness creeps closer.

"It's fine," I murmur to him, and the shadows start to recede.

"You're a dick," Essos snaps. "Maybe this is why your wife became a murderous sociopath—because you don't know how to be a good partner. I let my fear rule me, and it almost lost me my place in my wife's bed. I'm not going to make that mistake again."

By the time Essos is done speaking, the shadows have completely receded, and the bright sun is shining into the room again.

"Does this posturing have anything to do with your indiscretions?" Xavier sneers. He's on a roll for pushing my every last button.

"And what does it matter if it does?" I snap. "You would know plenty about having a wife deal with indiscretions. You wonder why I want you to stay away from Cat? *That's* why. You're incapable of keeping your dick in your pants. The last thing I want is for her to be saddled with you for the rest of her life while you make her miserable by fucking anyone and anything that looks at you!"

Now Essos is holding me back. During my tirade I actually jumped to my feet to yell, but I can't find it in me to feel bad for hitting below the belt with Xavier. His shitty attitude is wiping out every good thought I've had about him over the past few days.

Xavier clenches his teeth, eyes narrowed on both of us. "Tell me again why you're here and what you want from me."

"We're going out, publicly, to see the people. Talk to them, hear their grievances," I explain. "I want to inspire hope."

"What does that have to do with my ex-wife?"

"I'm sure if pretty princess Posey sees us out and about, she's going to want to come out and grandstand." I can't keep the contempt from my voice.

"Why are you eager for a confrontation?" Xavier moseys over to the bar cart and pours himself a drink, offering one to Essos as well. Never mind the fact that it's not even noon.

"Because she shouldn't have bested me the first time. Because she cheated, and she can't cheat if there are other people around." I cross my arms, and Xavier laughs at me. My cheeks warm at his response. "Because when she came to Finn and me on the streets in the mortal realm, she seemed more off than before, and I want to know why."

"Oh, you sweet spring child. She will *always* cheat. It's what she does. She doesn't fight fair. She hid her *entire* existence from the God and Goddess Supreme! She murdered my father in cold blood. What about that screams *fair*? I don't doubt she'll use the same tricks on you."

"Your problem, Xavier, is that all your wife has ever wanted is to be loved—by you, and by the people. She's not going to kill me when her smear campaign against us is going so well. I'm the Traitor Queen. I'm the Bitch Queen. I'm the Murderous Queen. And let's not forget the names that they're calling Essos."

"The Pussy-Whipped King is my personal favorite," Essos adds with a dry laugh. "Hard to fight the truth." He winks at me.

My eyes roll so far into the back of my head that they might get stuck there. Gods, I love this man.

Xavier takes a moment to study the united front we present. I might be frustrated or even angry with my husband, but when it comes to most things, we work together. When we work in tandem, we can accomplish anything and everything.

"You're not going to let this go, are you?"

"Not a chance," I confirm.

Xavier sighs heavily, and his casual grey sweatpants and T-shirt change to match the suit that Essos is wearing, one brother in black and the other in light grey. If a white suit didn't give me flashbacks to prom, I would say Essos should be in one. He always was the better brother.

Xavier gestures at the door, and we depart, looking for a fight.

12

I don't know what I expected when I stepped out of our building, but this wasn't it. Hardly anyone is outside. Our favorite bistro across the street is closed. Even our lobby didn't have anyone behind the counter.

It's an early morning on a weekend, and usually there would be a small street fair where people would be hawking their goods, including one of my favorites, a booth that made moth necklaces with gemstones. Occasionally, when small children would come and poke their noses over the table to peer at the jewelry, the artist would make the moths come to life.

I can faintly hear the tinkle of the children's laughter as we walk past the spot where that vendor was.

"Excuse me," I call, stepping toward the first person I see. We made it five blocks without running across anyone, and I'm deeply unsettled. "Where is everyone?"

The man starts to snarl at me, but once he gets a good look at me, he must realize who I am because something akin to pity flashes on his face. Then he turns his attention to Essos and Xavier, and his entire posture changes. He stands up taller, no longer trying to make himself as small as he can.

"You shouldn't be out here, Majesties," he warns.

"I appreciate your concern, but where is everyone?" Essos says.

"Her Majesty, Queen Posey, has instituted a curfew," the man replies, averting his gaze. Essos and I exchange a look. We knew this, but we expected the curfew to be at night, not in the middle of the day.

"It's not even noon on a Saturday," Xavier points out.

The man's entire demeanor changes rapidly, moving straight into panic. He surges toward me and grabs my upper arms, his dark eyes frantic.

"She's–" His words die in his throat...because he turns to stone, his hands still clutching my arms painfully. I look at Essos, trying to keep the building terror from showing in my face. I don't want him to see my fear, because I'm sure he'll become unhinged about it. He never wanted this, he never wanted me out of the safety of our home, and now I'm going to have to deal with the incessant reminder that he was right.

"Daphne, love, you need to relax," Essos tells me, his hand on the small of my back. It's a soothing gesture, and I try to relax into him, but I don't want to hurt this man either. The only way I can imagine Essos getting me out of this is to shatter his hands. My breath starts to come faster and faster, until I'm on the verge of hyperventilating. "Daphne, please." Essos sounds so panicked when he says this, I can only nod.

I take a deep breath that comes out shakier than anything else. I have completely forgotten about Xavier until he comes to my other side, his hands bracing around the man's. I watch helplessly as they both channel their magic into changing the hands that hold me from stone into flesh again, long enough for me to step away before they revert once more to stone when Essos and Xavier let go and step back. Their powers together are not enough to override whatever this twisted Fate wants. Not long-term, anyway.

How many others are stuck like this? Posey's the cat in this game and we're all mice running around for her to torture.

"Why would she do this?" My voice is shaking more than I want. Essos steps closer to me, offering his comfort should I want it, and I do. I lean into him, fighting the urge to rub my upper arms where I'm sure bruises are forming.

"Because it's how she can control people," a female voice says from behind us.

We all spin, and a vine dagger forms in my hand before I even think about it. Gods, I can't wait for the days when needing weapons is no longer second nature.

"Relax, you three. I come in peace."

I shouldn't be surprised, but I am. Essos and I share a look before I meet my mother-in-law's gaze.

Octavia looks just as put together as she did the last time I saw her. Her long, blonde hair is pulled back into a severe ponytail, and a black dress form-fits all her sharp lines and pointy edges. She is every bit the woman I remember her to be...except for her bloodshot eyes and red nose.

She's been crying.

It seems my unwillingness to bring back Galen is sinking in. Essos and I still haven't told anyone about her offer to become a turncoat in exchange for the monster from my nightmares.

Maybe it's the pregnancy hormones or I've gone a little soft since being a human, but I realize the pain she must be in. Her son and husband were killed on the same day. Even if Octavia and Titus were estranged when he died, they were together for eons.

Essos breaks our eye contact when he steps between us.

"What do you want?" Xavier demands.

Essos's hands are loose at his sides, but I see the urge to clench them into fists in the set of his shoulders. I'm surprised when Xavier steps up beside his brother, shielding me as well.

"I was hoping to see my children. Is that too much to ask?" I hear her heels as she steps forward, closer to us.

"We need to know whose side you're really on," Xavier prods.

I shift so I can see between the brothers.

"You really are the densest of my children. If I wasn't on your side, why would I approach you?" She shrugs one dainty shoulder. "Daphne knows what I want."

"I can't imagine what you could possibly want from me that your favorite daughter-in-law can't provide, seeing as she has the Scepter of the Dead, one of the God Killer blades, and all the souls from the Underworld."

Octavia's eyes narrow on me. I do know what she wants from me, but Xavier doesn't know that.

"Don't forget all about the newly dead souls too. It's a shame she doesn't have the *right* God Killer blade." I hate Octavia's tone and the haughty look on her face.

"Mother," Essos hisses, "what do you want?"

"I want my son back." Octavia's voice cracks as she says this. Even though I already knew what she wanted, hot and cold chase each other all over my body like I'm feverish. Galen *can't* come back. I don't want my child to live in a world with him in it.

Essos and I both knew this demand was coming, but Xavier ignores his mother's plea. "Do you even care what that bitch has done to us?" he asks, and I wish I could see his face. I've spent so many hours with him over the past few months that I can hear the hurt lurking within his words.

I reach out and press a hand to Xavier's shoulder.

My mother-in-law's laser focus narrows on me. "What, enchanting two of my sons wasn't enough? You have to go for the royal flush? Were Titus alive, would you see if you could bring him to bed too?" Octavia's words cut off suddenly, and I peer around Essos to see her mouth has been sealed shut, similar to what I did to Ellie.

Sometimes I wonder if Ellie still has no mouth, and then I find that I hope that she doesn't and that she's suffering for it. With no real lips, she'll think twice about setting her sights on my husband.

The ground beneath our feet shakes violently, and even Octavia looks afraid before Essos speaks and I realize that the shaking is his doing. "Enough, Mother. Insulting Daphne is not the way to go about getting what you want. So kindly—and I mean this respectfully—shut the *fuck* up about my *wife*."

I slip my hand into his and, again, I need to focus my unreasonable pregnancy hormones. Even with so few of us around, I'm positive that I cannot jump him in the middle of the street. His mother *is* standing right there.

The rest of my body doesn't get the memo, because his simple act of power and fierce protectiveness has my inner walls clenching, desperate to be filled by the man inciting these feelings.

"Why should we help you? Galen murdered me." I thought I was done having to explain this to people, but I seem to be stuck in some sort of hell loop where all I do is listen to people act like it's no big deal Galen killed me. Maybe I'll get lucky in this circuit of the loop and have a man tell me I should smile more.

Essos frees her mouth to let her answer me.

"Because he was my son, and I thought maybe I could appeal to you, mother-to-mother."

My hands fly to my stomach protectively. Xavier takes another step forward.

"That might carry weight if you hadn't just insinuated I was a tart who spread her legs for anything with a dick," I snap. "Oh right, and if your child *hadn't murdered me*. Honestly, is there some sort of weird space-time continuum where his crime has been erased from everyone's memory? Is there some sort of sound vacuum that those words disappear into whenever I speak them?"

"What sort of mother would I be if I didn't forgive my child for his mistakes and try to protect him from the consequences?"

"A bad one. Maybe that's why Galen never learned the word *no*. Maybe you're the reason that he felt *entitled* to me, so entitled that I was kept from being reunited with my husband—you know, your *other* son?" I can feel threads of power unspooling from me in ways I can't control, because my growing anger and resentment refuse to be chained any longer.

"Daphne," Essos warns, his hand coming to my forearm as I march straight up to my mother-in-law.

"No, Essos, let her speak her mind, regardless of how ignorant she sounds." Octavia lifts her chin and peers down her nose at me.

Xavier scoffs.

"What was it about Galen that had you bending every rule, ignoring your other children just to soothe his ego? I heard it was Galen who you consoled at my funeral, not Essos. What was it about him that made him so special that you would go so far as to think no consequences for him was good parenting? You are the perfect model of how *not* to parent. Gods, if my child wound up as spoiled and self-centered as Galen, I would think I failed as a parent!"

"Clearly, you spent too much time with the humans if you think that." Her tone is clipped. I turn my back on her, knowing that Xavier and Essos are watching. It's the best sign of disrespect I can put out there, letting her know I don't think she's a threat, even as my heart rate climbs higher the more I let my anger churn.

"Is she out of her fucking mind?" I ask them.

"I'm thinking I want you to give me my son back. It's the same trade I offered you in the Underworld. If you bring back Galen, I'll help you with Posey. I'll make sure you're rid of the Fate once and for all. If you need more encouragement, I'll give you a little token of good faith. The reason you can't call the souls of the dead back is because the gates to the Underworld are closed right now. Every time a soul tries to gain entry, they get turned away. Reopen the gates, and it will solve your zombie issue. Once the gates are open, you can call the souls back—at least, the souls that Posey hasn't consumed."

I look over my shoulder at Octavia to judge her sincerity. She already told us about the gates to the Underworld, which we've been investigating, but she's given us more details than we've been able to find in all the damn books we have. Posey consuming souls is new.

Octavia's viper-red lips spread into a calculating smile. "That's right. She's been consuming the souls that had no physical form to return to in the mortal realm. Some of the oldest and baddest. Like I said, reconsider my offer."

It's a struggle not to wince, knowing that we withheld that meeting from Xavier. In hindsight, of course, we should have told him. Xavier and Helene both deserved to know that their mother contacted me to bring their brother back from the dead. It wouldn't have mattered what they wanted, because at the end of the day, Essos has the dagger, and neither of us want Galen back in the world.

I'm upset about the betrayal I see in Xavier's eyes when I look at him, but the vise-grip around my chest at the thought of facing Galen outweighs the guilt I feel for not telling him. The mental image of what Galen will do to me—what he will do to my child if he's released from that stone—erases all the guilt.

I need to fight these thoughts because once they grab hold of me, they will drag me down, down into the watery depths of despair, and I can't stand, can't breathe, because he will get me, he will kill me if he has the chance, and the only way that he has a chance is if I let him out of the stone. Which is not an option. I won't let it be.

Essos's blue eyes ground me, and once we lock gazes, I realize he's squatting down in front of me. I don't remember dropping to my knees, but I must have in my panic. His hands on my arms ground me. The all-consuming, messy kiss he presses to my mouth pulls me back to land, back to air I can breathe, except I can't breathe because Essos's mouth is on mine, moving like I've died and he's just gotten me back and he will not lose me again to these poisonous thoughts of his brother. His hand slips into my hair, undoing my braid as the kiss deepens.

He pulls back, tugging my lower lip between his teeth. I whimper, forgetting where we are, what we were doing, as he gazes into my eyes. He looks away from me, up to his mother. All the love I saw when his eyes were on me is gone. His gaze is solid and hard and unforgiving of the woman who birthed him and ignored him.

"How can we contact you with our response once we've had a chance to discuss?" Xavier takes over, letting Essos be my husband and not a king or a son.

"If you insist on being stubborn, I will find a way to contact you."

Octavia is gone in a blink, and the absence of her is staggering. I know that if Essos wasn't holding me, I would have collapsed in on myself. The bravado that had me ready to face Posey is gone. Where did it go? Exhaustion and failure weigh on me. Given how I handled that confrontation, I can't say I blame Essos for trying to shield me from it.

An unspoken conversation passes between Essos and Xavier. I catch it in how they look at each other before Essos scoops me into his arms. I don't bother to object.

I cling to him, my arms thrown tightly around his shoulders as I bury my face in his neck. The need to be far away from here is burning us both, so strong that we're caught in the pull of each other, trying to drive our destination as we wink out of Solarem.

Our landing is hard, and I spill from Essos's arms. I scrape my elbow as I try to brace my fall. Essos scrambles to me right away and pulls me back to my feet. The panic attack is still holding me, and it's enough to negate the nausea from transporting home. The pain keeps my mind from going to that dark place where there wasn't enough air and the threat of Galen coming back was as real as the ground beneath my feet.

"Are you all right?" Essos checks me over, turning me around so he can get a better look at where I'm hurt.

I rub my elbow absently. "I'm fine," I reassure him, trying to get our bearings.

"You're not fine. You're bleeding," he's quick to point out.

I stop looking around and face him. His attention is totally on me. I clutch his forearms, forcing him to look at me. It's my turn to be the strong, reassuring one. When I look at him, I can see the evidence of his panic in the tense set to his mouth. "Essos, I'm an immortal. It's going to heal."

"Daphne—" He uses a condescending tone, which I am *not* about "—stop acting like you're invincible. You're not."

I swallow all the things I want to say and change the subject instead. We're both overly emotional and likely to say things we'll regret. "Where are we?"

Finally, Essos looks away from me and surveys our surroundings. We're near a beach somewhere on a road that runs alongside a cliff. There's no one on the road, and below us I can hear the waves crashing.

There is something familiar about the cliff beside us, and I cross the road to touch the spot where metal is crushed against stone. I can almost feel the reverberation it would have made—feel it in my bones. I can feel it, because it's part of me...a part of my memories. This mark made me who I am. The bus that touched here, that corrected too far and plunged into the ocean below, was the bus that carried me back to Essos.

"We're in California," I tell him, walking back to where he is.

His hands are shoved deep into his pockets by the time I get to him. "I did it again, didn't I?"

"Did what, my love?" I ask, leading him to the scenic view pullout from which Sybil first collected us.

"I'm trying to force you into a box where I can protect you without considering what you want or need." He sounds genuinely apologetic.

I perch on the guardrail, looking at the water below. Essos sits beside me, his arm wrapping around my shoulders.

"You are, and I get it. I'll never stop getting it. And I reserve the right to get annoyed about it. But before that, getting me out of Solarem—that was the right call. I needed that."

"All those scary thoughts that were going through your head when my mother was talking to you? I was having the same ones."

"How do you know what I was thinking?" I rest my head on his shoulder. His head drops over mine, and I inhale the smell of the ocean and him—vanilla, cinnamon, and sandalwood. Home and comfort.

"My love, I know most of your thoughts, but when it comes to Galen, I could feel you change. I watched your shoulders slump in, and I don't think you even knew you were reacting physically to the idea of him coming back."

"I know we talked about it, briefly, when she first made the offer, but I think I was still so caught in the freshness of it that I never really considered it a possibility. Now that Xavier knows, I'm afraid we might have to do it. I'm not sure I can stomach it if we do," I tell him, lifting my head so I can look at him.

"Then we don't do it. We'll find another way to beat Posey. We can and we will beat her. We don't need my mother." Essos wraps his arms around my shoulders, holding me closer to him.

"Don't we? If we can end this faster, then why wouldn't we? Why wouldn't we do everything in our power to end this? Don't we owe it to the people in the Underworld? In Solarem? Don't we owe it to the lost souls wandering the mortal realms? I can't in good conscience let this go." I know full well I'm fighting with myself now. Essos will go along with what I need, but my needs and the needs of the Underworld are so different right now. Being queen means foregoing my personal comfort.

"I can. If it means your mental health? If it means my wife being able to sleep at night? Then we will absolutely not do this. *I* will sleep better at night knowing you're safe, both of you." He rests one hand on my stomach, a reminder that every decision I make is not made for me alone. I am deciding for Essos and for our child, and that scares the daylights out of me. I've spent thousands of years preparing to be a mother, waiting for this day, and now, as I inch closer to it, I worry that I'm not ready.

But is anyone ever really ready to be a parent? Are they ever ready to take that dive and be responsible for another life?

The thought of Galen coming back makes me break out in a cold sweat. A shudder racks my body, and Essos hugs me tighter to him, trying to save me from my thoughts. I'm not sure it's possible to escape them at this point.

My priority has to shift. I would have said that I need to do right by the souls of the Underworld, but a child changes everything. Will I be able to get past Galen's return emotionally?

"If he comes back..." I let myself trail off, unsure what I want to say. I want to ask for assurances that Essos can't make.

"If he comes back, you'll never be alone with him. In fact, you may just never be alone again," he tells me, trying to make light, to make me smile. I reward him with a small tilt of my lips.

It's like the weight of the world is on me, and I might break under this decision. But that's what being a leader means—it means having to do things that you personally might not like, might not be comfortable with, if it's the right thing for your people.

"Would you be mad if I said maybe we should do it?" I watch his face. He doesn't give anything away; it's impassive, the way it is when we adjudicate cases. "I mean, I hate the idea of him being free, and you're right, I might never sleep again, but Posey froze *all* of us, including your father. Beating her is not something that we can do easily, and I don't see why we should risk more lives when we don't need to."

Essos rubs his knuckles down my cheek. I lean into his caress, needing the confirmation of his touch, his presence. "Love, I won't hold either decision against you, but maybe, let's wait to make one?"

"Why?"

"Because now that Xavier knows, it means we're going to have to discuss it with everyone else anyway."

It's a discussion I had hoped to avoid, but Essos is right. Even if I think bringing Galen back is the right thing to do, that doesn't mean the others will agree.

It's just one more battle I'll need to fight.

Once I've had a chance to get my head screwed back on straight, we call everyone to the house. Telling them about Octavia's offer is going to be one of the hardest things I ever do.

Cat and Zara are already in the library with Sybil and Estelle, pouring over all these new books to try to find an answer to restoring the veil and dealing with the Underworld. At least with Octavia's revelation, we have a jumping-off point.

It's so stupid and simple, I don't know why we didn't think of it earlier. No, that's not fair, I know why. The gates—the entrance to the Underworld itself—are something I took for granted. Of course, they would be in the same position they've always been. Why would that change? If I wasn't already maxed out on transporting today, I would have made Essos take us there so I could see them for myself, but I think even that would have been a step too far. Cat has bestowed her blessing so that nothing natural can harm the baby, but she's still untried, and neither of us wants to take an unnecessary risk.

I'm not waiting for long before Essos strides in with his siblings and Finn and Dion. Kai sits and pulls Helene onto his lap, and everyone goes silent, waiting for us to break the news. Xavier goes straight to the whiskey tumbler and pours himself a healthy serving.

"We saw Octavia today, in Solarem," I tell everyone. "She said she would help us."

Xavier stays silent as I lead the conversation. He looks miserable, sipping his drink and casting furtive glances at Cat, who is studiously looking everywhere but at him. I don't know if I owe his silence to Cat or to his desire to see how this is going to unfold.

"What does she want?" Helene asks, tone sharp. Mothers and daughters have a complicated relationship. I never expected theirs would be any different, but the open hostility is a surprise.

"What any mother and Goddess Supreme wants, I imagine. Peace on Earth and her children happy," Finn wagers. We're a small club, those of us who are not directly descended from the God and Goddess Supreme.

"Close," Xavier mutters into his whiskey.

"No," Helene says when she realizes just what her mother wants. She stands abruptly, but Kai pulls her right back onto his lap so he can hold her.

"Yes," I confirm, digging my nails into Essos's hand. He squeezes back with less strength to show he's here; he gets it.

"You mistake me. That 'no' was not because I'm surprised. That 'no' is an abso-fucking-lutely not. We just got rid of that nightmare. You of all people should be glad you're free of him. You never have to deal with his shit again. You never have to look over your shoulder and wonder if the big bad wolf is lurking in the shadows."

"I am considering it," I confess, my voice small. I thought I was ready to have this conversation, but I'm not coping with it well at all. I want to explode with rage and shower Octavia and Posey in the acid rain that would bring forth.

"*We* are considering it," Xavier corrects, looking to his twin..

"Even with a lead on where Posey is keeping the dagger, we don't have it yet," My eyebrows lift in surprise when he doesn't out us for having had this offer on the table for longer than a few hours. "That bitch killed Dad, and he was probably our best shot at not having to do anything about her, but really—think about that. She killed our father, the man who created life. We're immortals, and we should have been scared when Daphne died. I reasoned she was a minor goddess, so what killed her couldn't touch us, but then the two-faced whore showered us with Dad's blood and laughed about what we thought we knew. There is no going back, sister. We need every ally, and if that means bringing back Galen, then I think we have to do it."

"I'll consider it when you say her name," Helene hisses, getting back to her feet.

Kai doesn't pull her down him again. "Starfish..." he warns, reaching for his wife's hand.

"Who? Octavia? No problem. Octavia."

"No, Posey. Your *wife*. The woman you fucked over so thoroughly that she killed our father just to screw you over. I want you to say her name, because it's been weeks since it happened and I haven't heard you say it. You know she's not Bloody Mary; she's not going to appear if you say it too many times."

"Fuck you, Helene," Xavier snarls.

"No, fuck *you*. If you hadn't been so incompetent, maybe Daphne wouldn't have had to die, or Dad, or Galen. But you thought with your dick, and now there's a body count."

"But then I would still be stuck in a loop," Cat points out, getting to her feet and setting aside the book she was reading. "Galen would never have stopped pursuing Daphne, and I think if he hadn't been able to kill her, he would have done much worse. Sybil and Estelle would still be stuck too. The Fates—the very beings that you place all of your faith and belief in—would have stayed trapped. You can't have it both ways. I'm so sorry you lost your father. I am so sorry that your brother is dead and that your family has changed, but I am here now, and you have Daphne back. You can't just put all of this on your brother."

My eyes mark every step Catalina takes until she's standing beside Xavier, resting her hand on his shoulder. He goes still at her touch, as if he might startle her away by breathing. We had so many bombs dropped on our laps the night of the wedding that Cat being Xavier's intended from the start has been mostly overlooked.

"Cat, I'm glad we have you and that Estelle and Sybil aren't stuck with their mediocre jobs, but my father is *dead*."

"And I've had to live through countless of my own deaths. I'm not expecting you to get over it in the approximately five minutes it's been. I know you're not prepared for immortals being able to die and all, but stop blaming that on your brother. He doesn't deserve it." Cat's words come out fiercer each time she speaks. Warmth radiates off her in waves from her anger.

"The issue at hand still stands. Do we allow Galen to come back?" Finn asks.

"I don't think this should be an individual decision," Dion says, sitting up now. He rests a hand on Finn's shoulder. Dion wasn't here during the Calling to keep me from playing into Galen's hands. Both he and Finn carry so much guilt about what could have been prevented.

"We can't discount the fact that Posey sawed off Cassius's head in front of all of Solarem," I interject. "She's losing her mind, and if Octavia is to be believed, it's because she's consuming the souls of the dead. Who knows what kind of repercussions that will have?" My heart feels flayed open as we discuss which is the worst of two evils.

"So, what? We flip a coin?" Kai asks with a laugh. The smile leaves his face immediately when his wife cuts him a glare. He coughs into his large fist.

"We vote. It's the most diplomatic way," I hedge.

"Wait, aren't the Fates supposed to be able to tell you all about this? Isn't their thing seeing the future?" Zara's question is valid, and both she and Cat look at me expectantly.

"Posey saw the future," Sybil tells us.

I remember what Luminara said about each Fate having a different role. Three sisters, one to spin, one to measure, and one to cut. It was Sybil to spin, Estelle to measure lives, and Posey to cut the thread of life.

I echo what I learned. "It's how she knew which thread to cut and at what length. As Sybil spun each life, Posey saw their destiny spread out before her."

"That's convenient," Cat mutters, moving away from Xavier and back to her seat at my side.

"It's how she knew which threads would unwind the entire tapestry. She would cut the thread of mortal life. But that power wasn't enough for her." Sybil sounds sad when talking about their sister, and I realize that we've all lost something at the hands of Posey. Some of the losses are more tangible, like the deaths of Titus and Cassius, but Sybil and Estelle were betrayed by the person they were supposed to be closest to—their sister.

"There isn't enough power in the universe for her." Xavier turns his attention to his twin. "She takes and takes and *takes*. You think I'm not mad, sister? I'm furious. She took my family, she took everything, so I'm sorry if saying her name feels like I'm invoking the devil herself." Xavier drains his glass before pacing back to the decanter.

"Does anyone have any actual debate around resurrecting Galen? Do we even know how?" Finn questions.

"We know how," Sybil and Estelle intone together. A chill skitters down my spine.

Essos leans over to me. "I so wish they would stop that."

I squeeze his hand in agreement, and he smiles.

"I think him being a raging psychopath is reason enough." Helene crosses her arms and drops onto her husband's lap. His hand rubs circles on her back.

"I am the last person who wants to advocate for his return, but am I crazy? Doesn't it make more sense to come at Posey with all we have? If that means bringing Galen back, then maybe that's what we need to do." My insides twist as I speak, like even they can't believe I'm considering this. "At this point, he's the devil we know. I certainly never would have thought Posey capable of cutting a god's head off."

I hate that my words feel like I'm advocating for Galen to be resurrected. I *don't* want him back.

"Who's to say it will be faster with Octavia on our side? Titus was cut down in a heartbeat," Finn says, getting up from his seat. Everyone is restless, like their bodies are looking for some way to escape this option. Watching everyone pace makes me want to jump up and pace alongside them.

"Daddy never stood a chance," Helene points out. "She had all of us frozen and bewitched. You really can't bring him back?" I don't think a day has gone by that Helene hasn't asked about it. Zara mentioned it while we were catching up, but I never wanted to let on to Helene that I knew. Her pride is precious to her, and she would hate to know we were talking about her behind her back.

"Helene, if we could, we would. Gisella is still looking to see if there is something, anything, we missed, but the only other person with the knowledge would be Octavia." Sybil sounds sympathetic, but my eyes narrow on them and their new tune. This is the first time they've mentioned that Octavia might be able to help. I'd like to think it's a new development, but there's something I don't like in their brown eyes as they glance about the room.

"So, you're saying the only way I get my father back is to bring back my brother?" Helene sounds hopeful, and it crushes me that this hope comes at the expense of my sanity. I know I was the one arguing for doing it, but that doesn't make the bitter pill of this situation any easier to swallow.

"It's possible," Estelle hedges, cutting a look at Sybil.

"All those in favor?" Helene asks, ignoring the caveat and thrusting her hand in the air.

I observe the faces around the room. Sybil raises their hand first, followed by Estelle. Zara's eyebrows tilt apologetically before she raises her hand. I can hear the groan of the wood on my chair as Essos grips it. It's not a surprise when Kai stands behind his wife and raises his hand. I can't say I blame him but remembering how Galen beat him bloody during his trial, I'm still stunned that he agrees we should bring this man back.

Cat makes a show of putting both hands on the table, and Xavier mimics her, leaning forward in his seat.

I haven't decided how I want to vote, but I don't have to decide. There are eleven of us in the room, and Dion brings the count to six in favor. The air is suddenly suffocating, and I think someone turned off the oxygen, because I'm not able to breathe. One of my worst nightmares is coming true.

The wood of my chair splinters as Essos crushes it in his grip. "I am the only one who knows where the dagger is. We don't have to do this." His hot breath stirs the baby hairs on my neck.

I turn to face him. "That wouldn't be very democratic of us," I point out, trying to bury the queasy feeling working its way through my body.

"I would do it for you, love."

I reach out and cup his cheek, and he leans into my touch. "I know you would, but I think we have to do it. I might have voted for it too."

"Do you honestly believe we should? After everything he did to you? Did to *us*? I am willing to look past it, if it is what you truly desire, but I don't think it's right."

"It's the best option," I tell him, the small quake in my voice betraying what I really think.

As we're getting undressed later, Essos grabs my wrists, stilling my hands as I'm buttoning up my night shirt. I look up at him, confused.

"I need you to trust me," he tells me. Essos's chest is bare, and I want to reach forward and run my hands over him and pull him against me, but the look in his blue eyes gives me pause. He's deadly serious about whatever is on his mind.

"I do trust you. I've never not trusted you," I reassure him. He gives me a pointed look, a wry twist to his lips. "Since getting my memories back, I've never *not* trusted you," I amend.

"I have to go somewhere, and I don't know how long I'll be gone. I'm going to try to make it quick."

I drop onto the bed, trying to keep my posture erect. Essos doesn't hesitate to cup my face so I can't look away from him.

"Can I ask where and why?"

Essos kisses my forehead, long and hard, before meeting my eyes. "You can ask, but I can't tell you. I promise to explain when I get back, but I made a promise to someone else, and I have to honor that."

I get it, I do, but I crawl away from him to get to the headboard, hurt that there is still so much that happened that I'm not privy to yet.

He eyes me warily as he moves around the room to climb onto his side of the bed. "Are you upset?" He tugs back the covers so we can both nestle under them.

I slide across the cool sheets so I'm against him. I've been warmer than usual lately, but that doesn't mean I don't crave Essos's touch. I fold against him, slotting into the same spots I used to fit, one arm folded against his chest, one leg wrapping around his, my small bump cradled between us.

"No, I'm not upset. I'm just not excited about being apart again. I feel like I've just gotten you back, and now you're leaving *again*. I'm not even allowed to know where you'll be. What if you're in danger and I don't know it?" I hate how emotion clogs my voice, and I have to close my eyes to stop the tears that threaten to spill.

"I can assure you that I won't be in any danger. I will come back to you whole. This—what I'm going to do—is to help us. I wouldn't do it if I didn't think it would help." Essos strokes my shoulder with one hand while his other grips my wrist.

"I trust you," I assure him, before plunging the room into darkness.

14

Essos is gone when I wake. I have a vague memory of a brief kiss on my lips before he departed, but my mind tumbled back into my nightmares too easily. Because of that, rising for real is harder than I hoped. I spend several minutes staring at the indent Essos left in our bed.

A gentle *woof* has me looking to my other side, where Dave is happily thumping his tail. He doesn't hesitate to jump onto the bed and shower my face with kisses.

"Dave," I giggle, trying to push him off. He finally settles down next to me. "Did Daddy send you to watch me?" I ask, rewarding him with scratches behind his ears and under his chin. Curled in the cradle of my lap, Waffles lazily turns his head toward the dog before resettling, too comfortable to move and too used to Dave's antics.

Dave sheepishly lowers his head, the closest I'll get to an acknowledgement from him. I've missed my furry companions, but I've wanted to make sure that Cat and Zara had the physical comfort. I had Essos, but they didn't have anyone but each other.

"Not just Dave," Cat says from the doorway. She's leaning against it, watching me carefully. Just past her, I see Shadow sitting patiently. It makes me miss Spot, but I know he's safe with my parents in the mortal realm, and I know they're safe because of him.

"Are you just going to stand there, or are you two also getting into bed?"

Cat looks down at the pit bull at her feet. "What do you think? Is that bed big enough for all of us?"

Shadow takes this as her command and sprints to the bed, trying to secure a suitable spot. She's mindful of not stepping on me as she clamors over to lick my face. Dave lets out a plaintive howl that Shadow echoes. I have no doubt they're missing their brother.

"So, Essos has you on babysitting duty now?" I sit up in bed as she climbs into Essos's spot. I summon two breakfast trays for us, but mine is sparse; I don't have much of an appetite. I can't decide if that's the pregnancy, or if it's nerves. This time, the baby doesn't fight me on the food. There's a pomegranate and some blessedly plain toast on my plate.

"He mentioned to me he wasn't going to be around and thought maybe we could use the time to talk." Cat lifts a few pieces of bacon and drops them on my plate. I fight my scowl but lift a piece of toast and take a bite.

"I thought I was giving you space?" I point out. Cat takes a big bite of sausage while she mulls over how to answer me.

"You were giving me space, but I'm pretty tired of the space, especially since Xavier is also staying in the house while Essos is away. I miss my best friend too much for all this space."

"Was there an email that I missed?"

"It was actually on the news last night, a breaking-news special report." She grants me a smile.

"I missed you too," I confess. "But I am a capable adult. Everyone doesn't have to baby me." I mull it over. "I would actually prefer that you all didn't baby me."

Cat bumps me with her shoulder. "I'm sure you wish that, but it's simply not happening, so it's time to put on your big girl panties. Finn's taking me out for some training with my powers."

"Why? Want to see if you can get him pregnant too?" I snark before biting my toast.

Cat scowls and lifts a pillow from a chair across the room, then tries to hit me with it. She's getting better at control, but since I can see it coming, it explodes into petals around us.

I don't expect how exhausted that one move makes me feel. I was warned that my pregnancy would use more and more of my energy as it went on, that my body is working itself to protect the baby without my needing to direct energy to it. It's still worlds better than when I found out Ellie was trying to bind my powers. Another plot that Posey was probably behind.

"You're getting better!" I exclaim, squeezing her hand. Cat looks sheepish and gives a halfhearted shrug.

"I have been practicing. Honestly, though, Rafferty did help. Having him box up my past life memories or whatever has helped me keep a clear head."

"Good," I tell her.

"Was he able to get your memories back?"

"No. I'm going to get dressed so we can go make things explode." My lost memories are something else I haven't let myself think about. I like to think Rafferty would have helped me if he could have, but I can't—no, I *won't*—let him dig through my mind at his leisure. I'll make do.

I nudge Dave out of the bed so I can get changed. No use showering if I'm just going to work up a sweat. I pull my hair into a high ponytail and put on comfortable loungewear, which I notice is getting a little tight around the middle. Even my shirt is tight around my belly, so I grab one from Essos's drawer instead. Before I emerge from our dressing room, I take a moment to admire the swell of my belly. Until now, I've tried not to look too closely at it. That kernel of fear has always stuck with me. Looking at it now makes it feel very real.

Cat grins at me from the bed before rising and looping her arm with mine. "So, why can't he help you?"

I lead us from the room, not able to look her in the eye as I explain. "Because like all things Posey does, she didn't block my memories right. I probably wasn't even supposed to remember what I did during the Calling. Anyway, Rafferty said he can only do something about it by digging around in my brain and targeting specific memories. I said no thanks."

"Why do you think he could work his magic on me?"

"Probably because it was an actual block. When Posey pulled you from the tapestry, she didn't remove your memories, she just made it so you didn't exist to begin with. Rafferty just blocked what was there from your past lives."

"I don't get it. The whole thing is a disaster all around."

"A Posey specialty." I hold her gaze. "This conversation about memories is all fine and good, but you know you're going to have to talk to me about Xavier sometime soon. And how you feel about the fact that you were supposed to be Queen of the Gods."

Cat's steps falter. "What is with that? Why is it just Queen of the Gods? Why isn't Queen of Gods *and* Goddesses? Seems sexist."

"Queen of the Pantheon?" I offer.

Cat pauses like she's mulling it over. "I can support that."

I chuckle, feeling light for the first time in months. Just the sensation of the warmth of the sun on my face gives me a dose of energy I didn't realize I needed.

Finn is ahead of us on the beach, pulling weapons from thin air the way Galen pulled the blade that he ran through Cat's heart.

We must startle Finn, because he spins and launches one at us, but Cat's reflexes are improving and she casts it aside immediately. The weapon imbeds itself in my deck before it vanishes.

"You shouldn't sneak up on people," Finn scolds. He crosses to me, ignoring Cat entirely. "Are you all right?" His gaze rakes over me for any potential injuries.

"I'm fine. It didn't even touch me," I tell him. "Besides, I think Cat handled the challenge excellently."

"I shouldn't have had to. Essos would kill you if he knew that you threw an actual weapon at Daphne," Cat snaps.

"It was an accident. My humblest apologies." Finn's voice drips with sarcasm.

"Whatever." I wave a hand dismissively. "What are we doing? It looks like object creation?"

"Yes. If we're bringing that son of a bitch—and I do mean that literally—back, then I want to be able to keep him in line." I admire Finn's bravado as he summons another spear and hurls it down the abandoned beach.

"Motherfucker!" someone screams from the direction the spear was thrown. Kai emerges with the weapon protruding from his shoulder. "What did I say, Phineas?"

Finn blanches at how Kai snarls his name and gives an unintelligible response.

"I didn't hear you," Kai snaps. We collectively wince as he pulls the spear from his skin. I have to close my eyes and fight back the urge to vomit.

"I said I didn't see you there."

"If you didn't see me, it's because you weren't looking. I'm kind of hard to miss."

Just because we are gods and immortal doesn't mean that injuries don't hurt. Kai strips his shirt off and wades into the water to speed his healing, casting deadly looks at Finn as he submerges himself.

"Right. Before that oaf comes back, Catalina, how about you make us a wall—preferably along the entire coast, about sky-high so the fish man doesn't drag me off to the seabed?"

"Walls don't work," Cat tells him but creates a single brick before making a small barrier, one brick at a time. It's short enough that Kai can just step over it when he emerges. Slowly, she works at it, making it longer and taller and wider.

While she works, I turn to Finn. "How is your arm?" It's still bandaged, lovingly wrapped by Dion, no doubt.

"Eh, I'll survive. It's not that bad. I just had no idea that wounds itch when they heal. It's terrible. Dion said I was lucky it wasn't super deep. After seeing what Posey can do with that blade, I'm glad I still have my arm."

When Kai exits the water, he looks over Cat's wall approvingly.

"Good. Now blow it up," he orders.

I create an Adirondack chair and sink into it while Cat works herself hard, sweat beading on her forehead. I watch her focus, her hands clenching into fists before the wall explodes. At the last second, Kai throws up a barrier in front of me and Cat, preventing us from getting hit with debris. Finn is not as lucky and gets clipped in the forehead by a particularly large piece.

Kai shrugs at him unapologetically.

"I want to see her block, if you will, Kai." Xavier's voice comes from behind us, and we all turn to face him. He gives me a cursory nod before focusing his attention on Cat. He moves toward her, and she takes a step toward him before seeming to remember herself and drawing back, closer to me. Xavier takes the hint and passes her to stand at Kai's side.

Kai yields to Xavier, sweeping his arm out. Xavier forms something in his hand, never taking his eyes off Cat, and she never takes her eyes off him, either. It's something to behold as they dance around each other, inexplicably drawn to one another but resistant to that pull.

He pulls his hand back and lobs the sphere at her, but she doesn't block—she doesn't have time to before she's hit in the face. Her annoyance quickly gives way to amusement.

"A snowball?" She wipes frozen water from her face.

"Would you prefer I threw a baseball or a golf ball at you? This way, if you fail to deflect, I'm not hurting you." His voice gets quiet at the end, like he doesn't want to admit to having a soft spot for her.

"Again," she orders, moving into a defensive position. She raises her hands in front of her and shifts one foot behind her. Xavier catches her off guard and nails her in the hip. She frowns but gestures for him to do it again. He obliges her again and again, until she's more frustrated than anything else.

"Have you had enough?" Xavier asks, careful to keep any inflection out of his voice.

She lets go of her restraint, and roughly thirty snowballs fly at him. He sees them in time, I know he does, because I watch his gaze dart around the onslaught. He could throw up his defenses, but he doesn't. Xavier lets himself get pelted with the snowballs until snow and ice is sluicing off his person.

"Do you feel better?" he asks, wiping it off.

Finn has moved to stand behind my chair and is leaning against it. "He never looked at Posey like that," Finn points out to me quietly.

"Like what?" I ask, playing dumb. I twist to look up at one of my oldest friends.

"Like he would burn the world down for her and make her Queen of the Ashes."

I study how Xavier approaches Cat once she's nodded her acceptance of his help. Still, Xavier hesitates before touching her, trying to guide her through finding her own power within. I get to my feet and create my own snowball then hurl it at Kai. He's so intent on what Xavier is saying and offering his own tweaks that I nail him in the side of the head.

"You know, I'm not afraid to hit a girl," Kai warns.

Xavier finally glances away from Cat to see what chaos I'm causing.

"She's not the only one who needs to be stronger and better," I point out, a sword lengthening in my hands. I twist it around before holding it in front of me.

Kai presses his lips together. "Is this really the best idea?"

I straighten. "Why wouldn't it be? Because I'm a goddess, or because I'm pregnant? Because if either of those are the reason, I'm really going to kick your ass."

"It's because we're all going to protect you, Daphne. Nothing is going to happen to you," he tells me, still not brandishing his own weapon.

"Because everyone did such a great job of that the first time around?"

Kai flinches, and I might not be looking at them, but I would bet money that Finn and Xavier do too. I lower the weapon a fraction. "You had no problem training me before. I want the same treatment now. I need to be able to throw down with Posey."

Kai doesn't respond. He strikes, swinging his sword at me with vicious accuracy. Metal vibrates in my hands as I block the blow. We parry, going back and forth, Kai showing me how to advance, correcting my form as I go. When we pause to get water, I see Catalina and Xavier talking, still working on building her defenses. Finn comes up behind me, and I surprise them both by swinging my blade just in time to block him.

"Again," I demand, lifting my sword for another round. I should be taking it easy; there's a tightness in my core muscles that I attribute to not only carrying around a baby but also swinging a sword.

After a half hour, exhaustion pulls on me, and I step out of the fray, leaving Finn, Kai, and Xavier to coach Cat. I rub my stomach, afraid I pushed too far. Why did I push? Why did I insist? Was it my own pride, my own hubris, that I'm better than everyone expects?

A hand on my shoulder startles me from my thoughts. "Are you all right?"

I look up and meet Xavier's ice-chip eyes. "Fine. Just tired. I thought I might take a relaxing dip." I gesture at my outfit, which becomes a green bikini, putting my bump even more on display. Xavier's eyes linger over my swollen stomach before he meets my gaze.

"I think I'll join you." Xavier doesn't bother waiting to see if I'll object. He just strips down, his pants turning into swim bottoms. His fingertips graze my spine and I can feel warmth thread through my body, soothing the muscles around my belly. He pulls his hand back just as quickly.

"If you insist." I turn to Cat. "Do you think you can handle a metamorphosis, or would you like help?"

"I can try it first?" She closes her eyes, no doubt attempting to envision the outfit she wants to be wearing. I give it my best effort to hold in my snort when her outfit changes not into the bathing suit she probably intended, but a clown costume.

Finn is less gracious and bursts out laughing. "Unless you want to go swimming as Bozo, you might want to reconsider letting us help," he tells her.

Cat's green eyes open, and she looks down at the colorful baggy jumpsuit, complete with stripes and odd shapes and ruffles around the sleeves. Her lower lip sticks out in a pout.

"You're probably overtired," Xavier tells her gently.

Finn, however, is intent to make this worse, and reaches out to squeeze the big red nose she gave herself. "How did you manage this?"

"I was trying to focus on not making a fool of myself," she whines.

"May I?" Xavier offers, stepping toward her. She scowls at him before nodding. The clown getup is gone in a blink. In its place is a chic black one-piece with a plunging neckline and nearly nonexistent back.

I look away from Xavier and Cat when I catch the heat in his eyes while he looks at her. I walk toward the water, heading for a small tide pool, with Kai following close behind me. I'm so grateful to be able to ease in and lounge in the small, wide pool without being worried about waves crashing in my face.

"Where is your wife?" I ask, turning to face Kai as I settle into the water. It's going to be a disaster and a half getting out, but I wouldn't trade this comfort for the world. Absently, I stroke my bump, finding solace in it.

Kai settles in beside me, smiling at how I'm touching my stomach. "She's looking for her mother, trying to figure out what her end game is. You're really not going to find out what you're having?"

"Nope," I confirm, looking at the horizon. "I've been disappointed too many times before to find out. I want to hold on to my hope, but keep it at arm's length. I'm trying to temper my emotions."

"You shouldn't have to. I know I'm no fertility goddess, but this feels different. May I?" He gestures toward me, and I nod, grateful that he asked. In the mortal realm, people were always touching baby bumps without asking, like there was some invisible magnet between the belly and people's hands. When I was human, I knew that I would hate that.

Kai's hand is calloused and much larger than Essos's. The whole of my bump fits almost entirely in his hand, and it's so soothing and relaxing to feel that warmth and know that I'm safe—that we're safe—that I close my eyes and let myself melt into the touch.

"I think it's going to be a girl, and I think she's going to have Essos wrapped around her tiny finger the moment she's brought into the world. I think she already does, and he just doesn't know it yet," he prophesies.

I let myself imagine it. I imagine Essos holding our baby in a way I never let myself envision before, her tiny hand around his finger. I can see him using shadows to lift her in the air and soothe her while making dinner, keeping her close to him while she naps. My eyes slam open and I try to clear those images. I try to erase them, because I don't want to see what may never come to pass.

My heart kicks into overdrive, and I need to run and hide and protect this future I'm dreaming of.

Kai must feel the change in me, because he's holding my face, blocking the sky from my view. "It's okay. You're okay. Nothing has happened. You're all right, Daphne. Nothing happened. You're safe."

Then I realize why he's saying this to me. It's because I'm crying, and not only crying, my whole body is shaking with sobs. I clutch his wrists, trying to get my breathing under control. Kai starts to take deep breaths until I catch the rhythm, and I blow out shaky ones. I'm still on the verge of falling back into that fear, of falling back into everything that scares me, but Kai's focused breathing keeps me from tumbling from the precipice into an abyss I'm not sure I have the mental strength to pull myself from. These panic attacks are happening too frequently for my comfort.

Once I'm breathing normally and the tears have stopped, Kai pulls back.

I sit up fully and bury my head in my hands. "No one ask me if I'm okay." My words are muffled by my hands. I feel the water slosh against my side as Kai gets up.

He's quickly replaced by a slender arm draping around my shoulder and pulling me into her side. I don't have to look up to know it's Cat.

"Do you want to talk about it?" she whispers so only I can hear her.

"No. I don't. I'm fine." I wipe at my eyes, banishing the tears, before turning to Cat with a broad smile on my face.

"That is the fakest fucking smile I've ever seen from you, and I saw the smile you plastered on your face after catching Essos and Zara making out."

"I am emotionally vulnerable, and you decide to bring up my husband making out with another woman? Rude."

"I'm just pointing out that I know when you're lying, and I thought you weren't married. Isn't that a big controversy?"

I lower my hands and splash her. "Now you're just being mean. What did I do to you?"

Cat eyes me, but a smirk lifts her face. "You were crying during my training montage. I needed to bring the mood back up." She twists so we can look at each other face-to-face. "Seriously, are you okay?"

I splash her again. "Was I not clear about not asking? I'm not okay—I'm one bad taco away from a total meltdown. I don't know if things are ever going to be okay again. What I can control is people telling me that I'm not married, so stop telling me I'm not married!"

"Did I hear that we're planning a royal wedding?" Finn suggests hopefully.

"That could be a good way for you to get your mind off Essos being gone," Cat says casually.

I struggle up by first leaning forward so I'm on all fours before getting to my feet. I can only imagine this getting worse the more swollen I become.

"We're about to resurrect Galen, make a truce with the literal she-devil, and endeavor to kill a Fate, all while trying to end the Zombie apocalypse and close the gates to the Underworld. But sure, let's plan a wedding."

"We should probably plan on getting the veil back in place before the mortals try to nuke us," Finn points out. Xavier shoots him a glare.

My sarcasm must not be strong enough, because Cat actually claps in excitement before getting out of the pool. "You won't regret this," she assures me.

"I already do."

THE NEXT DAY, I hate myself for it, but I hide from my friends. Their cheer and encouragement are nice on a small scale, but it's getting overwhelming. I take a ton of older books from the library and go sit in the stables with Abbot and Costello. The horses graze while I read about raising the dead. It was always a risk, raising the dead while ruling the Underworld. There were schemes by the dead, once, shortly after Essos and I came to power, where they attempted to return to the mortal realm, but we were able to quash the rebellion. It led to some much-needed changes. We altered the criteria for each level of the Underworld, making it fairer.

My experiences with the mortals, as a mortal, may even

encourage me to change things further. They're faced with impossible decisions every day: free-range chicken or going vegan? Eat the healthy farm-fresh strawberries, even though the carbon footprint of getting them from California to New York is ghastly? How much activism is enough? How many good deeds are enough?

How many souls are in the wrong place because of shitty judgement or accounting? I want to fix this, but to do that, first I have to reopen the gates to the Underworld and get the souls back so they're not aimlessly wandering Earth.

My feet are tucked under me as I read. Occasionally, Costello nudges my cheek, looking for a sugar cube. Dave races around the enclosure with the horses before returning to my side.

I don't know how to solve this. One chapter in particular keeps calling me back to it, but I can't figure out its significance.

"It calls for the blood of the King and a queen." I startle at the voice and slam the tome shut before twisting to face my mother-in-law.

"I *am* capable of reading," I snap.

"I wasn't certain—you seemed to be stuck on the same page for the last forty-five minutes." She brushes a strand of blonde hair away from her face as she looks around the paddock.

Beside me, Dave growls. Octavia glares at him until he whimpers.

I snap in Octavia's face, drawing her attention back to me. "Hey, leave my dog out of this."

Octavia turns her stare on me, one perfect eyebrow arching. "Do you want my help or not?"

"Galen isn't back, so I'm not sure what you're doing here." I try to force as much annoyance and anger as possible into my voice. I don't want her to know how afraid of her I am. She radiates waves of raw energy in a way that Titus never did. Titus used specific shows of power to demonstrate all he was capable of, but Octavia loves to make sure everyone feels her power all the time. She already choked me once till I blacked out, and I may be immortal, but until my baby takes their first breath, they're not.

"I came to make another show of good faith. My daughter suggested it, since my first one wasn't good enough for her. So, I'm here to tell you that to complete the spell to start returning the dead to the Underworld, you need the blood of its king and a queen. That will reopen the gates of the Underworld and call the loose souls home."

"You keep saying *a* queen, like anyone would do." I wait for her to fill in the blanks and gesture to the other side of the table where I'm seated. She looks at the picnic table with disdain, but I don't know what she expected, considering we're beside a barn.

"Yes, Helene's blood would satisfy the requirement, as would Posey's, but to keep the gates to the Afterlife open, it would be best to use the blood of the Queen of the Underworld." She perches on the very edge of the bench in her black pencil skirt and Louboutin shoes.

"But I'm still not technically queen," I say more to myself than her. I twist the problem in my head like a Rubik's cube, trying to find all the different ways that I can make this work. Maybe I need to go along with the ridiculous idea of getting married to my husband in the middle of this conflict.

"I never liked you for my son. He was a prince, and you insisted on holding him back and keeping him down. That drama with the that nymph girl was embarrassing. Do you know how many nymphs and goddesses and mortals my husband fucked? I'm sure the ends of your hair would curl from shock."

"Just because that's how your marriage was doesn't mean that's how I wanted my marriage to work."

"Of course, you were always too good for us. My son was in love with you, infatuated, and it ruined my family."

I realize that she's no longer talking about Essos. I meet her eyes defiantly. "Is that why you wanted me to do my own Trials? To derail my marriage to Essos?"

"It would have been simpler if it had. You and Essos would have never married, and I could have chosen a more appropriate wife for him to rule the Underworld by his side. Anyone would have been better than a little spring goddess. You would have moved on from my sons eventually. I thought my son would tire of you faster if you just did what was expected and gave in to him."

"So, you would rather I had rolled over for Galen? That I spread my legs and just let him get it out of his system?"

"Nothing so crude, but you promised him one date."

I push up from the bench, no longer interested in her help. "Your family is un-*fucking*-believable. Essos is your son too. Did you not care for his pain? Did you not care that his wife was dead? Never mind my personal stake in this whole thing, but what kind of mother chooses to comfort the man who murdered her other son's wife? I know parents play favorites and claim not to, but that is some next-level shit, Octavia."

"The kind of mother that wants to protect her only child who was born of love," she shouts at me. Her careful demeanor is gone, shattered. The sky above us darkens with storm clouds. Dave hops off the bench and growls at Octavia, baring his teeth at her.

"Heel," I order him. He looks at me dubiously but sits.

Octavia rolls her eyes. "Those dogs are a menace." She crosses her arms.

"The only menace here is you. If you came here to talk all about your son..." My words trail off as I finally realize what she said. "What do you mean, *only* child born of love?"

Octavia freezes. I hold my tongue, knowing that if I remain silent, she will fill the void... and she does.

"Titus wasn't Galen's father. Lairus was." Now it's Octavia's turn to wait for me to fill the silence. The God of the Sun being Galen's father has me stunned.

"That's why Esmaray left," I muse, thinking of the moon goddess. So many things slot into place—how Galen never quite fit, how Titus never gave him a kingdom. "Did Galen know?"

"No, but Titus did. After the twins were born, intimacy wasn't something we shared again. Esmaray had caught Lairus and me together after Galen was born, and so she left. Titus had more important things to deal with than his wife's infidelity. It was never something we discussed, and once the boys were settled with their roles, we stepped apart from each other. I never liked you for my son—"

"You said that," I snap.

She scowls at me. "I never liked you for my son, but you were good for him. You made Essos happy, and I assume you still do. I just wanted the best for Galen. He was never given the same chances as his brothers. He was fixated on you, and I thought perhaps you could give him that same happiness."

"Octavia, he shoved a knife into my heart and danced over my body while I bled out. You're never going to convince me that Galen is the wronged party here."

She sits back down, her posture deflating. "I never meant for any of this to happen." She looks up at me, her eyes red.

"Did you give Galen the knife?" I ask carefully. The storm clouds are still above us, loosing small, steady raindrops.

"What? No." She denies this too fast, and her gaze darts away. Dave growls, and I pat his head.

"Want to try that again?" I ask, keeping the waver from my voice.

"I didn't give him the dagger, but I also didn't hide its existence from him. He asked me questions about the two God Killer blades and I answered them. I mentioned they were being kept in the family vault in our home."

The fucking vault that they all had access to. I get up from the bench and approach Costello, attach his lead rope, and walk him back toward the stable.

Abbott huffs at me, and I shake my head. "I'll be back for you, I promise." I pause and look at Octavia. "Why are you telling me any of this?"

"Because I want my son back, and if that means ripping my heart out for your pleasure, then I'll do it. He doesn't deserve death. You're about to be a mother. Surely, you can understand."

I look away from her, squeezing my eyes shut. Now it's my turn to face her with tears in my eyes. "I would have been a mother long before now if your son hadn't killed me. You're making your case to the wrong woman." I may have already agreed to bring Galen back, but I haven't told Octavia that yet. When her children decide they want her to know, they can tell her.

I settle Costello in his stall before coming back for Abbott.

When I do, Octavia is gone.

15

Cat stays with me most nights while Essos is gone. He and I have been back together for only three weeks, but his absence makes it difficult to sleep.

Cat and I have movie nights, and when Zara is free from helping Sybil and Estelle, she spends time with us too. Now that we have a plan to deal with the zombies and we know about the ritual Essos and I need to undertake, I try to find a solution to putting the veil back in place.

Much as I hate to admit it, it's thanks to Octavia that I'm on the right track. I keep finding books flipped open to passages I should read left scattered around the house. The information is too precise to be from anyone else, and if it was a friend pointing things out, they would just do it.

"I know planning your last wedding was no fun," Cat starts, flipping open a binder. It's the kind of thing I expected from Posey, not Cat. She would have one for her own wedding for sure. But mine? "But maybe we can make this one better?"

"Catalina, I love you for wanting to throw this baller bash complete with—" I flip to the dessert page, which features a donut wall "—special desserts, but I want low-key. I already had my own version of the red wedding, and I'm not interested in a repeat." Just the mention of the scene has me clutching my abdomen in sympathy pains. The brutality of the show made my womb ache when I was mortal.

"But you deserve a big wedding, like an all-out bonanza! I want to release doves, and have them shit glitter all over the party, and I just...I feel like we all need a win. We all need *something*. Everyone is so depressed, and bringing Galen back is only going to make it worse. Give us some joy, damn it."

"Is the life I'm growing not enough joy for everyone?" I ask.

Cat reaches out and touches my stomach. "Of course, it is. But weddings are also fun."

I fall back into my pillows with a sigh. "Fine, fine. Let's plan my wedding."

Cat laughs and claps. We send Dave for Zara, who makes the effort but still seems subdued after the visit to her family. I try to draw her out, asking her opinion on each detail and sending flower petals in her direction.

I'll admit to having more fun planning this wedding than my last one. I make Cat practice her magic to summon samples of things. I assure her that I will do all the floral arrangements, though she does make me create a few different types for her and Zara to approve.

Zara eventually leaves us to help Sybil with something, and after sitting there for three hours, I need to use the bathroom. I throw back the covers and get to my feet.

"Where are you going?" Cat inquires, breaking her focus on the cake topper.

"To pee. There's a tiny god or goddess who is crushing my bladder."

I make my way across the room to the en suite bathroom and open the door. Darkness greets me, and I fumble for the light switch as I step in only to find there's nothing there. I have no chance to call out before I go weightless, like I'm falling.

My feet hit the ground, and pain shoots up my legs. My landing is too sudden. I could have softened it had I been expecting it, but now I'm using all my energy not to fall over.

"Oh, don't be so dramatic," a high-pitched voice whines.

I look up to see that I'm in the entrance hall to Posey and Xavier's house. Posey is seated on a makeshift throne beside a bubbling fountain modeled after her naked body. Water shoots out of the likeness's stone mouth and down her breasts while she raises her hands to the sky. Ostentatious doesn't even begin to cover how vain it is for Posey to have a fountain...of herself...inside her home.

"Says the woman sitting next to a fountain of herself. What do you want, Posey?"

Posey doesn't look as manic as she did the last time I saw her, but there is still a gleam in her eye that tells me she's not quite right. She ignores my question and gets to her feet. Her stilettos tap as she crosses the marble floor to me. She reaches out to touch my belly like we're old friends, and I step away from her even though pain flares in my hip. I should heal myself, search for the root source of the pain, but I need the be ready to focus my energy on an attack against her.

"I wanted to see how everyone is doing and make sure you're getting used to the new world order." She walks in a circle around me, no doubt taking in the hole in my leggings near my ass.

"You mean the world order where you rule with an iron fist and take away my T-bird because I had fun, fun, fun? What happened to wanting to rule side by side as queens?"

"Yes, but that's the point. I gave you a chance, and you basically spat in my face. Now I'm the only option. Not Xavier. Is he still pining over that lost little mortal?"

"She's not a mortal, in case you forgot. She's a goddess you punished on a whim."

She crosses back to her seat and settles in. "How could I forget my husband's new plaything is a goddess? You know, I always wondered if you two ever..." she winks at me with a sly grin "...you know, did the deed behind my back."

"I *never* slept with Xavier." The very idea is offensive, and my stomach cramps. "Tell me what you want."

"I'm going to make you an offer you can't refuse." Posey does her best Brando impersonation. There's certainly room for improvement.

"Right. And what kind of offer do you think you can make me that I'm going to find so irresistible? The last one wasn't enticing, so I guess the only way from there is up. Please, go on. I'm actually going to listen to what you have to say."

Posey stares at me, maybe surprised that I agreed. "You know what? I think I'm a little put out by your attitude, *Daphne*. You haven't been very sporting."

If I didn't know her well enough, this might shock me. "Golly, I wonder what sort of things I have to be sporting about. You orchestrated my murder. You decided to play Fate and keep my best friend from being able to live her real life. You've kept me from my husband for over a thousand years. Pray tell, Posey, what exactly is it that I should be thanking you for? Should I thank you for killing Cassius?" I decide I'm not going to wait to hear her out. I form a sword in my hand and hold it firmly in front of me.

She looks almost bored by this. "You know, if you kill me, someone has to step in as the new Fate. Are you ready to do that? If you do, it means losing the life growing inside you. That tiny form can't handle the amount of power you would have to absorb." This gives me pause, and she senses my hesitation. "Besides, a normal sword isn't going to kill me."

"I'm willing to test that theory. Having your head cut off seems like a difficult injury to recover from." I readjust my grip on the sword and step toward her, ready to lunge, but the sword vanishes from my hand.

"You're right. Your former lover won't be putting that smart mouth to use ever again. Did you know it took me almost thirty minutes to cut his head off with that dagger? It would have been a lot faster if I could have used a normal weapon, but I wanted his death to *stick*. Even though you're an ungrateful bitch and turned your nose up at my last offer, I'll give you another chance. I'll grant you mortality, and you won't have to worry about me hunting you down. This offer is for you and Essos and Xavier and everyone else, out of the kindness of my heart." She gestures with her hand like she's turning her face toward a camera, highlighting how amazing she is. "*And* you don't have to bring Galen back to life. I know Mommy Dearest wants her favorite back, but I can save you from that trauma."

I try to even out my breathing to make it obvious that I'm not considering what she said. The fact that she knows we've been talking with Octavia does not bode well for our plans.

"I don't know what you're talking about," I say, feigning ignorance.

"Daphne, please, *please* don't insult my intelligence. You're much too smart for that. Don't you know there's nothing that gets by me in my kingdom? You'd know a thing or two about that if you actually, you know, tried to lead, but you don't. Instead, you're too busy trying to ruin things for me. So, I'm going to put this to you one last time. You all can be mortal. Live your sad little lives however you want to live them without my interference. And in exchange, you don't have to bring Galen back to life."

She leans back in her chair, pleased with her villain's monologue. I try to pretend I'm actually considering this deluded woman's offer. But there's no way. There's no *way* I'll allow her to be in charge. There's no way I'll let her get away with the things she's done. Even if it means I have to work with Galen, even if it means I have to accept Octavia's help. Even if it means giving away a little bit of my soul.

I'm not going to let her win.

"So, let me get these details straight." The throbbing in my hip causes me to shift my weight to my other leg. "We become mortal, Galen doesn't come back, or else...what?"

"I kill you all. I'll start with your friend Catalina and work my way up to you, and I'll give you the honor of dying last so you can watch your husband—sorry, your *lover*—die before your eyes the way he had to watch you fade."

Around us, the plants start to wither as my anger gets the best of me. I need to shove that feeling down, even if she's making me want to level a forest. The name of the game is deception.

"You know, for this to be a worthy deal, you have to actually offer me an incentive." I shouldn't push, but I do it anyway. It's what she expects.

What I don't expect is the head that she rolls my way like a bowling ball. I don't even know where she got it from, but I'm never going to get the image of Cassius's foggy eyes and grimace of pain out of my mind. I thought seeing the act was bad enough, but this is so, so much worse.

"I can't make this decision alone." I let my voice quiver, try to seem genuine in my unease. I have to drag my gaze up to Posey. At least my revulsion and panic are genuine. She eyes me up and down as if trying to decide whether or not she believes my act.

Something about it must be convincing enough, because she tuts at me. "Well, I suppose you'll have to talk to that traitorous husband of yours. I helped fix that problem you created for his old secretary. As I understand it, he loved the wicked things she would do with her mouth." The twisted grin on Posey's face is enough for me to want to do the same to her, but that's a fight I will lose. "But if you know what's good for you, do think twice before attempting further retribution against Ellie."

"Enough," I snap, glaring at her with enough force that the fountain sputters. "Enough of this insinuation that my husband is cheating on me with Ellie and Lucky and whoever else. I don't care. He's *my* husband. What happened while I was dead happened while I was dead. Move on. I have."

"Oh, dear. I'm not talking about old news. Well, I'm not talking about *that* old news. I'm actually talking about something a fair bit more recent, perhaps this whole week." When she looks at my blank face, she grins. "Oh, you don't know where your husband's been lying on his back? Well, I'm sure you'll find out soon enough. From what I understand, that's his favorite position—girl on top."

She has the last word, not giving me a chance to respond before she sends me back to my house.

I land with the same jarring force as I did at Posey's. Pain lances up my leg, and I cry out as the familiar scents of home surround me. My knee gives out, and I clutch the door handle for support.

"Daphne!" Cat comes running, her arms locking under my armpits so she can help me to the ground. She follows me onto the tile floor.

I'm so glad it's heated as I sink onto the warmth. "I'm fine," I assure her, reaching for my ankle. I tug up my leggings to see that the joint is already bruised and swollen.

"That doesn't look fine." Cat scoots around to study it. Gingerly, she lifts my foot onto her lap, and I wince.

"I'll call a healer to come look at it." I try to get to my feet, but Cat slaps my arm.

"Stop it. I don't know how you managed to do this in the five seconds it took you to cross the room, but I'm going to call for Finn." She cups her hands together and blows into them. When she opens them, a dove flies out.

"When did you learn to do that?" I ask as the bird passes through the pane of glass and vanishes into the night.

"Finn's really been helping me learn my powers, and he showed me a few tricks to make it easy to contact him if there's trouble." She looks away from me sheepishly.

"Good. I'm glad you're learning. But really, I still need to pee and don't want to do it with an audience."

Finn is in the doorway before I even finish my sentence.

"What in the Underworld happened?" He looks at my rapidly-swelling ankle.

"Captain Disaster over here broke her ankle walking to the bathroom," Cat answers.

He squats down and lifts my ankle with care. I can barely feel his fingertips and wonder if he's using magic to keep his touch so light.

"That's not what happened, but I really have to pee and this position isn't working for me, so, if you guys could leave the bathroom and close the door, that would be awesome."

Finn looks at me dubiously but obliges. "Are you sure?" He helps me onto my good foot, and while my bad leg hurts like a motherfucker, if I want any hope of peeing in peace, I need to pretend the pain isn't blinding.

"Yes, leave me." My words are shaky as I order them away. I hobble, trying not put too much pressure on the weak leg.

When I have finished relieving myself and washing my hands, I emerge to find my bedroom stuffed with people.

Xavier surprises me by stepping forward and scooping me up, one hand firmly around my waist and the other cupping my knees. I yelp but don't want to show how welcome this is. He deposits me on the bed before sitting beside my bad foot. This position is almost worse, though, because now my hip is hurting too, and taking several deep breaths isn't enough to keep the tears from my eyes.

"I feel like a freak show. I hurt my ankle. It isn't cause for an inquisition."

As he lifts my ankle, my brother-in-law's voice is whisky smooth. "How, Daphne?"

I sigh, noting the concern in Xavier's eyes. "Well, since you're all here, I might as well tell you. I saw Posey."

Everyone starts talking at once, demanding to know how I got it in my head that visiting her was a good idea and why I would confront her on my own.

I let everyone get their initial reactions out of their system—the outrage, the questions—before I bother answering them. "I didn't intend to see her..." I lose my train of thought as my ankle warms in Xavier's hand. I want to flinch and pull my foot away, but I know he's healing me, so I don't.

"Then what happened?" Xavier's voice reaches me over the din.

"I went to the bathroom, and she...*pulled* me to her house. I was there for ten, twenty minutes before she dropped me back here. And by dropped, I mean, she literally dropped me."

"I'm going to reach farther up your leg and toward your hip to make sure she didn't fracture it. I wouldn't put that past her." The dark tone in Xavier's voice makes me tremble, but I nod, trusting him.

I'm not sure if it's being away from Posey, his affection for Cat, or a combination of the two, but he's been much acting more brotherly toward me, to the point I can even call it affectionate.

My ankle is still throbbing, but it becomes a different sort of pain. His fingertips ghost along my leg, touching only the outside and top the closer he gets to my hip. The peanut gallery has gone suspiciously quiet, but I don't take my eyes off Xavier. I giggle when he touches a sensitive spot along my hip just below my stomach. I see his lips twitch at the sound, but he frowns when he presses down on each hip bone.

I wince, and his frown twists into a scowl. He repeats the process down my other leg before sitting on the bed at my feet.

"I didn't know you were so adept at healing," I whisper. I know he healed Cat, but I didn't know he had more than a rudimentary understanding of healing.

"What need does a king have of healing? I'm not skilled in it by any stretch of the imagination." The bitterness in his tone makes me flinch, and I suspect that's something he heard a time or two or a thousand from Octavia and Titus. I have to disagree, because he does seem to know what he's doing. "You might have a hip fracture, but I'm not confident enough to try to do something about it, not with the baby. You'll be all right for now, but I want the healer to check you out first thing in the morning."

"What did Posey want?" Helene asks.

I settle into my pillows, and both Finn and Cat jump up to plump the ones behind me so I'm more comfortable. Cat is still pointedly not looking at Xavier. Whatever personal progress they made during training has lapsed again. He's also trying to focus on me and my tale of woe, but whenever Cat moves, I catch Xavier's head twitching in her direction.

"She wants to cut a deal, and she seems to know that Octavia is working with us, so I'm not sure we can trust anything the Goddess Supreme has to say. She could be playing Benedict Arnold." I tell them of Posey's offer and of Cassius's head. None of them seem the least bit surprised, nor are they chomping at the bit to accept.

Kai has folded himself into my reading chair. The long chaise lounge usually swallows me up, but he hardly fits. Helene is perched on the armrest, looking at her nails. Waffles emerges from whatever dark hole he was nestled in and settles himself on the giant's lap. Kai immediately starts to pet him, and Waffles purrs so loudly I can hear him from across the room.

"I mean, obviously, no." Helene looks almost bored as she says this.

"Obviously," I respond dryly. "Does anyone actually know where my husband is?"

Glances around the room confirm that wherever he is, he didn't want *anyone* to know. I hope he gets back fast.

"You really threatened to cut off her head? That's not an exaggeration?" Finn asks with a laugh.

"I really did," I confirm.

"She was right," a new voice answers from the doorway. Zara is standing there' with a book held close to her chest. When all eyes look to her, she shrinks back. I beckon her forward.

"What was who right about? I'm lost," Dion whines, and sips directly from the bottle of wine in his hand.

"Lost in the bottom of that bottle," Helene mutters. Finn throws a pillow at her that she explodes into feathers, but he anticipates the move and the feathers become birds that fly at her.

"Enough." My voice comes out firm and commanding even as I rub my temples.

"Posey was right. Killing her will create a void. Gisella just brought me some old books that she dug out of her personal collection, and I was struggling with the translations, but this one deals with the creation of the Fates and the need for three. Posey's death would create a void, but rather than risk the collapse of the world, Titus and Octavia built in a failsafe." Zara's voice has grown stronger.

"What sort of failsafe?" Cat presses.

Zara clears her throat, looking at everyone. "Whoever kills Posey will take her place as a Fate, unless someone else takes her place willingly."

"Does your book cover how exactly to do that?"

At Finn's question, energy and hope drain from the room.

"I'm not sure. I'm not there yet. Sorry." Zara sounds it too.

I shake my head emphatically. "You have nothing to be sorry for." Given the lack of volunteers, I assume no one in this room wants to be a Fate. We're happy with our lives, and adding in this potential new power, this unknown, is like throwing dice into a board game and shouting *Yahtzee* when you're really playing chess.

An uncomfortable silence descends on the group. We glance at each other, waiting for someone else to speak up.

I decide to drag the attention away from Zara, who is squirming. "If you think I fractured my hip, why aren't I in pain?"

"Because your ankle was worse?" Xavier answers my question with a question. "Because you're lying down? Because when I healed your ankle, what I did to numb it stopped you from feeling pain? Take your pick. I already said I'm unskilled. If that's all, everyone should get out. We can regroup when Essos is back and see what we can do about what the she-devil knows and how we can attack the situation." Xavier's word is the last on the subject, because everyone complies, getting up and leaving.

Cat and Xavier stay behind. Cat's already settling herself on the bed beside me, and I can see him watching her from the corner of his eye.

"I can stay," he offers, shoving both hands in his pockets.

"No, go." I swat at Xavier. "You're being too nice, and it's weirding me out. I like it better when you're bitchy to me."

Xavier acquiesces, dipping his head in a show of respect before making his way to the door.

"Wait!" I call, and he stops. "Can you help me get under the covers? I may have lied when I said I wasn't in pain." A lie seemed easier than having everyone clucking over me.

"I can get a healer here now."

"No, it can wait till tomorrow. It's the middle of the night. Please, don't make this a big deal."

Xavier makes a strangled noise of exasperation, lifting his gaze to meet Cat's. They seem to have an unspoken conversation, then he scoops me up much the same way he did before so Cat can draw the covers back. He settles me back down, and I try to fight a whimper when he slips my foot under the covers.

"I'm going to stay," he announces once I'm tucked in like a child.

"No, you're not. You can check on me tomorrow, like a normal person. I just need rest."

"She could come back for you at any point. I'm going to talk to Sybil and Estelle about how we can prevent this from happening again."

"Good, go do that. Just get out of my hair."

"I've got her," Cat promises. Even the dogs are more on guard, Shadow positioned at the foot of my bed and Dave on the floor on my side of the bed, afraid, I think, of hurting me. Waffles makes his way onto the bed and settles near my head.

"Send Dave if you need me," Xavier says.

Dave lifts his head and woofs in response.

I give Xavier a small, grateful smile. "If I promise, will you leave?"

"Yes."

"Then yes, I promise. Now go. This is a no-boys-allowed space until my husband returns."

With my agreement, Xavier leaves. Grateful there is no one else to keep on a brave face for, I collapse into the pillows and cover my face with my hands, a small sob choking me. Cat doesn't say anything, just molds her body to mine, holding me close. She's mindful of my hip and my foot as she does this.

"You're okay," she swears as she strokes my hair, letting me cry until I've exhausted myself.

What I didn't tell everyone about was my fear of how Posey got to me. How there was nothing I could do when she did have me.

That feeling is the fuel for my anger.

Fingers gently touching my hair and face wake me from my nightmares in which I was faced with a hallway with hundreds of doors, a child crying behind one of them, as Posey chased me. As my eyes open, the bad dreams slowly recede into a memory to be forgotten, but the feeling of fear, of terror, lingers.

Essos looks down at me with a grim smile on his face. I melt deeper into the pillow and reach a hand up, my fingers grazing his cheek.

Relief burns through me. "Why do you look so serious?"

"Because it's been a seriously long time since I kissed you." His words are smooth, and then he covers his mouth with mine. He cups my face, his thumbs caressing my cheeks. I open my mouth to him, our tongues flicking against each other. I'm more desperate for him than I thought. I forget everything about Posey, Essos's mother, and my injury and try to sit up to match his ardent kisses with my own. The movement sends a wave of pain radiating from my hip.

I gasp in pain into his mouth, and he pulls back immediately, concern overwhelming his features.

"What? What's wrong? Is it the baby?"

I shake my head, because I'm beyond words. Xavier wasn't kidding about his healing masking the pain. I grip Essos's forearms just to have something to squeeze though the agony. My own powers of healing must have dulled the pain while I slept. I remember Helene once mentioning that her personal healing was slowed when she was pregnant because her powers were focused on the baby, leaving her injuries neglected. That would certainly explain why I was slower to heal during the Trials.

"No. Not the baby. You missed a lot," I manage.

"Good thing I had Saima make you a batch of macarons to ease the pain of my absence." His thumb smooths along my cheek.

Essos doesn't take his gaze off me, but I feel the presence of someone else entering the room. My head snaps up, and shock surges through the pain. I'm glad for it, because it takes my mind off the torment.

"Callie?" I breathe. The woman's black hair creates a halo of natural curls around her head. She always had impeccable style. She disappeared long before I died, though I'm hard-pressed to put an actual timeline on it. Her dark skin looks luminous against her cream-colored silk blouse, and her dark brown pants have been pressed so there isn't a wrinkle on them. Full lips and big brown eyes always made Callie irresistible to every person she met. There was a reason she was the Goddess of Beauty and Sex. She was a siren calling to all; no god was immune.

"Hi, Daphne." Her voice is just as sultry as I remember.

"It's been a minute," I tell her, which is quite possibly the understatement of the millennium. This earns me a chuckle from the elusive goddess.

"As much as I'm loving this touching reunion, my pregnant wife is in pain. Can you help her?" Essos looks imploringly at Callie.

Her brown eyes shift from me to him, and she nods and sets aside her giant purse. One wouldn't put healing in the wheelhouse of beauty and sex, but she once said it was an important skill to have when married to the God of War and Suffering.

"Of course. What hurts?" She pushes Essos out of the way, and he practically snarls at her. He moves around the bed to his side and sits where he usually sleeps, and it feels like déjà vu when he grabs my hands.

"Xavier said I may have fractured my hip, and I did something to my ankle," I inform her. I hate the strangled sound Essos makes, but when I look at him, his face is perfectly calm. He lifts our joined hands to his mouth and brushes a gentle kiss along my knuckles.

Callie gestures at the covers, peeling them off when I nod. She does the same things that Xavier did, her only tell a small wrinkle in her brow as she examines my ankle and hip. "I didn't know that Xavier was a healer." Her tone is neutral when she firmly grasps my hips.

"The things you don't know about him could probably fill a book," I say with a forced laugh. At every turn, it seems another layer of Xavier is pulled back and revealed.

"This is going to hurt for probably just a second, and then I need to undo what Xavier did to your ankle." There is a pitying look on her face when she says this.

"Will it hurt the baby?" Essos asks before I can.

"No. Daphne has a hairline fracture in her hip, which could be problematic if she were giving birth right now, but she's not. Trust me." Her tone is so confident that I do, even without knowing where she's been all this time.

"Go," I order, bracing myself against the pain. Her hands warm as she presses them down. My teeth clench and I close my eyes, not wanting Essos to know just how much it hurts, but he can feel it as I squeeze his hand. He uses his free one to brush the hair from my face.

"This is just practice. We'll be ready for when you have the baby. I already know where I have to be and what I have to do," he declares, whispering in my ear. I can almost envision it, my feet up, sweat dotting my forehead as I push.

Before I can have that, I need to kill Posey.

The pain ceases abruptly, and I'm able to breathe again. My breaths are haggard and shallow, and Essos moves so he's sitting behind me, cradling me to his chest.

Like Xavier the night before, Callie lifts my ankle and places it on her lap. Essos's lips brush the shell of my ear, and I melt further into him.

"Do you want to tell me how this happened?" he whispers just for me, but Callie lifts her head to hear my response.

"It's a long story. Can I get a macaron first?" I mutter, squeezing Essos's hand in anticipation of the pain. Callie doesn't delay, getting right to the business of healing me. When she's done, I'm panting from the pain of having her undo what Xavier did, but Callie looks as effortlessly lovely as before.

"I'll give you two a minute. If you need me, I'll be in the kitchen getting a coffee." Just as quickly as Callie reappeared, she's gone again.

Essos gently slides out from under me and presses his lips to mine with a fervor unlike the gentle kiss of earlier. It's deep and consuming, and I want to keep giving and giving and giving all of myself to him. I pull him back onto the bed, onto me.

We lie there for a while just holding each other, relishing in an intimacy that goes beyond sex. Do I want my husband between my thighs? Absolutely. Do I want him to just hold me, in a small assurance that we're both okay? Also, absolutely.

"I missed you." He nuzzles his face into my neck.

"You're just saying that because we're in bed together."

He lifts his head to meet my gaze so there is no mistaking his intent. "I am saying that because you are my *wife*. I am saying that because I have missed you for a thousand years, and every minute, every second away from you chafes at my soul."

My heart breaks again for him, for what he's lived through. There are emotional scars that are too deep for anything but time to heal. It doesn't mean I won't stop trying with every kiss and every touch. I try every morning, every night.

"I missed you too," I assure him, pulling him back down into my arms so I can hold him and just enjoy the feel of his body next to mine.

When we get these quiet moments, we have to enjoy them, because we don't know how long they're going to last.

It's still morning, but barely, when we finally emerge, showered and clothed. Everyone else is gathered on the back porch. Cat subtly gestures at my neck, and I scowl, feeling the tender skin that Essos had been so focused on before we came down.

Essos isn't looking at me now. He's back to being all business, including dressing in a suit. I changed into a loose, flowing floral skirt and oversized sweater. Something about the last few days has made me want to hide myself, hide my bump and my baby from all dangers.

I tense up even though we're among friends and family. Essos doesn't miss a beat, slipping his hand into mine.

"Thank you for looking out for her, brother," Essos greets Xavier, extending his hand.

"So, this is why you left for a week?" Xavier questions, releasing him and looking at Callie. She's leaning against the railing, sipping from a small espresso cup. Just seeing the dark liquid makes me want a coffee in the worst way.

"I wasn't willing to come quietly. It took him a few days to convince me," she supplies, glancing at me and what I'm sure is my hickey. I have to fight the urge to touch it, even though I want to. I could heal it or cover it up, but it causes a weird mix of pride and desire to wear my husband's mark for all to see.

"What did convince you?" Helene asks from her chair. Her legs are crossed, and she's leaning forward toward our sister-in-law. She's so casual, as if it hasn't been a few thousand years since Callie disappeared. Between the two of us, we've been gone a suspiciously long amount of time.

"Galen is dead." Callie shrugs one delicate shoulder before looking around at both familiar and new faces.

"You are aware we're going to change that, correct?" Finn clarifies.

"Yes, Essos was very clear what my role is going to be." Callie is just as tight-lipped as I remember. When we would spend time with her, she was often quiet and reserved. On the rare occasion all the siblings would get together, she would remain glued to Galen's side, doing what she could to dim her natural beauty, something difficult for the Goddess of Beauty and Sex. From what I can remember, whenever I would try to engage with her, she would close up, rarely giving more than one-word answers, whereas I would see her holding longer conversations with Helene. In retrospect, I understand why she was aloof toward me. Who would want to befriend the woman your husband was obsessed with?

"Which is what, exactly?" Cat questions. She leans closer to me so she can whisper, "You need to eat."

I frown at her. It's not that I'm not hungry—I'm actually ravenous—but I'm afraid of missing even a second of Callie's comeback. "I'll eat when our conversation is done."

"Who are you again?" Callie questions, dark eyes boring into Cat's.

Xavier steps into her line of sight, blocking Cat from Callie's view. "I believe she asked you a question first."

"I'm going to keep Galen in line by dangling what he wants on a string."

"Out with it, Callie," Helene snaps. "I'm getting bored of your evasive answers."

Callie turns on her. The change in her is subtle, but I can see the sharpness in her features. Her cheekbones, once fine, are more defined. Her eyes, once doe-like, narrow in anger.

"I will not be bullied by you people any longer. I spent centuries being pushed around by your brother—being ignored and belittled. What makes you think I'll give you any satisfaction?" She whirls on Essos, pointing an angry finger in his face. "You told me they were different. You said they would be accepting, but your sister is the same bitch she's always been. I don't need this in my life, Essos. I came for you, but I don't need this. I was *happy*."

"You came back because you have a duty. I helped you flee Galen. I kept you safe when he asked where you went. I traded in favors and chips I didn't need to cash in to hide you. I am asking you to step in now, and damn it, Callista, you're going to stay and you're going to do this."

"Why should I?" she demands.

He laughs, but it's not a happy sound; it actually sends a chill down my spine. He releases my hand and steps forward so they're toe-to-toe. "Because you swore to come when I called. Because your husband murdered my wife. Because your children were given a chance to grow up free from their father, and I want my child to do the same."

Callie's gaze drifts over his shoulder to me, regret and tears brimming in her eyes. "I am so sorry for what he did to you, but you have to understand. I am free of him, and being here comes at great personal cost. You don't understand what you're asking of me."

"But I do," I say. jumping in. "You left to protect your children, and they're grown now. I'm asking for the chance to be able to raise mine. My husband kept what he did for you a secret, even from me. If that doesn't scream that he is loyal to you, I don't know what will." I put as much gusto into my words as I can. A mix of pride and hurt blasts me, knowing that Essos kept something from me, but I can understand Callie seeking out Essos to help her.

Callie straightens her spine, nodding. "I have twins. When I found out I was pregnant with my sons, I went to Essos for help. I left before Galen found out. Essos spirited me away so I could raise them without their father around. I came back so you can dangle the location of my sons over Galen's head."

"How did no one know?" Finn asks. None of us are surprised that her reaction was to run—hiding from Galen was the right step to take.

"Rafferty," Cat suggests.

We all move to sit at the long patio table. We're short one seat, and the table accommodates us by lengthening and adding a chair. No one confesses to doing it, but we all settle in.

Essos nods. "Yes. He made it so when people thought of Callie, they wouldn't think too hard about where she was. It's a debt that Rafferty is not ashamed of lording over my head, even as I ask for more favors.

"Tomorrow, we will summon my mother. Tomorrow we will see exactly what is required of us to bring Galen back," Essos tells the group. He's sitting too far away from me, and that churns my stomach, especially since he's not going like what I'm about to tell him.

"About that. We should wait to bring him back."

Essos twists in his seat so he's facing me.

I lean toward him, trying to soothe the worry from his eyes. "It's just that while you were gone, a few things happened."

"I don't like the sound of this," Essos interrupts.

I place a finger to his lips. He nods, letting me go on.

"Well, first I was visited by the ghost of evils past. Your mother came to plead for Galen's life again. She also told me that, in order to open the gates of the Underworld, we need royal blood."

My husband closes his eyes and lets out a slow breath. "Of course, we do. Swell. Xavier and I can do it." His tone is sharp.

I grit my teeth in an effort to not snarl at him. "For the doors to *stay* open, it needs to be the blood of the King and Queen of the Underworld. I verified her statements from a research book. So, before we do anything, we need to get married again."

"We're already married," he tells me sternly, even though we've had it confirmed by several people that we are not, in fact, married in the way that counts for the ritual.

I hold up my hands defensively. "I am not the one you should pick this fight with. Rafferty confirmed it. Your mother confirmed it. Everyone has confirmed that declaring ourselves married does not make us married. You need to get down on one knee and put a nice big rock on my finger." We haven't discussed what happened to my rings or my old body following my death. He hasn't offered, and I haven't asked.

Essos grabs my ringless hand and presses a solitary kiss to my ring finger. "I shall remedy that oversight, posthaste. Do you have any other requests?"

"We will be married at the end of the week, so as a wedding gift to me, we're pushing back reviving Galen. I want to make sure your mother's proposed solution actually works before we do what she wants."

"Because there isn't a bomb hanging over our heads waiting to explode, Daphne needs to exploit her vanity," Xavier snarks, lifting a glass of dark amber liquid.

Essos snarls at his brother, all goodwill with Xavier ended by those words. I shoot out of my chair, letting it slam to the ground behind me. With the action, everyone else gets up, seeming unsure which side of the conflict they're going to fall on.

"*I* asked for the wedding," Cat pipes up, "so if you want to blame anyone, blame me. One week isn't going to change anything."

"I disagree," Kai interjects. "People—humans—are dying, and they have nowhere to go, so they're left wandering around, rotting and traumatizing their friends and families. Unnecessary deaths are occurring, and there are spikes in suicides and murders and who knows what else. We were in the mortal realm for less than an hour and witnessed a massive hoard moving into a small neighborhood. You weren't there as Helene and I did what we could to fortify those borders." He'd been so quiet this whole time I actually forgot he was there. "I understand why Essos and Daphne need to be married, but we can't wait. It's not just the humans left in limbo—dryads and other minor creatures in our world are dying too, turned to stone by Posey for stepping out of line. We don't have the luxury of time."

I move close to Essos, wanting the security that he offers me, and his long arms fold me against him in a tight embrace. "So, we wed tomorrow, but I'm not spending another night away from my wife."

"Fine," Xavier concedes.

"Just want to make sure I'm putting this in my calendar right—wedding tomorrow, open the gates to the Underworld the next day, and following that we're raising my brother from the dead. Did I forget anything?" Helene asks.

"At some point, I'm going to kick Posey's ass into next week," I add.

We settle back into our seats, and I wave a hand at the table. Snacks appear in front of us. I don't want to admit it, but Cat was right, I do need something to eat...especially now that I have to tell Essos about my conversation with Posey.

"Is that all?" Essos asks, glancing from the food to me, knowing the answer.

I grab a piece of toast and butter the bread carefully before I look at him. I snag a few pieces of sausage and bacon too and a fried egg and some fruit. "Not quite. I got hurt because of Posey."

Essos goes statute-still, his nostrils flaring.

He must realize I'm alarmed at this reaction, because he clenches and unclenches his hand before his eyes flick to mine. "I'm waiting for you to elaborate before I react, so please do, before I assume you went after her with some half-baked idea about ending all this."

I lift my chin, anger flooding my veins. "Why should I, since it seems you've already made your assumption?"

"Daphne..." Essos warns, never breaking eye contact.

I take an obnoxiously large bite of toast to stall. If he wants to be an asshole, I can be one right back.

I finish chewing and take a sip of orange juice. "I was going to the bathroom, and I stepped through the door and right into Xavier and Posey's house."

"She called you to her, no warning?" Callie asks.

I can understand her surprise and fear. Summoning another god isn't something we can do, but evidently Posey the Fate can. She must be enjoying her cat-and-mouse game.

"Yes, I think the first landing was jarring and hurt me because I wasn't expecting it. When she sent me back, it was much the same. She made me an offer—well, she offered all of us mortality in exchange for not having to bring Galen back."

"What kind of offer is that?" Callie asks with a laugh, pouring herself a fresh coffee.

"The kind of offer she expects Daphne to take because she's traumatized by Galen murdering her, attempting to murder her, assaulting her, and really just being Galen in general," Finn offers. He grabs a muffin and rips off the top, then hands it to his boyfriend before eating the bottom of it. Dion happily accepts, breaking off a dainty portion and popping it into his mouth before giving his boyfriend a kiss.

"She underestimates my desire to kill him again," I grumble around another bite of toast.

"You're going to have to beat me to it, my love. You had your turn. Now it's mine," Essos vows with a grim edge to his voice. Why this sends a bolt of desire through me, I don't understand, but I'll let him keep up with this caveman act.

"We're not taking my ex's offer," Xavier states, his tone final.

"No one thought we were, big guy," Finn teases with a laugh until his mouth is sealed shut in a similar fashion to Ellie's. The retaliation from Finn is swift, because the teacup Xavier was holding in a rather dainty fashion falls out of his hand when Finn removes all of his fingers.

I can see Xavier's eyes turn red with fury, moving to act out, but Cat beats me to it.

"Enough!" Her voice is commanding and firm when she shouts, and a small gust of wind blows around us. Xavier and Finn exchange a look and, without needing to be told, they revert the other to their original form.

"What does this ritual to open the gates of the Underworld entail? I can't say I'm excited about the prospect of bleeding my pregnant wife." Essos rubs his eyes, looking so tired when he asks his question. This is all so much that I don't blame him. When it's all over, I think I'll sleep for a year. Except not, because hello, bun in the oven.

"We have to be in your throne room, and we need a magicked blade so our wounds don't close right away. It's probably going to be more blood than you're happy about, but I'm not positive. Zara has been working tirelessly with Gisella, Estelle, and Sybil to get the details. They were trying to figure out what Posey did to damage the veil and what else she might have up her sleeve, but I asked them to switch gears so we can clean up this mess with the souls."

Essos looks disheartened when I tell him this.

"We have the other God Killer blade. We can use that," I suggest, my voice small. This of course, is the blade that has Galen stored in the stone.

"Right," Essos confirms, squeezing my knee.

Kai pipes up. "Does anyone else feel like Posey has us chasing our tails on purpose?"

"Probably. I mean, I know I'm the new kid on the block, but she seems more methodical than casually making that garbage offer. There's no way that she honestly thinks you all would take it, right?" Cat's voice is tentative as she breaks off a piece of bacon and eats it.

"No—being new means you have fresh eyes," Helene says. "We're all colored by centuries on centuries of expectations around her. She basically just pulled a rabbit out of a hat, and when we looked closer, it was actually a cat. Posey has been misleading us all for so long."

I refuse to gawk but that might be the nicest thing that Helene has said in the history of ever.

"So, what is her end game?" Essos muses out loud. He leans back in his chair, running his thumb over his bottom lip while we all sink into a contemplative silence.

I grab a scone. "What if she already told us? Think about it. She wants power. She's been trying to amass it for millennia. What if making us all mortal *is* what she wants? Maybe she knows we'll say no, that we'll all be laughing behind her back at what a stupid offer she made. And then she'll strike."

"You think this is the bluff to end all bluffs? Telling us she has literally nothing, not even a pair of twos, when she's going to take it all from us anyway? I just don't get why she would do that," Essos says, still trying to puzzle out the theory.

"There is no way she's that good at faking it. Her orgasms were as fake as silicone boobs," Xavier attests with a laugh.

"That...makes me uncomfortable," Dion says, grabbing his wine goblet. Sometimes it's easy to forget that he's Xavier's son.

Xavier blows out a harsh breath with a nod. "It's the sad truth, son."

I give a hard whistle, and Dave appears at my side. He sits perfectly straight in business mode, ears forward and alert.

"Get me Zara and the Fates," I order. He shoots off into the house like a rocket.

Essos eyes me questioningly, sitting up.

When Zara, Sybil, and Estelle emerge, they all look mildly put out at being summoned. Estelle grabs a scone and takes a bite. It must not pass her approval, because she turns to the side and spits it onto the deck, where Dave happily hoovers it up.

"I'm going to need to go into those kitchens and knock some sense into that new chef," she bemoans, tossing the rest of the scone to Dave. He doesn't have the same issues with quality, because he lies down and lazily munches on his treat.

"Can Posey make us mortal?" I ask, ignoring Estelle's dig about the new chef. The new chef who happens to be Estelle's former sous chef that she personally trained.

Sybil looks taken aback. "Why would you ask such a thing?"

"That's not an answer," Helene points out unhelpfully.

"In theory, yes, but she would need our assistance, or some other source of power," Estelle cuts in.

I lock eyes with my husband. We must both thinking the same thing, and it turns the food in my stomach sour.

"Could she do it with trillions of souls and the Goddess Supreme?" Essos questions, beating me to it.

I rub my hands over my stomach, trying to soothe the nausea. It feels like the stomachache promised by parents to children who eat too many sweets. Only, it's been brought on by the possibility of Octavia double-crossing us and working with Posey once she has her son back.

Xavier presses his lips into a thin line while studying his brother. "You're thinking this is a long con? Get Galen back for Mom? Get all of us out of the picture, including Dad? You think Mom is capable of that?"

I hate the skepticism in his voice, the concern that their mother would betray them like that.

I realize that I never revealed Octavia's secret, and now seems like as good a time as any.

"Titus isn't Galen's father. Lairus is."

I'm startled by the reactions around the table. Everyone starts heatedly debating if they knew this or not. Essos seems dejectedly accepting of it. Finn and Dion are startled and surprised. Helene tries to put up a defense, but the quiet murmur of "Starfish" by Kai in her ear gets her to sink into him.

"How do you know?" Essos asks me, not because he doesn't believe me, but because he does.

"Octavia told me. She said it was why Esmaray left. Octavia told me because, according to her, she was appealing to the heart of a mother." I rub my belly again, hating the fist of anxiety that seizes my heart. All this stress and anxiety is not good for the baby, and the perpetual feeling of heartburn isn't good for me.

"She always was a monster-in-law," Callie says, trying to support me, but I can't look at her, at this woman who got away from it all and barely wants to help now.

"I guess if this was a long con, the question is, was Galen in on it and was the goal to get to Callie and his sons?" Cat asks.

I don't like where she's going with this question, and we all look around the table as if someone will have the answer to how nefarious Octavia, Posey, and Galen were.

"I think Galen was a pawn. I don't think Posey ever counted on Callie or Octavia," Dion says.

"You lot sound like conspiracy theorists," Finn groans.

"Doesn't make us wrong," I point out.

"I still don't get what she's hoping to achieve," Xavier grumbles. I think it has more to do with his inability to see his ex-wife as anything more than who she's been—a vapid, deranged bitch. Oh wait, nothing has changed.

"So, what is this spell to open the gates going to require?" Essos asks, looking to his former second-in-command. During my death, Sybil was the one who kept him together; they made sure the Underworld ran as smoothly as possible. The only good thing about losing them is that there hasn't been an Underworld to manage. Our jobs are obsolete without souls to shepherd.

"It requires the near death of the monarch. You need to bleed out almost completely for the ritual to work," they tell us solemnly.

I can't help the laugh that bubbles out of me. Heads around the table swivel to me, and the laugh changes from a small giggle to full-out hysteria.

"Love, are you okay?" Essos asks, touching my shoulder, then my face.

"No. Yes. No. Don't you think this is ridiculous? I haven't had a moment of peace." I stumble over my words. "There is no moment of peace for our child. Of *course,* I have to nearly die. Of course, I need to risk my child's life. I don't know why that wouldn't be the case! I don't know why I let myself get attached to this life, or why I thought something was going to work out for me. Getting you, Essos, was the best thing to ever happen to me, but it feels like fate doesn't want me to be happy."

My laughter transitions to tears seamlessly. I'm alone on my chair as I lean forward, my face pressed into my hands while the tears come and come and come. A pair of strong hands encircles my wrists before pulling them from my face. Essos is kneeling before me.

"Fuck the Fates." He glances over his shoulder at Estelle and Sybil. "No offense."

"None taken," they intone at the same time.

"Fuck the fates. They haven't had anything to do with our love story. You were always meant to be for me. There was nothing in the world that could keep you from me, not even death." Essos's voice cracks a little, and I hate, I *hate* that my pain is causing him pain. But this is the way of love, is it not? Sharing not just joy but sadness.

Sybil helps to fill in the blanks. "Posey tried to keep you apart. She used her power as a Fate to read into Essos's insecurities and placed Ellie in front of him. I believe the restaurant you went to for your first date flooded. She's been trying to keep you from each other, and nothing has been effective." Their words only make me feel worse.

"You know I can heal. I will help protect your child," Callie vows, which only sends a fresh wave of tears from my eyes.

"We can always find another way to do this. We can wait to deal with the Underworld, zombies be damned," Essos offers.

I remember the way he reacted after he had to destroy those souls when we were at Zara's. I won't make him do that again.

"No. We cannot find another way. We cannot wait. Our people—the people we are meant to serve—are suffering. The people of earth are suffering. Callie and Xavier will have to monitor the baby. They're healers. I trust Xavier." I trust that he will protect me and the baby, if for no reason other than to not let Cat down.

"Are you sure?" Xavier asks, sounding skeptical.

"Yes. I'm tired of hiding. I'm tired of being the fragile child of Spring. I'm tired of being underestimated. Being pregnant doesn't change who I am; it just means I need to be more cautious."

"Of course, my queen," Essos replies, a touch of pride in his voice.

17

Essos lazily strokes my stomach as we lie in bed. After our unofficial meeting, he ordered everyone out. Xavier, Kai, and Finn took Cat to the water to practice again. Dion, Callie, and Helene stayed on the porch to watch, and the Fates returned to the library with Zara, eager to sort out this ceremony.

"I don't love this," he starts.

I swat his hand and turn on my side. "Then you don't have to touch it."

"You misunderstand. I love *this*." He rubs his hand along the curve of my stomach then up to my breasts to cup my face. "I don't love you risking your life." He's been quiet about the conversation from this morning. He hasn't brought up again how he hates any plan that involves both of us bleeding out. I haven't asked him about finding Callie and the secrets he kept. I know when he's ready to tell me about it, he will.

"We both are," I point out, covering his hand with mine.

"Two lives are not on the line as I bleed." He pauses. "I'd like to ask my mother to be there for the ceremony."

I sit up abruptly. Essos closes the distance between us.

"What for?" I ask. Even before this whole mess, she was never the person he would call in a crisis.

"Because she's a skilled healer. She has the power to keep you and our child alive. She needs to do this to prove to us that we should bring Galen back to life."

I sink back, accepting his argument. I wouldn't mind having the Goddess Supreme on hand to keep me and my family alive. But I don't trust her—I can't—and it would be a lie to say that this idea doesn't cause me any fear. "Did you know? About Lairus?"

"You picked up on that, did you?" Essos dances around my question, brushing at some lint on the bed that I think is visible only to him.

"You're my husband. Of course, I did. I often know what you're thinking before you've had a chance to think it."

He smirks. "I suspected. I mean, it was plausible that Galen just took very, very strongly after our mother, but even Helene had the same eyes and nose as our father. Galen had nothing. I can't remember the last time I saw Lairus, though, so if I ever thought Galen's father might be the Sun God, I couldn't say."

"You think this is why your father summoned Kai from the seas?"

"I would bet money on it. Sometimes, I forget he's gone. I forget that Posey killed him." There is sadness and pain in his voice. There is so much we still have to talk about—Titus's death, what happened with Galen during the Trials, my missing memories, but we ignore these subjects like the elephants in the room that they are.

"I don't feel great about Sybil and Estelle changing their tune about bringing Titus back. They were very clear after saving Cat that they couldn't do it."

"I don't either, but if it keeps Helene motivated and open to working with Octavia, maybe it will be enough."

I frown. "You don't find it cruel that they're willing to play with your sister's desires like that? How long did Posey dangle me in front of you like a carrot, but all you got was a stick?"

"But I *did* get you back," he whispers, brushing a kiss against my lips.

"That makes it worse, Essos. Helene won't get her father back. She'll get hit with a stick, and it's going to bring her fury down on the world we will have just worked hard to fix."

"What would Helene do that is truly so bad?"

I give Essos a gentle smack, my lips twisting into a wry smile. "Have you never heard of the phrase hell hath no fury like a woman scorned? It doesn't have to be a man that does the scorning. This lie will hurt her in ways I don't think anyone is prepared for."

He contemplates my words, what it would mean to hurt Helene so deeply. She's strong and has the support of Kai and the rest of us, but I'm not sure she would ever forgive us for going along with this farce. I know I wouldn't.

"I'll speak with Sybil separately and find out exactly what they're thinking about the possibility of bringing Titus back. But that will happen after our nuptials and after we've properly consummated our marriage." Essos shifts so his face is buried in my neck. I giggle as he kisses me. His teeth scrape against the hickey he left me earlier.

"I think it's a little late to consummate. I am already with child, dear," I point out with a laugh.

"Yes, our beautiful baby. I don't want to be that guy, but I think it's going to be a boy." He kisses down my body and over my shirt before lifting it so he can press his lips to my bare skin.

"Who do you think you are, Henry VIII?" I giggle as he blows little raspberries on my belly. I writhe against him, and heat suffuses every nerve in my body. I want to be writhing under him for an entirely different reason.

"No, I have just the one wife. I wonder if he's one of the souls sent back to earth?" Essos jokes.

"I doubt he's back. His body was too decayed for his soul to return. Most of the reanimated corpses were souls that had a body to return to."

"The King is back in Graceland?"

"Performances are nightly."

Essos rolls off me again, propping himself on his elbow to watch me. "You've been very on top of this." His eyes are too studious. With this one look, he's stripped me bare.

"I'm trying to keep on top of something. This is all my fault."

A growl escapes the back of his throat. "I'd rather you keep on top of me, but we have to talk about that comment. My love, you're really starting to piss me off. How is this your fault?"

"How is this not my fault? You asked *one* thing of me. One thing—that I trust you during the Calling—and I couldn't do that. I didn't do that." I close my eyes against the painful memory of Essos nearly begging me to trust him, knowing he didn't have a leg to stand on but doing it anyway.

"Enough. I love you, and I don't want to hear another word about it. Flagellating yourself over this isn't helpful. You didn't do any of this, and Posey made that abundantly clear. She has been manipulating us all from the beginning. You are *not* responsible, so stop, or I will have to spank you and punish you for going against my order."

"Is that a threat or a promise?" I ask, my voice dropping low.

Essos rolls over me so he's between my legs. I wriggle against him, finding his cock already firm. I reach for him but he grabs my wrists and pins them above my head.

"It is whatever you want it to be," he whispers in my ear before nipping at my earlobe. I arch my back, desperate to feel him against me, feel him inside me.

"Kiss me," I demand.

A wolfish grin slowly spreads. "As you wish."

Then he does, grinding against me in every right spot. I want to pull my hands down to touch him, to feel him, but he holds fast to my wrists, transferring them to one hand so he can touch me properly.

He barely grazes my breast and I moan into his mouth. Essos seizes the opening, his tongue darting inside in a torrid kiss, raw and intense. I want to melt into the mattress and let my body come apart for him. His hips press against mine, and I moan again.

"You are so responsive," he teases, releasing my hands so he can touch me all over. I reach for him but find my hands still bound to the bed. When I arch my back to look at them, Essos takes advantage by capturing my nipple in his mouth. He finds the skin puckered even more so now that my shirt is also damp in that spot. Above me, my hands are bound by shadows. Essos, who hates to use his powers even so much as to make dinner, will use them to hold me under him.

"That seems like cheating," I challenge.

Essos pauses his slow descent down my body to look at me, one brow raised. "Is that a problem?"

There is a hint of seriousness hidden in the dark desire he gets from having me tied to his bed, beholden only to him. If I did have a problem, the bindings would disappear without a moment's hesitation.

My lips tug slowly up at the corners. "Not at all."

"Good."

Essos continues his exploration of my body, touching places on my waist often forgotten in favor of erogenous zones. The featherlight sensations light up my body and tickle me as he pushes my shirt up. He's going slow, so torturously slow, and I want to scream at the need for him to speed up. It's foreplay of the best and worst kind as he exposes my breasts, my nipples already pebbled and aching.

His tongue traces the outline of one dusky pink nipple, spiraling until he reaches the peak. I cry out, arching into him. While I'm focused on this action and sensation, he slips his hand into my bottoms and touches 'my clit. I buck against him, desperate for more.

"You're so responsive, and so fucking wet, my queen."

My eyes nearly cross when he slips a finger inside me, and his soft chuckle is my only indication he saw that.

"I can't control how my body reacts to you," I practically pant as he grinds the heel of his hand against my clit. His fingers don't stop their steady pace, moving instead with more fervor as he sucks at my breast before moving back to my neck. Essos is about to give me a hickey in an entirely new spot, but the thought that I should care about going into my wedding day with not one but two hickeys comes into my mind, and my body clenches around him.

I can't string a coherent line of words together. There are a lot of *fucks* and *gods* and *Essos* as I come with such an intensity, I'm positive that having him inside me might break me.

As my breathing slows, I feel Essos work my pants off my legs. He kisses the inside of one knee, tickling me gently before kissing up my body again. I open my eyes to find him watching me.

"I don't think a man has ever loved a woman quite as much as I love you," he whispers. The bonds release my wrists.

I sit up, my shirt falling back down over my chest as I grip my husband's face. "No man has ever loved a woman with as much devotion or strength. I know that for every square inch of love you have in your heart for me, I have it tenfold more for you." I crush my lips against his, feeling a tear drip from my closed eyes.

Essos pulls back, cupping my face now, his thumbs brushing at errant tears as they fall. "No tears, my love. I promise I will save some worthwhile sweet nothings for our vows."

"Don't," I demand, my voice more ragged than I expected. The tears are flowing freely as I hold onto him with desperation.

Essos tilts his head questioningly. "Don't?"

"Don't save them for tomorrow. We've already given them all so much of us, so much of who we are and what our love story looks like. Save them for me, and just me, tomorrow night. We will tell each other of our love with our words, with our mouths, with our bodies tomorrow night when you properly bed me as your wife again."

"Is this your way of telling me to stop thinking about how it will feel to be inside you tonight?" There is no anger or malice in his words, not even quiet resignation that he won't be getting off.

I push him back and straddle his hips. "That is not even remotely what I am suggesting."

If he can use magic to cheat, then so can I. His clothes vanish, and his hands are bound, not by shadows, but by vines that crept off the wood of our headboard. His arms are spread, and there is a fierce undercurrent of desire in his eyes, along with love. It tugs at my heart to look at this man spread before me, willing me to do my worst and best to him.

I don't have the patience to test and tease him the way he did me. I will have fun with him for a little, though. I grip the base of his cock loosely.

"Is this how you like it?"

Essos narrows his eyes. "I think you know very well that I'm not fragile."

"Tell me what you want me to do to you. Do you want to fuck my tits? Do you want my mouth or my hand, or perhaps a graze of my teeth? Does it make you hot to think of coming inside me or my mouth? Which would you prefer?"

He studies me for a second, his gaze hooded and dark. "First, I want you to take that bead of liquid—"

I touch my finger to the tip of his cock, where a small bead of precum has been waiting. I slide my finger along the head, circling and circling the way he did with my nipple, until I reach that slit and slide my finger along it. He groans, keeping his eyes on me.

"What would you like me to do with this?" I ask, my voice foreign to my ears, low and sultry.

"Fuck, Daphne, I can't think straight. I need you to let me go so I can fuck you so hard you forget this little game."

I grin, taking a different sort of pleasuring in knowing I'm driving him wild. I lick along my finger and suck it into my mouth so my cheeks hollow out before I release it with a pop. I grab his base again and stroke him before lowering my mouth along his length. When I feel him at the back of my throat, I swallow, loving the cry he gives in reaction. He talks about how responsive my body is. I would snark at him, but instead I'm pumping my head steadily before stopping abruptly.

Slowly, I crawl up his body, licking and kissing as I go, letting my breasts graze the head of his cock.

I run my hands up his torso, barely grazing skin, until they reach his hair. I caress the silky locks while I kiss his neck, making sure I bestow a matching hickey. I let my core graze against him, fully aware of what it's doing to him, and his hips twitch up, looking to sink himself deep inside me.

I refuse to torture myself any longer. I grab the base of him and center my body over him. I slide down, my head dipping back in pleasure. I need a second, my body adjusting to his size and the feel of his cock within me. I slide back up over him, holding eye contact before Essos bucks into me, and I ride him in earnest.

I'm too undone by the feel of him to keep the bindings on. He must sense my lack of control over my abilities, because he keeps his hands right where they are. I can see on his face his desire, his need, to touch me, but he won't give in.

My nails dig into his chest as my second orgasm rocks through my body. When my release hits, pleasure breaks free from me, and it makes my head light and my ears ring. Essos roars his own release, his hands finally finding my hips while he thrusts harder and faster up into me until we're both spent.

I collapse forward with Essos still inside me. One of his fingers traces the curve of my spine, slowly, until my breathing steadies and my heart rate is normal.

"We did it again," he bemoans.

"My love, at this point, we've done this lots of times," I tease. He reaches down to give me a gentle spank, and I yelp, slipping off to lie beside him.

"No smartass. *This*." He gestures around us, and I realize what he means. The room is no longer a bedroom; it's a bed within a garden.

Last time I lost control over my abilities like this, we were in our apartment in Solarem, and I was going to have to marry Galen and figure out a way to get my family back. I had covered many of the surfaces in the apartment, but not to this extent.

Now there are trees and bushes in full bloom. Butterflies drift lazily through the room, batting their wings slowly. The only original things around us are the window and the bed, and I wonder if the lush foliage extends throughout the house.

Nothing like having to apologize for the orgasm garden you created. Nothing screams *I made love to my husband* quite like this, and I was already embarrassed about the hickeys.

"I think it's because you're finally letting go and tapping into the deep reserves of your powers." Essos has one hand folded over his chest and the other behind his head as he watches me climb out of bed.

I stride across the room, giving little care to anything as I get to the window.

"Oh!" I exclaim, my snarky reply about him wanting to take credit dying on my lips. Below, the entire backyard is blanketed in greenery. There are lily pads in the pool and palm trees where the umbrellas used to be. I think I even see a frog hopping from pad to pad.

Essos's hand on my hip is the only thing grounding me when he comes up behind me to see what I'm seeing. "Wow."

It seems I've shocked us both beyond words. I look at him over my shoulder as he hugs my body against his.

"At least I'll get the garden chic wedding I always wanted?"

"That's my queen, always finding the positive in a shocking situation." We're silent for a moment more. Then Essos says, "To sleep. I need to bed you properly tomorrow and see just how far this garden will go."

Essos spanks my bottom gently, spurring me back to bed. I swat at him but oblige, secretly excited to see what else I am capable of.

"My love," Essos whispers in my ear, nudging my cheek with his nose. I shake my head, reaching for a pillow that my head is not currently on. My fingers brush the velvet of a spare throw pillow. I intend to cover my face with it and burrow back into the sheets for another few minutes of dirty dreams, but the pillow tries to slip from my grip. Startled, I swat it in the direction of the tug and let go.

"Oof," I hear Essos cry.

I open my eyes to find him hugging the pillow to his chest.

"Is this setting a bad tone for our wedded life?" he asks.

"Depends. Was that not the softest pillow you've been hit with?"

Essos dips his head and plants a row of kisses along my neck to my jawline. "What type of dreams were you having that involved you moaning in the middle of the night?"

My eyes flash to his. He's trying look serious, but his eyes are alight with desire.

"The kind that involves my husband's tongue and lips and fingers and cock."

"All at once? What kind of woman am I marrying?" he growls,

pulling the blankets back so he can ravish me with all of those things. I make the mistake of turning my head to the side so he can better access my neck only to see the time.

I shove him off me and move quickly toward the bathroom. His laughter chases me into the shower.

"What am I supposed to do with this now?" Essos hollers after me.

"You have two hands and a mighty fine imagination!"

I emerge from the shower to find Cat, Zara, Helene, and Callie waiting for me. I tug my towel tighter around my middle.

"Why do I get the feeling I'm not going to like what happens next?"

"Oh stop, this is your third wedding. You know the drill when it comes to getting ready," Helene admonishes with an eyeroll.

"Only one of those other two counts. I never made it down the aisle for the second one." I glance at Callie apologetically. "That wedding did not end so well for the groom."

"And I almost died!" Cat adds helpfully.

"You *did* die," Zara points out.

"I heard." Callie's hands fidget in her lap. "Helene was telling me all about everything I missed. Have I apologized profusely enough for my husband?"

"Have I apologized yet for almost marrying your husband?"

Callie snorts. "Right, because that's what deserves the apology between us all." She pauses a moment before squeezing my shoulder. "I haven't considered him my husband since long before I left him. My boys are the only good thing to come out of my 'marriage.' I certainly didn't consider myself married when I took new lovers."

That earns a laugh from me. When this is all over, I hope she and I can form some sort of friendship.

Cat directs me into the bathroom to primp for my wedding. I never expected the nervousness that bubbles up while they get me ready. It's not nervousness over getting married; Essos and I have been married, and we both consider this a ridiculous technicality.

But there's still something thrilling about walking down the aisle to be joined with the person you love with your entire existence.

The dress that Cat picked for me would have been fine if I weren't nearly five months pregnant. It's tighter than anticipated in the breasts, making me explode out of the sweetheart neckline. There's a gentle dip between them covered by lace floral appliques.

The empire waist with a full tulle skirt makes the bump less noticeable, and the off-the-shoulder sheer sleeves make me feel like I belong in some gothic romance.

The tears in Cat's eyes are of joy this time instead of sorrow. She will not be leading me to Galen to possibly lose my life. Instead, I'm wedding my true love. The man I am meant to be with.

"What do you want to do with your hair?" Helene asks, combing out my wet strands.

"She's going to say she doesn't care," Zara hedges. She's been quiet, still focusing on our chatter, but I can tell she's torn about something. She's got a book in her lap, and I recognize it as the tome that I was reading when Octavia spilled her love story.

"Did you know about Lairus?" I ask Callie, dodging the question of my hair.

"Don't answer her," Helene jumps in. "She owes me an answer first."

I roll my eyes, unable to keep my reaction invisible. Helene smacks the back of my head, glaring at me until I answer her. "Leave it down."

"To hide your hickeys? I count one, two...and three," Helene teases, poking each one as she goes.

I swat her hand, delighted by the audible smacking sound it makes. "You're a brat. If you already had an answer, why bother asking?" I snap.

"Because making you focus on the wedding makes this whole thing more fun," Helene tells me.

"That's not true, because I've been planning this wedding for a week. But it would be nice if you did enjoy this morning." Cat has a touch of hurt in her voice.

I spin around to face these women who are trying to help get me through this week. I will not take them for granted even remotely.

"I'm sorry. I *am* enjoying this morning. I'll do better about showing it. I just..." I look around the room, which still has evidence of the garden I made last night. "I'm afraid that this is where my story is meant to end again."

I haven't even expressed this fear—that fate does hate me—to Essos. Not specifically Sybil and Estelle, who I consider family after all we've been through together, but the larger design of fate. I know Posey does for sure, but the idea that I might not get tomorrow weighs heavily on my mind.

"My gods, goddess, I want to slap you," Helene huffs. She conjures a chair and drops into it. "If you think a single one of us is going to let you die *again*, you're very, very wrong."

"I know. I trust you all. I just don't trust that the wedding will happen. I'm terrified of having the rug pulled out from under me. It's been one fight after the other for months," I explain.

"Forgive me, because I'm new to the gods and the goddesses and the whole dynamic around here, but I do know one thing. I know that Essos will burn this world down before he lets anything happen to you again." Cat's words ring true, and my hormones take hold and make me want to cry.

"Can I see him?" I ask, a little mad at myself for giving up this girl time, but what is a few moments when you have eternity? I could say the same about my desperate need to see Essos, but I need him here—I need him to soothe the frayed edges of my nerves.

Helene twists the shell on the chain around her neck three times. No one answers before the door swings open, revealing Essos. He stops short, not bothering to glance at the others, and gapes at me, his mouth opening before he closes it again without saying anything.

"Can we have the room?" he asks, not bothering to wait for an answer before he is by my side.

"How did you get here so fast?" I ask as my friends clear out, leaving us alone in my dressing room.

"I'm never far from you, love. What's wrong?" He moves a tendril of hair back from my face, twisting it around his finger as he does.

"I just wanted to see you. I just wanted to hold you. I'm terrified that this wedding will go the way of the last one."

He tugs me to his chest, one hand cupping the back of my neck. "Do you plan to stab your groom in the heart this time?"

I lean back, resting my chin on his chest. "To be fair, I didn't start that wedding with the thought that I would stab him. Circumstances just aligned."

"Well, I have no intention of giving you a reason to stab me in the heart." He waits a beat, and when I don't respond, he continues. "Do you want to tell me what this is really about?"

"This is about how afraid I am that we're entering the part of the story when the hero and heroine are torn asunder and have to fight to get each other back. I'm afraid that's just our story now."

"I hate to spoil the ending, but we've already passed that part of the book. We're at the part where the hero and the heroine defeat the bad guy and live happily ever after, and you can't tell me otherwise."

"Bringing back the villain of our story doesn't feel like we're entering the happily ever after part."

Essos draws me toward the bench I sit on when putting on my shoes. He sits first and pulls me onto his lap. "Can I tell you something?"

"Anything," I swear to him, twisting so I can look him in the face.

"I'm trying really hard to be as brave as humanly possible for you, but I'm terrified of everything that's going to happen next." I open my mouth to cut him off, but he silences me with a quick kiss. "I'm terrified, but I'll be damned if I let anything happen. I'm trying to anticipate every move Posey's going to make, and I don't think she expects you to actually go through with letting Galen come back. I think she underestimates your strength, and she will expect you to be too traumatized to do it. I think you're going to prove her so wrong, she's not going to know what to do with herself.

"I want to show you something that I hope will help you with the coming days."

His hands touch my temples, and he closes his eyes, instructing me to do the same. I comply, my eyes drifting shut.

I'm looking down at myself...and that's when I realize what Essos is doing. This memory is his, from shortly after we moved back into this house. It's been a few days since I killed Galen, and I've been restless when sleeping. I can feel Essos's feelings, and the impact the past few days have had on him. I can hear his thoughts, so I quiet my own and just listen.

My thrashing in bed has stilled, and my face looks serene in sleep, the worry lines that started to form between my brows smoothed away. Essos's hand reaches out and his thumb gently rubs the tense spot between my eyebrows the way I've done for him. I let out a contended sigh, my body giving the illusion of sinking deeper into the bed. Flowers bloom along the headboard, an indication of my mood. He's watched them shrivel at night, a physical manifestation grown from my nightmares. Essos has seen wolfsbane grow and for a brief moment, a corpse flower bloom, its scent so strong, he woke immediately. That night it was more difficult to chase the bad thoughts away.

It's comforting to see that my mind can 'find such beautiful things, like the tiny plumeria that dot the bedposts. It's a testament to my strength that I'm able to keep going. When all was bleak and he lost me, it was months before he was able to get out of bed, before Helene had to stop actually spoon-feeding him just to force him to eat. My own mind clings in sorrow to this thought of his and how miserable he was before, and there is nothing and was nothing that I could do to alleviate that pain.

His head dips closer to mine, and he breathes in deeply, the scent of magnolias and clementines fresh and clean and romantically sweet. He banned the flower and the fruit while I was gone; the scent of it was over-

whelming and undid all the progress that Helene and Finn were able to manage.

Now, though, he yearns to smell it. Even just a whiff of it settles Essos in a way that he never expected to feel again. It's a reminder that his wife and his life are back the way they're supposed to be. Mostly, anyway.

He wonders how he got so lucky to be on the receiving end of a smile, even in my sleep. I can feel a small amount of self-hatred that I've repeatedly been in danger, that my life has been lost or at risk, so, selfishly, he wants to enjoy this time and not share me, even if it means earning my ire or that of anyone else.

I snuggle closer to him, one hand falling to my stomach protectively. Essos wonders if I'm dreaming of the baby, or if it was an unconscious move for comfort and he's reading too closely into something that isn't there. What does matter is how our lives are growing and his determination to protect us, regardless of the cost. He failed once. He won't fail again.

My breathing changes, and I start to wake up. I can feel his lips tugging wide, smiling at the knowledge that I belong with him and that I am right where I need to be. He's lucky that he gets these moments, waking before me so he can admire everything that we have together without the outside world invading his thoughts.

My eyes blink furiously, and then I'm looking into the eyes of my husband. Those blue eyes are full of that same love and awe I've seen from him before, but now I understand. There is something magical about being able to see myself through his eyes. I wasn't something that needed to be protected. He sees a strength in me that I've never seen in myself.

"Why did you show me that?" My voice cracks.

"Because I think you're forgetting again how strong you are. You keep having these amazon moments where you conquer the world, and you'll cut down anyone who tries to take what we have. But then your fear digs its claws in and drags you down. I don't blame you for that."

There isn't anything I can say back that will change anything at all, so I wrap my arms around him. His firm body softens around mine as if trying to absorb my burden, all of my stress, like, if he could let himself soften enough, he could allow his body to enfold me entirely.

"I think we should get married. I think there are a lot of feelings here between us and I think we have a solid foundation for exactly that–an amazing marriage," I tell him through choked tears. My words are muffled by his shirt, but he just threads his fingers into my hair and keeps my head close to him, where I can listen to the beat of his heart.

"I think that's a great idea. Are you free this afternoon?"

My heart is beating in time with his, but I pull away to meet his gaze. "Today is looking good."

"Then what do you think, love? Should we go do this?"

My anxiety was so high that I didn't even realize Essos was already in his tuxedo, complete with tails. He offered to get this dressed up for our first wedding, but I'd told him the more casual the better—Octavia had already taken charge and made it into something I didn't want it to be.

My husband takes me in, seeing what is left to do. My hair is still untouched and my makeup isn't done. I twist two clumps of waves back and away from my face so my hair otherwise hangs free. No makeup for today.

Essos gets up. Once he has my shoes in his hand, he tugs his pants at the thighs and drops into a squat before me. He helps slide my heels on, probably the last time I'll be wearing them, if I have anything to say about it. They're almost like glass slippers, formed from a clear shell with diamonds all along it. His fingers deftly snap the closures around my ankles.

He rises and holds his hands out to me, and I take them, knowing that he has always been the best decision I could make. Essos keeps hold of one hand as we walk downstairs to where everyone is waiting for us.

I don't know where Cat planned for the ceremony to be held, but Essos must, because he leads me outside to my gardens. I had wanted our first wedding to be in a garden, among my plants, but I was overridden. The urge to jump Essos for this, for making sure my actual wants and desires were seen to, is strong.

"When did you do this?" I ask him, squeezing his hand.

"Cat asked me yesterday where you would want the ceremony to be held and what you really wanted for the wedding. She said you were rather distracted when she attempted to plan while I was gone."

"So, you told her?"

"So, I told her everything." He plants a sneaky kiss on my cheek as we approach the entrance to the garden. There is a small table where my bouquet is waiting along with a boutonniere for him.

The flowers gathered with a matching lace ribbon are colorful wildflowers. There are yellows and oranges and pinks and blues and whites, and they're heartbreakingly perfect.

"These are the same flowers..." I trail off, unable to stop looking at them.

"The same flowers that followed your every step the first time we made love in the meadow."

Our eyes meet, and I know I'm already crying. Today, this man has given me our love story in little slices. The first time we made love, I was a bundle of nerves because I knew he was much more experienced. We had gone out, a bottle of Dion's new wine in our hands, and I'd insisted we take a nice, long walk to the meadow where I like to test new flowers. My nerves created a trail of wildflowers with every step I took, but Essos never commented. He didn't comment when I laid the blanket out for our picnic, and he didn't say anything when I pulled the strings that bound the front of my dress before letting it slide off my shoulders and then my body.

The touch of his eyes on my skin made me feel like I might burst into flame before he even touched me. It wasn't the first time he and

I had done something sexual, but it was the first time we were taking this monumental step.

As I pulled his shirt off, tentatively, Essos asked if I was sure. He asked again as I worked his pants off, and again when the tree above us exploded with flowers and fruits. He never stopped making sure I was okay. He watched me closely, letting me set the pace and try what I wanted with no judgement. There was no judgement either when the field filled with wildflowers and our walk home was littered with different types with every step I took.

Now, with a smile, Essos places a peony on his lapel before kissing away my tears. “Shall we?” He doesn’t offer me his arm but his hand, because, when we do this, we will be hand in hand.

The maze leading us to the center of the gardens grows with each step. Essos doesn’t take his eyes from me, and I wish I could read his mind, see what it is he sees that has him grinning like a damned fool.

Before we turn what I expect to be our last corner, Essos stops me. “Sybil and Estelle are going to perform the ceremony. I wanted everyone else to enjoy themselves. It’s not often we get to appreciate a wedding without the unnecessary trappings.” Dave and Shadow are sitting there, waiting to lead the way down the aisle. While I wish Spot was here too, I know he’s doing something equally important.

I squeeze his hand. “Are you going to leave me now to go to the altar?”

He shakes his head. “Not unless you want me to.”

“I don’t,” I assure him.

“Then we do this like everything else—together. Whenever you’re ready.”

“I was ready yesterday,” I blurt out with a laugh.

His lips slant over mine for a stolen kiss before we walk around that last corner and face all those we love.

Our group is small, but it doesn’t feel lacking. Everyone we need is right here.

We walk down the aisle hand in hand, my bouquet clutched

close to my heart as Essos and I approach Sybil and Estelle. The dogs walk ahead of us, their heads held high. Dave has little necktie on while Shadow wears a collar of the same wildflowers that make up my bouquet.

Flower petals start to fall from the sky above us. I look up with a laugh, my heart so, so full. I hand my bouquet off to Cat before stopping in front of the Fates.

Sybil starts off, "I don't think that anyone is surprised by the love that these two share. I know that in terms of everyone here, aside from Cat and Zara, I never got to see the deep love that Essos and Daphne shared before their worlds were—ahem—changed." Sybil gives the group a wry smile, and I have to laugh, because the only alternative would be to cry. If I cry on my third wedding day, it's going to be only happy tears.

"I got to see it," Estelle interrupts, "on mornings when Essos would wake early to bring Daphne breakfast, and on nights when they would kick me out of their kitchens to make food themselves. It was and still is obvious to anyone who sees them just how deep their love for each other runs."

Sybil looks around at the group. I turn to take in each person seated around us. They're in a semicircle so that everyone can clearly see. Directly opposite Cat is Xavier, who alternates looking at us and looking at her. Zara sits beside her in a matching lavender dress.

My gaze snags on an unexpected pair—my mortal biological parents, Ron and Linda. It's been odd reconciling the two lives that I've lived, one a life where I grew up a goddess, the other where I grew up a mortal who had a childhood on earth and went to human college and did things like binge drink and study calculus. My mother, with her head of dark brown curls that match mine, is actively crying and clutching my father's hand. My father looks like he's attempting to stay stoic, but his eyes are teary and his nose is red. They're only half of my earthly parents, but their presence here matters to me. Essos follows my gaze, twisting so he sees what it is I'm looking at.

He releases my hand so he can cup my cheek and soothe away my tears. I use my free hand to swipe at the other tears, because I know once the waterworks start, I won't stop.

"At this time, we're going to pause so the bride and groom can say their vows to each other," Sybil tells the crowd, turning to Essos.

"No," he says, his tone not short.

"No?" Sybil asks, confused.

"No, my wife and I will express our vows to only each other, tonight," Essos confirms, giving me a full smile.

"In some cultures, they just call that getting laid," Finn says with a little laugh.

"Phineas!" Helene scolds, simultaneously reaching over and smacking Finn on the back of the head while stepping on her husband's foot as he guffaws.

"Well, if you have no intention of saying your vows now, then I suppose all that's left is the rings." Estelle sounds disappointed as she holds out her hands to bless the rings.

"First the blood bond," I blurt out, surprising Essos. He said he wanted to forgo most of the traditions, but this isn't one I want to skip.

"Of course," Essos agrees. He conjures a small knife and slices the palm of his hand without hesitation before handing the blade to me. "With this blade, I slice my skin, so that you may have a part of me with you always. It will be your reminder that my love for you will last an eternity, and that as long as there is blood pumping through my veins, I will be yours."

As he speaks, I cut my own skin with only a brief hesitation. Sybil cups their hands under ours, catching our blood as it drips.

"With this blood, I bind myself to you," I say. "Everything I have in me, so too shall you. With each beat of my heart, know that it beats for you."

We thread our fingers and press our cuts together so that our blood mingles. As it does, our cuts slowly seal. For those seconds, I feel full to the brim, not just with love for Essos but for everyone in attendance here.

Beside us, Sybil and Estelle press their hands together, mirroring our actions, until there is a flash from where their hands are joined. They press their heads together and speak in the old language. I don't recognize the rough words any better than I would have recognized Latin in my old life.

Essos reaches into his pocket and pulls out something else. With shaky hands, he slides two rings onto my finger, first a simple band braided with small gemstones all the way around, then a band showcasing a sizable oval opal flanked by two small amethyst stones and diamonds embedded the rest of the way around.

When I really look at them, my heart nearly stops beating. They're the same rings we were married with long ago. I want to lift my hand and stare at them, but Essos tugs it close to him and slides on a third band. This one is different, a ray of half a dozen marquis diamonds designed so that when it settles against the opal, it looks like a crown.

I'm so entranced by how the rings fit together that I almost forget we're in the middle of something. I hear a sharp intake of breath from someone in the crowd, but Essos silences them by lifting up one hand. He lets me ride the wave of emotions coursing through me from seeing something so familiar.

I wonder if they needed to be cleaned of my blood.

I close my free hand tight, squeezing my eyes as I make a fist, letting my nails dig into my skin. When I open my hand, a small seed rests in my palm. I look away from it and focus my thoughts and energy on my love for Essos. From the small seed, a vine grows and winds its way around Essos's finger, twisting and twisting until the entire digit is encased. Slowly, the coils press together until a thick wood band circles the base of his finger. I blow on it, and a mild gloss covers the band.

Knowing what's coming next, I join our hands again, a new vine wrapping around them both.

Sybil starts to close off the ceremony. "With the rings exchanged, you are now bound to each other, your lives together entwined. Your immortal lives are forever linked by this rope, or, because Daphne is a showoff, this vine. While this binding is temporary, at the end of this ceremony there will be a permanent link, and nothing can come between you. Your blood bond and blood-blessed rings are a further sign of your commitment to each other. By the powers of the land and the Supreme power of us all, we declare your union blessed by the Fates. You may now—"

"I don't recall getting my invitation," Octavia says, walking down the aisle toward us. She's in a dramatic form-fitting white gown with a stiff white rose constructed over one shoulder, the other one bare.

"You are a *literal* Disney villain, mother," Helene hisses, getting up to block access to Essos and me. Her twin and husband flank her, Xavier slightly behind her so he's closer to defending Cat. Essos takes one small step so he too is between me and his mother. Callie shrinks back like she wishes my hedges would swallow her right up.

"My child is getting married. I was overlooked for the other wedding. It doesn't seem fair that I have to miss the event twice." Octavia winks at me. "Come now, you can all relax. This is the best part."

"You mean where you curse me to prick my finger?" I snap. I feel Essos's hand wrap around my wrist, ready to hold me back.

"Oh no, darling. You are going to need to bleed a whole lot more than just a prick on the finger. No, have your kiss, and just remember who's going to be keeping you alive tomorrow." Octavia conjures a chair and settles herself in.

My annoyance and hormones are out of control. The hedge grows out, boxing her in the corner with two fresh bushes. With that extra cover, Essos turns to me, dipping me backward into a dramatic kiss. My leg extends out straight so I can keep some sort of balance, but I know that he won't drop me.

This kiss is different, and it feels it. My body feels tight and loose all at once, and it's because something finally goes right.

With our lips pressed together, I *finally* remember.

I remember nights with my old friends at Solarem University. I remember holding Helene's children when they were babies, and how I felt during my coronation. There are nights of tears and days of laughter. I remember family dinners and adopting Dave, Shadow, and Spot. I remember *everything*. This must be what was needed to unlock me fully—Essos and I being wed again.

My hands tangle in his hair, and I give the kiss my all. By the time his mother gets free, Essos and I are standing again, a little flushed but both grinning like idiots. I can't wait to tell Essos about my memories, but it can wait till later. Octavia is so angry I wouldn't be surprised if steam left her ears, but there are notes of pride and disappointment on her face too. She might want to have a better relationship with her children, but she is only poisoning the well further by acting like this.

Essos leads the way out of the garden, still holding my hand like we're teenagers. Whenever I catch a glimpse of my left hand, I smile, knowing that I've truly started to get my life back. We gather as a group on the beach, one long table set up for us all to sit around and enjoy a meal.

Cat and Zara embrace me together, prompting Essos to finally drop my hand. He winks at me before facing his brother and shaking his hand firmly. I have to remember to tear my eyes away from him, knowing that he's keeping an eye on his mother.

"I always said you'd be the first of us to get married," Cat teases, pretending to wipe away a tear.

"That is *so* false." I nudge her with my shoulder and go still when my parents approach. Nervous energy clenches my heart, and I smooth my hand over my stomach to soothe myself. As amazing as it was meeting them a few months ago, I don't really know them. I still hug them, though, laughing when my father wraps both my mother and I in a bear hug.

"I'm so happy for you, baby," my mom tells me while holding my face in her hands. I open my mouth to say something, anything, about how different things are, but my father shakes his head.

"Essos told us. After some fancy party, he came to see us and said he needed us to come with him for safety because he was no longer in power. He filled us in on everything he wasn't able to tell us when we met you the first time just in case one of us slipped and told you something we shouldn't."

I gaze at Essos, thankful to him for thinking of things I couldn't when I was too pre-occupied. In my defense, there was *a lot* going on. But that's what makes a partnership so important—he anticipates things I need before even I do.

My mom interrupts my dad. "It's me. I would have slipped. I mean, I gave birth to a literal goddess—I thought you were an angel when I had you, and it was the smoothest pregnancy I think ever known to man. I couldn't get enough of fruits and veggies, and I wanted to be outside in nature the whole time. It was unreal, but Essos explained it all. And I *definitely* would have let it slip, so that was smart of him."

"You don't think it's weird that I'm a born-again goddess?" I ask. I'm thousands of years old, I have wisdom beyond words, but standing in front of the people who were supposed to raise me, I am a mortal child again left alone in the world, sacrificed to the foster care system by circumstance.

"I won't say that having you turn out to be a goddess was at the top of my hopes and dreams list, but Queen Daphne has a nice ring to it. And my baby is having a baby!" My mother gestures at my stomach, beaming and crying at the same time.

Essos chooses that moment to come up beside me and wrap an arm around my waist. "I'm glad I could finally get you three in a room together again."

There's something moving about Essos greeting my parents with respect, like he's not an immortal being who watches over the lives of the dead, like he's not a king. He's treating them like a man should treat his in-laws, regardless of rank.

"I appreciate all you've done for us and Daphne," my father begins, holding out his hand to Essos, who takes it with a loud clap, "but I can't say I'm exactly thrilled that my little girl was pregnant before you walked her down the aisle. What does that say about your level of respect for her? What sort of precedent is this going to teach our grandchild?"

I swear to the Fates, my cheeks burn so crimson I can see the color behind my eyes. Finn, Kai, and Xavier are actually laughing behind their hands like gossiping schoolgirls. I glare at them before turning back to my parents.

"Dad!" I scold, exactly when my mother hits his arm gently. "We *are* married, we *were* married, and we thought we were *still* married. Not that it matters, and I shouldn't have to correct your antiquated thoughts about virginal marriage beds and pure daughters. This was a technicality."

"I can promise you, Ron, that I have nothing but the highest regard for your daughter. I've loved Daphne from the moment I saw her and will support her in all things, even if I don't strictly agree with her. Her life is her own, and I think it goes without saying that I would lay down my life for not just her, but our child, even if it means making a deal with the devil." Essos may be saying these words to my father, but his eyes are glued to mine, and his words are meant for me. I have to *not* look at Octavia when he says it.

"Can we go back to the baby? How excited you both must be. Are you finding out what it is? Have you picked a name?" I love my mother's infectious excitement, but I also want to hide from it, want to curl my body around my stomach, because now is the only time in my baby's life that I can provide absolute protection.

With Octavia there listening to every word, watching our interaction, I can't show my fear.

Octavia, naturally, has to chime in with her own two cents. "It's bad luck among the gods to choose a child's name before their birth. We believe that the Fates bestow their names when they're born. With Essos, our first, we let the Fates name him, but after that my late husband tried to name our children before their births. He wanted to name Helene 'Crescent,' and like most vain men, he wanted Xavier to be named after him."

"And what does Essos's name mean?" my father asks.

Dion has made his rounds with glasses of champagne for everyone, and when I take my glass, I see a subtle shift in the coloring. I relax into Essos once the ginger fizz touches my tongue.

"Glorious purpose," Essos supplies, and sips his champagne.

"Such expectations," my mom says, clearly uncomfortable with the direction of this conversation.

"Thankfully, it's easy to fulfil them when you become a king, isn't that right, brother?" Xavier wraps an arm around Essos's neck and attempts to dig his knuckles into his skull, but my husband ducks away with the practiced grace that only a brother can have.

"Shall we eat?" I ask, turning to lead everyone to the table. "I was so rushed this morning I haven't had anything."

"Oh, let's fix that right away!" My mother turns to see who she can find to supply us with food.

"Mom, we're all gods here. Just sit down and the food will appear."

She laughs nervously and looks at Cat as if trying to find someone else who is mortal to strike up a conversation with. Her gaze passes over Zara, the only actual remaining mortal. That's unsurprising—there always has been something otherworldly about Zara's beauty.

"So, you're one of the girls from that messy Calling business?" she asks Cat.

Down the table, Finn actually chokes on his drink. I glare at him, and he holds up his hands in defense. I wait to see how Cat wants to address this query.

She looks to me, checking to see if it's all right to answer. I give her a small nod as Essos steps behind my chair and pulls it out for me to slide into.

"It's a long story, but I'm also a goddess. I'm just much newer at it than everyone else. My powers are less predictable." Cat's voice wavers as she answers the question.

"That's not true. I'm sure you could conjure me a nice meal—I'm thinking chicken cacciatore with a side of polenta," Finn calls to her.

Cat's cheeks pinken a little, and there's a blink-and-you-miss-it moment where Xavier squeezes her knee under the table.

She gives a small nod of acknowledgement that she's going to attempt it. Her green eyes shut. It's important at the beginning of using your power to visualize what you're trying to do. A hush falls over the crowd, until a loud cluck escapes from the chicken on the plate in front of Finn.

Cat turns even redder, but Xavier swoops in. "I believe that's Catalina for, 'Do it yourself, asshole.'"

Kai laughs, reaching for the chicken. The animal gives an undignified squawk as he sets it on the ground. Dave and Shadow are curious about the new animal. Dave takes the lead, sniffing closest to it until the chicken pecks his nose. My fearless protector whines and drops onto his stomach, his tail tucked between his legs. His bravado approaching the beast is gone and now he won't get any closer to the chicken.

"I'm the only mortal," Zara says, diverting attention from Cat, who looks like she wants to cry.

Octavia makes an annoyed noise.

"Mother," Essos warns, his voice low.

"Well then," my mother says with a nod. My parents have given up trying to hold their own among the gods, who are now bickering over the chicken.

I lean into Essos's side and kiss him on the cheek. "Thank you. I'm embarrassed that inviting them didn't even cross my mind with everything going on."

"It's what I'm here for—to make sure your every need, anticipated or otherwise, is well attended." His kiss is soft and sweet, and his words make my body melt into his. I want to feel his hands on my bare skin. This dress, as beautiful as it is, is stifling my ability to feel my husband on me. Essos must read the desire on my face, because a knowing smile spreads on his lips.

"I wish my other parents could have been here." It's funny how quickly my thoughts and feelings about them have changed in the face of centuries of experience. I was so distant with Phil and Melinda when I lived under their roof, but now I miss them.

"Bringing live mortals to the Underworld didn't feel like the right call. Your birth parents are only two souls, so it's easy for me to tether them to me and protect them the way I would protect the girls during the Calling. I wanted you to have at least one set of the parents who loved you here."

I kiss him again, wishing that my touch could ease some of the burden he carries. The kiss moves from sweet and reassuring to desperate and hungry, until I have to break away just to get a breath in.

"Eat first, play later." He nips at my earlobe, and I turn to my plate. My taco craving lasted all of three days, and now I'm back to my early pregnancy craving for Essos's carbonara. Even before I knew I was pregnant, I wanted it all the time.

I grab my fork, ready to dig in, when the meal in front of me changes from the carby goodness of pasta and cream and pancetta and peas into a spinach salad.

I love a good salad. There are times when I still dream about an amazing cobb salad I once had in Disney World, which wasn't so much of a good-for-you salad as it was delicious. I also love a solid beet and goat cheese salad that hits that savory spot. But I do *not* want a salad right now, and I do not want the one in front of me, which is the kind of halfhearted salad that has no soul. There are three sad-looking cucumbers on top, and a single cherry tomato on a bed of spinach. If I were a betting woman—and I am—I would say that there is just the barest drizzle of dressing.

"What in the fresh Underworld is this?" I'm trying to keep my cool, because beside me, my husband has already started to dig into his pasta carbonara. There is even fresh garlic bread in front of us, but when I reach for it, my half turns into a stalk of celery. Essos glances up to see what the problem is, his noodles lifted halfway to his mouth. My carbonara is always served over long noodles, like a spaghetti or an angel hair, but Essos loves to eat his with a penne or a rigatoni so the sauce can clump inside the noodles.

Essos's head snaps toward his mother, who is daintily cutting up her veal saltimbocca, looking smug. As she lifts the fork to her mouth, my anger takes over, and it turns into a raw artichoke. All conversation around the table stops again.

"Did you do this?" I ask, hardly able to keep the fury from my voice.

"You need to eat better for the baby. All that fat product isn't good for your arteries or the child. Until you've settled back into your immortality, I worry that your mortal weaknesses will harm my grandchild."

Octavia meets my eye, daring me to set her straight.

"Mother," Essos snarls, getting to his feet. "There is a very set, very finite amount of patience I have for you, and for you being in my home. I have acquiesced to your ridiculous demands, including but not limited to resurrecting your other son who *murdered* my *wife*." Essos pauses his diatribe to look at me. "You're right, it is like shouting into the void when you say that." Essos releases a calming breath before he turns to face his mother again. "Understand this—decisions regarding my wife and my child are no concern of yours. Every time you think you have something to say regarding them, I want you to envision how it felt for me to find her dying."

Octavia flinches and I wonder if he projected that very image to her. Across from me, my mother looks stricken. There is no amount of information beforehand that can prepare a mortal for what it means to walk among gods. My father is rubbing circles on her back, a feeble attempt to keep her inevitable tears in check. We all sit in silence, waiting for Octavia's response. Essos look at my pitiful plate and replaces it with an even bigger helping of the pasta.

Octavia looks at my plate again, one eyebrow arched. "I see," she murmurs not meeting her son's eyes. "If my presence is not appreciated, perhaps I shall go inside and see if there is someone who will care about my opinion." She places her fork and knife at the sides of her place, the huge artichoke still attached to the fork's prongs.

"Mommy," Helene whines. "Don't be like this. We are trying to celebrate Essos and Daphne. You're being a drama queen."

Essos drops back into his seat, his hand going to my back, mirroring my father in providing comforting strokes to my bare skin.

"Stay or go, Mother, whatever you want, but I'm not interested in playing games. Today is about Daphne, and about the Underworld—whatever is left of it—having its queen back."

"She hasn't been coronated," Octavia points out, and I have to laugh.

"Octavia, what are you really trying to achieve by being here? Do you want to reconcile with your children, or is it just about Galen? Because if you only care about Galen, then leave. I'm serious. You've put your other children through enough grief with your blatant favoritism, and I'm not willing to stand for it in my house. You and Essos have some sort of deal for you to help tomorrow to keep me and my child alive, and I respect that, but your narcissism and emotional manipulation will not be tolerated any longer." Essos squeezes my shoulder gently, silently supporting me. When Octavia doesn't respond, I pick up my fork and twirl it in my pasta, then take an unnecessarily large and messy bite that has Essos fighting a smile. By the time I'm done chewing and have wiped my mouth with my napkin, she still hasn't said anything. "If there's nothing else, Octavia, I would like to enjoy this meal."

"Nothing else," she responds, her voice small, and some stupid maternal part of me realizes that her feelings are hurt. An urge to comfort her rises in me, but I tamp it down. She is the enemy, and I won't comfort the enemy, even if I can feel tears prickling at the back of my eyes when I notice the ones slipping down her cheeks.

I force myself to look away from her and down at my food. I've been dying to eat a bowlful of this dish, and yes, because it is so high in fat and carbs, I try to limit how much of it I eat, because I am growing a tiny god or goddess. I might be an immortal, but eating spaghetti carbonara four times a day will still make me feel awful, and the baby probably not great. But it's my fucking wedding.

A few looks are exchanged around the table, and Finn asks my parents rather loudly how they feel about being dead and the current state of the Underworld. I would like to hear their explanation about how Essos pulled their souls from the Underworld and stored them in a penthouse in New York City while Galen went through the Trials, but I'm too busy looking at my hands, because now the pasta is making me sad, and in my attempt to bury my tears, I've started to cry.

"Oh, what is it, love?" Essos asks, angling himself so that his mother is blocked from seeing me. He's catching my tears again, and I'm cursing all these blasted hormones that are flooding my system to the point that I am crying over fucking pasta.

It feels childish, but my lower lip quivers from my suppressing my tears. "I just wanted to enjoy my pasta, and now she's crying, and I don't want her to cry, because it's awful how unloved she is by her own children, but it's her own doing. And Essos, what if I'm just like her? A terrible mother? What do I know about parenting? I was born from a flower. Growing up as a goddess, I wasn't raised by anyone. What business do I have raising a child?"

"My love, having that concern, being worried about how good of a mother you are going to be, puts you leaps and bounds ahead of my mother. You can't listen to her. You're also going to have something that my mother never had—a husband who will be involved. There are moments that are going to be ugly, and we're going to fight, and we're going to doubt ourselves at every turn, but we have waited many, *many* years for. Your fears are normal, and we will survive becoming parents. I'm less certain of surviving my mother."

I laugh through my tears, and he draws me against him, still protecting me from the curious faces of our friends and family. I let myself cry for a moment longer, just to try to work out the emotions.

"It's okay. Take all the time you need," he murmurs, still rubbing my back. There is an odd, muffled sound to his voice, and when I look up, the world around us looks distorted, as if we're looking through an old pane of glass that's warped.

"What did you do?" I ask. No one is trying to look at us, their conversations dampened by whatever is happening to us now.

"I used some of my abilities for good, to shield my wife so she can have a moment to break down in peace without worrying about her mother-in-law or her mortal birth mother crying about it. I'll do anything in my power to protect you, even if it's just from your own hormones." He kisses the tip of my nose, then below each eye, catching more errant tears.

A wave of exhaustion threatens to topple me. There has been so much to do, so much stress and so many emotional waves that I could sleep till tomorrow. "Do we have to stay?"

The thought of tomorrow makes me even more exhausted, and I may have been doing a lot of it lately, but I just want to lie in bed with Essos. Not even for sex, just for his nearness. After spending centuries apart, even having him away for just one week felt like another century of absence.

"I do have one last surprise, so if you can hold out, then I'll have some cake brought up to our room. Estelle made it special for you."

I give him a small nod and sit up. The sounds come back to us all at once. My mom grins from across the table, and I know I need to have a conversation with Essos about what he's going to do with them and how to keep them far away from Octavia.

"Xavier," Essos prompts with a nod. Xavier gets to his feet, and Essos pulls me to mine and leads us to his brother, where everyone has a clear view of the three of us.

"Please kneel before me," Xavier commands, using a deeper tone than usual.

My eyebrows rise. "I don't know what you think is going to happen, but I am not about to give you a blow job in front of everyone we know on my wedding day."

Essos chokes on a laugh, covering his mouth with his hands.

"It sounds like that's not entirely out of the question, though, just not today," Xavier points out with a smirk. He's waiting for my volley back when thorns burst out of his skin. He yelps, and I quickly retract them.

"I'm sorry," I apologize, rushing forward to grab his arms. He's wearing a suit, but I can see the rips along the sleeves and blood dotted there too. I swallow hard. I was annoyed, not mad enough at him to hurt him.

"It's okay," he says, but when I don't stop fussing, he grabs my hands, stopping me. "I've got thicker skin than that. I'm fine."

"Evidently not, if I just made you break out in thorns." I'm brought to the brink of tears again.

"Just, be a good girl and get on your knees," Xavier orders again, with a halfhearted smile.

"Still doesn't sound any better," I mutter, but comply with Essos's help.

"If it's any consolation, I sanctioned the whole thing," Essos whispers, stepping away once I am kneeling tall in front of Xavier and looking up at his face to be sure I do not look directly at his crotch.

"It's not, although it's nice to know who to blame when these photos go viral."

"Would you quit being a wiseass? I swear, this is the last nice thing I do for you," Xavier bemoans.

"If you think having a girl suck your dick is a nice thing for *them*, then you really need to have your priorities checked." Sometimes I can't help myself.

"Daphne!" Essos and Xavier scold at the same time.

I hold my hands up in surrender, waiting for Xavier to go on.

"It has been too long since the Underworld has had a queen to sit beside its king. There are many things that a king can do alone, but all realms are better ruled when the power is shared, the burden divided, and the decisions made together. This is a much shorter version of the speech usually given, but I'm afraid my dear sister-in-law might burst into tears or giggles if I take much longer." This earns an undignified snort from me. "By the power vested in me by the Fates, and as King of all Gods, I am pleased to crown you Queen of the Underworld...again."

I feel the weight of a crown settle on me, and I have to lower my head so it doesn't tumble off. Both Essos and Xavier help me rise to my feet.

I don't much care what the crown looks like or what everyone thinks of this shotgun wedding, but as the world shifts back into its rightful place, I know this is where I am meant to be.

Finn was right about the night of the wedding. The vows Essos and I exchange are less about the words and more about the touch of the other. Essos's mouth explores every part of me, my new curves around my hips and waist and the lower swell of my stomach. In return, I track his hard-earned muscles with my tongue.

All of that, of course, came after a nap that I desperately needed, and it was followed by another nap.

It's the middle of the night when I wake, surprised to be alone in bed. I reach out to feel if Essos is just out of reach, but I know he's gone before I find his side of the bed cold.

"Essos?" I croak, sitting up. I can see him silhouetted against the large bay windows. His back is to me, and I can barely make out the scratches I left there earlier. Essos has no shirt on and is wearing sweatpants that hang dangerously low on him. He twists to face me, but he's shrouded in shadows. I haven't decided yet if they are shadows of his own making or just from the night.

"I'm here, love." His voice sounds as hoarse as mine. Bioluminescent algae blooms around the window frame. It's not the most ideal lighting, but it's the best I can do without lighting the candles or the fireplace. I want to maintain the illusion that I can lure him back to bed and sleep. His footsteps are quiet as he crosses back to the bed and slides between the sheets again. I yelp at the cold touch of his skin but relax into him all the same.

"Penny for your thoughts?" The question is out of my mouth before I think better of it. Obviously, tomorrow is on his mind. Tomorrow we will have to descend into the dark caverns of the Underworld where Essos and I will spill our blood. It's the very subject we've both been ignoring.

Essos splays his hand on my abdomen. "I'm thinking that I don't think I could bear to lose you again." I already knew this was what he feared, but a shudder still wracks my body.

"I'm immortal; you won't lose me." I twist in his grip so I'm facing him.

"Our child isn't, and I'm afraid of what comes if we were to lose this one as well."

I grip his face in my hands. "I like to think I'm a stronger woman, stronger goddess, than I was before."

He's not wrong in his concerns. If it were my fault that something happened, I might lose myself. Not immediately, though I couldn't promise him that either, but when this was over, when Posey was defeated, I would blame myself, and in turn Essos would blame himself, and we would be stuck in a vicious cycle.

"I know that, love. I just don't trust my mother."

"If she fails us, then we don't bring Galen back. We don't need him—we never did. Maybe the answer to stopping Posey is in opening the Underworld." I say this like it's not a conversation we've talked ourselves around and around and around.

"It's not." His words are nearly inaudible. I wait, silent, knowing that he has more information than he is divulging. "The souls that Posey releases are newer ones, yes, but if what Octavia said is true and she's consuming those older souls, I don't know that we can get them back. Never mind the issues with the Underworld. I don't know if we can get the trust of the citizens of Solarem back."

"They're terrified of her right now. I would think we're a shoo-in for being better than her."

"You're not wrong, but she's also sown so much distrust toward the royal family that she's presenting herself as taking a hard line right now, and once we're all eliminated, she'll relax things. Killing Cassius in front of everyone served two purposes. She made everyone afraid, and at the same time proved that she can kill us too. Coming clean to the other gods that you were also killed solidified her claims."

"How has she gotten this far?"

"Fate." A wry smile splits his lips.

"That's not funny."

"I'm not kidding. She's a Fate. Her powers may not be complete without her sisters, but she's formidable. Even if what Rafferty said is true—that she's tapped into her siblings' powers too—that's all the more reason we need to view her for what she is. A veritable threat." Essos waits a beat, watching my face. We're illuminated by the bluish glow from the algae. "Xavier was able to get the information from the drop Cassius made. He wanted to wait to make sure it was actionable intel before making a move. Octavia confirmed where Posey is keeping the dagger and scepter."

I snort. "Posey also knows that Octavia is working with us. There's no way she's kept it in the same place. Cassius dropped that information to Xavier weeks ago."

"We have to try to get them," Essos pushes, his fingertips digging into my hips, pulling me closer. "If she's consuming souls, I have to think there are still some to save. It's just like with baby gods—the power has to be absorbed slowly. She all but admitted that to you when she said if *you* killed her, the resulting influx of power would kill our baby. What if it's like that for her? Souls could be trapped in that dagger, human souls that don't deserve this. We have to help them. They could be fading because they're not where they're supposed to be. None of this has happened before."

I push away from him and climb out of bed, agitated, then grab the robe from the post on the footboard.

"How, Essos? How are you going to do this? When? Before or after we're both bled nearly dry trying to reopen the Afterlife? What about before or after we bring your murderous brother back from the dead? You have so many inopportune times to pick." I huff out a breath. "I don't want you to do this."

I tie the robe around myself as I pace to the window. I hear Essos murmur something, but I don't catch it.

I spin on my heel to face him. "What was that?" I demand.

He gets out of bed, and I swat at him when he reaches for me. Finally, I let him make contact. He grips my upper arms gently and stoops so he can meet my eye.

"I said this is why I shouldn't have told you. You have enough stress to handle without my making it worse. Finn and I have a plan, and we'll take care of it."

"When?"

"We don't have a when yet. We were going to decide after tomorrow. Regardless, you're going to need time to rest, and I want to be here while you do."

I have to rein in my tide of emotions. I pull out of his grip, and he offers no resistance. I slip into a chair beside the fireplace, a chair meant for only one, and I let my anger ignite the wood behind the grate. It roars to life, and Waffles, who was lying on his bed in front of the grate, jumps up with a hiss. He eyes the fire, backing away slowly until he scurries to the bed and jumps on it.

Essos sits on the ottoman at my feet, which I curl under me and away from him.

"Talk to me," he pleads.

I look from the flames to him. I can see the bags under his eyes, the burden that he has been carrying longer than he wants to admit. So much has been resting on his shoulders, and he refuses to share that burden with me. I'm not sure which part makes me madder—this stupid plot, or that he wasn't going to tell me about it.

"I don't want you to go. We will get them, but we need to be smart about it. Going to get the dagger and scepter now is most certainly a trap. You made a vow to me for eternity. You're not going back on that the day after you made it."

"I'm not going back on it, but if we have a chance to get the scepter and dagger back, we need to take it. It could tip the balance in our favor."

I bite on my nail, staring into the fire. "I don't trust Octavia not to be on Posey's side." Maybe it's time to have one of those difficult conversations we never seem to have. "Remember when Xavier showed up at our apartment in Solarem to tell me I was being sanctioned again?" I glance at Essos, who nods. He seems to understand that this is a serious conversation, and he pulls the ottoman closer in front of me.

"Yes," he confirms, and the wariness in his voice tells me he remembers exactly *why* I was sanctioned.

"After Kai's Trial, that night..." Gods. How am I supposed to tell Essos what *almost* happened? Because the thing that has gotten me through every single day has been the reminder that it was an almost. It was a close almost, but it was still an almost, and when I have so much to carry on my shoulders already, is it so bad that not thinking about it is how I choose to survive? "Galen came to my room. He thought he deserved something from me he didn't." I still can't get the words out. I glance at Essos, who has gone so still. "He was unsuccessful in trying to force himself on me. I defended myself using a letter opener that Bria gave me."

The Goddess of the Hunt is a firm believer of being armed to the teeth. When she first gave me the letter opener, I laughed at just how pointy it was, but I'm grateful every day that it was sharpened like a true weapon.

"I remember her giving it to you. It was when we opened the

Underworld offices. She said she knew you were never going to open mail, but it was still nice to have a weapon on hand."

"I remember too," I tell him. "I got my memories back, *all* of them, during the wedding." This causes him to sit up straight in surprise. I slide my hand into his, needing his physical comfort. "We can discuss that later. But that night, I stabbed Galen, and he was bleeding everywhere, and I was in a panic. I called for Ellie, Zara, and Miranda to help me clean up, because I didn't have my powers at the time. Miranda, who turned out to be your mother, provided the bloody sheets to the Council to sanction me. I know they would have done it anyway—Posey would have found a way to push her agenda—but your mother could have helped me, and she chose Galen and his deplorable actions *again*. She's going to disappoint us all when she does it after we bring him back. Octavia refused to even acknowledge Callie; did you see that?"

For a minute, Essos doesn't answer me, but he steps forward and scoops me into his arms, holding me tight. It's what I need, the physical reminder that the man I love is here and he won't let me wind up in a position like that again. But he can't be everywhere all at once.

"I can't be sorry enough that I wasn't here to protect you from what went down during the Trials. Galen and Octavia are both monsters. I do not support either of them, but right now our interests align. I will do everything in my power for you."

"Then why keep this plan from me?" I feel better getting that off my chest, and it's helped me realize what my problem is now. It's Essos's insistence on keeping things from me.

"There are enemies pressing down on us while the world below us crumbles. We can't be king and queen if there is nothing to rule over. We have a new goddess learning her errant powers, who is more liability than aid, and we have a looming vacancy among the Fates, one of whom used to cook our food. I am doing everything in my power to keep you safe, and if that means keeping things from you so you will sleep at night, just for right now, then I'll fucking do it. You saw that memory I showed you this morning. You think that was just a one-time thing? It absolutely isn't. You still do it. You want to know why I was out of bed? Because no amount of my touch would soothe your corpse flowers. I love you, Daphne, with every part of my soul, and there is nothing that I wouldn't do for you."

"Telling me the truth is one thing," I point out.

Essos's face goes blank before he rises. It startles me, and I struggle in his grip. If we're going to fight about this, I would rather be on my own two feet.

"Stop struggling, or I *will* drop you," he warns. I comply, shoving his shoulder for good measure, and he smirks down at me. "Close your eyes," Essos whispers.

I listen to him because, even if we're fighting, I trust him entirely. I feel the world drop out from under us for a flash of a moment.

The seawater is the first thing I notice before I feel the biting wind blowing off the ocean. I open my eyes, and Essos sets me on my feet. He's standing in the surf, and now I am too, the waves gently licking up my legs.

"Why are we out here?" I press, crossing my arms. The cold air puckers my nipples, and I wish I were back inside by the warm fire.

"Because being in that house is driving us both mad. I got away for a week, and before that, I was out of it for several months, but you've been a hostage of that place for almost a year. I thought some fresh air might cool your temper."

I glare. "My temper, Essos, is not the problem."

"No, your problem is that while we've been able to blow off steam in any number of creative ways, you still haven't had fun in how long?"

Essos invades my space, and I don't stop him as he pulls open my robe, exposing me to the elements. His hands slide over my shoulders, pushing the robe off. He casts it into the air, letting a draft of wind carry it safely to the shore. He shirks off his own bottoms, which I'm delighted to discover were the only thing he was wearing. Similarly, Essos balls them and tosses them toward the beach, where they land beside my robe.

"What exactly is this naked fun that you plan on us having that is different from all the other times we've done the horizontal tango?"

"For starters, it's going to be the vertical tango. And secondly, we're just going to go for a swim." Essos hoists me into his arms, knowing that I will not get into the frigid water unless I'm being carried. My legs lock around his hips, but I'm still skeptical and send a quick prayer to Kai to let the water be warm. I thank the Fates for my brother-in-law, because a bubble of warm water follows us as Essos wades farther into the water while I cling to him.

I let go of his neck, my body falling back. His hands anchor me to him, and I relax, knowing he has me. My temper has already cooled in the breezy night air. My astute husband is right. I can't remember the last time I genuinely had *fun*. And yes, I'm still mad at him for withholding his stupid plan, but I need this too.

"I'm going to keep you both safe," Essos swears. He moves one hand to the small of my back, firmly holding me, while the other skates up my body, over the swell of my stomach to my breast. His thumb rubs over my nipple, which is firm and alert thanks to the water and cool wind that kisses my skin. We're bathed in a sliver of moonlight that I swear is made brighter thanks to Esmaray, wherever she is.

"Can we not talk about it? Can we pretend, just for a night, that life is normal? At least, the old normal we knew before there were god-killing weapons and everything happened with your brother."

Essos releases me, letting me swim away. At first, I'm too short to reach the sandbar, but then I feel the sand come up to meet my toes as they stretch. Another Kai move to be thankful for.

"We can pretend anything you want."

His need to touch me wins out, because even though he's just released me, he swims up behind me to hold my back to his chest. He peppers kisses along my shoulder.

We tread water and swim until I submerge myself entirely. Essos remains where he is, but I swim around him and pinch his butt. He jumps a little but catches me before I swim away.

I yelp as he pulls me out of the water and presses a fevered kiss to my lips.

"Should we discuss names?" he asks, breaking for air.

"No." I don't offer any further explanation, but my husband knows my heart. There is no need for me to tell him why.

"Shall I regale you with reasons I love you, instead?" he offers, dragging my mind away from the dark places in my head that the fear lives in.

"I'll never say no to that."

Essos presses a soft kiss to my pulse point, and I feel my heart speed up in response to him. The smile I feel spread against my neck tells me he feels it too.

He opens his mouth to speak, but I cover it with mine.

Between kisses, Essos fills the quiet night air with tales of what I missed mixed with pulling out favorite memories of our shared life.

Gradually, I see exhaustion weighing on him. His blinks get longer, and his speech slows.

"To bed with you," I whisper in his ear, my arms wrapped around his shoulders. He grips my wrists gently, dropping his head onto my shoulder, our clothes forgotten on the beach.

"To bed," he confirms. I close my eyes, knowing what comes next. The world drops out from us in the water, and when I open my eyes, we're in our bathroom, dripping wet. Essos grabs a plush bathrobe and wraps it around me.

It's just over my shoulders when I push it off and lunge for the toilet to throw up. He's right behind me, pulling my hair back into a clip with a twist. Essos rubs my back until I'm done.

I sit back on my haunches, reaching forward to flush the toilet. In my peripheral, I see a glass of water appear in his hand.

I grope for it, nearly missing it entirely, but Essos holds it tightly so I don't drop it. I lean against the wall and look up at him.

"Did you miss having such a sexy wife?" I ask, my throat burning when I talk. I take a sip of the water and swish, then spit it out. Essos sits on the floor in front of me, having thrown on his sweatpants again. My stupid pregnant libido marks each ripple of his abdomen as he joins me on the ground, and I remind myself that I could probably just hook my leg over him and ride him like the stud he is.

"My love, if I wasn't afraid you would throw up all over again, I would lay you down on this cold tile and worship you the way you deserve." He kisses me, ignoring that I was sick only moments ago. "As it is, you're still looking a little green."

"I'm feeling much better, but you're probably right."

As much as the idea of jumping my husband's bones appeals to me, I'm hit by a wave of exhaustion and hunger, and the desire to have sex is gone just as quickly as it came.

My head falls onto Essos's shoulder. His free hand reaches up and traces the curve of my cheek.

"I think we've had enough excitement," he says. "Let's get you to bed."

I don't object, even knowing what we will face tomorrow.

If the Queen of the Dead is needed for this ritual, I'm going to dress the part.

Essos is still asleep when I wake up, and the moment I take to study him is too brief. His rosy lips are parted gently, and his normally tame hair is wild and mussed from the ocean and sleep. He looks peaceful with a dark curl on his forehead as he lies on his side, reaching for me. The thin sheet manages to cover just one leg and ass cheek. The rest of the covers are bundled on my side, stolen away in the night. I admire his exposed body, his normally tight muscles relaxed in sleep.

His arm is extended toward my side of the bed, but I was too far away from him to be touching. Curled by his arm is Waffles, who will never admit it when Essos is awake, but clearly has a soft spot for my husband.

By the time I get out of the shower, he's awake and sipping from a coffee mug.

Essos glances up, his gaze raking over my body. I'm already dressed in a form-fitting black gown that showcases my bump instead of hiding it. It's a floor-length dress, and the scoop neck is unnecessary with my now ample breasts. Such dresses used to give me a little boost, a little allure, but now I've got the goods on full display.

"Good morning," he greets, not looking away from me as he sips his drink. I want a coffee. Gods, I want the caffeine more than I want anything at this moment, but I hesitate. Today will be enough stress on my body.

I slip onto Essos's lap. He moves his mug out of the way to make space for me. We're silent, soaking in the morning. His other hand is on my hip, rubbing it absently.

"What time are we doing this?" I ask, nuzzling my nose into his neck. He shivers under my body, and I relish the surge of power in knowing I can make him tremble under me.

"Noon. We're going to all meet at my office and then go down to the throne room."

I think of the throne room that helped reunite my friends Tiffany and Steve. It's not a friendly space. It's cold and dark. We designed it that way intentionally and chose to use it next to never.

"Are you going to get changed?" I ask, settling further against him.

"I would, but I'm otherwise engaged at the moment."

I move to get off him. "I could go..."

Essos snags me around the waist and tugs me against his chest more firmly. I give him no resistance. This is exactly where I want to be.

"You're not going anywhere without me saying so," he growls into my neck.

"Is that what you think?" I ask, dropping my voice low as if appalled at his audacity. I wiggle on his lap, pleased to feel his arousal.

"That is what I know to be true." His mouth is on mine, hot and demanding, and I lean into him. I want more of this, more of the forgetting. If I let my thoughts run wild, I'm not sure I'll be able to make it down those stairs without someone dragging me.

I grind against him, and he moans into my mouth.

Then I get off his lap abruptly.

"You need to get dressed," I insist, offering him my hand.

"I hate that you're right," Essos mutters. He drains his coffee and rises, then presses a chaste kiss to my lips. I drop into the chair as he slips into his dressing room. When he emerges, he is the King of Night and Death and Shadows. Essos has his hair slicked back perfectly in a way that makes me want to run my hand through it and pull on it as he makes me scream in pleasure. The look he gives me tells me he knows exactly what I'm thinking. He doesn't bother hiding his smirk as he holds out an arm to me.

I slip my arm into his as the familiar weight of a crown settles on my head.

We make our way downstairs. Everyone looks grim in the dining room, with unfinished plates of food before them all. Essos guides me with his hand on the small of my back to my chair beside him.

"I hate to be that person, but if we're going to drain your blood, then we need to make sure you're fed," Helene urges, pushing a plate toward me. It's stacked with eggs and bacon and toast. On a good morning, the scent of all these things would make my mouth water. Even on the roughest mornings, toast would be more than enough to help get my appetite back.

I begrudgingly accept the food, taking a small bite of the cheesy scrambled eggs. Beside me, Essos hums in approval. I want to glare at him, but I know that this is all for my own good.

"What were you all talking about before we ruined the party?" I ask, folding some of the eggs onto my toast. I rip off a piece of bacon and hold it under the table, where Dave gladly takes it, nibbling lightly at my fingers. Essos glances at me but opts not to comment on my feeding of the dogs from the table. It's been a debate for ages, one that he will never win.

"There's been...unrest...in my kingdom," Kai remarks delicately.

"There is unrest everywhere," Xavier grumbles, not looking up from his paper. When his eyes do lift, it's always to gaze at Cat.

"What sort of unrest?" I ask, placing a piece of bacon on my tongue, letting the greasy goodness melt into my person.

"The sort of unrest that has people wondering if perhaps we're to blame for Posey's continued anger and that maybe we should turn ourselves in," Kai answers solemnly. "Our children are attempting to handle it, hoping that fresh young faces will calm the masses. It seems to be working thus far."

"I can only hope we have a chance to do better than before." My voice is small for words that need to mean more. I do want us to have a chance to do better, but that chance means defeating Posey. That chance means ending her. I'm sure my niece and nephew can hold the fort of the Ocean kingdom, but they shouldn't have to be put in this position.

Octavia purses her lips, finally taking the hint to not interject with her own thoughts and opinions.

Essos eyes her warily, his blue eyes narrowed. "Do you have something to add, Mother?" He lowers his fork and knife.

"Is my opinion being requested, now?" she asks, acting put out as she sips her tea with a pinky raised.

I open my mouth to ask if she needs an implicit invitation on letterhead, but Essos covers my hand with his, shooting me a look to be silent. I narrow my eyes.

"Gods, yes, Mother, that is what Essos is asking. Are you trying to make Daphne turn you into a plant?" Helene snaps.

"No need to be rude. My opinion wasn't welcome yesterday, but today it is. I'm just making sure I understand when it is and isn't acceptable."

"Mother," Xavier warns, looking at her.

"My point was just that your hopes mean nothing to the people who are suffering now because of Posey. Neighbors are turning on neighbors, and there is rampant fear. People are losing their businesses. Without a real plan for how to fix this, you're going to be in much the same position as you were, disappointing the people who depend on you. The status quo was survivable before because that was just how things were, but for the few short weeks before Posey took things to such extremes, people had hope. Hope that they would be given a voice in how things were run."

"What would you know of it, Octavia? You were never here," Finn points out.

"I know that your little programs to help people start small businesses and pave roads were meager in the face of what people wanted—a government that would answer to them and rulers who did more than fuck all day."

I slouch in my seat, looking at Octavia, hating that she's right. "So, we have another thing we need to figure out, on top of overthrowing a tyrant Fate, installing a new Fate in her place, opening the gates to the Underworld, summoning the souls back to the Afterlife, shutting the veil between realms, and bringing my murderer back to life. But sure, let's add developing a new form of government for our people." I can't stop the hysterical laughter that bubbles out of my throat.

"One thing at a time, my love," Essos murmurs, kissing my temple.

"Besides, you forgot that we have to get the dagger and scepter back," Finn adds. I can see the glint in his eyes—he wants to go for it. I can only hope that after we open the gates to the Underworld, I'll be able to talk him out of the idea. Both he and my husband are obsessed with their desire to get this threat eliminated. They *need* a cooler head to prevail.

I am not the only one that glares at him. Sybil, Estelle, and Zara drift into the room, all looking somber. Their usually bright tunics seem dull for the day, and I know that everyone is worried about what we're about to do.

"We're ready whenever you want to begin," Zara tells me, and my whole body goes still. I'm not ready for this. I'm not ready for what is being asked of me, but what ruler ever is? What ruler walks into every situation knowing what they're supposed to do, and then going about it? A fake one; one that is posturing.

I rise, knowing that this is what I have to do.

The men all shoot to their feet when I get up and I want to hug them for it. People can say what they will about these gods, but I know they have my back. Essos literally touches my back, glancing at my plate, which I did a decent job of finishing. I feel like a child whose parents are checking to see if I've finished my peas before I can go play. Except this is eggs, and it's not for playtime, it's so I can nearly die and hope I don't take my child with me.

"Only if you're ready," Essos whispers to me and only me.

I gaze into his blue eyes, wishing I could read his mind. "Let's just get this over with, shall we?" I slide my fingers into his and lead our group to the stairs I took so long ago, most recently to adjudicate with Essos during the Calling, and to hear Steve's case for why he should get a second chance with Tiffany. There has been some good and some bad in that room, and I don't expect this will be any different.

I let Essos guide me with my hand in his, and we take the thin spiral stairs together. I try to take a deep, calming breath, slowly pushing it out, but I can't find it in me to get the sort of depth that might help.

When we step into the room, I stall. I haven't been down here since Steve came from the mortal realm with his guitar to plead for Tiffany's soul. It looks very much the same as it did then, dark and cavernous. Once, I tried to breathe a little life into the room with flowers and vines, but nothing can live in this darkness.

Above us hangs a heavy metal chandelier. It's all black with hundreds of candles dripping wax that never makes it to the ground. Directly underneath it is a circle of black and red wax candles. If I didn't already feel like a human sacrifice, this would certainly seal the deal. My steps falter, and Essos waits for me to go forward again. Knowing everyone is at my back, I have to do it. I have to get this over with.

The makeshift altar has a book spread in front of it with a curved dagger waiting.

"What do you need us to do?" I ask, forcing a brick wall of strength into my words.

"Both of you need to move into the center of the circle." Zara's voice shakes as she instructs us. She brushes past me to look at the book again, ready to pour over the words, to make this perfect and precise. I have absolute faith in her and her ability to pull this off.

I notice two large gold bowls set on the outskirts of the circle, no doubt meant to catch our falling blood. I nearly choke on my own breath, unable to force one foot in front of the other. Essos patiently waits for me while our friends move to stand by the walls of the room. Only Zara, Sybil, and Estelle are gathered near the altar, with Octavia hovering close.

Cat is beside Xavier, and I notice her slip her hand into his. Good. He'll be there to anchor her, because I have no doubt that this will be hard to watch.

I recognize the blade as the one that holds Galen's soul in it. I wonder if Octavia can feel the presence of her favorite child's soul in the room. Sybil shoots me an apologetic look as they handle it with the utmost care.

"No one but them can step inside the circle," Estelle warns, giving pointed looks to Finn and Callie. She knows, of course, about Callie's promise to act as a healer. I can only hope that Xavier and Callie, along with Octavia, will be enough to keep the small fragile heart in my womb beating.

My hands cradle my stomach, and Essos's hand follows mine, pressing against the swell. The baby hasn't quickened yet. I was told I should start feeling movement any day now, but I know they're there, waiting. I just hope they're strong enough to survive.

I take one, and then two steps forward, crossing the barrier of the circle. Essos follows me into the space. Sybil joins us in the circle; apparently, Estelle's warning doesn't apply to them.

I try to focus on their soothing voice as they explain what to do. We kneel in the center of the circle, nearly knee to knee. They place the dagger in Essos's hands, and I'm taken aback by the length. Now that it's right there, I can see that it's nearly as long as my forearm. I'm grateful Essos is listening, because there is only a ringing in my ears. I want to be sick; I feel clammy all over. Too hot and too cold all at once. It was one thing in the abstract, but now I'm here, kneeling with my husband in the middle of a ritualistic circle.

Sybil steps out of the circle again, and the chanting begins.

"Nothing is going to happen to you. I swear it," Essos promises. With the knife held far away from us, he uses his free hand to grip the back of my neck and pull me in for one last searing kiss.

The candles around the circle are all lit at the same time, the flames climbing higher and higher like some fancy special effect from a supernatural movie. I grip Essos's hand, trying to follow the ancient language. Sybil, Estelle, and Zara start chanting, and I'm impressed with Zara, not only for her pronunciation, but for how she's able to follow along.

"I love you," I tell Essos through gritted teeth.

I try to fight a tear, but it rolls down my cheek anyway. A matching tear runs down Essos's face. He takes my wrist gently and turns it over. His blue eyes flick behind me, where I know Sybil stands. I don't know their response, but Essos grips my wrist with a bruising force. He meets my eyes, an apology written in them, and digs the tip of the dagger into my arm.

I bite my lip and try not to cry out, and he keeps mouthing his apology over and over again. I reach out with my other hand and wipe his tears. My arm burns with each move the blade makes from my wrist up to the inside of my elbow. He turns my arm over, twisting my wrist down so the blood flows more freely.

I can no longer hear the chanting, only the plink of my blood dropping into the metal bowl. It starts slowly, and then I feel the blood being pulled from my veins. Essos turns the dagger over to me and holds out his arm. I don't know how I missed it, but both his sleeves are rolled up.

I hesitate, pressing the knife to his skin and nicking him a few times before I commit, pushing the knife too deep into his wrist. He winces, but when I look up at him with apology in my eyes and on my lips, his focus is on me with grim determination. He gives me an encouraging nod, and it's all I need to drag the knife up to his elbow. I hate the resistance I feel from his skin. It's small, because this knife has been sharpened so well—too well.

Essos lets out a grunt when I twist his wrist the same way he did mine. There isn't the same plink from his blood, because mine has already created a base layer. The sound is more of a drip as our blood blends.

We repeat this process again on our other arms. I'm surer of my cut the second time. Once we're done with the second round of slices, we toss the dagger out of the circle. I don't know if Galen's soul could ruin the ritual, but it's not a risk I'm willing to take.

Essos and I press our cuts against each other so our blood is combined as it drips.

I can't look away from Essos even though I want to see where Callie and Xavier are. Instead, Essos and I are' stuck nose to nose, and I can feel the magic dragging the blood from our veins.

I think there's sweat on my forehead, but I can't reach up to touch it. Our arms are bound with a garish red ribbon that keeps tightening and releasing to keep the blood flowing. My head falls forward onto Essos's shoulder.

"Stay with me, my love," he whispers in my ear, a desperate edge to his voice.

"I'm always with you," I reply, hearing the dreamy, faraway quality to my voice.

I'm not sure if I'm imagining it, but I think that the bowls of blood are lifting in the air as the chanting gets louder. I'm trying hard to keep my eyes open, but the room is so warm as the flames climb higher and higher. Either I'm spinning, or the bowls of blood are spinning, but I know that I haven't had a case of spins this bad since I turned twenty-one.

I lift my head to look at Essos and find him looking pale. There is a thin sheen of sweat on his face. I want to brush a damp strand of hair from his brow, but I can't move my arms. I've forgotten why I can't move my arms until I glance at them and see the binding that's forcing them to stay outstretched.

It's raining blood, and I don't understand why there is blood everywhere. I know I should be worried about something, but I don't remember what. I try to focus on Essos again, but my vision is blurry.

I see Octavia close to the edge of the barrier, coming closer and closer before she kneels right at the circle. My vision gets worse, and there are two of her until it narrows and narrows and narrows and everything goes black.

"Why isn't she waking up?" Essos's growl is the first thing that breaks through my dreams.

"Let her rest. Her body is healing, and all this fussing isn't helping her," is Callie's low reply.

I want to respond to them, tell them I'm here, I'm awake, but my mouth feels dry and like it's glued together. I couldn't lift my hand if I wanted to. I feel Essos close to me, brushing my hair from my brow.

The room is warm and shrouded in darkness. I want to turn over, but the weight of the blankets is too heavy. I can't move, and I briefly wonder when we got a weighted blanket.

"I just don't know how I'm supposed to tell her," Essos's voice is anguished when he says this. I decide I don't want to know what he's talking about, and I let sleep pull me back under.

My dreams are plagued with flowers and Posey and people

without mouths and eyes. The dead are making their displeasure known, grabbing at me, leaving me bruised. I have two long angry red lines the stretch from the inside of my wrist all the way to my elbow, but I don't recall how I got them. A chain of flowers unfolds along my forearms, watercolors mixing with the ink on my skin.

I'm admiring them when my body feels like it's slammed down into a box, and I have to fight and claw my way out. I've been buried alive, and I don't know how to get out, how to survive this.

Hands grab me from everywhere. They hold me down and try to drag me further down and down and down. Voices keep telling me that they're taking me where I belong, that I've died again, and I don't get a second chance. Screaming doesn't help, but then I can't stop screaming, my throat growing raw, then wet, as if I have screamed it bloody.

"Daphne. DAPHNE!" Essos's voice is pleading.

My eyes open, and I realize I've been flailing. I wasn't being dragged into the Underworld by the dead.

Essos is practically on top of me, his hands gripping my shoulders gently but firmly. There is a wild look in his eyes as he tries to see if I'm awake. Even in my dreamy haze, I can feel his panic; it's evident in the way his hands tremble.

"Oh gods," I moan, leaning into his arms so I can sob. The terror from being buried alive still has my heart racing. I hold on to him like he's my lifeboat in the storm.

"You're all right, my love, you're all right," he whispers into my hair.

Once I've stopped crying, I'm able to get a feel for the room. The sun is just rising outside our window, and all around me is evidence that this is where everyone has been congregating. There are mugs and plates piled on surfaces, with remnants of various meals. For gods, they're all so messy.

Essos lets his body relax onto the mattress beside me. "What do you need?" he asks, his voice quiet now that I'm not shouting.

"A bath," is the first thing to come out of my mouth. My memory is coming back gradually—the ceremony, the blood, the feeling of being bathed in it. Essos's words about not being sure how to tell me. I don't know what he has to tell me, but my hands fly to my stomach, and I look at him with bewildered panic.

"She's safe," he swears to me. He grips my face, brooking no room for uncertainty. Essos wants me to see the candid truth in his features.

"She?" I ask, feeling my eyes well with tears.

"Fuck," he swears with a laugh. "Callie accidentally spilled the beans when she was checking you over after the ritual. I wasn't going to tell you, but I've been thinking about how fucked I am, having you and a little girl. I won't know a moment's peace for the rest of my eternal life."

He scoops me up, looking buoyant with the news, and I can't help but smile back. I hold on to that good mood and don't ask all my burning questions, because I want to preserve this moment of terrific news and peace.

The tub is already full of lukewarm water. As he carries me toward it, I register that I'm in nothing but a camisole and shorts, decidedly not what I wore to the ritual.

"How long was I out?"

Essos sets me on my feet and teases the camisole up and off my body.

"These are new," he remarks, confused, turning my arms so the insides of my forearms are face up. Inked over the scars are the tattoos I dreamt of, only, intermingled with the pink watercolor flowers are black ones ringed with shadows and stars. At the wrist of my left arm is the same skull that tops Essos's scepter. His fingers gently touch the skin, and I flinch at how sensitive the tattoos are. Quickly, he pushes up his own sleeves to show matching ones that hide his own jagged red scars. The ones on my arms were precise slashes, but I hesitated and went too deep on him.

His tattoos are both unique. On his left arm, he has a miniature replica of his scepter. Where the red ruby eyes are on the real thing, there is instead a peony in the left eye. The right eye still has a ruby that burns and gleams in the terrifying skull topper, and wrapped around the shaft are the same flowers that decorate my arms. Essos's left arm features the dagger we used to slice into our skin, lying on a bed of flowers.

"Complimentary tattoos," is all I can say. It's not clever or funny, but it's all I can think of to say as I shimmy out of my shorts and slip into the water. Essos is close behind me, unwilling to be far from me at any given moment.

"It's certainly better than the scars I've been sporting for the last few days."

I nestle between Essos's legs as his arms wrapped around my shoulders. He presses a kiss to the bare skin along my neck.

"I was out that long?"

"Three days. I was out of my mind. I refused to leave the bedroom in case you woke. Callie's been here most of the time too, monitoring you and the baby. Everyone has popped in at one time or another. I refused to let you be alone when you woke up."

I contemplate what it means for my poor husband to be spread so thin. I hate that I keep doing this to him. At every turn since I've come back, I've caused him so much anxiety.

"Did it work?" My heart pounds in my chest. Surely, if it didn't work, he wouldn't be as calm as he is.

"Yes. I called back all souls trapped in their decaying bodies, and your father, Phil, has used this to explain to the President and other world leaders that we have no ill intent. They're holding off launching any missiles for now. We've readjusted the tithes to their original amounts. Now the only souls in the Inbetween are those contesting their placement. And before you ask, I already had your parents reinstalled in their appropriate Afterlife. I had Sybil see to it personally."

Essos kisses my neck again before pushing me forward gently. I slide along the bottom of the tub so I can wet my hair. My body is fully submerged, the very tips of my knees peeking out as I lie there.

When my lungs can't take it anymore, I emerge and take a deep breath of air.

I slip to the other side of the tub so I can lounge against it and study Essos.

"What don't you know how to tell me?" I ask, fighting to keep my voice from wavering.

He brings up a wet hand and runs it over his face. His other hand comes up, and he rubs his eyes before looking at me.

"While you were out, we made a move."

I lean forward, drawing my knees up to my chest. My arms fold around them so I'm hugging myself, waiting for the other shoe to drop. Someone is dead. I can feel it. The only move they would have made is to get the scepter. The very thing I warned Essos about, the thing we fought over. I release my legs and grip the edges of the tub, my gaze locked on his face. His eyes are closed now.

"Finn." His voice breaks, and I lean forward to grab his hands.

I can already feel the tears welling and my heart breaking. I'm not strong enough to hear this. I'm not strong enough to know. I don't think I can handle looking at him when he breaks this news to me. Water drips down his face, and I mark each drop, knowing that it's not just bathwater, but tears.

"No," I choke out, covering my mouth with one hand while the other grips his wrist.

"He's alive," he swears.

I can read between the lines. Just barely. I'm not sure I can stomach knowing what happened to Finn.

Essos reaches forward and tugs me closer to him. The bathwater splashes over the sides of the tub as I glide back easily. My heart won't still. My mind won't stop.

"What happened?" I ask, my voice small. It's how I feel right now —small and insignificant, reduced to a nervous, shaking mess. The tub is full of warm water, but I feel so, so cold.

Essos kisses the palms of my hands. "She took his eyes using her God Killer blade."

I don't comprehend what Essos has said at first...then I can see it happening. My clever friend, who has sticky fingers and never backs down from a fight, has been maimed. It's not going to change how I feel about him, but knowing that I'll never again see his bright eyes brimming with mirth leaves me bereft. I can't imagine how he must feel.

"Where is he?" I demand, ready to get out of this tub to tend to him.

Essos holds tight to my wrists as I start to push to my feet. "Sit down," he demands. It's a tone he never uses with me, and I'm so surprised that I comply. His eyes burn into me, seeing past my bare body and into my heart and my intentions. Essos knows that I would run from this room, ignoring my own exhaustion, to tend to my friend.

"Yes, sir." My voice is dripping with sarcasm as I settle back into the water.

Essos's eyes flash with desire before his whole body softens to me. "I know you want to go to him. Dion is with him now. Finn hasn't been alone, and right now, you're my concern. So please, indulge me further." Essos pulls me to him and turns me so my back is pressed against his chest. I do as he urges, not minding when his ankles hook on the insides of mine, spreading my legs. He doesn't do what I expect; instead, he scoops my hair into a clip and starts to wash my body. I close my eyes, luxuriating in his devotions to me.

"I would prefer if you didn't scare me like that again, love," Essos whispers, kissing my cheek.

"I would prefer to not have to do that whole ritual again, so I think we're agreed on that point." I lean my head back to rest on Essos's shoulder. I let myself slide briefly into the darkness that must have consumed my husband. What it must have been like to witness the love of his life, laid out and unconscious, and then his best friend return blinded. I want to hug him and kiss him and tell him that everything is going to be okay.

His hand gently strokes the bar of soap in small circles over my stomach, working his way outward. He rinses away the suds with his bare hands.

"Finn is going to be all right," he promises, but I think it's more for him than me. He has a rough edge to his voice, my husband who hasn't gotten enough sleep, who has had worry consume him for days. I want to gather him in my arms, be a comfort for him, but when I try to twist around, he holds me tight where I am.

"He will be." I'm silent a beat. "Did he succeed?" I hate asking the question.

Essos sighs, kissing my neck. "No. I knew it the minute he returned. When I touched the scepter, it felt...wrong somehow. I didn't even try to use it. I'm afraid it's a cursed object."

I sink further into the tub, wondering how I can help Finn. He'll hate it; he'll feel like I'm making him a project, but he's one of my oldest friends and I can't let him slip away.

Essos warms the water and summons a platter of fruit. He grabs a strawberry and holds it to my lips until I take a bite, and juice runs down my neck. Essos leans forward and licks it, trailing up to my mouth. Each fruit he feeds me is ripe and juicy, strawberries and pineapple and blueberries.

We rest like this until we're both prunes. Essos climbs out first, careful to help me and wrap me up. A full meal waits in our bedroom, and even though I've eaten my weight in fruit, I'm ravenous. My husband, my dream man, my everything, has tacos here for me, and my gods, I want to jump him.

Wrapped in a plush bathrobe, I sit down and grab one. The second I'm eating it, my stomach starts to churn. A smirk pulls at Essos's lips, but he smooths it away as I lower the taco. I have to force myself to swallow, and I glare at the offending food as I set it back down on my plate. I reach instead for Essos's plate, which has a well-seasoned chicken breast sitting on a bed of polenta.

"Baby girl doesn't like tacos?" he asks, fighting the smile in his voice.

"Baby girl has decided that she is not interested in tacos *today*."

Essos takes the tacos from me and leans back with a laugh. My mind and body relax, and I try to forget about the world outside our bubble.

"Penny for your thoughts?" Essos asks as I lean back and rest my hands on my very full stomach.

"Just wondering if you're excited about a girl. Wondering what we're going to name her. Feeling guilty."

His brow furrows. "Why do you feel guilty?"

"Because we're enjoying this moment of bliss, and Finn's been blinded. It feels wrong to be happy."

"He would be mad at you for that. You've sacrificed enough in the name of this crusade. You're allowed to take a breath after nearly dying. And, of course, I'm delighted we're having a girl. I'm excited to see all the ways she and her mother are going to bring me to my knees."

I rub my stomach to soothe the bloat I feel from overeating. My heart wants to bask in its fullness, that our family is growing and we're together and well. But the nagging truth hounds me; we are at war, and there is still more to do.

"What's next?" I ask, getting up. I untie the robe and let it drop to the floor as I walk to my closet. A glance over my shoulder assures me that Essos's eyes are where I want them—on my ass as I put one foot in front of the other. My ability to walk without waddling is swiftly coming to a close.

"Don't you worry; I'm watching," he assures me. I hear him clamor out of his chair to trail me, his own towel still wrapped around his hips. It's slung low, and I love how his muscles writhe as he makes his way to me. Desire curls low in my belly, my need for Essos trumpeting in my veins.

"Well?" I ask, turning to him, aware of the affect I have on him. He's drinking in his fill, his gaze tracing my collarbone down to my heavy breasts. My nipples pucker under his stare. He doesn't stop there, his gaze sweeping around my swollen stomach to my sex. I think he's going to lay me on this floor and fuck me until I forget my own name and his name and everything in between, but then he looks at the fresh tattoos on my arms and shuts down.

"Next? I'm going to coax you back into bed for another night of rest. Hopefully while you're unconscious, Sybil or Estelle or Zara will find a spell that I can use to have you locked in this room away from any prying eyes."

"Essos!" I scold, putting my hands on my hips. He only grins at me wolfishly, his eyes doing another sweep of my body.

"Daphne!" he mimics, crossing his arms. "You can't expect me to gladly invite danger where you're concerned. I will do what I have to in order to keep my family safe."

I turn my back, keeping the disgusted snort I want to make inside. "I thought we got past this. We talked about it, and you were going to let me help."

"That was before I thought I lost you, before I had to hold your body to mine while you were unconscious and bleeding out, and I had to tell Callie and Xavier to stay back so the spell could finish. I had to wait, praying to the gods that you were alive and would stay alive so that it wouldn't be for nothing. You think I wasn't disgusted with myself for making that choice? If I let them in and the spell was ruined, you would have been in danger for *nothing*. You think I didn't spend the past three days fearing that you weren't going to wake up? Wondering if I made the wrong call? So, no, Daphne, this is not up for discussion. I will not put you in danger again."

I stop rooting around for clothes. My strong husband is bowing under the pressure of the world. So much rests on his shoulders, and I want to take it from him.

Essos's knees give out, and he drops to the ground, burying his face in his hands. In two steps, I'm across the room to him. We're knee to knee again, and I hold him to me, smoothing his hair down when the first drops hit my chest. His body shakes as he lets go of all the pent-up emotion from the week.

Essos releases his face to pull me against him, and we sort of fall to the ground on our bottoms, holding each other. He cries in a way I don't think he's let himself in a long time, and I can't even imagine what it was like for him to hold his pregnant wife as she was dying in his arms *again.*

"I understand," I whisper in his ear, because I do. I understand why he's putting his foot down, why he's trying to hold me back from everything that is happening. But I won't let him. This is so much bigger than just me and him and our child. This is bigger than anything we know. If Posey asserts this power, if she is able to make the gods mortal, who knows what type of havoc she will bring?

When he's cried out, I help him to his feet and lead him out of my closet. I gesture at the fireplace, and the fire roars in response. We slide into bed and meet in the middle. We don't say anything else, letting the would-be argument rest until tomorrow. When my recovery from the ritual isn't as fresh, I'll convince him that this attempt to protect me is wrong.

Together is the best chance we have of defeating the monster in the dark.

22

I wake in the morning feeling refreshed. My strength isn't where I want it to be, but it feels like the day after a workout, when I'm both energized and exhausted at the same time.

I'm afraid to see Finn because I don't know what I can possibly say to him. His condition feels like my fault. I know it isn't, but I keep putting everything that happens on my shoulders, for better or worse.

I've lost four days between unconsciousness from the ritual and a day of recovery with Essos. I'm ready to tackle whatever comes next, even if that is bringing Galen back. I don't want to do it. I don't want to have worry about my murderer lurking in dark corners in my home, but we assured Octavia we would do just that, so now I have to stall with her as long as I can.

Given the recent developments—my being unconscious and Finn's injury—maybe I can get away with it.

Essos has already gone to his office to get in a few hours' work before we start training. My workout clothes are tight, and I relish the sensation of my bump pulling on my bottoms. I went with a sports bra instead of a top, because I want to show everyone just how much my little pomegranate has grown. I want to wrap myself up in this feeling of fullness and never forget it.

My carefree attitude slams to a stop when I walk into the dining room and find Galen sitting alone at the table. He lifts his head from where he was cutting up his eggs.

My stomach bottoms out. It's wrong, I shouldn't give any indication that he affects me like this, but I grip a chair all the same, needing the support.

He flashes me a scary wide grin as his gaze roves over my body with the familiarity of a lover. The way his focus lingers on my bump is predatory, and I want to scream. I want to scream until my throat bleeds from how raw it gets, but I can't.

I can't, because there is no air in my lungs. I can't, because I can't breathe past the rising panic. It's like when I was on the streets of Solarem and that man grabbed me, only this is so much worse, because Essos isn't here to ground me; he isn't here to keep me safe.

I gasp in a sip of air, and it manages to clear the fog, just enough for me to let go of the chair. I can't let Galen know how much he affects me. I can't let him see how much his existence hurts me, even though it does hurt me; it hurts and scares me, because I don't know what he will do to me. He's taken one child from me; he won't take another.

I will kill him again first.

That single thought cements my resolve and I take a deeper breath. My shoulders shift back, and I hold my head high. His mouth spreads into a manic smile, and I have to bite back the urge to scream again. I *should* scream, should let everyone know that he's back and he's here, but I don't.

I don't, because screaming will show him that he scares me, and I'm going to be the scariest motherfucker in this room. The mystery of *how* this happened will have to be addressed later. Obviously, Essos had no idea he was back, or he would have said something to me. Gods, I doubt Essos would have ever left our room, or at least my side.

I grab a plate and start to pile it with food, anxious just from being around Galen, but turning tail and leaving isn't an option. I don't want to show him that weakness. I should have walked out as soon as I saw that I would be alone with him. I should have turned around and waited for Xavier or Essos or Cat or literally anyone. I won't stay; I'm going to grab my food and leave.

"It's wonderful to see you've decided to carry our child."

Galen's words chill me, and I almost drop the tongs I'm using to grab kielbasa.

"You're fucking delusional," I hiss, wanting to find it in myself to look up and meet his eye, but I can't. Not when he's looking at me like he owns me. I can feel his gaze on me like a tangible touch.

I'm afraid that leaving now will just embolden him. I don't want him to know that he scares me enough to send me running in my own home.

"Am I? I seem to remember the feel of your tight little body under mine."

The reminder of that night makes anger burns through me, white-hot. That night, Kai had lost the second trial, and Galen thought that my active participation in the charade of our engagement meant he was welcome in my bed.

"I seem to remember nearly cutting your dick off that night. No, this baby is my husband's, through and through." I finish loading my plate and turn to leave him behind and sit outside, away from his toxicity.

Galen moves quickly from his chair and stands beside me. He grips my arm tightly. "We can always start over, you and I. No need for this animosity to continue any further."

I turn my head a fraction toward him...and then my actions stop being my own.

I pivot toward him completely. Pursing my lips, I blow in his face, then watch as his eyes turn totally white.

He lets go of me as if burned, his head whipping around frantically like he's unable to see anything. I step back, terrified of what's happening. I don't understand it myself, and I back up until I hit the buffet table against the wall. There's an acidic smell in the air, and I notice a dark spot growing on Galen's shorts.

"Essos!" I cry, the plea a mixture of fear and concern. Whatever is happening here warrants a scream. Dave gets to me first and places himself between Galen and me, barking his head off.

Essos appears at my side and immediately checks me over, but he's quickly distracted.

Galen is screaming and scratching at his face. He's drawing bloody gouges down his cheeks, and then all at once...it stops.

"Galen?" Essos says, his voice low, nearly a whisper of shock. He stays glued beside me.

Galen lifts his head and looks at me in wonder and fear. "What did you do to me?" he demands.

"Me? Nothing, I...I..." My words falter as Essos turns to look at me. His gaze rakes over me, pausing at my arm where Galen grabbed me, and his eyes darken.

"You should go, Daphne," Essos tells me, voice low and lethal.

"The things I saw...I was never going to escape...it was dark, and they were on me. What did you *do*?" Galen sounds haunted, and then he leaps for me, his arms outstretched.

"Nothing. I didn't do anything!" I maintain, dropping my plate and scuttling back.

Essos lunges forward and grabs Galen by the shoulders, then hauls him off the floor and throws him onto the dining room table, which collapses under the force. My husband is on his brother in a heartbeat, pulling him up by the lapels of his shirt. Galen hangs dumbly from his hands until Essos nails him with a right hook to the jaw, followed by another punch.

The brothers start to grapple, and it's not for fun. This isn't boys being boys. Essos is taking out all the rage and frustration he's kept on a tight leash for centuries for the better of the realms. He takes a left hook but deflects the next and manages an uppercut that sends Galen sprawling. There is no hesitation before Essos is on him again, whaling on him. My husband's fist comes back bloodier and bloodier with each strike, and I'm not sure whose blood it is anymore.

Galen starts to laugh and keeps laughing long after the sound of flesh pounding flesh has stopped. Essos lets him go and stands up straight, rubbing the back of his hand along his mouth to catch whatever blood is there. I step forward and put a hand on my husband's shoulder, hoping to soothe him.

"If you so much as *look* at my wife again, I will carve out your eyeballs with the God Killer dagger and feed them to you. And if you lay a single finger on Daphne without her express permission, I will leave you with bloody stumps and gift your hands to you as a fucking necklace." Essos's ragged breathing is finally calming. He tugs on the bottom of his suit jacket, straightening it, as he glares at his brother with murderous intent.

"Someone sounds worried that maybe this baby might not actually be his," Galen taunts, then spits a mouthful of blood.

Essos doesn't hesitate to cock his fist back and hit his brother again and again. I hear the crunch of bones breaking and worry it might be a knuckle.

All this commotion finally draws the rest of the family, except for Finn and Dion, down.

Essos snarls in Galen's face. "Give me a reason, asshole, please. I don't care if it upsets Octavia. I will carve you into pieces and dump you into the bottom of the ocean, and I'll sleep better for it." My husband straightens up, breathing heavily.

When it becomes clear no one is going to help Galen up, he struggles to his own feet and staggers. His face is swollen and already turning mottled shades of purple and blue. "Why shouldn't I run to Posey now, take the Goddess of Spring, and leave with all I want? It's clear that you fuckers aren't ever going to respect me or listen to me."

Essos growls, taking another step toward Galen.

This dumb fuck actually won't get the message, and I think only the painful removal of a limb might teach him a lesson. Whatever I cut off will grow back, but it will be slow and agonizing for him.

"You won't do that if you ever want to meet your sons." Callie's voice rings out clear as a bell as she pushes to the front of the group.

Shock isn't a sufficient word for the look on Galen's face when he sees his wife. Her arms are crossed defensively over her chest. Callie taps her index finger on her bicep, and I'm proud of her for holding her head high as she faces this monster.

"We didn't have any children." His words are barely a whisper as he watches her walk closer.

During the Calling, Xavier talked about Galen's children with another goddess—the Goddess of Strife and the God of Murder. With my memories back, I remember who they are. Both of the children were born just after Galen and Callie were married. Their mother is the Goddess of Pain, Aiden. Aiden hated Galen long before they were born and, from what I remember, he had nothing to do with raising his children.

"We have two sons," Callie tells him confidently.

Galen turns his murderous glare on Essos. "What, one sloppy second wasn't enough? You had to fuck my wife too? Make her a pawn in all this? Are there no boundaries, *brother?*" Galen spits a wad of blood at Essos's feet.

"I was pregnant when I left you. It's *why* I left you. Essos was the only person who could make me disappear, and he did." Callie's smug, even when Galen rushes her. Essos steps between them, but Galen's arm shoots out, and he grabs Callie by the throat in a move that feels all-too familiar. In the group, Cat staggers back a few steps, having been the one in that position before.

"Tell me where they are," Galen growls, squeezing. Gods may be harder to kill, but we still experience pain. Callie doesn't flinch, her smile only growing as he becomes more and more frustrated.

"Try to kill me and you'll never find them. They have instructions on what to do if I don't return when this is over. I've raised your sons to know *very* well what their father is capable of."

"You fucking bitch. You took my sons—*my sons*—and fled?"

"She didn't fucking mumble," I snap, crossing my arms.

"I am going to carve that child from you and make you watch as it takes its dying breath," Galen swears, turning his gaze on me. My body starts to shake at the very *idea*.

The room fills with thunder, and Galen is blasted back, his spine cracking against the wall. I look over my shoulder to see who attacked the God of War, and it's Cat who is striding toward us. No, not striding—floating.

Cat's eyes are red with rage as she moves across the room, and I know that I need to calm her down. Her magic is still too new, too fragile, and she could bring the house down on us all. Beside me, Essos's Adam's apple bobs as he seems to come to the same realization.

"Words against that unborn child will be the last you ever utter if you keep up this fuckboy act. You will do no such thing to Daphne or her infant," Cat intones. Her voice doesn't sound like her, and it sends a chill down my spine.

Essos tucks me into his side, ready to haul ass outside with me, consequences be damned.

"Plot twist," Galen muses as he really looks at my best friend. The last he knew, she was dead, having died in my arms after taking a dagger, thrown by Galen, to the heart.

"Catalina." Xavier's voice is calm as he steps into her path.

She turns her red eyes on him. "He cannot be allowed to make such threats. He is not allowed to intervene in the actions of another god. *I* am the one who made that life possible." Her hair is starting to lose its static look. She's still hovering in midair, but she is no longer focused on Galen.

"No one is going to let him harm that baby, I promise." Xavier holds out a hand to her, displaying a patience I never knew him to have. Cat starts to drift down before placing her hand in his.

When she's firmly back on two feet, Essos loosens his hold on me, and I relax when I see the color return to her eyes. Cat looks almost scared over the depth of her powers.

With our attention off him, Galen seems to think he can slink away, but I shoot a hand out toward him, wrapping vines around his ankles.

"I really hate when you do that," Galen whines.

"You will help us, and we will let you live," I tell him.

"I want assurances. I want to see my sons," Galen demands. "They're legitimate children, not ill-begotten bastards." His voice might be intimidating if his face didn't look like it had been through a meat grinder. Scratches still mar the area around his eyes. They look more macabre set against the bruises and swelling inflicted by my husband.

"Good behavior earns gold stars. Gold stars get you rewards," I tell him with a saccharine smile. "Touching me today the way you did does *not* earn you a gold star."

A wave of exhaustion nearly knocks me off my feet, but I lock my knees and stand tall with an eyebrow raised. I don't take my eyes off him, and even though it takes a considerable amount of my energy to do so, I bring forth two vine creatures from the ground. They're large and strong, made from dense wood.

Essos steps behind me and places steadying hands on my shoulders. How he knew I needed the strength to remain upright impresses me.

"These are your new bodyguards," Essos says for me. It's good, because the ability to speak is beyond me. Even trying to open my mouth is getting to be too much. "Try to kill them, and we'll know about it. That is not gold star behavior."

"You don't need to talk to me like I'm a child."

Helene scoffs. "You insist on acting like one, baby brother. Of course, we're going to treat you like one."

Essos's hand slides possessively across my chest, pulling me against him so my back is flush with his torso. It looks like the tender touch of a husband, but I know it for what it is—support when my knees want to give out.

"Enough bickering," Xavier hisses, turning away from Cat for the first time. Her small hand is still wrapped in his, and she lets him lead her back to where we all stand.

"Do you have a cell for me as well?" Galen growls, looking at the united front before him.

"That can be arranged." My voice wavers too much, and his focus narrows back on me.

"If you behave, you won't need one," Essos tells him coldly. "Tomorrow, we will discuss what you know of Posey and how we can defeat her. For now, I'm sure Octavia would love to dote on her favorite." Essos lets the comment hang like it's a kindness, but we all know what it is, a thinly veiled threat. Octavia might love him best, but that doesn't mean her love isn't smothering.

I step away from Essos's grip, needing to show to Galen that I can stand on my own. "I suggest you go to your room." I don't know where the strength comes from, but I don't question it.

Galen steps into my space. He raises one hand slowly, not to strike, but it looks like to stroke against my cheek.

Essos grabs Galen's arm and twists it so it's bent at awkward angle before he punches the back of his elbow.

Galen cries out, glaring at his brother. "I didn't touch her!" he shouts, cradling his arm.

Essos threads his fingers through Galen's hair and lifts his head so he has to look at me. I can see the strain of the position in Galen's throat. His Adam's apple bobs as he finally looks at my face. There's a flicker of fear there.

"That bruise on my wife's arm says otherwise."

I lift my arm to see what Essos is talking about. Where Galen grabbed me earlier, there's a dark bruise in the shape of a handprint. I didn't think he grabbed me that roughly, but I must have been wrong.

In all the years I've been with Essos, I've never seen him like this, and I'm not afraid to admit how turned on that makes me.

"Take him to his room," Essos says to my vine guards. "Quit crying, Galen. You'll heal." He lets go of Galen, shoving him forward a little. The guards each grab one of Galen's arms and drag him from the room. Once he's cleared of the doorway, Essos runs his hands through his hair before turning to me.

With the exact opposite treatment of his brother, he takes my elbow and lifts my arm so he can get a better look at the bruise.

"Are you all right?" Essos asks, his finger brushing the bruised flesh. It fades immediately, but that doesn't seem to be good enough for him.

"Fine. Confused? Shaken?" I voice my thoughts, but I don't know how loud I am. Essos pulls me to his chest and kisses my forehead. I turn my head slightly to better fit against him and see our family awkwardly standing around us.

"Why don't we all sit outside?" Cat suggests, gesturing to the back door. My dining room table is in splinters, so there's really nowhere for us to sit anyway. I let myself be led, trying to puzzle over what happened.

When we're mostly seated and everyone has food, Essos hovers over me. I'm still too frazzled by what happened to be hungry, but I take a bite of a flaky croissant just to please him. There's so much pent-up tension in his body that he can't sit, and I don't blame him. If I wasn't exhausted from making those creatures, I would still be standing too.

"How is he back?" I ask, looking up at Essos. I feel fragile.

"The dagger was misplaced during the ritual to reopen the Underworld," Xavier supplies.

"Misplaced?" Essos snaps, eyes blazing with fury. He slams his already bruised and bleeding fist on the table, cracking it. "How the *fuck* was it misplaced, and why am I finding that out after Galen has come back and accosted *my wife*?"

"There are a lot of reasons, Essos, and you need to calm down," Xavier tells him, getting to his feet.

"When in the history of ever has telling someone to calm down *actually* led them to calm down? The man who murdered my wife was just alone with her and could have killed her again with the very weapon that is currently *missing*. Do *not* tell me to calm the fuck down, because I can't. You wouldn't be calm if it was Cat in that situation! You know what it's like, brother, to hold the person you care most about in the world as she bleeds out. I don't understand how you can stand there and expect me to just relax like it's a fucking day at the beach!"

Essos is screaming now, and we're joined by Kai from the water and Dion from the house.

To his credit, Xavier does manage to stay calm, but the mention of Cat's death seems to subdue him. "There was a lot going on. The Fates thought we had it; we thought the Fates had it. Remember: we had to carry both of you from the throne room. Then Finn was injured. It was an oversight, one we never should have made, but there is no going back."

"Are we operating on the assumption that Octavia took it during the ceremony and brought Galen back?" Callie suggests.

Essos grabs a water and puts it in front of me, and I greedily drink it down.

"It makes the most sense," Helene agrees. "Mom has never been patient. She's always done what she wants when she wants. She probably saw a golden opportunity and took it. What else did we miss?"

I fill them in on coming downstairs to find Galen sitting at the table, how he grabbed me and I blew in his face.

"You just blew in his face, what, with your breath?" Callie asks, sipping her mimosa.

I'm jealous that I can't self-medicate the way she can to deal with Galen's return, but I have a better way to relax; I have Essos.

What I need right now is to be bent over a table and fucked until I can't remember my name.

Maybe I should drag Essos out of here so we can do just that.

"Yeah, and I felt a little weird before I did it. He was in my space, and I just sort of...reacted." It's a weak explanation, but how do you explain the unexplainable?

Everyone is quiet.

"Could it have been the baby?" Cat asks, gnawing on her lower lip.

Xavier looks at her, gaze drifting to where her teeth are pressing into her flesh, and I get the impression that he very much wants to be the one biting that lip.

"Could be," Helene agrees, thinking it over and nodding her head. "When I was pregnant with Kristis, whenever I sneezed, it rained."

Xavier snorts. "I remember that. Posey banned you from all events."

I let the memory wash over me. Helene had just been starting to show, and Posey was hosting a garden party. I stared enviously at Helene's bump every time she smoothed her hands over it. Between my envy over Helene's pregnancy and my annoyance at Posey, I was in a ripe mood. The only thing that made it better was when Helene sneezed just before greeting Posey, dousing her in a quick spritz of rain. Since the rain came from Helene, she was left totally dry, but Posey was not so lucky. Her white dress was drenched to the point of becoming see-through. It was dismissed as a one-off until Helene's next sneeze ruined the cake.

"It's not like that stopped me from coming. I'm a queen too, and I swear she forgets that sometimes." Helene's trying to lighten the mood, and I appreciate her beyond words. Essos cups the back of my neck and begins stroking soothing circles on my nape.

"So, what, we think the baby can terrorize people?" I ask, alarmed.

Essos chuckles. "If our little girl can terrorize men by blowing a puff of breath in their faces, I will be one happy father."

"You think that now," Kai warns. "Until she's sixteen, and you've banned her from going to Solarem for a party and she uses that little party trick on you."

Essos covers my ears. "Shhh, don't give her ideas."

I chuckle and slip some bacon to Dave, who has been whipping me with his tail. Essos watches from the corner of his eye but doesn't scold me.

His trailing finger makes its way to my ear, and he gently tugs on the lobe. "I'm going to steal my wife away," he announces, keeping his eyes on me.

I turn to him and smile.

"You know she's already pregnant, right? You're fucking like teenagers who just discovered sex," Xavier teases, but his gaze quickly slips from Essos and me to Cat, and I have no doubt he would love to discover sex in much the same way.

I push out of my chair. "He's training me, you asshole."

"Wow, if he's training you how to have sex, things are more dire than I thought." Xavier laughs at his own little joke, and I swear murder flashes in my eyes.

"Brother, you're playing with fire. I won't protect you from her wrath."

Dion surprises us all by slamming a fist down on the table. "We don't have time for cute games or banter. We don't have time for training. Finn told me he hasn't gotten a message to deliver all day."

"I don't see the problem," Zara says as she steps outside. "Sybil and Estelle sent me to find out what all the shouting was about."

"The problem, Zara, is that Finn would get messages all the time. Love letters and well-wishes that his little doves sent all over Solarem. I watched him show Cat how to create her own dove to send. He felt every message, every secret. He knew it all, but hasn't gotten a single one all day. Now do you understand?"

"No, I don't." Cat takes the lead even as she glances around to confirm that we're all just as lost.

Dion buries his face in his hands, and I have to wonder how much of the stress of taking care of Finn is getting to him. Not that I don't think he has a point, but I've never seen Dion lose his cool like this. "Either no one is sending messages, or he can't feel them anymore."

"Should Finn be worrying about sending and receiving messages?" Essos asks, a calm in his voice that's misleading. I can feel the tension in his body radiating off him. Finn not having powers is unexpected, to say the least.

"What, the almighty Essos doesn't have an answer to why he can't feel people's messages?" I flinch from the vitriol in Dion's voice.

"What do you want me to say, Dion? I *don't* have all the answers. I don't actually have any of them—that's why Zara and the Fates have been holed up in the fucking library only to emerge when they have an answer!" Essos shouts, letting go of me, the tide of his anger rising once again. "I can't be the one to figure everything out. You're all content to live in my house and let my wife and I come up with a plan for what to do next while you all, what? Wait for me to tell you what to do? Xavier's jerking off in my apartment. Helene and Kai come back from their kingdom to bitch and moan that we're not doing enough while they're not actually doing anything. You don't get to stand in my house and tell me I'm not doing enough, not after my wife just got the shock of her life and probably sacrificed her mental health because Galen is actually back without any of us being alerted! Now, if you will excuse me, I'll be ensuring Daphne has every weapon at her disposal."

Essos doesn't wait for anyone to respond. He slides his hand into mine and tugs me away from everyone else. When I stumble, he changes directions and leads me back up to our bedroom. Once the door is closed behind me, he pulls me into his arms, enveloping me in a crushing hug that I'm more than happy to stay in.

Slowly, our breathing and heartbeats match up until Essos

releases me. He moves toward the window, facing away from me as he runs his hands through his hair.

"I'm a monster for snapping at them, but I'm tired of the constant judgement. Maybe I was the protective big brother for too long, ready to jump in and take care of their problems at a moment's notice, but I can't do it anymore. I can't be everything to everyone. You and I can train tomorrow. I can practically feel you still shaking from the adrenaline letdown with Galen."

I tug on his hand until he spins around to face me. He crashes back into my arms.

"You are not wrong..."

"But I'm still an asshole."

"No, but you need to ask them for help. I'm sure if you had been specific about what you needed from them, they would have gladly jumped in."

"It's not my job to hold their hands. I'm navigating this situation with just as much information as they have. They have access to the same books."

"You're right. But I don't think yelling at them is going to make the situation any better. Finn is right; him not being able to receive message requests is a problem."

"You think I don't know that, Daphne? You think I'm not wondering what sort of implications that has? But I can't control that. In fact, I can't control anything outside of how I can help you prepare and better protect yourself. There was a moment, when you shouted for me, that I think my soul left my body because I was afraid something had happened to you again, and it very well could have. Galen was back, not on our schedule, but on Octavia's. So yes, I'm in a bad fucking mood right now, and I'm taking my anger out on everyone else. I'm usually pretty mild, I like to think anyway, so let me get this out of my system now. And tonight, after I've exhausted you in bed, I'll apologize."

"Okay," I tell him, because I don't know what other comfort I can give him. He's made it clear this is something he has to work through.

"Don't let *my* fear trick you into thinking you aren't strong enough. Knowing you can hold your own and wanting you to are very different things."

Essos tilts my head back with both hands. I meet his eyes, giving him this and refocusing on the task at hand instead of the things we can't control. He's right; it's easier when we have something smaller to contend with.

"I understand," I tell him, and I do. If all things were equal, I wouldn't want him in the middle of all this either, but we don't have that luxury.

No matter what happens, we don't have a choice over how entrenched we are and the consequences that come with that.

While Essos goes to work out some of his stress, I nap, something that feels too decadent an undeserved, but making those vine guards took a whole lot more out of me than I wanted to admit. Curled beside me on the bed are two of my dogs and my cat, who seems to be on edge too. Even as I go to the bathroom, all three follow me.

It seems Galen isn't the only one with guards following him. My dogs track my every step as I shower and move into the hallway in search of my husband. Knowing that Galen is around here somewhere makes me uneasy, but I won't be made to be afraid in my own home. I didn't give him that advantage during the Trials and I won't give it to him now. Having killed him almost feels like I've leveled the playing field. We're now tied one-to-one, and I'll take another win if it comes to that.

Dion is walking out of the room he shares with Finn when I emerge. His back is to me, so he doesn't see me approach as he walks away. It's probably for the best because I wouldn't even know what to say to him right now. Still, I'm going to take the chance that his absence has afforded me.

Not that I have a better idea of what I'm going to say to Finn, but I have to try. Gingerly, I tap on the door and then step inside without waiting for a response. Rude? Maybe, but this is my house, and I know Finn.

"Who is there?" Finn demands, his head cocking in my direction. The dogs enter the room ahead of me and his attention shifts toward them. "Daphne?"

I smile faintly before going to sit beside him in the chair there. He's on the bed, sitting up with the curtains drawn. His face is almost completely wrapped. There are tufts of blonde hair sticking up above the bandage.

"How did you know?"

"What? Are you expecting I'm going to tell you that I could *smell* you and know it was you? What a fucking cliché. No, I heard your dogs, and if what Dion told me is true, then I assume Essos isn't letting you alone, which means your guard dogs are with you, ergo, Daphne."

I snort. "I wasn't thinking anything like that, but thanks for dissuading me of that notion and for laying out your very clever powers of deduction. Shall I call you Finn Holmes from now on?"

"You can fuck right off, Daphne. I don't want to see anyone. I can only assume you saw Dion leave and that's why you thought you could ambush me."

"I didn't intend to ambush you," I say softly. "I'm going to touch your hand." I slide my hand into his. I expect him to pull away, but he doesn't.

Finn clasps my hand tightly. "Came to see the ruins of my beautiful face?"

"No, I came to see how my friend was faring with all this. Are you in pain?" I notice then just how tightly Finn is holding himself, with his shoulders nearly bunched up to his ears.

He opens his mouth, but hesitates before answering me. "Yes. Some."

I doubt his assertion that he's only in "some" pain. "Why don't you tell Dion? I'm sure he can get a healer. Callie would probably also help you."

"Because I don't want anyone to see me like this. Because no one is saying it, but I can *feel* the I-told-you-so's on the tips of their tongues. I was just so *mad* having to watch Essos cry over your limp body again. And then you wouldn't wake up, and I'm not blaming you, not even a little bit, but I was angry that Posey still seemed to have the upper hand, and we had this information, and I might as well check that we could do something about it. You were so still lying in that bed... I thought that maybe we couldn't save you. That we opened the gates to the Underworld, but at what cost? And Essos wasn't leaving your side, and they all told me not to, but I *had* to try."

As Finn is telling me all this, I'm growing herbs across the room that I can use as a poultice for his eyes. I may not be a healer, but I know the herbs that can help and I'm determined to do at least that.

I slowly release Finn's hand and wait for him to completely let it go before I start to make the concoction that should help aid with pain and healing.

"And you know what, Daphne? It was all for a fake. The fucking scepter I *thought* I had was fake. I know they're trying not to tell me, but the really awesome thing about losing my sight is that now my other senses are better, so when Essos was gently letting Dion down in the hallway, I *heard* all about my fucking failure. Because that's what I am, a godsdamned failure."

I sniffle, determined not to cry, determined not to make my feelings his burden. "It sounds like you're in the same boat we all are, getting played by Posey left, right, and center."

"I know I didn't particularly love Cassius, but no one deserved to die like that. Not even him. And now it was all for nothing. Posey still has the damned scepter and dagger, Cassius is dead, and I don't have eyes. And I have to listen to my partner cry in the shower like I don't know his heart is breaking. This is the punishment I deserve."

"It is *not* a punishment you deserve, not even a little bit. I'm going to take your bandage off and change it."

"Fine, whatever."

I start to slowly unwrap it while trying to brace myself for what I'm going to see. Nothing could have prepared me for the sight of his livid, red skin and the gouges along his eye sockets. I have to bite the inside of my cheek to stop myself from making an audible sound.

"You didn't deserve this, Finn. Not one bit of it."

"Spare me the platitudes, Daphne. What's the next thing you're going to tell me? That I'll get through this? That no one sees me differently? So funny since I can't see any more. I can't see a damn thing, so, kindly fuck off, Daphne."

I say silent, cleaning and re-dressing the wound. "You're not scaring me, Finn. I'll be here, even if it's just sitting with you."

"*Get out,*" Finn hisses at me. "I don't want reminders of what I've lost, so if you're done playing Florence fucking Nightingale, *get out.*"

Finn turns his head away from me, and for now, as he adjusts to life with his injury, I'll give him some space. It's still too fresh, and I would be an asshole to push him harder right now, but the best thing I can do is keep reaching out, and reaching out, and reaching out until he knows I won't give up on him.

I summon him a tea and place it in his hands. "This should also help with your pain."

Finn lifts it, and I flinch, thinking he might throw it, but instead he whispers something so faint I almost don't hear it. "Thank you."

I'm not eager to run into Galen, or anyone really, so I hide out in my bedroom all day. I try to give myself a mental break. If I don't, I'm going to lose it, so I chose to get lost in another book about Princess Lorelei.

I'm curled up on a chair by the window with Waffles on my lap and Dave on the floor at my feet when Essos walks in.

"How is my sweet, loving wife doing today?" Essos asks, planting a kiss on the top of my head.

"Tired. Trying some escapism. I think I'll see if Finn wants me to read to him, but it might have to wait."

"That makes sense. I talked to Dion today after his outburst. After my outburst. There were apologies, there were drinks shared. I think we're both feeling two different kinds of pressures, and I get it. His partner is hurting and he can't fix it, so I get."

"Any chance you got a hold of your mother?" The real elephant in the room.

"No, I think she's hiding from me."

"Good. She should be afraid," I say with a scowl.

Essos drops onto the edge of the bed. "When I get my hands on her, she's going to wish she hadn't crossed me. Tomorrow, we're going to try this training thing again."

"How about tonight we focus on seeing how close we can get?" I tease, putting my bookmark in. Nothing like a well-written threesome to get you in the mood.

Essos raises his eyebrow and grins. "I bet we can get pretty close."

He gets up, prowling across the room toward me, and I can't help my answering grin.

THE NEXT DAY, we try training again, heading out to the training arena uninterrupted.

Essos and I had a lazy morning in bed, until we heard something shatter in Finn's room. That got us up and going. The longer we delay, the worse things get all around.

"The amount of power I used to make those vine guards knocked me flat on my ass. I don't want to be that vulnerable, and I don't know if I can even come close to using that amount of power again," I tell Essos as I stretch.

"We will find new ways for you to do what you want without using the same amount of power. I want to teach you to work smarter, not harder."

With that, Essos creates a sword made from shadows the way I make them from vines. There's no hesitation when he swings it at my neck. I can parry or die—not that he would let that happen, but Essos is counting on my fight or flight response to kick in.

I create a sword and deflect just in time, only maybe not, because his sword grazes my cheek, and wetness trickles out. I watch him fight his urge to react to the cut before he swings the sword again.

Since he's fighting with actual steel and I'm not, I have just enough time to reinforce my sword with more wood before blocking him again. So begins this dance that has me on the defense. Every so often, I manage to impress the man. My movements lack the grace I had when I wasn't pregnant, my defensive moves more lumbering than artful.

Essos stumbles when I manage to cut him behind the knee. He's so proud, I can feel it emanating off him in waves, but he doesn't let up, not until I'm pinned under him with the blade at my throat.

"I let you do that," I pant, tying to ease air into my lungs. Essos doesn't have his full weight on me, but he has settled himself below my abdomen somewhat uncomfortably.

"Of course, you did, love." Essos tosses his sword to the side, letting it dissolve back to its natural smoky state before it disappears altogether. He holds out a hand to help me to my feet. I gladly take it, letting my own weapon dissolve to dust.

When I'm upright, I sway, the movement having been too fast. Essos's hand finds the small of my back, and he holds me against him until I feel less lightheaded. He presses a kiss to my forehead.

"I'm really fine," I swear, not at all feeling it.

"You feel warm," Essos hedges, loosening his grip on me. When he's sure I'm able to stand on my own, he lets go.

"Is that what you're doing every time you kiss my forehead—checking if I'm feverish?"

A glass of water appears in Essos's hand, and he holds it out to me. "No, not every time. Excuse me for trying to keep my girls safe."

I drink the water greedily before reducing the glass to sand and raising a new weapon.

Essos shakes his head. "No. I want you to practice fighting with your powers, and I have a gift for that." He drops a small satchel into my hands.

"What's this?" I ask. It's about the size of a large coin purse, but the insides move smoothly against each other, like a bag of rice. I don't need Essos to explain the contents to me. I can feel them calling out.

"They're seeds," he says, brushing a strand of hair behind my ear.

I look up at him, my expression telling him, *No shit*. "I know that, but why?" I tug open the drawstring and run my fingers through all the untapped potential. Each seed tells me what it can be, what it can grow into. They whisper what they can become and what they want to do. It's an interesting collection, to say the least.

"Tell me how you create your dagger and manifest your ability." His tone is patient as he asks me to explain.

"I draw power from the earth, and the seeds and gains of dirt become what I ask. My dagger is easy, because I can draw it from myself. But mostly, I have to manifest the creation from nothing."

"I think it will be less taxing on you to not have to draw it out from yourself. Those little beauties will be good for battle. These—" he drops another bag into my hand "—will be for practice."

I can hear the anguish from the seeds in this bag. They want to make beauty, not cruelty. I reason with them that even roses have thorns.

"What are you doing with seeds in the home of the Goddess of Spring?" I meet Essos's gaze and hate a little bit that I did. He looks sad, gazing at the small bag in my hands.

"I used them to maintain your garden." He pauses, letting this sink in for me before continuing. "I was more gifted with death than with life, but I wanted to keep as much of you as I could." A wave of his grief crashes against both of us, and I want to hug him and hold him. "Anyway, if there are other plants you want, we can get them for you, but let's start small."

I throw my arms around his neck, and he takes a moment to breathe me in.

"Let's see what you can do, flower girl."

Essos and I step away from each other, and I take a moment to think. I grab a small handful of seeds, tossing them at Essos and propelling them forward. They grow roots and bloom, and then I turn them to ash, so Essos is forced to inhale the remains of the flowers. It sends him to a coughing fit, his eyes watering.

I frown. I hate doing this to him.

When he doubles over, bracing his hands on his knees, I approach him. He must see my feet getting closer, because he holds out a hand, stopping me, then gives a thumbs up before he's upright once more.

"Again," he demands, his eyes still watery, but I comply.

He drills me for hours, and we work together, discussing what types of flowers and other seeds I can use and what I can do with them. We practice and practice and practice until I sway on my feet.

"I'm sorry," Essos sputters, running to catch me before I collapse.

I grab hold of him. "Nothing to be sorry for. I was just trying to see if I could get out of more practice by feigning exhaustion. Looks like it's working."

His brow dips in concern. "I'm sure you're not at all actually exhausted, but to go along with the charade, do you mind if I whisk you off to bed? After witnessing such impressive feats of power, I want to have my wicked way with you."

He wipes the sweat from my forehead, and I cringe. "Don't get rid of my glistening awesomeness," I object.

Essos scoops me into his arms, hugging me to his chest. "Are you possibly delirious, love?"

I wrap my arms around his neck, knowing what comes next. "Possibly," I admit, waiting for him to take me to our safe haven.

Before we can leave, Octavia approaches us. I thought I was exhausted, but now I'm squirming to get out of Essos's grip to give his mother a piece of my mind.

She speaks before I have a chance.

"Your dog is here, back from the mortal realm."

We don't hesitate to walk back to the house, sweaty and exhausted. I don't know how much more I can take of this seemingly endless day. The three of us enter through the back of the house to find Spot is curled up on his bed by the front door, watching Dion block the doorway.

"I don't care why you're here. *I* don't want you here," Dion is telling someone angrily.

"This isn't about you, Dion. This isn't even about us. This is about Finn. Helene wouldn't have called me if it wasn't serious, so tell me *what* is going on."

We pause before walking into the foyer. Essos and I exchange a look. I feel a little guilty about eavesdropping, but this *is* my house, and if what Spot needs to convey was urgent, he wouldn't be lying there eavesdropping too.

Dion is standing at my front door, gripping the doorknob so hard I think I can hear the metal crunch. Before him, I can just make out the form of a woman in leather pants. I know that voice. I know exactly who is at my front door.

Bria.

Goddess of the Hunt.

I still don't know what happened between Bria, Dion, and Finn while I was dead, only that they were together, and that ended during the time I was gone.

"Why did you stop walking?" Octavia asks from behind us. I forgot that I need to have words with her, and those words are going to be blisteringly angry words, but that needs to wait because now we've been caught.

Both Bria and Dion snap their attention toward us.

Bria's red hair is styled in twin French braids, and her green eyes survey me from top to bottom. "The Phoenix Queen."

There's no inflection in her voice for me to determine how she feels about me and my return.

"Bria, I'm surprised I didn't see you at any of the Trials," I say serenely.

She snorts, then crosses her arms. Slung over one shoulder is a duffel bag. "You know I have no patience for the bullshit of the Council."

"Daphne," Dion intercedes. "Would you please tell her to leave your house?"

"No, I'm here for Finn. You don't get to tell me that I need to leave," Bria snaps at Dion.

"Right, well, this isn't a spat I'm getting in the middle of," I say, stepping, well, into the middle of it. "Finn is asleep. You can come in for now. When Finn wakes up, ask him if you can stay."

Dion turns on me, brown eyes flashing. "You shouldn't get in the middle of something you know nothing about."

"You can tell me," I offer, expecting neither of them to agree.

"Yeah, why don't you tell her, Dion? Tell her how you told lies about me to Finn and ruined what we had."

"Only if you tell her about how you started to see—"

"*Enough*," I snap. "I don't actually want to hear your tit-for-tat story." It's a lie. I do want to get to the heart of their juicy little spat, but there is a strange tightness in my stomach. Or lower. Xavier emerges from the library and I address him. "Can you find Helene and see what she wanted to do about this?" I gesture in the direction of Bria before dropping my hand to my stomach.

Essos uncrosses his arms and places one hand on my back. "What's wrong?" he asks, placing his other hand over mine. The fight with Bria is forgotten.

Xavier is a half-second behind Essos, but he waits for my answer.

"I don't know. I feel off—not me, but my stomach."

Xavier reaches a hand toward me but waits for me to okay it. "Are you in pain?"

"No, it just... feels weird."

Xavier touches me, and I watch his face, waiting for him to give me something. There is a small tick up of his lips. "You're okay. It's just your baby moving."

Laughter bubbles out of me, and it's enough to relax everyone in the room. I stand up straighter, smoothing my hand along the curve of my stomach. "Right, of course, it is."

"I'll take care of this," Xavier offers, gesturing again at Bria and Dion.

"I am not something to be taken care of. I am here to help with Finn," Bria repeats.

"Go," Xavier gestures, ushering us forward.

Essos clicks his tongue, and Spot follows us toward his office. "You too, Mother," Essos calls, glaring at Octavia.

My husband is calm as he closes the door to his office behind us. He points at Spot and gestures toward a dog bed in the corner. "Sit," Essos snarls. I'm surprised at his vitriol, until I realize he's looking at his mother.

She perches on the edge of the couch. "I don't appreciate being spoken to like one of your dogs."

"Perhaps if you were honest and not sneaky, I wouldn't have to do so. Can you tell me, Mother dearest, *why* my baby brother was sitting in my dining room yesterday morning, where he accosted my wife?"

Octavia presses her lips together hard enough that they turn white. For a second, I think regret flickers over her face as she looks at me. "You weren't going to bring my son back, so I took matters into my own hands."

"You're telling me that instead of protecting Daphne *like you promised*, you stole the dagger to bring Galen back?" Essos booms.

I take a different approach. "Octavia, I was unconscious for three days. There was no delay for any reason other than we just needed to regroup."

"All you seem to do is regroup. You take one action, then discuss it while Posey is out there growing more powerful by the day. I decided I wasn't willing to wait while you hashed out what to do next. So, yes, I was, as you called it, 'sneaky,' because I didn't trust you to do what you said you would."

"If anyone is untrustworthy here, Mother, it's you."

We're all silent a moment, waiting to see if someone will crack first with an apology.

Octavia sighs. "I can't carry you and do all the hard work. Titus and I created Solarem. We created mortals. I gave up the love of my life so that you all could flourish. The mortal realm isn't what I thought it would be, and the rest of you have squandered what I've built. Excuse me if my willingness to help is spent. Galen's resurrection was my reward. The rest of the world can burn."

"What is it going to take for you to commit to helping?" Essos asks, still holding out hope for one of his parents to be the person he thinks they are. I walk to where Essos stands behind his desk and place a hand on his shoulder.

Octavia laughs bleakly. "There is no more help I can give you. The last thing on your to-do list besides kill Posey is to put the veil between the realms back in place. You won't be able to do it. You need the blood of..." She pauses, catching herself. "You need the blood of the God and Goddess Supreme together."

"You weren't at the wedding, so how did Posey manage to remove it without you?" I point out.

Octavia gives me a Cheshire cat smile. "Are you certain I wasn't there?"

I think back on it. I remember Miranda, who I now know was Octavia, disappearing from my wedding in all the chaos, but could she have given Posey her blood to use for the ritual that ripped the veil away. "Could the blood of your children work?"

"Their blood is too diluted for that. No, that veil is never dropping again, unless by some miracle you have some of Titus's blood lying around here in a vial somewhere."

Dread forms a lump in my stomach. We need to find a real way to make sure the mortal realm doesn't attack us. The threat of that adds a host of complications for our life that I don't think we're ready for, including maybe even needing a representative to act as an ambassador. A worry for tomorrow.

"Why are you being so difficult? There has to be another way," Essos nearly pleads.

"I'm not being difficult, Essos. I just don't care. I don't know what about that isn't clear." There is a slight relaxation of her shoulders. "I'm done. I'm done with Solarem and the mortal realm. I've spent eons of my life caring, and what did it get me? Not a whole lot, so I'm trying something new. I'm trying *chaos.*"

"Chaos isn't working for me, so I'll give you one last chance, Mother. Get on board, or get out of my house." Essos looks at Spot, almost purposefully avoiding the hurt look on his mother's face. "You can leave. My wife and I have much to discuss, and you've broken our trust." Octavia rises and heads for the door. "One last thing, Mother." She pauses and turns to face him. "If you don't turn the dagger over to Xavier by tonight, I don't care what promises we've made, I'll chain Galen in a metal box and drop him into the ocean so deep that even Kai won't be able to find him."

She clenches her jaw before walking out of the room.

I wait until Octavia has closed the door behind her before pulling Essos into my arms. Slowly, he enfolds me in his grip, squeezing just a hair over the line of uncomfortable, but if this is bringing him any amount of comfort, I can suck it up.

"I'm sorry," I tell him.

"You have nothing to apologize for." Essos presses a kiss to the top of my head.

"I'm sorry your mother is a monster. I'm sorry I've managed to come between you and your whole family. I'm sorry that Octavia won't help more."

Essos releases me to sit on the couch. "Come here, boy." He beckons to Spot, who leaps at the chance to smother Essos and jump on the couch. I smile at the sound of Essos's laughter before sitting on the arm of the couch. Spot takes this as his cue to climb over Essos and lave me with licks too. "You have nothing to be sorry for, my love. It's all circumstances we already knew about, all circumstances outside your control. I should have known she wasn't going to be helpful. She wasn't before now, so this isn't exactly a grand surprise."

"You're allowed to be disappointed that your parents aren't who you thought they were," I tell him gently, scratching at his scalp.

"Stop being insightful. It looks like we're needed in the mortal realm. We should shower and head there before I change my mind about forcing my mother's hand."

"Not going to lock this princess away in her tower?" I tease, pressing a line of kisses along his neck.

Essos pulls me onto his lap, where I land with a yelp. "While my brother is in this house? Fuck no." His gaze softens. "Be honest with me: are you all right?"

I give him a quick kiss before threading my fingers together at the nape of his neck. "I'll be okay. I'm a little shaken up at the confrontation, but mostly, I'm just relieved it's over. It's like she ripped off the Band-Aid while I was sleeping. Sometimes, anticipation is the worst part."

"You are appallingly relaxed about this."

"I wouldn't say I'm relaxed. I've just accepted that his coming back was inevitable. Now, rather than making myself sick wondering when it was going to happen, it's already happened. It's done."

Essos is silent, and I wonder what he's thinking. "Let's go. Your father is probably waiting for us. I also want you out of this house. Maybe we should move back into the apartment in Solarem."

I smack his chest lightly. "We will not be driven from our own home. We just need to come up with a way to keep Galen in line."

"That's why Callie is here. I'm the only who know knows how to get to her sons. If Galen wants any hope of being able to meet them, my brother will behave."

"Let's hope that is enough."

When I emerge from my shower, I find Cat sitting in my room.

She glares at me. "You scared the shit out of me."

"I'm sorry, but honestly, I think I did more damage to Galen this morning than he did to me."

"That's not what I meant. Having to watch you bleed out was scary as fuck. Every time I think I have a handle on being a goddess, something like you dying happens."

"Or you falling into a power rage that only Xavier can snap you out of?"

"I don't want to talk about it," she grumbles, but I get the feeling that, if I sit in silence, she'll spill like a waterfall.

"Okay, but I think there *is* something you want to talk about." I lean toward her, one eyebrow raised.

Cat turns scarlet. "I mean, you didn't miss much. There was a lot of fussing over Finn and you and Essos, and I gave Xavier a blow job, and Kai has taken over my training since Finn isn't up to it anymore, and Callie offered to help show me the ways of healing, and—"

"I'm sorry, way to try to bury the lead. You did what now with Xavier?" I conjure us drinks, hugging my tea close to my chest.

"Don't you want to talk about my powers? Helene told me I better get control over the fertility part of my powers before she and Kai get pregnant again."

"If you really don't want to talk about Xavier, we don't have to, but you wouldn't have told me if a part of you didn't want to."

Cat stews over my words for a moment, taking a sip from her coffee. She flicks her hand at my fireplace, igniting it. The room is suffused with warmth, and I readjust, assuming that she's going to start talking. The water on my skin starts to dry, reminding me that I *do* need to get dressed, but I don't want to interrupt this moment, so I notch my towel tighter and sit.

"It was so shitty of me, and I really shouldn't have done it, but I was crying, and he was comforting me because I was afraid you weren't going to wake up, and I just felt like...like I was to blame. He was holding me, telling me that it wasn't my fault, blah blah blah, and I could feel his dick pressing against my ass, and then I fell to my knees and licked him like a lollipop until he came in my mouth."

I'm silent, waiting to hear if there is more. Cat huffs and continues. "Then this asshole is like, 'If I had known you wanted me, I would have eaten some pineapple to make it sweeter for you.'"

"And did he reciprocate?"

"I didn't let him. I literally ran from the room. Not my proudest moment."

I study my friend in her rich purple gown as she tries to hide behind her drink.

"Do you want me to tell Xavier to get lost? He can be like a dog with a bone when it comes to women."

"You mean a dog with a boner? No, he's really been good about keeping his distance and listening to me and what I want. But what if he's just chasing me because of what the Fates said when Galen died? That he and I were supposed to be together? I've just discovered this whole immortal life, and he's already fucked his way through every woman and creature he's not related to, present company excluded."

"Are you saying you want to date around?"

"I'm saying he's had thousands of years to fuck around, and deciding on me is easy because I'm the second-to-last piece of tail he hasn't had."

"If you want time to sleep around, Xavier is going to be the last person who will tell you not to. And if he tries to tell you not to, then he can go fuck himself."

"I don't know. It's not like we've even talked about a future. And he's not acting like he's entitled to me; you know I wouldn't stand for that. When this is all said and done, I was supposed to be Queen of the Pantheon, but what does that mean? Will I have to marry Xavier? Share his bed? Give him children? I just don't know what I want. Rafferty actually propositioned me after he blocked my memories, and I scoffed. I told him if I wanted mediocre dick, I knew who to call. Probably not my finest moment, but I felt so out of control, and knocking his arrogant ass down a peg or two felt good."

"He deserves it."

"Rafferty couldn't help you, right?"

"No, but I actually got my memories back during the wedding when Essos and I kissed. We were so focused on the wedding, and then opening the gates, it's never felt like a good time to make confetti rain down because I can now remember that time Kai had no idea we were throwing him a surprise party, and he walked into the room dick out because he was ready for his birthday present."

Cat scoffs. "But like, was it as big as I think it is?"

I laugh. "Bigger. I truly don't know how Helene takes it. He's definitely rearranging her internal organs."

She and I are both in giggles when Essos steps into the room, fresh from his shower. His towel is slung low on his hips, and I can't stop my gaze as it tracks a solitary bead of water moving down his body.

"I'm going to leave you two *alone*," Cat teases, getting to her feet in a rush.

Essos chuckles. "Don't leave on my account." He runs his hands through his wet hair, accumulating water and flinging the droplets at me. I giggle again, because it feels so much like how things used to be that I start to see hope. I start to see what life could look like when we're on the other side of this.

Cat gives me a wink. "Nope. I have to go try to conjure a cake that doesn't taste like plastic. Wish me luck!" She gives me a kiss on the cheek before leaving and closing the bedroom door behind her.

I turn my attention back to Essos, not at all surprised to find his hawkish gaze on me. I point a warning finger in his direction. "We do not have time for this."

Essos crosses to me anyway and tugs on the knot holding my towel. "I don't see why not."

"Because Spot's been here for hours."

My refusal is half-hearted, because I follow it up by pulling Essos's towel from his hips and letting it drop to the floor. Really, I want this. I want to feel Essos bumping the back of my throat as he fucks my face, moaning my name through his release. I want to have a king on his knees before me, spreading my thighs as he feasts on me.

The training helped remind me that I'm not powerless. This will reinforce that I am a queen capable of making my own decisions. Others might try to force me back into the role of pawn, but this queen is fighting to defend more than just her king.

25

My dad opens the door before we can even approach.

"This is your home too, sweetie, you don't have to knock," he says, sweeping me into a hug before shaking Essos's hand. I chuckle, not bothering to point out that I didn't even have a chance to knock.

"Are we supposed to bow?" my mom asks, walking in from the kitchen. When she sees Spot, Shadow, and Dave at my side, she turns around and gets treats for them all.

Essos smiles. "Besides the fact that your daughter abhors such deference, I will also say it is not at all necessary."

"Is everything all right?" I ask jumping in. "We haven't heard from you since we last visited. I thought there would be more messages through Spot." I can't keep the concern out of my voice. The concern that maybe our timeline is getting more condensed. The concern that maybe the president will want to see if he can bomb us anyway, just to flex his military might.

"Oh, we thought it was a one-use only," my dad says with a shrug. "No, everything is all right. The president was hoping to set up a meeting with you all, eventually. See if you mean us any harm, or if we should expect zombies again. Also, no one really believes you're gods. It took a lot of favors to get me into the oval office. Besides, I think your mom enjoyed having Spot here."

My mom hasn't torn her gaze away from my stomach. "You've really popped since we saw you last."

"Right," my dad mutters. "Matters of national security, but let's focus on how much weight Daphne has gained."

My mom whacks him right at center mass, hard enough that he lets out an *oomph*. "She is pregnant; she's not putting on weight. And that is your grandchild. Have you thought about *that,* crankypants?"

He turns to her. "You might have been able to accept this whole situation like Daphne was telling you her favorite color is red, but I am still digesting the very large meal that is gods and zombies and reincarnation."

"And that you're going to be a grandfather," she points out.

"Yes, that too."

I smooth my hands over my stomach absently before asking, "So, you need us here to meet with the President? Will they even allow that? We're gods; they can't really frisk us. I can make a weapon in the time it takes someone to blink, and they can shoot me and it will hurt a ton, but we won't die."

Essos turns to face me, cutting my parents out of the conversation somewhat. "We need to put this off as long as possible. I have an idea, but we need to talk to Rafferty again."

I make a disgusted noise in the back of my throat. "You know he had the nerve to proposition Cat when he was in *our* home last?"

"I can't say I did, and I can't say that Xavier knows that either."

I muse over the idea of Xavier finding out. I wouldn't hate seeing Xavier staking his claim on Cat in front of the God of Memory, though it would probably violate some friend code, and I really *shouldn't* meddle, but damn it, I want her to have a happily ever after too.

"What is your idea?" I press him. My eyes search his face for any hint of what he's thinking.

"I'm thinking we need to see if your idea for helping the souls in the Underworld forget what happened to them could somehow be implemented in the mortal realm."

I can't help the gasp I let out. I mean, I've considered that it might be best if everyone in the mortal realm forgot too, but doing that has the same issue of needing a distribution system to get to everyone, and how to target these specific memories. It feels overwhelming to consider, and worst of all, it would require Rafferty, which brings us to the issue at hand.

"We would need Rafferty," I echo him.

"Indeed," Essos confirms rubbing his chin.

"What is a Rafferty?" my dad asks.

"The God of Memory," I absently explain. "But how are we going to find him?" He's hard enough to track down on a normal day. We needed Finn to find him before, and if he can't even get messages, what are the chances he can find the elusive god?

Essos turns to Spot and whistles. While the dog had been content in the dog bed my parents apparently got him, he jumps up and runs to Essos for his command.

"Find Rafferty, then find us," Essos orders.

Spot gives a small bark of acknowledgement before he's gone.

"I will *never* get used to that," my dad says, still staring at the spot where Spot disappeared.

"He would do it in the morning when it was time for his walk or for food. He would be in one part of the house one minute and the next...*poof*...he was by our side, leash or bowl in his mouth." My mom is squatting to pet Shadow.

I give my mom a smile. "Don't let him fool you. They can be fearsome things."

"Yes, I bet you can," she says not to me, but to Shadow, who has rolled over with her tongue flopping out.

"How have things been since the eradication of the zombies, Phil?" Essos asks. It's strange, not only that he's making conversation with my dad, but that it's about zombies. So many parts of my life that I never expected to intersect are colliding. I can only hope that, when this is all over, I'll be able to introduce Phil and Melinda to Ron and Linda, the parents who raised me and the parents who birthed me.

My dad turns to look at me, aghast. "Did you ever think the eradication of zombies would be a topic of discussion? With a god no less?" He turns back to Essos. "Did you do something about the clean up too? After the zombies all... died? I don't know what happened. They all stopped fighting, and then they just ceased to be there. It's been a little bit of a reset. That's why the president hasn't been too worried about dealing with your floating city, but to be honest, I know he's getting daily briefings about what you're doing up there."

"My siblings took care of the cleanup."

"Can the government see into Solarem?" I ask as my mom starts to herd us into the living room while we await Spot's return. I don't think he'll be gone that long, but at the same time I want to stick as close to the one-hour transportation wait time as possible. As our little pomegranate has gotten larger, I'm getting less afraid of something happening to her during this jaunt, but I also haven't been eager to leave the house. What was once my prison is now my safe haven.

My mom waves her hand generally at the sky. "I mean, they see your floating land mass or whatever the media is calling it these days, but it's not like we're able to see what your streets or technology or anything look like. From the reports I've seen, there's some sort of haze or mist around it. There may have been a few attempts to get close, but each time it's tried, the jets run out of fuel and fall. I think that's what scares everyone the most. You're hovering over us, and we're just waiting for the other shoe to drop. Well, not me. I know that you don't intend any harm, but the general world. But again, the zombies were sort of distracting," she explains. She sits beside me on the couch, then gestures at my bump.

"Of course," I tell her, responding to her silent plea.

She places both hands on my stomach and leans close. "I know you're going to be some sort of god or goddess and have a king and queen for parents, but that doesn't mean that your grammy isn't going to spoil you."

My gaze catches Essos's, and I can feel tears well in my eyes. "We'll figure out some way for you to see her."

"Her?" My dad asks.

"Yes, we're having a girl," Essos confirms, giving me a wink.

My dad brings out shots of vodka for him and Essos, and I have to hide my laugh behind my hand because my husband is not a vodka man, nor is he a shots guy, but he refuses to say no to my dad.

"I have to warn you, son, there's been discussion of a special mission. They haven't wanted to shoot a missile at you, because for now you haven't done anything but exist, but people are getting restless. They want answers. If you're planning something to hide your little island or make it disappear again, you should do it sooner rather than later."

My father toasts this claim with a third shot, after which Spot returns to us. My mom is more than happy to reward him with treats, which gets the other two dogs excited, and for a second, I can see it. I can see our happily ever after with my families all together. From having our baby fawned over by two sets of grandparents to having my dad discuss the merits of golf with Kai. I can see it all, and I want it.

I didn't need the encouragement to have something more worth fighting for, but it did give me a goal to work toward. That's why we let Spot rush us from my parents and to Rafferty.

I'm not sure what I expected from the God of Memory's home, but a dark cave off the coast of Ireland wasn't it. Spot takes us to a rainy cliff overlooking a raging ocean below. I can see the cavern Rafferty must be living in just ahead of us. The air around it looks oily, like there's a film over it that would force a mortal's gaze to avert.

"I feel like we're going to turn around and grumpy Luke Skywalker is going to emerge and lecture me about the force."

"I don't know what you're talking about," Essos whispers in my direction as he hedges in front of me.

I stop walking. "Seriously? You've gotten all my other pop culture references before now."

Essos stops walking too, so he can face me. "You misunderstand. I got your reference. I just don't acknowledge the sequel trilogy as canon."

"Okay, fine, but you can also not gaslight me about it. You don't like it...fine, but you understood my reference perfectly well."

"If you two are attempting stealth, I have to say, you're doing a shit job." The god we're seeking emerges and runs a hand over his head. "How did you find me?"

"Spot has your scent," Essos supplies. Beside him, Spot bares his teeth.

Rafferty steps farther into his cave, not denying us entrance, but we're still on guard. We walk farther and farther in. Above us, string lights brighten the darkness until we're in what feels like a living room. I expect the space to feel dark and damp, but it's warm and almost homey. The crackling fireplace certainly helps.

"What do you want from me this time?" Rafferty walks to a small teakettle and removes it from the warmer before pouring three cups.

Since I'm wet from being outside, I take it, but before I do anything else, I sniff it. After having Ellie and Posey attempt to bind my powers during the Trials, I'm wary of tea.

"It's safe. I may not be your ally, but I'm also not your enemy."

"We actually want to discuss a few things with you," I say, taking a sip and letting the warmth flow through me.

"Well, spit it out. I haven't got all day."

"It would be best if the mortals forget about the zombie apocalypse and that they saw Solarem," Essos tells him.

I suck my lower lip into my mouth before I jump in. "If the souls in the Underworld could also forget about what they endured while being released to the mortal realm, I think that would also be beneficial."

Rafferty sits but doesn't gesture for us to do the same. Our dogs sit themselves between Rafferty and us, seeming to be at ease, but there is a marked difference from how they were at my parents' house versus how they are now.

"You want me to come in and clean up your mess, is that it?" Rafferty gives the appearance of considering the request as he brings his cup up to his lips. I think we have him as his head starts to bob, like it's in a nod. "I'm going to have to pass, but thanks for thinking of me."

"My apologies, Rafferty," Essos bows his head in supplication, but then lifts just his gaze to the other god. "You misunderstand. This wasn't a request. We are here to come up with possible solutions to the problem at hand and to see how we can best achieve these aims. Or I'll have to have a conversation with my brother."

Rafferty snorts. "What care do I have for what you discuss with your brother? Which brother would that be, anyway? The one who killed your wife or the one that is the root cause of all our recent troubles?"

"Make no mistake, Rafferty, the root cause of all of this is Posey and Posey alone," I interrupt. "I have no problem having a conversation with Cat to convince her she needs to come clean with Xavier about how you attempted to abuse your position as the God of Memory so she would sleep with you."

"That is not what happened and you know it," Rafferty snaps, getting to his feet.

"I'm sorry, my memory isn't what it used to be, but who will Xavier really believe? His sister-in-law who is best friends with the woman destined to be his queen, or the hermit of a god who can't be bothered to do things for the greater good?" My tone stays perfectly pleasant as I push him.

When Rafferty narrows his eyes at me, I figure it's time to flex my powers. It's not my fault he chose to live in the side of a cliff. My power pokes and prods around me, looking for the best access, and then I find it—a tree root that's close.

I give it a mental tug, and the root reacts, driving into the ceiling. The root reaches for Rafferty, and I would be a liar if I said it didn't give me a perverse pleasure to watch him hit the ground to avoid the root.

"I don't want to deal in threats, but you've proven yourself unwilling to work with me, so that must mean you're working against me, against us." My voice is still sweet as can be, and I take a sip of my tea.

"I can wipe your memories with a single touch. I don't think threatening me is in your best interest."

Beside me, my husband chuckles like he's amused by Rafferty's attempts to threaten me. "You should try taking your own advice." Shadows creep around Rafferty, darkening the space until they're pressing him down into the floor. "Threats against my wife haven't worked out for anyone. We're here to ask nicely, Rafferty. You can do good with your ability. It is a difficult thing to be cursed as the God of Memory, meant to be forgotten. Do this, and everyone will know the good you're capable of."

Essos eases up on the shadows, and I send the root back to where it belongs. Rafferty gets to his feet and dusts himself off. "I'd rather they not know, if it's all the same. I suppose there's nowhere in the realms your dog won't find me?"

"Correct," Essos confirms. His shoulders relax as Rafferty moves back to his chair, this time gesturing for us to sit. When we do, Essos ensures he's between Rafferty and me so the god never has a chance to make good on his threat. I don't know that either of us take the threat seriously; Rafferty has been mostly bluster thus far. And it's one thing to threaten a queen of the realm and another entirely to act on it.

"How do you want this to work, if the veil is still gone?"

Essos and I glance at each other. "Let's start with clearing up the souls' memories. Your power is tactile, though I'll admit I don't know if you're capable of using it in other ways."

"I prefer to keep how my powers work to myself. You want the mortal realm to forget about the zombies? I can do that, and I will. The mortal souls in the Underworld will be different. Your realm is not as vulnerable to my powers. I'll work with the Fate that used to be your assistant. They already know how my power functions, and I'm fine with keeping them in the know."

"Sybil?" I ask.

"Yes. Now, fix the veil so I never have to be bothered by you people again."

Essos rises dismissively. "When can you work on the Underworld?"

Rafferty rolls his eyes, and I want to smack him on the back of the head. "Let's deal with the mortal zombie memory issue. I know where you live. I was being nice before. Now, get out of my house."

It only takes Rafferty attempting one step toward me for Essos to grab me and bring me home.

Essos wakes to find me sitting at my vanity, sliding on a pair of dark earrings. For a second, I soak in the sleep-bleary man watching me from our bed. The sun has barely risen this morning.

"Why are you awake?" he asks, his voice rough and low. The sound makes me want to crawl back into bed with him, but I can't. Today, I am a woman on a mission.

"Go back to sleep," I urge him, even though I want him on this journey with me. It's something we should do together, but I'd rather he be well-rested for what comes next.

"Not fucking likely. What are you up to, Daphne?" He sits up completely and rubs his hands over his face.

"I want to go to the Underworld." I spin on my vanity chair so I'm no longer speaking to him through the mirror. So he can see the desperation in my face.

He's silent, I hope contemplating my words, before he climbs out of bed in all his naked glory.

"Give me twenty minutes to wake up," he says, gripping my shoulders gently before pressing a kiss to my forehead.

I'm so startled, I lean back so I can look him in the eye. "No fight?"

"No fight. I'm too exhausted to fight with you, especially when you're right." Essos slides a hand along my cheek before planting a sweet kiss on my lips. "I'm man enough to admit it. We need to be seen by our people. We need to know what exactly we're asking Rafferty to fix. I'm going to shower, and you are going to eat a very hearty breakfast."

Essos walks into our bathroom, and I hear the shower turn on. In the time it takes him to wash, I summon a breakfast, but I'm only half paying attention to the food because I'm agonizing over something stupid—what to wear.

In my mind, I know that I it doesn't *really* matter, but I hate the idea of going to the Underworld dressed as a queen. It feels too on par with Marie Antoinette being tone-deaf to her people's plight.

That's why Essos finds me standing in my closet, a piece of toast in my hand as I survey my clothes.

"I don't recommend wearing nothing to the Underworld. I'm not sure even Dave can protect you from the masses then." He slides up behind me, his hands cradling my bump and pressing a kiss to my neck.

"Leggings and jeans feel too casual in the face of all their suffering, but going in a dress feels tone-deaf."

"How about we both wear jeans and a nice shirt, and we go prepared to get our hands dirty? The Underworld has been missing its queen for too long. The souls could probably benefit from space to grieve, even after Rafferty has done his fix."

I lean back against him. "Will the souls even remember me?"

"I don't know, but let's go and find out."

I SETTLE on jeans and a tunic, and Essos makes me a bacon, egg, and cheese sandwich in the kitchen before we go. The food turns in my stomach, and I wish I hadn't let him talk me into eating so much.

All three dogs come with us. When we arrive, it feels too quiet, and I have to wonder if something else went wrong. But no, it's just early for the souls in Paradise. Essos slides his hand into mine as we walk the streets between the homes the souls have established.

It was our goal that the Underworld would provide a perfect Afterlife for each of these souls. They would be near friends and family and have the ability to see others. Each time a new soul arrived, they would have a space designated just for them that would grow to accommodate their needs.

Paradise is usually so green and lush, fueled by the joy of the souls. No joy means the space feels bleak. I let my power unfurl, blanketing the walkway with rich green grass and expanding to fill empty flowerbeds with lush life.

I'm so focused on trying to infuse this world with light that I don't notice the souls that have stepped from their homes to greet us.

"Majesty," an older woman says, walking toward us. Her hair is silvered with age, the way she wants it. Margarita Reyes, passed in her sleep in her home in Madrid last year. I can tell all of this just by looking at her. It's a power I still had before being crowned again, and it's the reason I can understand her even though she's speaking Spanish. She holds out her hand to me, and I feel Essos tense, but I take it, trusting that she means no harm.

"Margarita," I greet, taking her hand.

"I killed my grandson," she tells me before she starts to weep. "I sank my teeth into his throat until he stopped screaming. Why did I do that? I want to forget. I want to forget. I want to forget."

I embrace her, and when her body isn't strong enough to hold her up any longer, I guide her so we're sitting on the ground together. Around us, I hear similar laments. Their neighbors, their friends, their families, strangers, the elderly, children. There was no limit to who was affected and how.

Tears are in my own eyes as I hold this woman, wishing I could hold them all. Essos places a hand on her shoulder, a calming wave relaxing her long enough for her to call to her grandson, the same one whose life she took, to come collect her.

"We..." I have to clear my throat because my voice breaks. "We will hear you. All of you."

I grow two thrones, not of the Underworld, dark and terrifying, but thrones meant for a child of Spring and her king, and then an equally comfortable seat for each soul to sit with us and share their story.

I listen to every single one while my back cramps and my butt goes numb. I don't move from my perch, even as Essos tries to catch my eyes between souls, even as I fight the urge to hold my stomach at some of the more gruesome stories.

"Daphne," Essos urges quietly, and I know what he's going to say. That I need to eat, that I need to get up and walk around, so occasionally, I do. I lead the souls through a garden and infuse it with alcoves for private grieving.

Essos follows, calming souls who are overwrought, but it doesn't feel like nearly enough for all they've gone through. Dave, Spot, and Shadow are all there too, providing emotional support in the form of licks and resting their heads on laps.

Even when I'm dead on my feet, trying to come up with other ways to help, it doesn't feel like enough.

Eventually, Essos puts his foot down.

"Daphne." There is censure in his tone now, because the line of souls never seems to end. "We will come back. We have to. But you can't keep going. You need rest, my love."

"We understand." I turn to the voice that said that, and my heart breaks all over again. Taylor Jade, a fourteen-year-old boy whose mother poisoned him, thinking that it was end times.

"How do you understand?" I ask him, choking down a sob.

"When I died, it was like my brain downloaded this whole 'how to be dead' guide that explained where I was and what happened. I know my mom is somewhere called the Deep, and I understand why, but I want to ask you to change that."

Killing her child, regardless of the reasons, would have been enough to earn her a one-way ticket to the Deep.

"Why?" Essos asks, squeezing my shoulder.

"Because she wasn't a bad mom. She didn't let me play video games after I was supposed to go to bed, which wasn't cool, and I know that what happened was her fault, but it also wasn't. She was scared. I want you to reconsider sending her there. I'll tell everyone why you have to leave for now, but please look at her case. Also, I think everyone is just excited to see you here. I mean, there was talk of a king and a queen, but to actually see you both in person...I mean, that's cool too."

"Who wrote this guide?" Essos mutters, mostly to himself. "We'll take it under advisement. I'm sorry, we must go, but I promise we will be back."

Before I can object, Essos pulls me flush to his chest and whisks me home. I don't object as he undresses me and guides me into the shower, taking care to wash my hair and my body. I don't object as he uses the towel to dry me before wrapping me in a plush robe and carrying me to bed. I don't object as he holds me close to him, waiting for my anguish to break through the numb barrier I had to erect around myself so I could hear their stories without putting the burden on them to comfort me.

I don't object as he squeezes me to him, and my own keening wail lets loose as the weight of what happened to the souls settles on my shoulders.

Taylor asked us to consider his mother's punishment, and I'll do that for the boy. "What are we going to do with Stacy Jade?"

"I'll get her file tomorrow and review it. I'm inclined to honor his request. His mother acted out of fear, not malice. I can't say a zombie apocalypse makes for clear thinking."

"You're not wrong," I agree, wiping my eyes before snuggling closer. "I hate her."

"Stacy?"

"No. Well, maybe a little bit. I can't imagine taking my own child's life. No, I want to kill Posey for this." My voice is raw.

"I know. I do too."

I press my face against his chest. "I don't think I can do it, though." Essos stays silent, giving me space to explain. "I thought I would feel better, having killed Galen, but sometimes I get flashes of his blood on my hands. I know he's back, and he's alive, now, but it feels like my soul is forever marked. I try not to think about it too much."

I try not to think about it ever, but sometimes it's unavoidable.

"I wish I could have taken that hit for you, because I would have. I would have killed him six or seven times over. We *will* figure out a solution to the Posey problem, but you won't have to take that hit again. You don't have to be the one to kill her, if it comes to that."

"How are we even going to kill her?"

"The God Killer blades. I don't see why they wouldn't work on a Fate just as well as they worked on the God Supreme."

"I want to face her with more than just a maybe."

Essos presses his lips to the top of my head. "I might have a trick or two left up my sleeves."

We visit the Underworld three days in a row, and for three days, I sit and listen only to go back to my room and cry. Eventually, Essos convinces me that we need to stay at the house and work on other ways to help the souls and end this cycle of pain once and for all.

I can't get enough of the sun after all the gloom that's inhabited my soul, so I'm sitting with Finn and Bria, sunning myself by the pool when Essos approaches from behind. I tilt my head back for a kiss that is long and sensual. My tongue flicks against his, and I groan.

"Where's my welcome kiss?" Finn asks. His mood is improving, but only because Bria forces him outside with her. He's learning how his other senses compensate for his lack of sight. Finn can feel when I'm building up my power, and he's starting to predict my attacks. In Finn's hand is the mobility cane that Bria made for him. Naturally, it's not just a cane; printed all around it are weapons and animals that will spring forth if Finn is threatened. Until he's comfortable enough with his new situation, as long as we're at risk, Bria wants him to have another form of defense.

Finn's power also still seems to be failing for a reason none of us can figure out. Whispers behind closed doors wonder if it has anything to do with his reaction to his injury. As if closing himself off from the world has closed him off from his powers.

"I can do you better than a kiss." Essos comes and sits on the end of my lounge chair and pulls my feet onto his lap. There's nothing quite like having a king rub your feet as he bends to press a kiss to your swollen stomach. I feel like I've doubled in size. Part of that is definitely the stress eating. I want to go to the mortal realm and check on my family, but Essos wants me to give my body a week to recover from all the transporting we did that day. He's playing it safe, and I understand, but *gods* it can be frustrating.

"Yeah, I somehow doubt that," Finn grumbles, crossing his arms.

When a new shadow falls over us, I turn and startle. "Tink?"

Standing at my back is a broad-shouldered man. He has a strong, square jaw and a playful glint in his dark brown eyes. I struggle to my feet as best I can. When I face him head on, he does a full body perusal, eyeing me from head to toe. There is a flutter in my stomach that I've come to recognize as the baby moving.

"Well, if it isn't Daphne, back from the dead." He scoops me up and spins me lightly while I laugh.

"Can we not manhandle the mother of my child?" Essos pleads, but it falls on deaf ears because Tink gives me a bone-crushing hug.

"Tink?" Finn asks, turning toward our voices.

"The one and only," Bria mutters, getting to her feet. It's fascinating to watch her and Dion fight over how best to handle Finn. Dion clucks over him like a worried hen, and Bria does her best to let Finn figure out his new limitations on his own. Somehow, they're striking a perfect balance that's not only getting Finn out of his room but making him more confident about his situation.

"Here on special assignment," Tink confirms, setting me down. News of his arrival seems to have spread, because before I know it, almost all of our cohorts have joined us. Cat in particular seems struck by this beautiful man, who gives her a wink when introductions are made.

"Is Tink your full name, or is it a nickname?" Cat asks, sliding her arm in mine.

"It's a nickname. My actual name is Ignatius. I can tell you it's not because I'm a petit pixie who dies without any attention. Daphne here takes that role," he teases, and I shove his side, but I'm quick to pull him back to me.

"Rude," I object.

"But it's so true," Cat adds with a wide grin.

"I like to tinker; that's why I'm here. God of Craftsmen. I come bearing gifts, but first, I want to know why I wasn't invited to join this little club, especially when there are such beautiful members." Tink winks at Cat for effect, and boy, does he get it in the form of an obvious eye roll from Xavier. What Xavier misses while he's pouting is how Tink deliberately doesn't look at Callie when he says that.

Galen chooses that moment to emerge from his room, where he's spent most of his time sequestered following his attempt at breaking the rules. He made one attempt to destroy one of my vine creatures before he was encased by the other. He's at least learned his lesson not to fuck with them.

Tink stumbles back a step. "Last I heard, you were dead." All teasing has left his voice as he faces Galen. Tink's eyes flash to where Callie has taken a step closer to the group, closer to Tink and away from her husband.

Galen doesn't miss the movement, his eyes flickering to her and then back to Tink.

In addition to hiding out in his room, Galen took his time to lick his wounds and heal while talking to his mother. I don't know if he's aware or not, but after that stunt she pulled, they've both been under constant surveillance. It's somewhat comforting that she turned over the dagger to Xavier, like we asked. I'm glad that we haven't caught them up to no good. For once, I would like something to be easy.

When he catches Galen eyeing me, Essos hands me my cover-up, and I slip the dress over my shoulders.

"Well, like some others here, it didn't stick. Are you here to join the merry band of misfits in their pathetic rebellion?" Galen sneers, finally taking his eyes off me only to narrow in on his wife.

"And if I am?"

"I'd suggest you pick the winning side. I'm here only because I have to be. You still have time to get out." Galen moves toward the table. He takes one step and finds Dave beside him, growling. Galen turns to me. "Call off your dog." He glances around at everyone contemptuously. "All of them."

Essos pauses before issuing a command. "Heel." Dave doesn't respond right away, not until my voice joins in.

"Heel. Come," I demand, and Dave does. He doesn't waste energy trotting over to me. Instead, he vanishes and reappears at my side. Essos shakes his head but smiles, looking glad that I have him near me.

"Galen, when you're able to put aside your petty differences, you can join us. Otherwise, the adults are talking. Do you need a nap?" Tink asks with a smug grin.

"Posey is going to pick her teeth with your bones. She has the dagger and the scepter, and when she wants to make a move, she's going to. And you're all going to live to regret it." Galen glances around as if taking inventory, and I realize that Kai and Helene are absent. "I have to wonder if she's not already made a move, and you all have no idea."

My stomach contracts, but I tell myself it's just the baby moving.

"If she's so powerful, why is she still alone, turning her citizens into stone? The gates to the Underworld are open, so what is she going to do with all those souls still stuck in the dagger?" I ask, already knowing the answer, but I'm curious to learn if he knows she's consuming souls. It's possible that Octavia told him, but it's also possible he has no idea.

Galen blows out a puff of annoyed air. "Why would I tell you?"

He drops into a seat, conjuring a drink. Dion turns the wine in the glass so Galen is left sputtering at the vinegar.

"You *don't* know," I hedge, stepping toward him. Dave stays glued to my side as I move around everyone. After being locked up with him for months, I've gotten to know Galen better than I ever wanted to. The man was never afraid to gloat when he had the winning hand, and he knows he doesn't this time.

"Of course, I do. I was her partner." He's still posturing, but now he's also sweating.

"Her partner in what? I was the steak she was tossing to keep the guard dog busy. She didn't need you, so she gave you something shiny to keep you out of the way. She needed the souls, and she needed you to get them. You have no idea what her plan was. Your existence is utterly useless to me." This realization makes my face twist in disgust. We didn't bring him back solely because he could have information, but it would have been a boon if he did. Maybe it's for the best that I need never interact with him again. If he's useless, we can lock him up and throw away the proverbial key.

Galen slams his hands down on the table, but I'm faster from all my practice, and a vine shoots up to wrap around his neck. He laughs, pulling on it. "You think this is going to hurt me?"

"No, but I'm hoping it will shut you up long enough for me to think," I snap, rubbing my eyes. Bringing Galen back will be for nothing if he was just Posey's pawn. I didn't believe he was truly her second-in-command, but I had hoped for at least a general of some kind. And honestly, Octavia has proven herself unwilling to help past pointing us in the right direction for opening the gates of the Underworld.

"We still have one of the daggers. If he's this useless, we might as well kill him again," Finn suggests.

Galen blanches at that.

"I'd like to try my hand at battling the God of War," Bria says, flipping a dagger in her hand. Galen glares at her. Those two often went head-to-head regarding who was the better warrior.

"No, we still have to see if my mother has any more helpful information. Her knowledge as the Goddess Supreme should finally come in handy." Essos crosses his arms, studying the panic on Galen's face.

"You think that's the real reason Posey killed Titus?" Cat suggests.

"Because Titus could take her down? Maybe. He would at least have more knowledge on ways we could fight her," Xavier muses.

"I can help!" Galen gasps out, clawing at the vine. I loosen it to let him talk. He starts an overdramatic coughing fit that no one acknowledges.

"How?" I prompt.

"I may not know her plan, but I am the God of War, of strategy. I can help you defeat her, but I want assurances. I want to meet my sons, and I want to live," Galen demands.

"Let's hear the genius plan first, and then we can discuss your terms," Cat pipes up. Xavier's eyes flash to her, appraising and proud.

"You still can't kill her. Whoever kills her will have to take her place as a Fate. She's counting on your selfishness to protect her. I know that much. I do know that she was planning to consume the souls for power, but she can't do it all at once. It would be like trying to eat too much at once. But she started to consume them long before the wedding."

"Which wedding?" I grumble. I try not to fidget, my lower back hurting from standing on my feet without support. These are the things no one warns you about when it comes to pregnancy. Or maybe they do, and I just never paid attention.

Essos passes me and plops into a seat before pulling me possessively onto his lap. Galen watches us, an angry scowl twisting his mouth. Out of the corner of my eye, I see Essos's mouth quirk up in a smirk before he starts to rub absent circles on my stomach with one hand and massage my shoulder with the other. I moan when his thumb finds a knot that has been causing me all sorts of problems.

"Ours, pet," Galen says with a self-satisfied smirk. I don't know what he's thinking he's won, since it ended poorly for him.

"Do you need an invitation to continue?" Dion asks, his tone indicating he's bored, but his posture says otherwise. He's tense everywhere else, a coil ready to spring.

"You need to get her off balance. I'm guessing you tried to steal the dagger from her? That's how Phineas lost his sight? She was expecting that. Posey expects you to go for the scepter and the dagger. I doubt either leave her person."

"How did you know Posey was a Fate?" I ask, narrowing my eyes at him.

Galen turns red. Another lie, it seems. I'd have to guess that Octavia told him, because there is *no* way that Posey did.

Essos tenses under me. I can't look at him. I can't give away that they tried exactly that, and yes, Galen is right about Finn losing his sight to a decoy.

"Thanks for that *genius* insight. We never could have cracked the case without you," Xavier deadpans.

Galen looks panicked that this information isn't good enough, and it really isn't. "She needs the dagger because it has special properties. It collects the blood of everyone it cuts. If she used it on Finn, then she has his blood. I also know that the red algae works on Fates."

My mind starts to race. The dagger she has also cut me during the wedding, as well as Essos. One glance at Finn, and I see him rubbing his arm that Posey sliced with the God Killer blade. How many of us have been cut with the blade, which is now imbued with our blood?

Unable to get further with that unknown, I focus on the latter half of his statement and think over the implication of the red algae. In all the chaos, I had forgotten about the attempt to poison me during the Trials. Posey had installed Ellie and "Miranda" as lady's maids to work for me, one of whom was dosing me with red algae powder, which slowly bound my powers. Of course, that was Ellie, the nymph who'd slept with Essos.

My brain hiccups again. The maids weren't just Ellie, my husband's former lover, but also Octavia, posing as Miranda.

Essos's stroking falters, and I twist to look at him. If I could will one power into existence in this moment, it would be telepathy. This is not a conversation I want to have in front of everyone else.

"Red algae?" Dion asks. Most of the group had been oblivious to it. Once I knew my powers had been bound, I hid that fact from everyone. The only reason I even found out was my father-in-law, Titus, who alerted me to it.

Essos and I fill everyone in on the substance, not bothering to sort out who knew what it was or wasn't. Tink stays quiet, watching us volley before he sits at the table as well, looking overwhelmed by everything he's learning.

"Ellie was slipping it into her tea," Cat pipes up.

"Ellie is Posey's second. She's who you need to get the upper hand on her," Galen suggests. I snarl at the idea, and Galen snorts. "Finally realizing that Essos isn't so perfect after all?"

I feel the growl reverberate through Essos, but I squeeze his knee to stop him. "You're wrong. Ellie's not clever enough to be Posey's second. She couldn't even handle sending memos correctly. She's a nymph, and not a very good one, if I remember correctly."

Galen sneers. "No, *you're* wrong. Ellie is Posey's daughter."

28

Xavier looks the most shocked of everyone at the table, and I can't say I blame him. He was an inattentive husband, but the idea that his wife snuck in a love child during their marriage seems unbelievable to everyone.

Once the shock has had a chance to dissipate, Xavier starts to laugh. It's full-body tremors, and he laughs so hard he doesn't make any sound at some points. It takes him several minutes to control his laughter, including time for him to get up and grip his chair as the fit nearly takes him to his knees.

"I'm sorry, that's just...outrageous," Xavier says, turning to his little brother, all amusement gone.

"It's not. It's why Ellie had the job with Essos to begin with," Galen insists.

Now I chuckle. His own words prove him wrong. "That can't be. Essos and I had already dealt with the nonsense with Ellie by the time Xavier and Posey were married."

"How do you know this?" Essos asks Galen.

"How do I *not?*" Finn asks.

"During the Trials, I overheard Ellie ask Posey when she would claim her as her daughter. I don't know who her father is, or how she managed to keep a kid from you during your marriage, but I know what I heard," Galen insists.

Essos leans forward and presses a kiss to my shoulder. "Can I talk to you alone for a minute?" he whispers so only I can hear.

I'm still trying to swallow this latest pill, so I nod. "Of course," I agree.

We step inside, not giving an explanation to the rest of the group. We leave them to strategize while we cloister ourselves in Essos's office. Dave is the only one who follows, prancing happily between us.

"I have a confession to make," Essos starts once the door is closed behind me.

I cross my arms and gesture for him to go on. He walks first to his drink cart and pours himself a whiskey, taking a moment before pouring another glass and offering it to me. My eyebrows shoot up. Now I'm worried. This revelation has to be bad if he's offering me booze to take it better.

I accept the cup but don't drink from it, moving farther into the room. A layer of moss pads the walls, giving us privacy.

"After the Calling Ball, after you agreed to wed Galen and I was on the run, I saw Ellie."

I inhale a deep breath through my nose, stung. We've been together uninterrupted for months. Why this is the first I'm hearing of it, I don't understand.

"Go on," I tell him, my voice shaking.

"Nothing happened, but she came to me, wanting to prove to me that she was the only one for me and that you truly did want Galen. I obviously never took her up on her offer, but what if we can use it?"

"Use it?" I whisper. My emotions are churning, and I set the glass down, unconsumed. Dave stands at my side, and I stoop down to scratch behind his ears. It sounds like it was a conversation, but if that's all it was, then Essos should have just told me, right?

"What if I can trick her into coming here—trick Ellie, and make her our hostage? Maybe we can leverage her against Posey. I doubt she'll expect that at all. Love, I think we can use this. Ellie is blinded by her obsession with me."

"Why does it keep coming back to Ellie? She was your side piece and then your main piece when I was dead, and then she chased you again after I rejected you. Why didn't you tell me?" My thoughts feel like they're going a million miles a minute, and I want to focus on all the good between Essos and I, but how can I do that when the *same* woman keeps haunting us? An errant tear escapes, and I brush my hand against my cheek to catch it. I can't even focus on the idea he's suggesting, because I just want this woman out of my life for good.

Essos steps toward me again, and Dave barks at him this time, feeding off my emotional turmoil. "When would I have had time to tell you? Between changing safehouses every other day? When I was here long enough to check on you only to catch you kissing my brother? I never had the time, and then I had you back and it didn't seem important. Clearly, it *is* important to you and I was mistaken, but Daphne, these aren't normal circumstances. She was never my main piece. She was the woman I fucked while imagining she was you."

I laugh, but it's humorless. "Is that supposed to magically make it better? Oh, I'm so sorry it was such a *hardship* for you that after I died, you literally fucked the one woman who came between us before, but I'm *so* glad you thought of me while you did it." My tone oozes sarcasm.

Essos cuts me a frustrated look, but he takes in a breath and rubs his hands over his face. "Obviously, that's not going to make it better. I'm not trying to excuse my behavior. She meant nothing to me. I haven't even thought about her since I got you back, that's why it never came up. This—" he gestures between us, earning another growl from Dave "—is why I brought you in here to tell you."

"So you didn't embarrass me in front of our friends and family, *again,* over Ellie? I bet everyone got a real kick out of her being my lady's maid. They saw me bring her to events and probably laughed behind their hands, knowing that she was my replacement, and I had no idea."

Essos lets out another calming breath, the only one of us committed to keeping a level head. "Ellie was never a replacement for you. She wasn't even a shadow compared to you. What is it going to take to convince you that I feel nothing for her? What do you need?"

I deflate a little at this, not knowing what I need. I don't know what it will take to repair this fragile hurt between us. "Let's see what everyone else thinks about us kidnapping your mistress. But if you think for one *second* that I'm going to let her into our bed or let you fuck her ever again, you're sorely mistaken." I don't even know where the idea comes from, but once it's out there, it's like I've finally put a face to what has me so on edge.

This seems to catch him totally off guard, and he lowers the glass he was raising to his lips. "Daphne, the thought never crossed my mind. I have everything I want right here. And more! I fought so hard to get you back. I'm not going to turn away from that for *any* reason. I would sooner let the realms burn."

"I understand that you sought her out to fulfill needs I couldn't because I was dead. I'm just saying that if you're tempted to do so again because of my condition, *that* would be inexcusable."

"Okay, there is a lot to pick apart there. First off, I didn't seek her out; she was just there. It wasn't because I was looking to get off. I wasn't looking for anything or anyone. Secondly, you're pregnant with our child, with our daughter. Our sex life hasn't waned since we found out; it's only made us more insatiable. I find nothing sexier than you. Is that it? You're insecure because you're pregnant?" As he steps toward me, he eyes Dave. My eyes widen and I step back from him, and I think he realizes what he actually just said to me, because he winces and deflates a little.

"Right, because all these problems can be marked up to the little lady and her insecurities." I pause. "I'm puffy everywhere. I'm just going to get bigger. I don't see why you *would* want me with her around."

"Can I?" Essos asks, reaching for me. I nod, and Dave backs off, still eyeing Essos warily. "I don't see any of that. I could show you what I see, but I don't think even getting in my head will be enough right now." His hands reach for the bottom of my cover-up, and he lifts it and casts it aside, leaving me in just my bikini. "I see the body of a woman who has survived so much. I see a goddess..." he tugs on the strap behind my neck, letting my breasts fall free without the support "...both literally and figuratively, who is carrying my child. Who has found new ways to manipulate her powers and explore the deeper well of them."

Essos continues to disrobe me, sliding my bottoms off my legs. I step out of them, a little embarrassed. He pulls my hands away from my sides so I can't cover myself up.

"If you won't believe my words, believe this." He guides one of my hands to his erection. "I wake some mornings in awe of you, wanting to get my fill of you, but you sleep so peacefully, I have to take matters into my own hands because if you so much as looked at my cock, I would come. And that's just all the ways you make me physically crave you. I love watching you apply lotion to your belly every morning. If it didn't look like you enjoyed the act so much, I would offer to do it myself because I can't get enough of touching you and wanting to be with you. I would glue myself to your side if I could, and we would never be apart. And that's just all the ways I physically desire you. When I'm in my office and you're in another part of the house, it takes all my willpower to not just follow you around."

He doesn't hold my hand there, it was just meant as a demonstration, but I take it further, stroking him. Essos moans as I take it even further, unzipping his pants and pulling them down his legs. He watches me, unsure what I'm going to do until I get on my knees before him and take him into my mouth slowly. I slide my mouth down him, reveling in the way his body responds to me.

Essos was right. It is my insecurity, but it always comes back to Ellie. I know his devotion is to me and this baby, but it doesn't make the thought of them together hurt any less. I turn my thoughts away from our argument and to the issue at hand, or rather, at mouth. I suck, letting my teeth graze his cock, eliciting a hiss a pleasure. His fingers thread through my hair, and he moves me at the pace he wants, matching my movements with the thrust of his hips. I cup his balls, humming as I go, knowing he enjoys the vibration, until he pulls me off him entirely.

Essos lifts me and crashes his mouth down on mine, and I let it burn me from the inside out, his deep reverent need for me. I fist his shirt, annoyed at how clothed he is compared to how bare I am. Quickly, I pull on his buttons before sliding his shirt off. Who this man is that he wears suits to the pool, I'll never understand. He changed during the time I was away.

Essos maneuvers us to the couch, where he sits. It's awkward how he has to slouch to make space for my stomach, but I slide down, impaling myself on him. We come together in a deeper way than we have, full of so much emotional turmoil. His hands come to my tender breasts, kneading them and pinching my nipples, heightening my sensations. I set the pace as I slide my body up and down his until the friction sends me careening toward orgasm and I let myself go. My fingernails dig into his chest and leave scorching lines down his skin. Essos's own orgasm rips through him, and he grips my hips, urging me at the pace he needs while my own aftershocks leave my body trembling.

I lean forward and press my forehead to his.

"You're all I need. You're everything I want. You're my eternity," Essos swears before kissing me thoroughly, reminding me that we are one heart and one soul.

When we emerge to join the others again, we both look exactly like what we got up to. Xavier wisely says nothing but smirks to himself. Galen looks enraged, even more when he catches sight of the hickey my husband left on my neck like we're teenagers. I don't bother trying to smooth down Essos's hair, glad to see it askew. One of the vine guards places a hand on Galen's shoulder after sensing my trepidation at his response, and the God of War only bats the hand away sullenly.

While we were gone, Kai and Helene appeared. Kai stands behind Galen's chair, arms crossed, while Helene stands behind Cat. I think I see the white of a bandage peeking out under the sleeve of Helene's blouse, but I don't question it.

"We have a plan," Essos starts.

"Does it involve fucking Posey into submission? Because I can smell the sex pouring off you both," Finn complains.

"No. We're going to kidnap Ellie," I announce with a grin.

Galen snorts. "Like it's going to be easy to grab her."

"Since she's in love with my husband, I should think it will be."

Murmurs start around the group.

Helene scoffs. "You would invite your mistress here to torment your pregnant wife? Brother, I'm so disappointed."

Helene taking my side in this warms me.

Essos levels her with a glare. "If you think a single soul exists who I would pick over Daphne and our child, maybe you don't know me as well as I thought." He sounds hurt that she wouldn't have faith in him to pick me.

I slide my hand into Essos's and give it a squeeze, hoping that it conveys to everyone that I am with him in this and in all things. Essos gives me an appreciative smile before turning back to our family.

"How do we get her, then? Last I recall, your lovely wife sealed her mouth shut, and she was running scared with Posey," Xavier points out, and he's not wrong. In the weeks leading up to my wedding to Galen, Ellie tried to turn the screws to me. She kept pushing and insinuating that Essos would choose her, that she was the one he loved more. Joke was on her—I sealed her mouth shut when she tried to object.

"Posey undid that," Tink supplies.

All eyes turn to him.

"And how do you know that?" Xavier demands.

"Because I've been at Posey's house, working with her on her whole take-over-the-world operation."

"And you didn't want to lead with that?" Bria asks skeptically.

Essos smirks, eyeing Tink before looking at the redhead. "You didn't think we left him out of our plans on purpose? He's been our inside man."

"It was just me you left out?" Bria gets to her feet.

"I didn't want you here," Dion admits, meeting her eyes.

It's not hard to see the flash of hurt before she covers it up. I don't know Bria that well, but it feels like whatever progress they had made has been undone. "Of course, not. You were too busy spreading more lies, I bet."

"Where's the lie, Bria? Please, enlighten us, because Finn and I didn't seem to matter enough to you to warrant an explanation when we broke up." Dion braces his hands on the table before standing up.

"The lie where you said I was cheating on you! And don't play the victim here. You're the one who took your assumptions as fact and ran with them. You decided to spin the narrative that worked best for you, Dion. If you wanted to cut me out of the relationship, you should have at least had the balls to say so to my face instead of telling Finn I was cheating on you." Bria's breathing becomes ragged as she yells.

"What did you expect me to think? You had a second apartment, you abruptly ended conversations when I walked into the room. I didn't know what else to think! Don't act like you fought for us. You shut down when presented with the evidence, and you. Walked. Away. So really, if anyone is spinning a narrative, it's you. But that's what cheaters do: they lie and manipulate situations for their own benefit." Normally cool and collected Dion is turning purple with rage.

"Enough!" Finn shouts. "We can finish this argument later. Perhaps when all of our friends aren't watching."

"I don't know. I'm sort of enjoying not being the center of an argument for once," Galen says, tipping onto the back legs of his chair. I use a vine guard to give it a tug—not enough for him to fall, though he would have deserved that. No, just enough to be a slap on the wrist for enjoying the misery of my friends.

"Right," Tink says awkwardly. "I, of course, came bearing gifts and information."

"You're just a regular Benedict Arnold," Zara proclaims, finally joining us. She eyes Tink, taking in the look of him. She purses her full lips before flipping her braid over her shoulder and taking the chair closest to him.

"Yes, well, down to the nitty gritty. Posey's trying to call Lairus to her side and get him to seek revenge for his son's death and steal back the God Killer blade that has, well, had, his soul."

"What if we kill two birds with one stone? Take out two of her allies at once?" I suggest.

Galen sits up straight, his brow furrowed as he listens to us talk this through.

"So, you're proposing kidnapping your mistress and the father of the man you killed. Really, team, awesome plan." Helene gives me a thumbs-up and a face that conveys she has no faith in us.

"I can take care of Ellie," Essos assures everyone.

"I can get to Lairus," Octavia announces, walking out to us and bringing everyone except the Fates into the fold.

I look around at this unlikely crew, wondering why I am cursed to have to work with two people I hate, but also so lucky to have so many people I respect and adore with us.

"Oh, good, we're relying on the benevolence of former lovers, because that never backfires," Xavier says dryly. He pushes a plate of fruit toward Cat, and she picks up a huge chunk of pineapple and levels him with a look as she takes a big bite. Xavier doesn't look away from her, and I get the feeling that we're all intruding.

"Lairus will want to see Galen. He's known all along," Octavia confirms. She moves to stand behind her golden son, running her hands through his hair.

"Lairus has known *what* all along?" Galen asks, looking around, confused.

I feel Essos's hand close around my wrist, ready to whisk me away at the slightest threat. Everyone in the room goes totally still, unsure what to do. No one wants to be the one to break the news, but someone has to.

Helene takes the plunge. "Galen, Titus wasn't your father. Mom confirmed that Lairus was."

Galen stares at Helene before twisting toward his mother. "Did everyone know except me?" Anger is radiating off him in waves of heat. Xavier edges closer to Cat, knowing that while she might have powers, she is next to defenseless if Galen strikes out.

"We all just learned for sure," Helene confirms, pity in her tone for once. "Like, right before we brought you back."

"That's it. That's why Dad, or Titus, was a bastard to me all the time. It's because *I* was a bastard." Galen's cry of rage sends out a concussive force. I feel time slow as Essos grabs me, stepping in the way of the blast and transporting us away from its radius. We land on the beach, farther out, so we only stumble when it reaches us.

"Are you all right?" he asks, checking me over for any possible injuries.

"I'm fine," I confirm, looking over his shoulder at everyone else. The windows along the back half of my house are shattered. It's an easy fix, but tiresome all the same. My vine creatures, his guardians, have been demolished, having been too close to Galen when it happened. I've never seen Galen demonstrate such a destructive power before.

We make our way back to the deck. Xavier is picking glass out of Cat's hair, and for the most part, everyone seems no worse for wear. Bria is tucking her wings back in from where she protected both Finn and Dion from the blast. Even as she shrugs them into her shoulders, I shake my head, having forgotten that she even *has* wings. Callie is burning with the same fury that Galen was.

"This, *this* is why I ran off with your sons the moment I found out I was pregnant! You and your temper. You may be the God of War and Suffering, you may be strong and powerful and whatever else you tell yourself, but at the end of the day, you're always the same little boy, throwing a tantrum and blaming everyone else for your own actions. You would hit me and then blame me, and you attacked Daphne and blamed Essos. You're going to blame this outburst on being lied to your whole life, and you've blamed your shitty attitude on Titus your whole life. I *know* you. I know the scum you are. *This* is why you don't know your sons. This is why they know what a monster you are."

Callie's visibly shaken by what happened, and she stalks away.

We're all surprised when Tink follows her, leaving his box of treasures behind.

TINK COMES to see me in my office that night. It's after dinner, and Essos is giving me time to try to find my way back into the swing of things. Now that souls are coming back into the Underworld, it's about finding the balance we had before I died. It's actually soothing to have this time. The rhythm is familiar, like putting on that pair of old sweatpants you love.

What I want to focus on is ensuring souls have a chance to recover from being zombies. I want to go to the Underworld again, but Essos isn't keen on the idea.

"Your Majesty," Tink teases with a bow.

I snort and gesture for him to sit. "Stop that. You were never one for such formality. Thank you for the help fixing the windows."

After Galen's tantrum, Essos and Tink repaired what had been broken. I put my energy into creating new guards that Tink helped to reinforce.

He offers me a kind smile as I lean back in my chair, taking my tea with me. I'm not there yet, but soon enough, I'll be able to use my belly as a table.

"It was my pleasure. You have quite the crew assembled. You should hear the things Posey is saying about you all."

I take a sip, giving myself a chance to decide how to proceed. "Do I really want to know?"

"No, but I'm glad Essos contacted me when he did, just before your second wedding, hoping that I knew enough to funnel him information. Posey is spinning quite the tale of what happened."

"Of course, she is." I tap my pen on the stack of papers in front of me. "I didn't see you at the Trials." I try to keep the accusation out of my tone.

"Some of us like to do what we're supposed to and spend time in the mortal realms, letting our presence be inspiration. I found a new inventor. He's no Da Vinci, but I think he has a lot of promise."

Annoyance flares in me at the insinuation that Essos and I aren't doing our jobs. "I thought you were the God of Craftsmen and not a muse?" My words are biting, and I try to soften them. "Is there something you needed?"

"I come with a gift," Tink tells me softly, reaching into his box and producing a pair of gloves and a belt. I don't have to touch the items to feel the plant life within them calling to me. Gently, he places them on my desk. I sit up and take them, sliding the supple leather of the belt through my fingers. It's thin for a belt, but woven into each stitch is a seed—organic material for me to pull on and grow. Etched along the accessory are acorn symbols, and when I touch one, I feel the energy in it thrum to life, waiting for me to manipulate it and grow it. I set the belt aside and pick up the gloves. Similar energy runs through them. They're not leather like the belt, but instead woven with roots and vines alike. Holding them in my hands has me imagining myself with dyed red hair and a green bodysuit.

"These are exquisite," I murmur, totally forgetting about Tink. I slide them onto my hands, the inside feeling like smooth, comforting suede.

"The acorns are actual acorns. You'll have the full power of whatever it is you do with trees. I tried to weave in as many different types of plants as I could." Tink slouches in his seat, looking very satisfied with his work. By his accounting, these should look like Frankenstein gloves, a mixture of colors and materials, but they're a lush green, the color of moss that carpets the forest floor, deep and rich.

"How did you know I needed these?" I ask, flexing my fingers. I tease some ivy off my hand, feeling like Spider-Man, only with more control. The vine stretches out, growing toward Tink, thickening. When it reaches his face, a single leaf emerges and tickles him.

"That better not be the poison ivy branch." Tink swats at it. "Essos told me that my expertise as a craftsman was needed, so here I am."

I withdraw the vine, smiling as it shrinks back into place. "Your timing is perfect." I slip off the gloves and set them aside. "Thank you."

"Yes, well, I'm glad to finally be of assistance. It wasn't fun, being on the outside." His mouth turns down slightly at the corners.

"You being there was helpful. Having someone here who knows what she's planning going forward is helpful."

Tink blows out a slow breath. "It doesn't feel like it."

"I'm guessing I'm not the only reason you've left Team Posey?"

Tink gets to his feet. "No, but Finn won't let me in. He says he's not seeing anyone at the moment. His exact words."

I can't help snorting at Finn's dark sense of humor. "This isn't something that he can get over, and even if you have something in your bag of tricks to help him, he's not going to be the same."

"No, but I can do better than just giving him eyes back. I can increase his sight like you wouldn't believe. He would be himself but with so many more abilities." Tink sounds frustrated, and I get it. We're gods; we have all the power in the world, and yet we're powerless to help our friend.

"Don't meddle, Tink. Let him come to you. At least you'll be ready for him, but for now, he needs to process what happened, and pushing him won't help. It will make us feel better, but that's all it will be—for us."

Tink lowers his head and runs a hand through his hair, the only acknowledgement I'll get that I'm right.

"I'm the only one who can truly understand what he's going through, but he won't let me help."

I can't help it; my gaze drops to his leg. He was born without a limb from the knee down on the left. He toyed with prosthetics over the years, different styles and making them with different materials. I remember him once coming to a party at Helene and Kai's with an eyepatch and a peg leg. He's been good-natured about it for so long that I forget at one time he hadn't been. His prosthetic now looks so real that, at a quick glance, it's hard to tell the difference, but looking at it, I can see the slight shine to the skin-toned metal that slims into a moveable joint. To prove his point, he lifts his foot and rolls what would be his ankle.

"I think, since you understand best, you know that I speak the truth."

His sigh is heavy but full of confirmation. "Your husband is looking for you," Tink tells me before slipping out.

"He knows where to find me!" I shout at the door as it closes behind him.

Waffles pokes his head up from the couch, where I hadn't noticed he was sleeping. He lets out an annoyed *meow* before glaring at me and plopping back down.

I needed solitude when I retreated to my office after eating. There was too much going on, too many voices clamoring to put forth their ideas. My trust in Essos is firm. I may be hurt and disappointed that he didn't tell me about seeing Ellie after the ball, but I know him—I know our relationship—and I know she will not be the thing that divides us. Death couldn't even do that. I don't think some nymph with her sights set on Essos will achieve what my murder couldn't.

Essos must sense that on some level because he may be looking for me, but he doesn't seek me out. He knows precisely where I am, and he doesn't find me. I'm grateful for my space, even more so when he doesn't stop me when I finally step out to get some fresh night air. I feel his eyes track me as I pass him in the living room. When I glance at him, he gives me a devil-may-care wink before looking back down at his own paperwork. I can't say I blame him for seeking a change of scenery.

I crave solitude and walk out to the beach, where darkness reigns. There is no moon tonight, only the brilliance of the stars lighting my way to the water. I discard my sandals as I go so my feet are completely submerged. I let go of the sky-blue dress I'm wearing, letting the hem get soaked.

"I'm going to get us out of this," I whisper to my stomach, rubbing it. Ever since finding out we're having a girl, a small part of me has started to worry about what comes next. I can protect her now, while she grows inside me, but what about after that? I've seen the terrible side of men and life. I've seen what disadvantages a girl can be at, and I can only hope that I raise her to be strong. If we're right—if what happened to Galen when he tried to claw his face off truly was her powers at work—she will be a force to be reckoned with. She hasn't shown any sign of using her powers again, but there hasn't been a threat to me like there was that day.

"I'm sure you will," a soft female voice says from behind me. I spin around in a panic, gathering my powers. When I locate the voice, the surge of power clashes.

"Esmaray?"

The woman is petite with iridescent white eyes that glimmer against her pale skin. Her hair is a rich mahogany with a single streak of silver, styled in a single braid down her back. The likenesses of her in books don't do her justice.

"Yes, my little flower. In the flesh. Come out of the water before you catch your death." The smile she gives me is peaceful, and all I want to do is comply, but I don't move.

"What are you doing here? You haven't been seen or heard from in...I don't know how long." I'm too stunned to move, but I hazard a glance around to see if anyone else is witnessing what I am.

"I've heard you plan to seek out my husband. I wish to help."

"Help," I repeat dumbly, and she grins at me.

"Yes. As the Goddess of the Moon, I'm able to see all. I may be hidden in the dark, but I am always there, always observing, like I did when you were a child." Esmaray walks to me and lifts my chin.

"When I was a child?" I sound like a parrot, capable only of repeating what she says back to her. Like Octavia, she has power thrumming through her body, potent and old. Somehow, it feels familiar, and I wonder if that's because Esmaray and Lairus have similar magic and I've been around Galen. I think back to when she's referring to, but I don't remember a childhood. I remember emerging fully formed from a flower. I went to school to learn how to hone my abilities, but I was never a child in the traditional sense.

"We have much to discuss, and not enough time. Titus and Octavia would prefer you believe that they created all the gods and goddesses, that even if they were not born of Octavia, it was their ability to create that led to the birth of the universe and the realms as you know them. That's not true, but those of us who know better don't care to refute them. We are called Titans, Titus and Octavia and Lairus and me. The Fates know better, though they will never confirm the existence of Titans. The status quo is fine for them. But I will never forgive Octavia for what she took from me."

I wait, enthralled with her tale. Since my death, we've learned so much about the order of the world, from the true powers of the Scepter of the Dead to the existence of not one but two daggers that can kill gods.

"Lairus never wanted a child." She smiles wistfully, looking away from me to toy with beads that hang off her silver skirt. "It was for that reason that I grew the moonflower. It would bloom for me, and I would tend to it myself while my husband chased the sun around the earth. It was the moonflower that you were born from."

"What are you saying?" The question barely leaves my mouth. The world is spinning around me. If she's saying what I think she's saying, then I need her to *say* it.

"I'm saying that I am your mother. You were born from my love of the moonflower, and so it is fitting that you would be the Goddess of Spring and flowers and earth. I returned one night to see the moonflower open, and you were there, just a babe, lying in the center of it. You loved to bask in my light, trying to reach out to catch me. Lairus knew. It was a transgression for me to create life, not because he didn't want a child, but because Titus and Octavia wanted to be in charge of it. But I had found out about his tryst with Octavia, and so I leveraged that to ensure his silence so I could keep you. Titus was a jealous god. He was allowed his trysts but Octavia wasn't allowed another lover."

I finally step out of the water, but only so I can stumble to the sand and listen to her story.

"Lairus told her about you one night, as they discussed their spouses and complaints. Octavia came to me and said I had to give you up or she would kill you, as was her right as Goddess Supreme. Never mind that I was older than her and could have destroyed the earth and all she held dear, including her young son whose eyes were flecked with gold like the sun of his father. She and Titus had created the daggers already, and Titus had the scepter forged for their quiet, dark-haired son. Lairus would never agree to create opposing weapons, and so I had to coax my sweet, beautiful girl into her flower bed with a sleeping draught. I had to let Octavia decide what your fate would be."

My heart is racing, trying to remember those nights, trying to remember her as my mother. Her story sounds like just that, a story, but something about what she's saying feels right.

"You wept until I promised to lie down beside you. You were only five, still a child, and I had to leave you. I thought Octavia would take you with her, but she kept you asleep in that flower until she decided to let you out. For what purpose, I don't know. A wife for her son, perhaps. I don't know why she released you when she did, but she did. The next time I saw you, you were grown, having emerged from that flower as an adult goddess with no memory of our time together. I never forgave Lairus for telling Octavia about you...not because my husband chose to lie with another and father a child when he wouldn't father one with me, but because his indiscretion robbed me of what I loved so dearly."

"I can't... I..." I cover my mouth with my hand. I don't want to face this realization alone. I'm afraid I'm about to start hyperventilating from system overload. "Essos," I whisper, and then he's there, kneeling beside me. I don't know how he knew, or if my words were carried to him on the wind, whispering my desperation for him.

"What, my love? What's wrong?" Essos smooths my hair away from my face, and out of the corner of my eye, I see Esmaray take a step back. Alerted by the movement, Essos spins, ready to defend me, but seeing the Goddess of the Moon standing there makes him falter. He starts to rise but stays instead by my side.

"King of Death," she greets coolly.

"*The* Dead—I'm God of the Dead. Why doesn't anyone see the distinction? And more importantly, why is my wife trembling while you stand there?" Essos glances between the two of us. Indecision is all over his face; he wants to stay by my side, but he also wants to interrogate Esmaray.

"I made some revelations to Daphne that she will have to be the one to tell you about. I just wanted to offer my assistance. I understand your plan is to get my husband to help you by using his son. Lairus has known that Galen is his child since he was conceived. It was quite intentional that they had him. My husband will betray everyone, including Galen, to appease Octavia. It is in your best interests to ensure that your goals align with hers."

"Does Lairus not care about my brother?" Essos asks, standing up. I slide my hand into his and use him for leverage to get up myself. Not once does he break his focus on Esmaray.

"He does, but for Lairus, Titus's absence means that he can finally be with Octavia without your father meddling. If anyone were to stand in the way of that, he will forge a new dagger with her and use it to eliminate that threat to his happiness. Take this." Esmaray tosses something at Essos, and he manages to catch it. He looks warily from what's in his hand to the woman claiming to be my mother.

"What is this?" He holds it up toward the luminescence given off by the moon goddess, or should I say, Titan, hoping the light will filter through enough to discern the contents. It looks like a reddish liquid inside a small vial.

"It took the blood of two Titans to tear down the veil. The blood of two Titans will put it back in place. Be safe..." Esmaray hesitates, and I can hear the word left unsaid hanging in the air. *Daughter.*

She's gone before Essos can question her further, and I'm left trying to reconcile the different tales I've been told. We go inside and walk slowly through the house, not saying anything to draw attention to ourselves. My husband waits till we're in our bedroom before he starts to interrogate me over what just happened.

"Start over," he says, running his hand through his hair.

"According to Esmaray, I'm her daughter, and she's something called a Titan. It seems the God and Goddess Supreme are not the only ones with the power of creation."

I'm standing beside Essos, but barely, as he tries to change the geography of the puzzle in his mind. There are revelations that came with this day that none of us expected. When I sway, Essos gathers me into his arms.

I let him undress me and bring me to the shower as I consider what Esmaray said. That she's my mother. My origin story as a goddess was that I emerged from a moonflower, fully formed, an adult who went to Solarem University so I would learn of the other gods and different powers.

Essos pushes me onto the shower bench before squirting my shampoo into his hand. My eyes drift shut, and I let him lavish attention on me.

"It could make sense," he muses, so quietly I can barely hear him over the sound of the shower.

"What could?"

"I always told you that you were more powerful than we thought. What if this is why? What if, because you were put to sleep in that flower the way you were, you were never able to realize the full depth of your powers? You were never aggressively ambitious, so it would make sense that they remained mostly untapped."

"I wonder if your parents knew it when we were dating, and that's why they were so opposed to us being together. Kai was pulled from the depths of the oceans for Helene. Posey, as far as anyone knew, was just another goddess. The same for Callie. What if my true parentage was why they wanted me to do the Trials? Our union could put us on par with them power-wise. Maybe your parents saw that as a threat. I don't know how it works. Our being the children of Titans is certainly something I never saw coming."

Essos's hands still in my hair. "That feels devious, even for them." He lets go of my hair and pulls the shower head over to rinse it.

"Does it? Or does it feel right? Just how powerful do you think our little pomegranate is going to be?" My hands fall to my stomach even as my head tips back so Essos can massage my scalp with the shower head.

"I think her birth will make the realms tremble."

30

Panic surges in me as the gag in my mouth is tied tighter. I let the tears leak from my eyes, knowing that my makeup is most definitely not waterproof. I struggle against the bindings on my hands and feet. The only thing I have to be grateful for is that the chair I'm tied to is comfortable.

"Shh, you're all right," Essos promises me, stepping into my line of sight. He reaches forward, presumably to smooth away the tear streaks, but I shake my head.

The throne room somehow feels darker now than when we were spilling our blood. I'm not sure I'll be able to use this room ever again. Maybe Essos can be convinced to make our ballroom the new throne room. It's certainly warmer and brighter.

"Leave them. The tears make this more believable," Cat suggests, crossing her arms over her chest. She looks between Essos and I, her mouth twisted in a frown. None of us are happy about this setup.

Essos nods, clenching his teeth before looking away. In his hand is a dagger made to look every bit the real thing. We've gone over this plan several times in the last week, but it makes it no more comfortable.

"Take away the cushion," Xavier says before reaching under me.

Essos puts a hand on his chest. "No. She's pregnant, and we don't know how long this is going to take."

We had to lock Dave away, not that he let something as insubstantial as a door hold him. He's never had to do it, but he's capable of growing to ten times his size without his siblings, outweighing even the griffin that Galen fought during the last Trial. If Dave were here, there would be no way Ellie or Essos walk out of this room again, at least, not whole.

"I'll be fine," I try to say, but it's so muffled and I think I'm drooling into the cloth.

Essos turns to look at me. "No. I have to put my foot down somewhere. You convinced me to tie you up and not in a fun, sexy way. Fine. You convinced me to gag you, again, not how I would have imagined doing it, but you think this will sell it. Now you want me to remove the one thing you can have for comfort? I can feel your heart racing, you're trying to keep calm because you have to, but this is scary and if keeping a cushion on your seat means that you're even remotely comfortable, I'm going to do it because at some point, I'm going to have to hold this to your throat." He waves a dagger between us. "And *I'm* not comfortable with this."

"It's not real," Xavier whispers to him. Their blue eyes lock, trying to survive this battle of wills.

"It's real enough," Essos tells him, shaking his head.

I make the decision for them both and the cushion disappears. Essos's gaze flashes to me and he rubs his eyes. Knowing now that Ellie is the daughter of a Fate, we don't know how much of her powerlessness is real and how much of it is just an act. It's best if this setup looks as real as possible.

"The rest of you, get out. I mean it. Get out now before I change my mind." Essos' order has the desired effect, and everyone leaves us to wait for Ellie. There weren't many here to begin with, just Helene, Xavier, and Cat. We wanted the fewest number of people involved.

Essos presses one last kiss to my forehead before he changes into a different person.

Gone is the husband I know and love. In his place is an aloof king with a crown perched on his head. There is a matching tiara on mine, a prop to sell this. I struggle again against the binding, and the baby gives a light kick in response. We're doing this for her and I have to keep reminding myself of it.

Essos sends his message, dropping it into a bowl of water, leaving us both to wait. We have no idea how long this is going to take. Ellie may be in love with my husband, but if she's feeling put out by his rejection of her, she may not jump when asked.

I try to focus on other things, like how my growing bump strains against the low-cut watercolor dress I'm in and how glad I am that I decided to empty my bladder before I sat down. The quiet contemplation has a negative affect too. I have to think about Esmaray and her proclamation that she's my mother.

Ellie doesn't make us wait long. She springs forth from the ground. As a nymph, her mode of transportation is different from ours. Where we can move, appearing and disappearing at will, she grows forth from the ground like a tree. Nymphs fall under the nature hierarchy, and I've typically felt a deeper kinship for them. She's one of my own kind and it makes the cut of her infatuation with Essos so much deeper.

"Essos," she's trying to sound calm and cool, but her eyes are bright when she spots me. She looks good for someone whose mouth was sealed shut. She's in green leggings and a black tunic, not exactly ready to be faced with her lover. I wonder if she debated changing before appearing before him.

"Ellie." I recognize the tone in his voice. It's the same one he uses when he says my name, and I try to ignore the flutter of my heart. We discussed how this was going to go. We discussed every step that was going to come next.

I know it's coming when I watch him cross the floor to her, sweeping her into his arms and kissing her like she's the wife he's been missing for a millennium. The anguished scream I try to release is not an act. I thought I could handle it, that I was strong enough to see him fake this kiss, but it doesn't feel fake. It only makes me feel like a fool.

Fake, fake, fake. I have to keep chanting the words in my head, but I also can't be too convincing because I still need to sell his betrayal.

Tears begin anew, and when he finally releases her after scooping her up, he won't meet my eyes. Essos nips her lip hard enough to draw blood and he soothes it away with his thumb, flicking it at me. He keeps his focus on Ellie, kissing down her neck until he sets her down.

"What is this?" she asks, finally looking at me with a triumphant sneer. She walks toward me and Essos trails her like she is his master. My eyes flash to his and I convey everything I can in that look, the hurt and the betrayal at seeing that kiss and nearly feeling the heat pouring off them both.

"A gift. My apology gift." Essos places his hands on her shoulders as he stands behind her.

She's wary of me and Essos. I can practically see the gears turning in her head as she calculates if this whole setup is legitimate or if it's too good to be true.

"What changed your mind? Why now?"

Essos trails kisses down her neck. His hands rove over her body possessively, one hand reaching for the hem of her dress to stroke her thighs. The tears leaking from my eyes are very, very real. It's not hard to let myself believe what I'm seeing in front of me because my husband is excellent at selling it. His hands never stray to her breasts or her pussy, and maybe if her mind weren't clouded by his touch, she might see this for the trap it is.

She doesn't let him answer. She spins in his arms and kisses him again, pressing her body against him. He moans into the kiss and it's one that I feel in my bones because I've heard him make that sound while making love to me, and this all feels too, too real. When she breaks it off again, she turns to look at me, her eyes blazing with lust and triumph.

Ellie doesn't look at Essos. She just keeps her eyes on me. I'm not prepared when she pulls her hand back and punches me in the jaw so hard the chair rocks to the side. I don't fall, and I'm glad. There is a binding circle on the floor around me so I can't jump from the space we're in. It's to sell that I'm here against my will, but I need her to step into it. We've made the space around me the Hotel California; you can drop in, but you can never leave, at least, not magically. The flick of her blood onto the border of it coded it specially to her.

"She finally let a healer come to look at the baby and I realized I've been had." Essos's hard tone holds accusation as he glares at me. He moves toward me, pulling the crown from my head. I'm already seeing stars from the punch, so his pulling a few strands of hair barely registers. He holds the tiara out to her almost reverently.

"You've learned what a whore she is? I told the Council the truth. She and Galen slept together and she just tried to cover it up." Ellie sounds meek and apologetic, but vengeance dances in her eyes as she takes the crown, setting it on her head without hesitation. I'm glad it's one of my least favorite crowns because I'm not sure I can ever wear it again.

"It would seem that the bastard that grows in her womb is not mine."

I hate the layer of pain in his voice when he says this. The baby kicks furiously at this, like she can hear and objects to what he's saying. We're both trying to convince ourselves that this isn't an act to sell this to Ellie, and I can only hope we can escape this unscathed. Just hearing him talk like this is dragging up a lot of bad feelings, and we've crossed the line where my tears are not just for show. His hand fists in my hair and he tugs my head back, exposing my throat. Other than the initial tug, he's barely pulling.

"Do it," she urges when she spies the dagger in his hands.

Essos presses the flat side against my throat, and I want to cough. Ellie is so focused on me, she doesn't feel the bindings that are growing up her legs, ready to encase her.

"I want to hear her plead for mercy," Essos taunts viciously, and I feel the blade between my cheek and the gag. The fabric tears easily, but the zing of pain tells me he's nicked me.

Ellie takes a step closer. If he were actually going to slit my throat, she would be coated in my blood, and I think that's what she wants.

"Fuck you both," I snarl. Since I can't see it, I don't know that he has the blade to my throat again, so when I struggle, I feel it slice my skin. It's not deep, I can feel that much, but the blood there only serves to rile Ellie up. And then she's in my circle, and it's too late for her now.

I feel the chair being dragged back as soon as she's fully in and I tighten my fist so the bindings lock around her. Essos drops the fake dagger and kicks it away immediately before kneeling in front of me.

"Are you all right?" he demands, cupping my face, checking my chin and my neck. The wounds are superficial, already healing. Ellie, confused, tries to take a step forward, only to find that she's trapped.

"What the fuck?" she screeches, but we both ignore her.

Essos works first on my hands so we can both untie my ankles. When I'm completely free, his lips crash into mine for an all-consuming kiss. I start crying in earnest while holding him to my face, and it's not cute, but I'm like an exposed nerve. I'm hurting all over and not in a physical way. I need Essos to hold me, and rock me, and soothe me. I knew going into this that it would be difficult, but I never expected to feel like this, so worthless.

I melt into him, ignoring the tantrum Ellie is throwing from her new cage. When we come up for air, I rise on shaky legs.

"I'm all right," I assure him.

"You fat fucking slut!" Ellie screams at me, and I can only snort at her.

"I'm pregnant, you asshole." It is taking all my strength to not to scream at her or attack her, though I would be in my right to. Essos pulls me to his chest, his hand cupping the back of my neck.

"Yeah, with Galen's baby. She's a fucking liar. Galen told me that even before he killed her, they were sleeping together. He told me he only did it because she wouldn't leave you. They had a plan to try to get pregnant and pass the kid off as yours. That's all this is! An extension of that plan." Ellie is coming undone as she rants at us. She's moments away from actually pulling her hair out because there is nothing she can do to escape.

"Shut your mouth or I'll shut it for you... Again," I sneer.

The doors open and in comes the cavalry. Xavier has his hands shoved in his pockets, and Cat's dress looks mildly askew, but now isn't the time for questions. We agreed that it's in everyone's best interest if Tink and Callie remain our ace in the hole, so they are out of sight.

Galen, however, strolls in like he's on our side, copying his older brother with his hands in his pockets as well. When Ellie turns and sees him, she lets out an ear-splitting scream.

"What are you doing here?" Ellie demands, slamming her tiny, ineffectual fists on the invisible force around her.

"I'm choosing the winning side," he says pointedly.

Ellie turns around the room, glancing from person to person before she turns to Essos, a mixture of disappointment and hope on her face. Even after everything, she thinks he will pick her.

"That's not your baby," she warns him before placing a flat palm on the invisible barrier. "It's not too late for us. Let me show you what a true queen can be."

Essos glances up at her long enough to call my tiara to him, off her head. "I know what a true queen is. I'm married to one." He presses a kiss to the crown of my head before smoothing the tiara back where it belongs. I guess I will be wearing it one more time before I cast it into the surface of the sun.

"I can guarantee this child is my husband's." I smooth my hand with my rings over my stomach, not just because I need the calming reassurance of her presence, but because I need to settle my nerves. The adrenaline dump in my stomach makes me want to vomit, but I refuse to show that weakness in front of Ellie.

Essos places his hand over mine, and it does just enough to soothe my ragged emotions.

"Can we wrap up this episode of 'Who's the Daddy?' and maybe get down to business?" Xavier pleads. I catch his icy gaze registering the cut on my cheek and neck. He shoots a glare at his brother, who nearly stumbles back from the force of that look, before focusing on Ellie.

"What do you want with me if we're not getting back together?" Ellie asks. Her shoulders droop, her whole posture collapsing in on itself as the realization that Essos doesn't want her sinks in.

Kai grabs the chair from in front of me and slides it to Ellie, so she doesn't have to stand the entire time she's in there. It's a kindness she doesn't deserve.

"Nothing. You're going to sit there, like a good little hostage, and hope that Galen hasn't overstated your value," Xavier tells her while circling her cage.

Ellie spits at his face.

He takes a step back, letting it fly past him. Then he turns that cold, vicious glare on her. "Eliana, it is in your best interest to not piss us off. My sister-in-law has raging hormones, and who knows what she'll do to a rogue nymph? Unlike us, you can die with one bad thought. Or perhaps we can test how vulnerable the child of a Fate is."

I'm less concerned about what I'll do and more concerned about Helene and Cat. Both of them look like they're crafting clever ways to make her disappear and have no one the wiser. Ellie goes pale at the insinuation of her parentage, but I would love to have her confirm it for me.

I clear my throat. "I have to ask: did your mother throw you in Essos's path because you were just her pawn and she would have put anyone there or did you beg her to let you at my husband the way you begged for him today?"

"I have always loved Essos more than you. It's because of my love for him that my mother promised to keep him safe when she comes for you. And she will, Daphne. She will and when you're mortal again, I'm going to enjoy watching you grow older and older, forced to watch while Essos enjoys my body."

I see Xavier cast a glance in Essos's direction, a brow quirked, wondering what she means about everyone being mortal again. Does Ellie realize what she's let slip?

Essos steps toward Ellie and into her circle. "What gives you the impression that mortality is in the cards for Daphne again?" His voice is tender and sweet, as if he didn't just pull the rug out from under her. It's a little sad to watch as she sinks into his touch when he strokes her cheek. I might actually feel bad for her and all her delusions.

"The gods don't deserve their power, except for you, Essos. But your siblings, your traitorous wife, and your friends abuse their power. Mortality for them is the only way to level the playing field."

Helene looks over at me and scratches at the bandage on her arm. I can't remember if she was there when we discussed the dagger being used to collect the blood of those cut with it. If not, she's no doubt been filled in, but I don't like the way the sight of the bandage causes worry to creep up, making my whole body tense.

"And what is she going to do with the immortality of gods? She's a Fate. She doesn't need it."

Ellie's eyes are practically hearts even as Essos interrogates her. "She's going to take them the way she's been taking souls. If she's more powerful, then she can better protect Solarem."

"Why should we trust anything Ellie has to say? If she's dumb enough to tell us everything, what are the chances she actually knows anything truthful?" Galen prods. "You didn't even believe me when I said anything."

"That's because you were too narrow-minded. You only wanted

Daphne. Mother couldn't trust that you wouldn't turn on her to get what you wanted. She trusts me. I am her child!" Ellie shouts while stomping her foot.

"I still don't buy that you're the child of a Fate." Xavier leans close to her as Essos steps out of the circle and away from her. "Shouldn't you have even a whiff of power?"

"You were too busy with your own dalliances to even know. I'm the child of her and a dryad. My father raised me because he supported my mother's dreams. When I was old enough, she told me everything I needed to know about the royal family. She introduced me to Essos before she got me the job in your office. Before you started to see Daphne. You were on your way to meet *me* when you saved *her.*"

Essos seems to think about this. After saving me from the chariot, Essos insisted he walk me to wherever I was going. I had a study group I was going to, but Essos charmed me with an easy smile. We wound up taking a long, looping walk through Solarem for hours until the sun started to set. He made me promise him a dinner, and I agreed.

Essos's eyebrow lifts and he nods, confirming. He looks toward me. "I was going to meet someone for coffee, a blind date set up by my mother. She wanted me to start to think about settling down because every good king needs a queen."

My husband grabs my hand, pressing a kiss to my knuckles. Ellie makes a choked noise. I doubt there is much more we can get out of her, but I'm happy to leave that up to someone else to handle.

I create a creature similar to Galen's guards from a tree we placed down here for just this purpose. The tree creature lumbers toward us.

"Please guard Ellie and ensure that she is provided with meals." The creature doesn't give any sort of acknowledgement. I want to go upstairs and soak in the bath and wash all these horrible feelings off me. "If you don't mind, this fat slut has things to attend to, like the kingdom I rule. Because *I'm* the queen." I level a pointed glare at Ellie before walking out with Essos hot on my heels.

Once we're clear of the throne room and back on the main level of our home, a choked sob rips free. There aren't any words to soothe the pain of that situation, but Essos doesn't hesitate to scoop me into his arms and carry me to our room.

We clear the doorway and it's not a moment too soon for me to run to the toilet. Essos plops on the ground beside me in an undignified way. With one hand holding my hair back, he uses the other to rub my back.

"You're an incredible woman, you know that?" he tells me quietly.

I lift my head from the bowl long enough to glare. "Is it the vomit or the sweat that does it for you?"

Essos snickers. "It's your strength. I'm so proud of what you did today. Most women wouldn't have been able to handle it. Hell, I wouldn't have been able to handle it if I had to watch you kiss Galen."

I flush, then fall back on my bottom so I can look at Essos. "But you *did*. You did it while the Trials were going on. You stood back and did what had to be done. Don't act like I did some heroic thing today."

Essos climbs to his feet to start the shower and the bath. "Yeah, but you didn't have to hold a blade to my neck while you did it."

"It felt like every day I was holding a blade to your neck if I didn't do what was expected of me. Today felt a little too real," I confess.

Essos's back is to me as he strips off his suit, but I can see his shoulders bow in. "For me too. There was this look in your eyes after I kissed her, an anguish that felt too real."

"It was real. For a moment, I could imagine it, you picking her over me. I know you wouldn't, but I was afraid of it all the same."

"Never. Besides, apparently our baby girl has the ability to make big scary gods want to rip their eyeballs out. I'm not interested in getting on her bad side anytime soon."

Essos helps me to my feet. He snaps his fingers for dramatic flair, and my dress is gone, hung up behind me, leaving me naked for his perusal. He kisses where Ellie punched me and both spots where I was cut, which are already healed, before hauling me into the shower so we can enjoy our very short reprieve before the next problem arises.

31

Xavier requests an audience with Essos and I the next day. We're still trying to figure out how to get our message that we have Ellie to Posey without causing her to just smite us on the spot. I'm not sure it's something she's capable of as a Fate, but I don't really feel like testing it. My hackles are raised that Xavier is going about meeting with us officially, but I go with it.

He asks that Essos and I meet him on the beach, but when we get there, Xavier is nowhere to be seen.

"This is fun," I snark, looking up and down the beach.

Essos chuckles. "Give him a few minutes. He has been trying to do better." He rubs my arms as if to warm me, but I'm not particularly cold.

"Do better? Essos, he still doesn't have a realm to run, but has he offered to help us with ours? No. He's the same Xavier who just punted more and more of his work to us. I'm sorry, but we both have requests that could take the rest of our lives to process. I don't have time to wait around for whatever this is meant to be."

"I'm sorry if I'm wasting your precious time."

I spin around and find Xavier standing there. His face is too stony for me to tell how upset he is by my comments.

"No, Xav, I'm sorry—"

He holds up a hand to silence me. "You're right. I've been lazy and it shows, and I have to be better. If I were a better man, Posey wouldn't have been able to eviscerate me so completely when it came to our realm. Our people know who I am, and that's why they believe her so readily."

"This is a level of self-awareness I never expected," Essos says, eyebrows lifted.

"Like I said, I want to be better. It's why I got you this." Xavier had been covering something with an illusion, but when he drops it, I stumble back in surprise. Sitting at his feet is a baby gryphon. My heart lurches at the memory of the warm blood spraying my face during the final trial, and I have to swallow hard to keep my nausea at bay.

The animal coos, rising to sit on its haunches. The wings on its grey back are too small for it to take flight, but it chirps at me, its front claws scrabbling at the air. It has little spots that cover its bottom, and it decidedly looks disappointed that I have not picked it up yet.

Essos obliges the baby gryphon, lifting it into his arms. It shakes out its wings before nudging the God of the Dead with its little head.

"She's six months old, and I wanted to present her to you for your child." Xavier glances anxiously between us, waiting for us to say something.

I look at the beast, happily chirping in Essos's arms, her tail swishing. I reach a hand toward her, letting her close the distance if she so chooses. Her feathers are soft when she nudges against my hand.

Essos and I have a silent conversation about the creature that is moving her way up his chest so she can perch rather proudly on his shoulder, only to not understand her balance. She tumbles forward and Essos catches her with a groan. This only delights the beast more, so she does it again with a happy squawk, intentionally throwing herself forward to be caught.

"We might as well. What's one more when you have an infant, three dogs, and a petulant cat?" I tease, watching Essos wince as she digs her claws into his shoulder.

"Her name is Nightwalker, and I'll take care of her training and, of course, helping the baby with training."

"We're calling her Pom," Essos interjects, releasing Nightwalker to the ground.

"If you want to change her name, I'm happy to do so–" Xavier starts, unsure of what to do as the gryphon gets a running start before flapping her tiny wings.

"Not Nightwalker, the baby. I'm tired of calling her 'baby' and since we can't decide on a name, I went with what she's the size of. Right now, it's a pomegranate," I tell him with a laugh.

Xavier's eyes fall to my stomach. "May I?" he asks, gesturing toward my stomach.

I nod, guiding his hand to where she's been kicking. I'm not sure if anyone else can feel it yet, so far Essos hasn't, but soon I know he will. Xavier withdraws his hand just as quickly as he touched me, a look crossing his face that I can't name. I want to question him about that look, but he speaks before I can press him on it.

"I don't think you need me to tell you this, but your child only grows stronger every day and you're glowing because of it ."

His comment makes me shift uncomfortably, and I don't know what to say in response so I take the low hanging fruit, so to speak. I snort. "Pretty sure that's just the sweat from exerting myself, but I'll take it."

"Xavier, what Daphne and I were saying before..." Essos reaches out and grabs his brother's shoulder.

"No, you're absolutely right. I was a shit ruler and now we all have to fix it. Maybe eventually we can even figure out how. I just wanted to do this one thing for my niece." There is a tone of finality in his voice. Xavier pulls out of his brother's touch, but I rush forward, grabbing him.

"Xavier, you're going to be around plenty for your niece. She needs a stubborn, pain-in-the-ass uncle who will help embarrass her in front of her dates." I know he promised to help train Nightwalker, but something about his tone doesn't sit well with me.

"Let's clean up this mess first, and then we can talk about what I'll be around for." Xavier less outs a shrill whistle and Nightwalker comes bounding to him, screeching to a halt at his shins.

"Brother, we're going to come out of this. That's a promise you can take to the bank. I should know, I'm the bank."

I try to choke my laugh at the seriousness of Essos's words. Part of me can't help but wonder how long he's been waiting to say that.

"Do you two think I'm making some sort of suicide proclamation?" Xavier steps away from us, studying our faces with amusement.

"I, well, yes," I stutter, glancing at Essos. When his blue eyes meet mine, his shoulder lifts just the barest amount.

"You're both out of your minds. I'm not suicidal. I'm regretful. Gods, you two need to get out more. I have every intention of seducing Catalina and making her my queen."

If I wasn't secretly shipping the two of them together, I might have more of a problem with this proclamation. His inclusion that he also wants to make her his queen helps to save him from my wrath.

"If she doesn't want you, you can't push her. She's learning this world, this realm, her powers, all new. If I hear that she said no, and you didn't listen, I'll cut off your manly pieces and feed them to Nightwalker."

Xavier's whole face darkens as he purposefully utilizes his height to look down on me. "If you think I'm capable of something like that, then you don't know me very well at all." He looks away to the little gryphon. "I'll take Nightwalker back to the stables."

Xavier is gone before I even have a chance to form my objection. Of course, I don't think he's like that, but doesn't he understand that she's my best friend. I may not have trapped her in the endless loop her life was stuck in, but I was the reason she died. It was me, and only me, that can be blamed for her latest death.

The idea tumbles through my mind, but Essos distracts me when he pulls the collar of his shirt to the side, showing off all the tiny scrapes from Nightwalker's claws.

"She got you good," I tell him with a laugh. I press to the tips of my toes to get a better look, but rather than let me tend to him, Essos captures my mouth in a kiss.

"My brother was right, you are glowing, and it's getting harder and harder for me to keep my hands off you."

I laugh, looping my arm in with his, dragging him closer to the surf so we can walk with our feet in the sand.

"Good thing I'm amenable to letting you have me whenever and wherever you want."

"Even right here, on this beach?" he teases, drawing me closer to him.

"No, there will be no sex on the beach right now. I am not interested in getting sand all over my everything and then not being able to...just...no."

Essos lets out a hearty laugh. Even though we've been under such tremendous amounts of stress as of late, I've noticed that he's been getting lighter with each passing day, like being by my side every day has started to ease some of his pain. It may not ever leave him completely, but my presence is going a long way to fixing that hurt.

"I'll gladly clean wherever you want," Essos says before buying his head in my neck, laughing. It tickles me, causing me to laugh too. Between us, the baby kicks.

"Okay, you guys are actually mega gross," Helene says as she steps out of the surf.

I turn to look at her. She's dressed for her court, with pearls woven into her hair and a white Grecian-style dress draped around her.

"Now you know how it felt being around you and Kai during the Trials," I tease, nestling closer to Essos.

"Yes, well, that sounds like a personal problem, but I am here for legitimate reasons. Dion and Bria filled me in about the God Killer blade and its magical properties."

All mirth leaves Essos's from and he stands up straighter, crossing his arms. "I'm listening." Even his tone is harder.

"Kai and I decided to try to appeal to Posey ruler-to-ruler."

I can practically hear Essos counting in his head as he draws in a long breath before slowly letting it out his nose. In his defense, my own anger is rising, but I'm willing to give Helene a chance to explain herself, whereas her brother is always going to go straight into protector mode. I can understand why Helene bothered to try.

"*Explain.*"

"You and Xavier are obviously triggers for her. She hates Xavier and she hates Daphne for apparently also taking you from her daughter. I thought maybe we could try to come up with a solution."

Essos turns his back on his sister and presses his hands into his eyes. He takes in another shuddering breath. "And?"

"And she seemed receptive at first. We met at the cabin, on neutral ground." Helene is really dragging out her take and it's starting to push my patience.

"Spit it out, Hel. What happened?" I ask. I feel tense all over again, waiting for the other shoe to drop.

"Posey cut us. With the God Killer blade. She said she wanted to prove to us that she was open to negotiations by showing that she could have killed us, but didn't."

"She cut you," Essos says.

Shit.

I know better than to get between the siblings when they want to fight, but I can't help but feel for Helene. I've done my fair share of boneheaded, reckless acts while we navigate this, but the possibility that Posey has now taken Kai and Helene's power is a blow I'm not sure we can come back from. It's less their individual powers over the oceans and the stars and more their strength when it comes to fighting.

"Yes," Helene confirms. "Both of us."

"I can't fucking believe you would do something so stupid, so *reckless*, Helene. What were you and Kai *thinking?* She could have killed you, and we had no idea you were even doing this. You deliberately went behind our backs because you knew that Xavier and I wouldn't approve." He paces away from her before screaming, "*Fuck*!"

"You can't have it both ways, Essos. You can't lecture us on not doing anything and then take issue with how we do things."

"I absolutely can, Helene. We've been talking every move through before we make it to ensure that we're not stepping into one of her traps like you just fucking did. Do you understand what this means? No, of course you do. This happened two days ago, and you're only coming to me now. Tell me, what power of yours are you lacking? What is wrong that you realized you have no choice *but* to come clean now?"

"You can be such a sanctimonious prick, Essos, you know that?"

"It doesn't change that I'm right. I can't look at you right now, Hel. You should find our mother and start researching to see if there is a way to reverse what you've done."

"Fuck you, Essos." Helene doesn't bother looking at her brother as she stomps in the direction of the house.

I wait until she's inside before I look at Essos. "Do you think maybe you could have handled that better?" I ask.

He turns his angry glare on me. "Don't you start. What is with the insistence that confronting Posey is a good idea? It's not. It never has been, and it never will be. We know she has Finn's blood, very likely our blood from the night of your wedding to Galen, and now Kai's and Helene's too. Who knows who else could be at risk? Did she cut each of her followers? Did she get Tink or Xavier? We may never actually know. But we know there are still souls unaccounted for, and we know she's starting to consume power. So let me be fucking pissed about this, Daphne. I'm tired of us handing wins over to Posey and giving her the upper hand." He kisses my forehead roughly. "I am going to go work off some of this anger because I will yell again, and I don't want it to be at you because I like sharing a bed with you very, very much." He starts to walk toward the house, leaving me standing on the beach.

Essos pauses and turns to me. "I love you." He says it with such anger and surety that I have to smile at him, even as he turns and strides away from me.

This whole turn of events has me feeling too unsettled to do nothing. So, I do something I know will piss Essos off. If he doesn't like it, he can just deal with it.

32

Zara and Octavia are sitting in the library, arguing over something in a book.

Zara huffs in annoyance. "I think you're reading it wrong. This line here indicates that once the blood is used for better or worse, then it means that the blood can't be used for some other nefarious purpose."

"I think *you're* the one reading it wrong because *I* am the one who wrote it," Octavia argues.

"Just because you wrote it doesn't mean you aren't wrong," Zara snaps, pulling the book around to face her.

"What are you arguing over?" I ask. I expected Helene to be here, but it shouldn't surprise me that she wouldn't listen to her brother, not after he dressed her down so thoroughly.

"Your mortal thinks that her interpretation of an ancient text *written by me* is right and I am wrong," Octavia pouts.

"And where are Sybil, Estelle, and Cat?" I ask, pausing my walk around the perimeter. I stop at a shelf with well-loved paperbacks. I had seen the bawdy romance novels here during the Calling and had started reading the series then. I grab the next one in the series off the shelf and look over the cover, which pictures Princess Lorelei heavily pregnant while her two lovers embrace her. All three of their hands are touching on her belly while she is nearly kissing one and the other is kissing her neck. I hug the paperback to my chest and turn to face Zara and Octavia.

"Cat is with Bria and Finn, I think up in his room. Sybil and Estelle are down in the kitchens arguing about how they should be weaving without their sister," Zara supplies. She tosses her long, dark hair over her shoulder before pulling a book from the pile in front of Octavia.

"Octavia," I say her name sweetly, and she narrows her eyes. "I need you to fix the veil, and I need you to fix it now."

I place the vial of blood from Esmaray in front of Octavia. Just remembering my conversation with the Goddess of the Moon...no... the Titan...has my blood pressure rising and I need to keep it under control.

"You have the blood of...Ti-tus, just lying around?" From her tone, I can tell she knows it's not Titus's blood.

"This blood should be able to accomplish what you need. Now, I suggest you get to it. We want this to be handled as soon as possible, do we not?"

Zara has her focus of the book in front of her, but her ear turned toward Octavia and me.

The Goddess Supreme lifts her head and looks at me. I don't like the way she seems to be peering into my mind, and I have to wonder what else is not covered in these books about the God and Goddess Supreme.

"Go get my son, your husband, and we will do it now. The less you need from me, the better."

I nod and walk out of the room to go hunt for Essos. I know he's angry with Helene right now, but my hope is that he's mellowed out some. I check for him the first place I expect him to be.

When I push open the door to his office, calling out his name, the world shifts to black, and I'm falling again. I try to hold on to the doorknob, but it's no use. Posey's magical pull drags me to where she wants me.

I land hard on my feet again, unhappy with the feel of my hip popping. Thankfully there is no resulting pain like last time. My ability to hold back my hurl is totally shot, and I might add a little more force than necessary when I throw up directly in front of me.

It's too bad Posey isn't right there. Instead, she's watching me from a small dais. Her upper lip curls at the mess I've made, and she wipes the floor clean with a magical flick of her wrist. The white gown she wears makes me wish even more so that I had gotten some on her. She actually looks...awful, and the thought isn't from somewhere petty. Her skin looks sallow and there are black lines along her face and arms where her veins would be.

I look around at the garden I'm in, surrounded by other minor gods, goddesses, and nymphs. The sycophants look like they're out for blood, namely, mine. One face among the many that surprises me is Cassius. The sight of him nearly sends me reeling. I didn't mourn him particularly hard, but I had still thought that he was dead, and I felt guilt and sorrow that his life had been lost.

And here he is, probably has been since he was beheaded, well, fake beheaded. I doubt he would have been willing to actually cut his head off, which means the head that Posey showed me at our first face-off was also a fake. Fucking bitch.

Cassius has two women nearly dripping off him, but his face is blank. He glances down at my pregnant stomach, then away. Our very own Judas. I'm glad we only had the one meeting with him there. I wonder how long he's been here, and it's fortunate that his beheading happened early on in this game of chess we're caught playing between two queens.

It's then that I notice one of the women dripping off him is Lucky, a sick glee on her face. The hedges are tall with white and red roses blooming, nearly dripping with blood. I bite my tongue, waiting for Posey to speak first.

"You insolent bitch," she snaps. She doesn't rise from her chair, but her cheeks are pink with fury.

"Do you want to itemize the things I've done to wrong you this time, or shall I guess?" I shouldn't antagonize her, but sometimes she makes it too fucking easy. I'm glad I just gave the Titan blood to Octavia. Zara will ensure nothing happens to it.

Posey makes her second mistake by trying to attack me with the wooden staff beside her. She lifts it, ready to propel it at me like a javelin thrower at the Olympics. The bushes behind her swell in size, reaching out to snatch the staff from her grip. I have half a mind to skewer her on it like a Posey-kabob, but I keep my temper in check, letting the wood be reabsorbed.

"Where is she?!" Her voice is shrill as she jumps to her feet, advancing on me with renewed vigor. I refuse to take a step back, even when I notice the God Killer dagger in her hand. I'm not naive enough to think she won't use it on me. Visions of Finn's freshly carved face swim in my mind. Posey is toe-to-toe with me, and yeah, I'm a bitch for it, but I grin down at her.

"You're going to have to be more specific." I hope my voice affects a calm that isn't currently in my repertoire. There is very little I can do if she decides to use that weapon on me, but damn it if I won't do every last thing. I try to transport myself home but can't.

"Where is Ellie?!" Posey hisses, giving whole new meaning to the term spitting mad. With grace and a touch of attitude, I wipe some of the spittle from my face.

I take the leap when I lean forward, pressing my mouth next to her ear. "You mean your *daughter*?"

Posey doesn't hesitate to thrust the dagger at my face, but I'm fast enough to dodge her. Maybe egging on the lunatic with a weapon wasn't my smartest move, but it was certainly a decision.

The blade slides over the exact spot that Essos cut me days ago with a fake dagger. The training with Essos and Kai kicks in, and I react, grabbing the hand holding the blade and twisting her arm far enough that I can feel the tendons on the verge of snapping, urging her to let it go. Posey grits her teeth, straining not to, but the move works and she releases the dagger. I catch it.

It feels like a lucky break that I can end this all, even if I don't kill her with it now. Having Ellie and having the weapon means that we're ahead of the curve for once.

The blade practically thrums with energy in my hand, and I can't help but turn my face to glare at Posey triumphantly. I have the weapon and I need to get out now. Quick as I can, I release Posey, but she's already realized that I have the upper hand, and she won't let me go that easily. Her hand twists into the loose fabric of my shirt, and I can feel the air being dragged from my lungs. It's not enough to feel so breathless, but I can feel the pressure on my windpipe as she squeezes.

No matter what I do, I can't get a breath. The pressure on my chest feels too much for me to compensate for. My vision is starting to go splotchy, black creeping in to suffocate the light.

"Let me show you how it was for your friend when he came trying to steal from me."

I have no choice as Posey pushes her memory into my mind.

She's sitting and waiting in her office like some sort of assassin lying in wait for her mark, but I suppose that's exactly what she is.

Finn appears in Xavier and Posey's old bedroom, and he glances around, looking for the trap to spring. It's written all over his face in the skeptical squint to his eyes and the tension in his shoulders. But Posey bides her time and waits until he's exactly where she wants him.

Every little bread crumb that Posey painstakingly laid is leading to this very moment and she's almost giddy with excitement. Small wings emerge from Finn's shoes and lift him in the air so he can hover over the bed to better access the safe hidden behind a portrait of Posey.

Finn glances around again, instincts probably screaming that this is too easy because it is, and this might be a memory, but I want to scream at him to run.

"Looking for these?" Posey asks, holding out the scepter and the dagger. She's transported to be right at his side. He startles back, but has just a second to grab one *of the items. He snatches the scepter because it's a hair closer to him, but it's that greedy moment where he thinks he can grab the dagger too that seals his fate.*

Three goons appear in the room. One throws their arms around his middle, pinning Finn's arms into place and hauling him off the bed while the other two rip the wings off his shoes.

He screams in agony as blood spurts from them. It's only a memory and I still gag, my heart breaking all over again for Finn.

He never sees who is holding him as Posey advances on him with the dagger, but I can see Cassius watching on coldly even as he holds down a screaming, crying Finn, his body thrashing as she carves one eye from his face.

To shut him up, she shoves the removed item in his mouth before she starts on the other one. There is so much wrong with this scene, but perhaps nothing more than the utter delight I feel from Posey.

"Perhaps the princes will think twice before sending someone else to do their dirty work."

Through the whole ordeal, Finn never gets go of the scepter, and the moment he's free, he transports himself out of that room. At some point he spit his eye out because both of them lie on the ground, seeming to stare at me in accusation for not helping my friend.

I WANT to scream and cry myself, but when I come out of the memory, I'm still being held in a chokehold. It's unclear what she hoped to achieve with showing me that memory, but it makes me never want to let this weapon go.

"You may not die, but your child will. Let go of the dagger, and I'll let you both live."

I wish my eyesight was enough to cook her with the fire of a thousand burning suns, but I'll have to settle for the next best thing. I stab the dagger into the hollow of her shoulder. The pain must be distraction enough because she lets me go as she stumbles away from me with the blade still embedded in her flesh.

We break apart, eyeing the other to see if we're going to go for another round.

"You want Ellie back? You'll come, *alone,* to my house tomorrow."

"Why? So you can spring a trap and kill me?"

I scoff. "You're the one carving people's eyes out. We would prefer to settle this amicably, but if you leave us no other choice, we will strike to kill. Show up. Otherwise, I'll turn Ellie into an herb and you'll spend the rest of your immortal life wondering if you're seasoning your meal with your daughter."

Posey rears back like I've hit her, but I won't give her the chance to respond. Whatever force Posey was using to hold me there is gone. I separate myself enough from her to return home.

If I were smart, I would have told Posey to come next week to give us time, or even said, *Don't call us, we'll call you,* to stop her from treating me like some sort of errand girl.

When I feel the sand beneath my feet, I finally start to relax, letting my knees drop to the sand. Now that I'm away from her and the adrenaline is done coursing through my body, I realize I'm shaking and really want to throw up. Again.

What she did to Finn...

This time I do throw up and it's mixed with my tears because it was all too close, too fucking close.

I need to get my emotions and breathing somewhat under control before Essos finds me and levels Solarem. The tide laps against my ankles, and I whisper a quiet prayer to the water to get Kai. I have to hope that even with his powers so diminished that he gets the message.

"Fancy meeting you here," Kai greets after approximately thirteen seconds. I want to collapse like tissue paper, but I don't. My fingers slide into Kai's outstretched hand and I struggle to my feet.

"Of all the gin joints," I joke. One of his large finger's prods under the cut on my cheek, wiping at the partially dried blood there. I can feel the water running off his fingertip, helping to clean my cheek so I look more presentable to Essos. If Zara was right and the blood was a onetime use only, I've just fucked myself by getting cut again.

"Want to tell me what happened?"

It's not that I blame Kai for prodding, but I would rather only deal with this once. I look up into his warm brown eyes and shake my head.

"Gather the council. We're going to war."

Essos is the first person through the door. I'm standing at the head of the dining room table, arguing about if we need to have food for this right now because I don't know if I have it in me to ever eat again, and Kai is doing his level best to distract me by listing different foods. I can still feel my body trembling. My husband spins me to him, pressing a kiss to my lips. It sears me to my bones and I reciprocate, grabbing his sides, opening my mouth for him.

Kai clears his throat and we step apart. "Where did you go? I just heard you say my name as you opened the door to my office and then you were just, gone."

I touch Essos's cheek gently. "I know. I'm fine. Posey magicked me away again. Her mistake. She showed her hand, at least part of it. She's desperate for Ellie back. I also saw Cassius and Lucky there, so we may have had Tink in our pocket, but she had her own people spying on us."

"Who? Posey?" Cat asks as she walks into the room. She's wearing a red gauzy dress and has an ethereal glow to her skin. The more she practices, the more she sharpens her abilities, the more clear it becomes that she's right where she's supposed to be.

"Yes, but I think she's desperate and sick. Posey wants, no, needs to get Ellie back. Maybe there is a bloodless way out of this. Maybe we just agree to give Ellie back if she promises to give us–"

Helene cuts me off. "Everything we want? You think she's going to hand all that over for one woman? Even if she is her daughter? Keep dreaming." Helene rests her hand on Kai's shoulder, checking him as if he was the one abducted by our enemies.

"I think she will. Her daughter might very well be her only chance at ending this. I think whatever she's doing to consume the souls is having an adverse effect on her. She looks like a walking corpse. This might be our chance to really end this." I wish there was a way I could convince Helene. I want her to understand.

"I think you overestimate my ex-wife's ability for emotion. She doesn't love, not even a child she failed to officially acknowledge. Ellie is just a convenient pawn in her play for power." Xavier grinds his teeth, meeting my gaze, trying to show me, what? That he's right?

But I doubt them all. I doubt they can really understand what I saw. I turn to Essos, cutting out the group. Essos's blue eyes fall to me, searching my face to see what I want to convey to them. His gaze catches on the cut, and he lets out a harsh breath.

"We have to try," he announces, turning to everyone.

Galen and Octavia enter, and the conversation dies down immediately. Suspicious glances are cast toward the mother-and-son pair, who ignore the unwelcome climate in the room. Octavia sits primly at the table, pulling apart a croissant she conjures. Essos's hand snakes around my waist to the small of my back and pulls me against him. One look at my husband's face and I can see him tracking every step Galen takes.

"We also don't have much time to come up with a plan," I admit sheepishly.

"Care to elaborate?" Finn prods when I don't say anything more.

"I told her to be here tomorrow so we can settle this once and for all."

Everyone erupts at once. Even Octavia pales at this admission. Everyone is talking over each other except for Essos, who is patiently watching me.

"I suppose you still want me to put the veil back into place today?" Octavia asks. As if she needs to but in all the different things we have to do on this short timeline.

Zara walks in, holding another book and the vial in her hands. "Ignore Octavia. It's actually a much simpler ritual than she wants to make it sound. We could even do it without her if we had some of her blood."

"Someone's been a busy little bookworm," Galen taunts Zara.

She glares at him for a fraction of a second. "Maybe if you tried opening a book once in a while, it would help your IQ. You certainly have nothing else going for you." She turns her back on the God of War and Suffering, dismissing him.

Essos is focused on me, and not the verbal sparring between Zara and Galen.

"I don't think you need stitches," he admits, gingerly pressing on my cheek. The bruise from Ellie's strike has finally faded, but this will serve as another reminder to him of my fragility, and I'm frustrated by it.

"I stabbed her in the chest. I should have stabbed her in the heart." I don't admit to him how she choked me, how she cut off my air so thoroughly, so completely, that I thought I was going to die.

"If you had stabbed her in the heart, you would have had to take her place and we might have lost Pom."

"We might have a plan, though," Zara tells me excitedly. "See? Book smarts over brawn," she throws at Galen over her shoulder.

"And it would seem just in time," Estelle announces, followed by Sybil, who rounds out their trio.

Hope blossoms in my chest, and I want them to give me an easy solution, one that we can handle tomorrow.

"Well, don't keep it to yourselves. Out with it," Xavier orders.

What remains of the Fates sits at the table across from Galen and Octavia.

Bria braces a hand on Finn's shoulder, and I don't miss how he threads his fingers with hers. Even Dion is standing a little closer to her now, and I wonder if they've started to sort out their problems.

Callie and Tink are the last to join the group and the table. Galen watches his wife move with confidence to the farthest point away from him, placing herself between Tink and Kai. Helene is perched at the farthest point from Essos, even if it puts her next to Galen. Xavier sits on the opposite head of the table from Essos and me, surveying our motley crew himself.

"Our plan is not just for how to handle the veil but how to handle Posey. We just need a new blade," Zara says with excitement.

"A new blade in addition to the two that are already floating around? That's a winning idea," Finn grumbles.

"What we need is the blood of the God and Goddess Supreme in order to shift the veil back into place and to forge a new weapon," Estelle says solemnly, and my anger spikes. My conversation with Esmaray was short but loaded with new information that I haven't had time to utilize, but now is the time for that.

"Too bad we're fresh out of blood from the God Supreme, what with him being dead," Finn snarks. If he still had eyes, I bet he would roll them. With how vocal he's being I can't help but think it was a good idea to have Bria stay. She's helping him even if it goes against what Dion thinks is best.

"You mean, you need the blood of Titans," I state dryly.

Sybil has the decency to look chastened as they glance up the table in my direction.

"Titans?" Helene asks, confused.

"Titans. As in the creators of our universe. As in your parents aren't the only ones." I level my glare at Octavia, who doesn't look the least bit ashamed, even though she won't meet my eye. I already revealed to her that I knew this, but it's the first time her other children are hearing it.

"I'm so lost," Helene says, glancing from me to her mother to the Fates.

"Why don't you give us a history lesson, oh 'Goddess Supreme?'"

Essos squeezes my knee under the table, and I wonder if my sarcasm is too much.

Octavia huffs before starting, "We were born from a kernel of the universe. There were six of us, but only three remain. We were Titans of the world, and we created the universe to be what we wanted. We added birds to the skies and water to the lakes. We created Solarem to be the safe haven that it is for people of our kind, and we molded more and more types so as to give the world magic.

"When the two other Titans chose to flood the world with their magic and become one with the realm, it left the remaining four with a question of what to do. We had nymphs and sea creatures. Out of necessity to serve the mortal realm, gods were being born. Werner, the God of Mischief. Gisella, the Goddess of Knowledge and Truth. I had Essos, then the twins. The other two Titans continued their lives happily."

I glare at Octavia, waiting for her to admit her indiscretion.

She continues. "I fell in love with the God of the Sun and bore him a son, and I was happy. I wanted to live the life I wanted with the man I loved, but Titus told me that I had to choose between my son and my lover. He didn't want me, but he didn't want anyone else to have me either. If I chose my lover, I would never see any of my children again, including Lairus's child. I would have been cast out and ruined. So, I chose the life I did, and I'm not mad that I did."

Octavia folds her hands on the table. It's not the whole story, and I trust it a lot less than I trust Esmaray's story. I can't say why. It's clear I don't know Esmaray better, but I know Octavia's character, and I know I can't trust her. I open my mouth to question her further, but Cat beats me to the punch.

"Who are the other Titans? You said three remain. You and who else? Can we get them to help?" I love Cat's impassioned plea. She hasn't been one of us for long, but she fits right in.

Estelle is tight-lipped before she finally speaks. "In the absence of the blood of the God Supreme, perhaps we can try with the next best thing. As children of Titans, blood from Essos, Xavier, Helene, and Galen should satisfy that requirement. The stronger the blood we have, the better."

"Mother, who are the other Titans?" Xavier pushes.

Cat turns her head in his reaction, still careful not to make eye contact. I stay silent, wondering if Octavia will come clean about everything.

"Could you use that blood to imbue another weapon to make it a God Killer also?" Essos asks, his train of thought on a totally different path.

"The blood *is* the metal of the God Killer blade. Using your blood is imperfect, but we will have to make do," Estelle answers.

I can practically see the gears turning in Essos's head as he rubs his thumb over his lower lip. I want to bite his thumb and lower lip and be anywhere but here.

"What about the blood of a fifth child?" My question causes Essos to frown. More blood drawn from my body. I lift one shoulder to him in apology but wait for an answer. My obvious preference would be to avoid that. I don't want to spill my blood any more than Essos wants me to, but if that will make it stronger, I will.

Essos pinches the bridge of his nose. "Why is bleeding my wife one of the first options? Why shouldn't a Fate bleed for once?" I don't think Essos really means it when he mutters that under his breath, but it raises an interesting question of using the blood of two Fates against once. "If the blood is the metal, then we can make another weapon."

Sybil must realize that I'm talking about me. Everyone else is exchanging confused glances. Sybil does what their sister is unwilling to do–they answer Cat. For whatever reason, Estelle has chosen to stick with perpetuating the lie of the God and Goddess

Supreme, even if all the cards are on the table. "Lairus and Esmaray are the other two Titans. The sun and the moon. It's been a closely guarded secret that we've held for eons." Estelle looks at Sybil with censure in her eyes. "What's the saying, sister? In for a penny, in for a pound? Clearly, the way things were working aren't any longer. It's time to try something new."

Essos tips his head at them in thanks while squeezing my knee under the table again.

Helene turns her attention on her baby brother, pointing a finger in his face. "Great. Galen, ask your daddy for some blood. I imagine it's going to take some time for this weapon to actually be forged, so chop-fucking-chop. It would be nice for all of us to be armed against Posey."

Finn cuts in. "I repeat, why do we want a third blade floating around?"

Sybil ignores him and addresses Helene's comments first. "She's right. This will take time. It requires the blood of two Titans to work. If we can get Lairus's blood to mix with Octavia's instead of the blood of the children, the blade will be stronger for it. We don't know that your blood will even work for a weapon or the veil." Whatever silent accord Estelle and Sybil had about information or the Titans or whatever, Sybil is done with it. They rise to their feet, ready to jump into action. This is the person I remember from the Calling.

"Why should Lairus bleed for the woman who murdered his son? You haven't even *asked* if I'm willing," Octavia spits, getting to her feet. She stares down her only daughter, waiting for a good enough response. She just doesn't expect it to come from the man sitting beside her.

"Maybe because I made her bleed first, mother." Galen's words echo in the quiet room. "Besides, it's not just for *her*. It's for all of us." He's not looking at me with apology in his eyes. He's looking at Callie apologetically. I don't know if I trust his words, but his intention is clear. He wants Callie and everyone to know that he's repentant for his crimes. At least, that's what I surmise. If he were truly repentant, he would use actual words to start.

Callie doesn't look Galen's way. She doesn't acknowledge him in any way, but I can see the barest movement of Tink taking her hand under the table and squeezing. I hope for both of them that her husband didn't see that. There might be no love for their pair, but Galen has always been the jealous sort.

"Is any of this bleeding even necessary? We still have one God Killer blade and I refuse to give up another piece of my heart for the weapons," Octavia whines.

Zara jumps in, ready with the answer. "Rather than the blade being forged to kill Posey, this blade will strip her of her powers. We don't need any more pieces of your heart, just your blood."

Finn grumbles under his breath, "Finally an answer to the question I've been asking for the last thirty minutes." Bria squeezes his hand.

"Can you convert the purpose of the stone to hold her power?" Essos asks, leaning forward.

"Maybe we can?" Sybil hedges.

"If you can work with me on it, I'm happy to try to develop something," Tink offers.

Zara grins at him. "Help is always appreciated."

"We still have the problem of needing another Titan," Dion says.

Galen turns to his mother. "Call him."

Octavia's lower lip juts out in a petulant pout. "No," she whines.

The back-and-forth between mother and son gets old quickly, but I'm not the first to lose my patience. Essos slams his fist on the table, causing a crack to split the wood. Everyone stares at it for a moment before I place my palm on the surface, fixing the damage.

"*Yes,*" Essos pushes back. "You demanded that Galen be resurrected and he was."

"Only because I took it upon myself to do so."

"Mother, you swore up and down that you knew how to defeat Posey and Galen was your bargaining chip. You brought back the man who murdered my wife, and I didn't immediately put him down like the animal he is because *you* demanded it. I have held up my end of the bargain. I have no trouble reversing that if you find you cannot uphold your end of our bargain." Essos's voice is lethal. Octavia shrinks back like he's slapped her, but Essos has no patience for her. "Call him, *now*."

Octavia purses her lips. "Everyone should close their eyes."

Begrudgingly, everyone does as she asks. Bracing for the reason that Octavia had us cover our eyes, Essos's hand finds my face, further darkening the world on me. Magic fills the room in a nearly suffocating amount, accompanied by a blistering heat. Just as quickly as the warmth came, it is gone. Dave whines under the table.

"You can open your eyes," a deep voice instructs.

I still hesitate to open my eyes, afraid of what I might see. When I do, I'm stunned by the man before man. He has rich tan skin and striking golden brown eyes with dark hair that's tied back with a simple frayed ribbon. He's remarkable and impossible to look away from.

Octavia spins in her seat and launches herself into Lairus's arms. He buries his head in the crook of her neck and breathes deeply. He's casual in his stance and dress. He's got on a faded T-shirt, shorts, and flip-flops. Where Esmaray looked like the ethereal embodiment of the moon in a gossamer gown with light panels flowing around her, Lairus looks like everyone's favorite dad, dressed and ready for summer vacation.

Galen gets to his feet, a slight tremble in his limbs. There is trepidation in how he holds himself and on his face while he watches his parents' reunion. When Octavia presses her mouth to Lairus's, Galen looks away, his gaze finally meeting mine. I refuse to be the first to blink, so when he does, shame coloring his cheeks, I count it as a victory.

"Lairus, this is your son." Octavia clutches the shoulders of both men, tears glistening in her eyes.

Essos rises, taking my hand, helping me up. There is nothing subtle about how he places his body between Lairus and me. We might be counting on him for help, but we don't know who he is or what his intentions are. Esmaray's warnings regarding Lairus and his love for Octavia linger in the back of my mind.

"Can we dispense with this episode of Maury and focus on the real issue at hand?" Xavier's cool voice calls. Everyone else in the room has gotten to their feet, and Lairus finally looks from his son and his lover to survey the room. Kai moves to step in front of Helene, but she stops him with an icy glare.

"I'm sorry, is meeting my son for the first time inconvenient for you, child?"

Xavier bristles at the insinuation that he is inexperienced and youthful.

"My brother doesn't mean to be rude. We're on a time limit and would deeply appreciate your assistance," Essos interrupts, trying his hand at diplomacy.

Lairus's golden eyes flick to my husband then to me before falling on my stomach. My reaction is instinctual. I smooth a hand over my belly protectively. I will not go down without a fight. It's the similarity to Galen's eyes that chill me to my bones.

"What is it you want from me? I was told to let the God and Goddess Supreme reign and that I was to only fulfill my job, ensuring that the sun rose and fell, and now you call me here, before the weaker share of the Fates, to ask for, what? My favor?" Condescension drips from Lairus's voice. I might hate him.

"Posey has been running roughshod over Solarem. She has plans that will shake our existence to the core. We want your help to craft another blade that will stop her." My voice is stronger than I feel. I step around Essos, unwilling to be cowed by Lairus. Beside me, the God of the Dead tenses.

"And you, the child of Spring, plan to end her? Do you plan to take her place as a Fate when you do?" He steps around Octavia to caress my cheek with the backs of his knuckles. I won't look away from him, even when he grips my chin with his pointer and thumb finger, tilting my face up so he can get a better look at me. Dave barks at the intruder, but Lairus ignores him.

"We have a plan for that," Zara bravely announces. I don't know what her plan is, but Lairus won't stop looking at me, so I can't even look to her to see what she means.

"You grow heavier with child each day," Lairus starts.

"Gee, just want every pregnant woman wants to hear, how she's gaining weight." My tone is dry, but I need to affect this feeling of cool indifference. I can't let him know how his hands on me bother me. They're warm, like one would expect of the man who is the sun incarnate. I expect the blistering heat from them, but it never comes.

"Do you know what joy it will be to see my grandchild brought into this world?" Lairus asks, lowering his face so I can feel his breath on my cheek.

Essos's tolerance has run out. Gently, he grips my wrist and pulls me out of Lairus's grasp. "The child is mine, not Galen's." Essos's tone is steely, brooking no room for argument.

"But she is mine," Lairus announces with a smug smile.

"I'm sorry. Excuse you?" I ask, but I sway in my place. Essos hooks an arm around my waist, holding me to him.

This time, the confusion rippling around the room is felt by all.

"What?" Octavia asks, disbelief in her voice. She knows of my origin. Octavia was integral to how I was taken from Esmaray as a child.

"Esmaray always thought that it was only her love that brought a child into the world. She thought that a moonflower meant that you came all from her, but fertilization is what brings forth children. I played the part of a bee, helping you come into being. It meant that Esmaray was happy. It meant that my wife was able to stop pestering me because of my relationship with Octavia. I let Esmaray believe that she alone had created you. I let her think she had the upper hand and was buying my silence. Only, her infatuation with you meant that she didn't care for me and how I spent my nights. It meant that I was jealous of a child. I never expected to miss how my wife would pine for me. So, I sold you out to Octavia, earning Esmaray's ire for my troubles."

Xavier snorts. "So, your son almost raped your daughter. Gods, you Titans got so much wrong."

I have to agree with his disgust. Gods, not only that, but Galen and I kissed and went skinny-dipping together. My whole body feels dirty suddenly, and even if we're only half-siblings, and not even in the traditional sense, I can't do it. I can't believe it. This is one of those traumas that I'm just going to have to sit on for the next hundred years because there is too much to unpack right now. Everything I thought I knew about my creation, my birth, was a lie. I thought I grew up without parents, but I had them. Only, one didn't care and the other had to give me up to satisfy Octavia.

The room shakes a little, and I don't know who is causing it, me or Essos or Lairus with the way he's looking at Galen, his brow crinkling.

"Is this true?"

As much as I want to see Galen get his shit rocked by the God of the Sun, or rather, a Titan, we are on a timeline, and I didn't give us enough time to deal with this.

I cut in. "Honestly, we can address that later in family therapy. We need your help and I want to know if you intend to give it or if you're more interested in playing games and manipulating all of the women in your life. You've already done wrong by me once. Do you plan to let me down again?"

"What is it that you want?" Lairus's tone is even when he responds, finally tearing his eyes from Galen to look at me again. The room stops shaking.

"Your blood. We want to create another dagger," Essos supplies. My husband turns his head toward me, surveying my physical state, trying to glean what he can about my emotions, but I don't want to think about that. Like everything else, I'll deal with all the emotional fallout when we've survived. No need to get worked up over something when I might be dead in a day anyway.

"Because the first two worked out so well for you?" Lairus deadpans.

"We also need to close the veil between our realm and the mortal realm. Our plan with the dagger isn't your concern. Are you willing to bleed for your grandchild, or not?" I snap. I lift my hand to press it to my temple, but I don't want to show weakness in front of Galen and Octavia and Lairus. It's true, they're playing their own game, and right now, I'm less worried about their games.

"Which vein would you like me to cut, daughter?"

I leave the more useful members of our group to puzzle this out. Essos tells me he wants to stay behind to ensure that this happens, and as much as I just want to crawl into his lap, I can't begrudge him this.

My progress toward my room is paused at the bottom of the stairs. I've been getting more winded the bigger the baby gets. My body is focused on building a nervous system and lungs, not on making sure I'm getting enough oxygen into mine.

"Escort me to my room?" Finn asks, cautiously walking toward me. He has a white cane in front of him, feeling for tables or anything that might get in the way. Once, Finn comes close to colliding with the doorway, and Spot gives a low growl beside him.

"It would be my pleasure." I take his hand, sliding it over my arm before progressing slowly up the stairs. I have to fight the mental image that works into my head of him screaming with blood pouring down his face as Posey shoved his eye in his mouth.

"Do you believe this will work?" Finn asks as we gradually get up to the second floor. Behind us, Cat and all three dogs are patiently watching, ready to jump into action if needed.

I try to keep a positive tone. “I hope so. It’s not like it’s over once we defeat Posey. We still need to rescue those souls that she consumed, if that’s even possible, and the ones that are locked in the stone. All for which we will likely need the Scepter of the Dead. This is not an easy fight. There is also the matter of convincing the people of Solarem that we’re not intending to hurt them.”

“Is it awful that I want to hurt her?” he whispers, shame burning his cheeks.

“No. It’s not. But if we can take her powers, maybe we can let her live out her life as a mortal.” I honestly hadn’t thought past that next step. It seems so improbable, that we will defeat her. That doesn’t mean we shouldn’t have a plan. Should there be a trial where all of our misdeeds are dragged into the open light of day? Do we reveal the existence of Titans and weapons that can kill Gods? Are we just setting ourselves up for more trouble?

“Daphne?” Finn asks. I realize then that while I spiraled down, down, down into the possibilities of tomorrow and the day after, Finn had been talking to me and I totally missed it.

“What was that?” I ask, walking again. Rather than taking him to his rooms, I walk him to mine, determined to keep him out of his room for just a little longer.

“I said, I think you and Essos should take over Solarem. You can find someone else to rule the Underworld. What Solarem needs now is a leader who will actually lead.” Finn’s steps falter when we walk past his room.

“I’m not ready to be alone. Come sit with me and Cat in my room?” I’m almost begging him.

Finn turns his head toward his room, then back to me. “Fine, but only if you consider it.”

“Essos and I have no dreams of leading more than just the Underworld. We want to be able to fix what was broken. It’s also been so long since I last ruled. You can’t expect me to step in and rule all of Solarem.”

“Someone has to. Xavier made it clear that he’s not that person.

We've all known it for a long time, but no one wanted to say or do anything about it. There is no better time."

"You're talking about a coup, and I'm not interested. Let's survive this and see what happens next. I have complete faith that Xavier will want to do better." I don't say that I think that part of Xavier's reluctance to actually lead had less to do with laziness and more to do with his aversion to Posey. She was the one that tried to push him to do more. She was the one that pushed him to take on more and more that he passed off to Essos.

"I plan on helping," Cat pipes up, taking a seat on the couch and helping Finn sit beside her. He turns his head toward her sharply.

"And what do you know of the politics of Gods?" he snaps.

A frown tugs my lips down. He might be one of my best friends, but Cat is my sister. I will defend her and fight the battles she doesn't want to. This might be one that she wants to take on herself, but I can't tolerate his tone.

"Whatever you will teach me," she says, playing on his pride before I can even open my mouth.

Finn's eyebrows shoot up in surprise. "You think I can teach you about what it means to be not only a Goddess, but a queen?" Finn scoffs, slouching in his chair. His sunglasses start to slide down his nose and he pushes them back up self-consciously.

"I think you can teach me what makes the people of Solarem tick. I think you can teach me about a lot more than you think, like what they want and how disappointed they have been in Xavier and Posey. You seem to know a lot about that personally."

"And do you think, Catalina, that just because the Fates said you were meant to be together, that all of the sudden the biggest man-whore in all of Solarem is going to keep his dick dry just because you told him to? His focus has always been on chasing a warm body to fuck and not on leading."

"Finn," I warn, but Cat holds up a hand to silence me.

"Isn't that what your Fates do? Pre-determine everyone's destinies and who they were meant to be with? I don't believe that this will change who he is, and I don't want to change him. If I'm not enough for him then we can face that, but maybe I don't just want to be with him. Maybe I'm biding my time to taste all the goods that Solarem has to offer. You said it yourself, you live too long to limit yourself to one gender. I've lived and died as a woman in love with straight men so many times, maybe I want to see what else life has to offer. Maybe I want to have several lovers. Maybe I'll have a queen's harem, but I know that I was born or created or however gods come to exist to be the Queen of the Pantheon, and I'll be damned if anyone will stop me from fulfilling my destiny. Actually, I take that back. I literally was damned to prevent that and I won't let it happen again."

Cat is breathing heavily by the time she finishes the tirade that she actually ended up shouting in Finn's face. I expect him to be turning various shades of reds or purples from being filled with rage, but he's not. There is an amused tilt to his lips.

"Sounds like someone is ready to do what it takes to be queen. As long as you're not going to step all over people to get there, you can. You forget, Catalina, I know you. I understand you. You're going to make a great queen and I know you will serve the people of Solarem well. We just have to survive long enough to get there."

"That means getting *you* into fighting shape," I point out, ready to be on the receiving end of his ire. Whatever fight is in Finn leaves him quickly and he deflates.

"You're talking about those gadgets Tink made, aren't you?"

"I am."

Tink never showed me what he made for Finn, just that he made something. I envision some horrible thing that he will have to use, but I'm not sure. The craftsmanship of the gloves and the belts was perfect. Maybe he has another way to do this without making Finn feel worse.

"I don't want to become Frankenstein's monster. I'm already hideously scarred and Dion won't touch me." His Adam's apple bobs as he swallows. "What if he won't have me? What if it makes me more monstrously deformed? Never mind that Bria is here now too."

I surprise Finn by cupping his face and pressing my fingertips to his temples He jerks back and out of my grip, but I see the change in his features. With one touch, I am able to give Finn a gift. All I'm doing is sharing with Finn what he can't grasp for himself.

He saw what I've been seeing. He's seen the last few weeks of Dion and Bria fussing over him, tears that I caught Dion spilling that I shouldn't have been privy to, and the general concern the rest of us have expressed about how to help him. There are moments of Bria consoling Dion and little signs of solidarity once they were able to get past their earlier animosity. None of our conversations have been about how horrible he looks or how we can't bear to look at him any longer. They're not full of pity, they're full of helplessness, knowing that he is our friend, knowing that we love him and there's nothing he will let us do until he's ready.

Finn covers his face with his hands, collapsing in on himself. I reach around his shoulders and hug him until he folds his body in half. Cat takes over from there, following him down to whisper something in his ears that I don't catch. I rub his back, knowing that for now this is how he has to cry.

"I'm trying," he grits out, sitting up so quickly, he nearly smacks his head into Cat's nose. She gets out of the way just in time.

"We know. I didn't show you that to make you feel guilty. I showed you that so you can understand what is going on outside your room. Dion knows he can't push you, that you need to do things when you're ready, and I'm not trying to push you to take what Tink is offering. But these problems you think are problems really aren't. They're all invented problems. I don't talk to Dion about your sex lives, but I would bet anything that he's just tired and doesn't want to push you on it. He wants to wait until you're ready." My voice is light and even. I know that if he could, Finn would cast a glare in my direction for what he perceives as talking down to him. I don't even mention Bria now because who even knows what is going on with that wild card?

"What do you propose I do then?"

I ignore Finn's condescending tone. "Try talking to him. You've been together for so long. It feels foolish to let communication break down now."

"Maybe," Finn grumbles, "but he has to stop talking down to me."

"Then tell him that!" Cat practically shouts. "You can't dance around each other without talking about it."

I look past Finn and raise an eyebrow at her, wondering if she's taking her own advice.

"Sure, sure. You make it sound so easy. What's the point if Posey is just going to kill us all?"

"Enough," I bark, startling them both. "We're not going to die. I'm going to have to deal with the emotional fallout of finding out that not only do I actually have original parents but they're Titans, rebuild an entire realm, and do this while keeping my blood pressure low enough that Pom doesn't come early."

The reminder that we all have something to live for, that we have someone to fight for, breaks them both out of the fatalistic stupor they were falling into. Cat manages to trap Finn into talking about the who's who of Solarem, and I take that as my chance to sneak out.

I'm not going looking for trouble, but I want to see for myself that the veil is lowered. I trust Essos to handle these things, but we're so close that I don't want us to forget anything.

Zara spies me first when I make it down the stairs and she gives me a small smile.

"This is going to work out," she swears. "And also, I hate to say it, but Lairus is a total DILF."

I scrunch my nose up. "That is not a mental image I want or ever needed."

"Well, you have it. Shouldn't you and Pom be resting?" she

teases, leading me outside. I trust her to show me the way since I don't actually know where this blade is being forged.

"Even if we were, you would mind your own business about that," I warn.

"I suppose I would, for I am but a mere mortal in the presence of a goddess." Zara barely finishes her sentence before letting out a laugh.

Slowly, we wind our way toward the paddock, where I can hear the sound of metal on metal with repeated clanging.

The group comes into view, and I can see Essos standing with his arms crossed. His back is to me, but I can see his fingers drumming against his side as Lairus sits with Octavia on his lap.

"Would you look at who I found just wandering the property?" Zara's tone is light, but Essos spins around on high alert. When he sees it's me, his gaze softens, and he welcomes me into his embrace. Any reason for this man to be touching me I am A-OK with.

"Have you fixed the veil?" I hate that we're not really going to have time to confirm with my parents that it worked before we face off with Posey, but I did this to us.

"Not yet. Give me another knife," Lairus demands, holding his hand out. Octavia pouts and then narrows her eyes in my direction.

"It was Esmaray's blood, wasn't it?" Octavia accuses me, shifting so she's practically grinding on Lairus's lap. At the mention of his wife's name, Lairus shoves Octavia off his lap so he can approach me.

"You've seen your mother and she's told you the truth."

"Her version of it, anyway," I confirm, craning my head to look up at him.

"She was always honest and would have no reason to lie. I delight to see the child you will bear. She is a third generation Titan and she will make gods cower in her presence." Lairus touches my stomach and it feels a little like a blessing he's bestowing. I hope she doesn't feel the weight of all these prophecies hanging over her.

I form a vine blade in my hand just to be sure I still can before I hand it over to Lairus. "What else do you need?"

"A worthy skill, child." He turns his back on me to face Octavia. "Come, lover, and spill your blood with me so we may make love and shelter Solarem from the mortals."

This brightens Octavia. "I know just the spot."

I had wanted to watch, to ensure the ritual is done, but there are some things I never have to witness, and the man who claims to be my father and my mother-in-law having sex in front of me is one of them.

Zara pulls the book out to consult it. "I don't remember that part being necessary."

Xavier is grimacing while reading over her shoulder before pointing to a word. "There: intercourse."

"I thought that meant combination."

Galen chuckles. "Yeah, combining fluids."

He seems to be the only one unbothered by them having sex, but a troubled look still crosses his face as he watches them wander toward the beach.

I shake my head before shuddering. "Nope, not thinking about them having sex on the beach at all."

"That's just because you wouldn't let us have sex on the beach," Essos teases, kissing just below my earlobe.

"When we've stripped Posey of her powers, then we can have sex on the beach."

"Tomorrow night then. It's a date."

When he finally comes upstairs, Essos climbs into bed as quietly as he can. I open my eyes just enough to glance at the clock and see that it's half past three in the morning. Annoyance would be my primary emotion if I wasn't still mostly awake. I always took for granted having him sleep beside me. On nights when he comes to bed late, it's nearly too hard to sleep without his presence. Even without that, knowing we're facing down Posey tomorrow means sleep is impossible.

I roll over to face him with as much grace as a turtle stuck on their back. When I finally turn to see him, Essos is fighting a smile.

"Don't you dare," I warn, but he chuckles softly anyway. He pushes my hair from my face clumsily.

"Why are you still awake?" he asks, his brow dipping down before kissing me soundly. I lean toward him as much as I can, and he closes the distance only to be foiled by the pile of pillows that have started to surround me.

"Because I needed my safety blanket to sleep," I admit, grabbing a pillow and tossing it aside. My fingers trail on Essos's bare chest before sliding lower to his hips. I'm surprised to find him without boxers on.

"You need sleep for Pom."

I finally notice the slight slur in his words when his hand starts to trace along my stomach. My T-shirt is stretched tight over my bump for once. All night, I had been fighting a losing battle, pulling it down only for it to ride up when I rolled over.

"Are you drunk?" I ask, my fingers tracing up to his face. He squirms when I skate over his ticklish sides.

"No, well, maybe a little. We had a few drinks, trying to figure out what we're going to do tomorrow with Ellie and Posey and what comes next. Helene had a crazy idea to add something to the blade and I don't know if it's going to work, and I don't want to think about it anymore." His hand grips my waist firmly before pulling me against him.

Essos studies my face like he's trying to commit it to memory, and I can't blame him. I'm doing the same thing. I need to go into tomorrow with hope and optimism, but it's hard to maintain that when I can hear the anguished cries of Finn as Posey mutilated him. There's been no easy way to tell Essos about it. It's not something I want to burden him with, but I need someone to understand just have terrifying Posey is now.

I watch as Essos's face transforms from adoration to concern as that silly wrinkle appears between his brows. "What is it, my love?"

"When I was with Posey..." Essos brings his hand to my face so his thumb can stroke along my cheek, soothing me as I prepare to tell him. He waits patiently till I'm ready to continue. "She showed me what happened with Finn." This gets his hand to stop.

"How do you mean?" he whispers.

"She showed me how she lay in wait, and how Cassius, *Cassius* was the one to pin Finn's arms while she used the blade."

"I am so sorry you had to witness that," Essos's voice cracks and he presses a kiss under each of my eyes, capturing the tears that have started.

"He never died. I saw him at her house, her base of operations. He was so cold when he did it. There was no emotion in him as he held Finn..."

"I saw it too." There is an emptiness in Essos's voice when he tells me this.

"You never said."

"Of course, I didn't. I hated that I had to push myself into his mind like that, and I wasn't going to scar you with what happened. It didn't do either of us any good, but I'm glad you told me. It's a terrible burden to bear alone."

"Then why did you? You always have to carry the weight of the worlds on your shoulders when it's not yours to carry alone."

Essos looks down toward my stomach before he starts to stroke it. "Because I violated my oldest friend's privacy by doing that. He came back injured and screaming, and I had to find out what happened, so I calmed him and looked at his memory to see how he was injured. The moment I saw the God Killer, I knew that we needed a healer who could help stop any possible further damage. I had, still have, no idea if a wound made by the blade can cause infection. It's not something I ever want to find out. I want to have both the blades and the scepter melted down for scrap metal when this is all over."

"Have you talked to Finn about it?" I ask him gently. I slide my hand around his middle to hug him close.

"Not a chance. Not yet. I want to, but I don't want it to be because I need to get it off my chest. I want it to be because Finn is in the right frame of mind to hear about it."

"When this is all over, we're all due for a long vacation from everything." I press my lips to his chest, trying to inject some levity to the moment. Because despite my fears, there will be a tomorrow and a next week. There will be a time when we can just live day-to-day and not have to survive from day-to-day.

"When this is all over, you and I are going to go somewhere very far away from everyone else, where all we have to worry about is the weather forecast and making sure that we are well stocked with food you want, because I plan on spending a solid three years where it's just me and you and no clothing." He kisses my neck, tickling me.

"You forget we'll have a tiny goddess to contend with as well," I point out.

Essos beams at me, and it's so blinding, I almost wonder if he is the child of the Sun God as well because he shines when he truly smiles. "We don't want our little pomegranate to be an only child. I hear you're most fertile just after having a baby." He grabs my ass, kneading it as he pulls me against his body.

I gasp into his mouth, but he descends on me like a drowning man looking for something to lift him. The hard length of him presses against my thigh. Desire floods my nerves, making every thought eddy out of my mind. Only he stays there. Essos is the only thing that I want. His hand slides down and around to my ass, which he squeezes before pulling my thigh over his hips. Essos' fingers dip between my legs and then into me when he finds me slick and ready for him.

The bigger I've gotten, the more awkward it's become, and I can only imagine how much more difficult it will be when I've swollen into my third trimester. I adjust so I'm straddling him, leaning down as far as I can get. The distance could be closed, but I enjoy the thrill of being the one in control, watching as my husband comes undone.

I slide my clit over his erection and Essos growls, his fingertips digging into my thighs.

"I want to be inside you," he demands.

I rock my hips again as I slide over the sensitive underside of his cock. "And I wanted you in bed hours ago. You're just going to have wait for me to take my pleasure."

He lets out a hiss when I lift my hips. "Then by all means, my queen, take your pleasure."

I reach between us, lifting up. His eyes light up, expecting me to take him into me, but instead, I slid my own fingers along my wet sex, and then inside myself, moaning. I grind against my hand, slipping a second finger inside myself, setting the pace that I know is driving me wild. This isn't sustainable, how I'm lifted above his body, but I can't get over the restraint Essos is showing. He reaches a hand out, grasping my breast over my shirt, one finger teasing my pebbled nipple. The rough fabric of my shirt sends my mind reeling.

My own impatience wins out, and I grasp Essos's cock, sliding my wet fingers along him, stroking leisurely. I fit myself over him and then let my body slide down, absorbing inch after glorious inch.

I gasp, never getting used to the feel of him. After centuries together, our coupling never got old, and it isn't getting old now as I move my hips back and forth.

"Fuck, Daphne," Essos grinds out. I grasp my shirt to pull it over my head, only for it to get stuck with my arms trapped over my head. Essos lets out a deep chuckle, taking full advantage to grasp both of my breasts with his hands. He kneads them, tweaking my nipples while I've trapped myself in my shirt.

"Help," I plead, which only makes him laugh more, even though I've stopped moving. Essos thrusts up into me and my head falls back in a moan at the feel of him bottoming out inside me. His hands graze my side, returning the tickling favor before gripping my hips.

He won't help me out of my shirt, but he lifts me lightly before bracing his feet on the bed and thrusting into me again.

"I like you right where you are, my queen."

I pant as he fucks me. I manage to get the shirt off just in time to grip his pecs, my nails digging into his skin as my orgasm catches me and carries me away. The look on Essos' face reveals that he's right there with me as we moan in tandem. My orgasm is so intense, it's like watching the creation of the universe the way stars explode in my mind. There is a violent ringing in my ears, and I have to blink to clear my vision.

When I do, I see one of the most perfect sights: my husband lying under me, giving me the secret smile of a satisfied lover. We might die in a few hours, but at least we have right now.

35

We do very little sleeping. When the sun rises, filling our room with its golden rays, we're both a little worse for wear. No shower or amount of makeup can cover the bags under our eyes. It doesn't stop me from trying while Essos watches me in the mirror with an amused smirk.

"I'm *so* glad you're entertained," I grumble, trying my best to smooth the cover-up under my eye. I could do it with magic but there is something soothing about doing things myself.

"Love, you're a goddess. If you don't want bags under your eyes, then make it so. For the record, I think you're beautiful and don't need all this fuss."

Essos pushes off from the doorway he's leaning against, stalking toward me like a predator. I think we've finally reached the limits of my pregnant libido. Still, I get a rush of desire admiring his bare sculpted chest, following the trail of his muscles down his Adonis belt, knowing full well what is waiting for me under his low-slung sweats.

"I know I don't need all of this fuss, but what is a little extra emotional armor against Posey?" It won't change the outcome of the day, but it will make me feel just a little better.

Essos grips my shoulders before letting his fingers slide down my arms. He hugs me from behind, pulling me to his chest and resting his chin on my head. The smile he gives me is sad and regretful and I know what is going to come next. It's the conversation I've been avoiding since he came to bed.

"Daphne."

"Essos," I interrupt, giving him a level look. He won't break eye contact.

"Dion is taking Finn to a safe house in the mortal realm. If things start to look bad, I want you to go. I want you to get to the mortal realm and then find him. You need to promise me you'll do this."

I shake my head, but he just hugs me tighter. One arm loosens and he presses a palm to my stomach. "No," I insist.

"You need to do this for Pom. Xavier and Kai are having similar conversations with Cat and Helene."

I scoff at this. "Let me get this straight: you're just sending the little women away. Getting us out of your hair so the men can risk their lives and leave us to go on without you. No. Essos, absolutely not." My voice wavers as hot tears spring to my eyes. He hugs me tightly again. I had known the talk about staying safe and out of the fray was coming, but the idea that he would be risking his life is one that I'd managed to avoid until now.

It would ruin me to lose him as much as it ruined him, and I don't want to go there. I don't want to think of those things, but he's planted the seed and it's grown down into my psyche.

"I'm doing what is right for my wife and my daughter. This is not how our story ends."

"Why is my life so much more valuable? What makes it okay for you and not for me?" I know the answer before he even says it. It's like she's heard my words and aims a kick for my side.

"Pom. You need to raise our daughter." His voice is full of regret for the future he is imagining. It's a future that doesn't have him in it.

I push up from my chair, unable to take the devastation on Essos's face. Words get choked in my throat, because it's not a future I can even begin to envision without my whole body wanting to shut down.

He pulls me against him, burying his face in my damp hair, breathing deeply. This is the only time we can let this happen. When we leave our rooms there will be no space for emotions or regrets. We need to act decisively today.

Essos holds me for as long as I need, and if I let myself, I'll indulge in his embrace for the rest of my life. There is nowhere in all the worlds that I would rather be than in his arms, but for today, we have an important mission, one that we need to deal with so that Pom has a world to grow into. Reluctantly, I pull out of Essos's arms with a kiss to his sternum.

Today is meant to be a peace talk, so I refuse to wear anything akin to battle armor. I don't doubt that the others in our group will dress differently, but I am trying to appeal to Posey, queen-to-queen, woman-to-woman. That doesn't mean I won't have my own protections in place, but lulling her into a false sense of security will work in our favor.

Essos emerges in a grey three-piece suit. He pulls back on the jacket to show me he's wearing Tink's belt for me, extended to fit his hips, to keep it innocuous while still accessible to me. He's carefully placing my new Tink-engineered gloves in his pocket when he looks up at me, a grim smile on his face. It's a nice change from his days of all black, and it makes my heart flip to see him embracing other colors. The grey complements the lavender dress I'm wearing that, admittedly, fit better in my pre-pregnancy days. All it takes are a few alterations and it fits more comfortably. The off-the-shoulder sleeves show off my collarbone, and my breasts strain aggressively in the bodice. Fine silver vines wrap around my torso, which is layered with tulle. I'm not totally naive and have a pair of leggings under my dress so if I have to tear it to fight, I can.

"Would you like a tiara?" Essos offers as I slip my feet into flats.

"How is that even a question? It's like you don't know me at all," I tease, waiting to see which one he will call forth. I'm surprised by the one that appears in his hand. It's not one I've ever seen before. The silver metal work matches my dress, but it's the crystal moonflowers that he's woven into it that have me clutching my chest.

I have to clench my teeth to stop my sob because this is everything that my husband is, thoughtful and a planner, and the thought that put down roots pushes against my mind that this could be the last thing he ever gifts me, and our daughter won't know what it is to be doted on by her father. I have to dig my nails into my palms to stop the sob in its tracks.

"I had it made for you when we found out about your mother. I thought this would be a nice way to honor her."

His consideration, both in having the crown made and how I might feel about it today, makes my heart melt. At the very center of it is a crescent moon with a flower resting in the curve. I don't give myself time to reconsider. I just slide it onto my head, rearranging my curls around it.

I hold my hand out to Essos and he takes it gladly. Both of us begrudgingly start our way to the door but I stop him.

"Essos, I love you. I love you with my whole heart. I've loved you across lifespans that most would only ever dream of. For me, there is only you. There will only ever be you." I cup his face and pull him down toward me. He only has to slouch for a moment before his arm comes around my back and he lifts me to the tips of my toes. I want to run my hands through his perfectly gelled hair, but that will only delay the inevitable.

I open my mouth to him, and he presses his advantage, his tongue brushing against mine. I clutch him like the life raft he is. We part, breathless and flushed.

"That is not going to be our last kiss, Daphne. Don't you dare think like that."

I know I should be embarrassed by how well he reads me, but I can't find it in me to be mad.

"Let's get this over with. We have a nursery to decorate." He can't leave me if we still have so much more to do.

HELENE IS the first one we encounter on our way to the throne room. My desire to be done with that space seems impossible, but I hope this is our last dealing with it for the foreseeable future. I questioned the decision to have Posey meet us there, but I was outvoted. It's a display of power and we need the upper hand where we can get it.

Everyone is lingering in the entryway of our home, waiting for me and Essos to descend. It only makes my stomach cramp like all this is on our shoulders to fix.

"I have to apologize for Kai's absence," Helene says. "He thought it was a good idea to tell me that if things start to look bad, I should turn tail and run. I've left him to sit in the corner to think about what he's done," She hisses, clearly still fuming from the same talk I got. "Here. Complements of my husband." She places a small pouch in both of our hands. I crack mine open and see a fine red powder inside.

I'm optimistic, and maybe it's going to be my fatal flaw, but I want to resolve this without violence. I'm sure Posey will be angling for it, but I just want everyone to come out of this whole and unscathed. What happened to Finn was horrible enough. I won't see another member of my family harmed.

"What's this?" Essos asks about to sniff the powder, but Helene and I both react to stop him. She pulls it from his hand and I cover his mouth.

"It's red algae refined into a powder," Helene explains. "Everyone is getting some to use against Posey, in case we have an opportunity to bind her powers. We tried adding some to the blade after you left, but I'm not sure if it will work that way to steal her powers, so this is a backup. Nice dress." Helene's tone implies that she does not, in fact, think that my dress is nice.

"Thanks! It has pockets," I tell her with a grin, shoving my hands into a pocket. It's just big enough to hold the small pouch. Essos closes his hand and slips his into his jacket. My other pocket has the pouch of seeds Essos and I have been curating.

Helene is dressed smartly in a blue tunic and black leggings. She has her own belt of gadgets and I have to wonder if I've made a mistake. Kai, who is apparently not sitting in time-out, joins us with a bandoleer crossing his bare chest.

I'm criminally overdressed and want to run upstairs to rectify this, but Essos grabs my shoulder, shaking his head.

Kai gives me a sly grin. "So, Daphne is going for mind games. We don't think you're enough of a threat, so I'm not going to bother with weapons. It's a bold decision," Kai teases.

"You're supposed to still be in the corner," Helene scolds.

Kai hugs his wife from behind, kissing her cheek. "Starfish, you can't blame me for wanting to keep you safe."

It's fascinating to watch Helene actually melt into his arms with just one small sentence. "It's cute you think that, but I absolutely can blame you." She pats him on his cheek with a fearsome grin.

"I'm guessing you all got the run-and-hide speech?" Cat asks, sliding down the banister. Essos is quick to catch her when her momentum is too fast and she nearly barrels into our group.

"We did," I confirm.

"I'm going to take Xavier up on the offer. I'm a liability for now. It's best to not have me here."

Cat's words seize my heart like a fist, squeezing. "You're not a liability," I protest.

"She is, and there is no harm in her recognizing that. There is strength in knowing your weaknesses," Kai says sagely.

I smack his arm with the back of my hand. "Stop making sense," I whine. Then I hug Cat tightly.

"I'm sure Essos already said it, but you should come with me. There is no need for you and Pom to be in the middle of this."

"I appreciate the concern, but if I'm absent, I don't think she'll hesitate to make it a massacre. I mean, she's probably already planning it but me being here might at least force her to think twice," I protest.

Cat brushes my hair behind my ears before pressing a kiss to my forehead.

"My mother and Lairus are gone, and the veil is in place," Galen announces. He's slow coming down the stairs and is followed by Callie, also dressed in leggings and a T-shirt, and Tink, who looks the most tired of us all. His hair is sticking up in every which direction, and his shirt is mis-buttoned.

I wish I could go to see my parents to confirm about the veil for myself, but we're short on time. After this, when we're successful, I'll go to them and confirm. I'm going to manifest that future by obsessively thinking it.

"When did they leave?" Xavier demands, emerging from the kitchens.

"Last night after the forging of the blade. They said they're not interested in the entanglements of minor beings." Galen sounds almost disappointed in them. He won't meet my eye, but when he looks around at us all, his gaze catches on my stomach.

"Well, they aren't winning any Grandparent of the Year awards," I grumble, leaning into Essos. He wraps his arms around my shoulders, tugging me close.

"For what it's worth, I agree with my brother," Galen says. "You should flee with Cat and Finn. You're pregnant."

I nearly hiss when Galen finds the balls to tell me what I should and should not be doing.

"That's rich coming from the man that murdered me the last time I was pregnant." My breaths start coming in rapid and shallow. It's not something I let myself dwell on when I think about what happened that day.

"That's right. I did that and I wanted you. Just imagine what someone who hates you will do to you. Posey will carve Pom from your stomach and make you watch as she slits her throat moments after taking her first breath."

"Enough, Galen," Essos demands. My husband places himself between us, breaking my line of sight of Galen, but it's too late, I'm hyperventilating. My vision is starting to narrow, and I can't. This is a terrible idea. I shouldn't be here; we shouldn't be doing this. I'm a terrible mother for thinking that I should do this.

"Daphne, love, I need you to breathe," Essos coaxes. He takes my hand and places it on his chest while holding my other hand to my chest. "Match my breath."

I try. I try to listen to him, but I'm just seeing that ghastly image that Galen has put in my mind and it's worse than any nightmare I could have dreamed up.

My vision goes stark white for a second, and then I'm in a meadow that's calm and quiet. I can hear birds chirping. I'm sitting on a blanket beneath a willow tree, my back pressed against Essos. I don't have to see to know that he's the one there, I can smell him–sandalwood, vanilla, and cinnamon invading my senses. Before me, a little girl with dark curls chases a butterfly. Her short, stubby legs means that she can never catch it, but she won't stop, giggling as she goes. Even when she stumbles to her knees, she's quick to get back up again.

"You think we're ready for more?" Essos asks, pressing a kiss to my shoulder.

"We don't have much of a choice, now do we?" I joke, taking one of his hands and pressing it to my stomach. There is barely a bump, but I know in my heart of hearts that we're having another child, a boy this time.

"No, you did promise me a whole football team once upon a time." His nose traces the span of skin from my ear to my shoulder as he pulls the strap of my dress down.

"I'll enjoy all the trying till we get there."

My sight returns and Essos is standing before me, looking bewildered. "Daphne, can you hear me?"

"Yes, why are you shouting?" My emotions are calmer than before, and I can't remember why I was so worked up. I know what we're doing and why, but the small girl chasing butterflies lingers in my mind. I look around our group to see we've been joined by Bria, who might be the most armed out of anyone here.

"Why am I shouting?" His laugh sounds crazed and he crushes me to his chest. "I'm shouting, love, because you were catatonic, standing here with your eyes pure white." Essos looses a shaky breath, unafraid to show our friends this side of him.

"It felt like a dream," I whisper, trying to puzzle over what just happened.

"Unfortunately," Xavier interrupts, "we don't have much time before the wicked witch descends with her flying monkeys."

Tink edges to close to where I stand, shoulder-checking Galen as he goes. "Besides, Daph is our secret weapon." Tink gives me a wink before gesturing at me. "May I?"

I have no idea what to expect, but I nod, watching him drop to his knee beside me.

"I hate to break it to you, but she's already married," Essos points out with an amused smirk.

"No reason it can't be a party," Tink teases. His sure fingers grip the side of my gown at the hem and tear it straight up along the seam. He draws the freshly-made dagger from his bag and sets to strapping it to my leg. There is a question in his eye, as he has to reach between my legs to secure it, and I nod, trying to give him the space he needs.

Essos frowns as he runs a hand through his hair, mussing it. "Is this necessary? I would like to keep my pregnant wife out of this as long as possible."

Tink tightens the straps before looking at Essos. "And that's why we need her to have the blade. Posey is going to expect you to keep Daphne out of this. She is going to expect Daph to be sheltered and protected. She's not going to see it coming when Daphne buries this into her side." Before sliding it into the holster, Tink hands the blade to me so I can get a feel for the weight.

It's heavier than I expected. It has a silver handle, and the blade is as red as the blood that made it. The handle is intricate, with skulls and flowers that I imagine was not strictly necessary. I enjoy the feel of the weapon in my hands. Sitting atop the hilt is the same stone that once held Galen's soul.

Tink nods as I inspect it. "The stone was surprisingly easy to snap off, but maybe those are just my big brawny muscles. You need to stab her with it and leave it in as long as you can for it to steal her powers. Cutting her with it won't drain her powers. Shoot for at least ten seconds, twenty if you can manage it."

I think of the last time I stabbed Posey, when I had to leave the other God Killer blade behind in her flesh. And how she crushed my windpipe during that same encounter.

"Will it kill her?" I ask, marveling at the blade. It's smaller than its twins, but the edges are curved in the same way.

"If you stab her in the heart or face, yes. But if you did something like slit her throat, she will probably recover, albeit slowly, and she will need a healer to keep her alive. She'll be left with a nasty scar, but the intent was not to kill, I thought."

Dave, Spot, and Shadow trot in, and I wish I had some sort of protective covering for each of them, but it doesn't make sense. If my great protectors are getting involved in this fight, they're doing it in their other form, and when they're like that, there is little need for protection.

"What did I miss?" Dion asks, strolling down the stairs. He has on a beige fedora that flattens his afro. His casual button down and shorts affect the look of a man headed to a vineyard for day drinking, not one that is headed to a fight.

"Nothing. Is Finn safe?" Essos asks. My husband has a hard time tearing his eyes from me as I slip the blade into its holster.

"Yes, I'm here for the last of my charges, Cat and Daphne?" Dion holds out a hand to Cat and she takes it. His head swings to me, and I shake my head.

"I'm not going," I reiterate. My heart thunders in my chest, knowing what today is going to bring, but I won't be away from Essos when it happens.

"Good, because I have one *last* gift for you," Tink interrupts as he pulls a small metal badge out of his pocket and affixes it to the front of my dress. This time, he's too focused on his task to ask if it's okay to touch me, and it's when his fingers brush the swell of my breasts that he realizes his error.

"Enjoying yourself?" Essos asks with an eyebrow raised.

Tink looks beyond my dress to where he's touching and lets me go immediately. "I'm so sorry. I should have asked."

"No, no, you've already started, finish what you're doing. Ignore my husband. If you keep touching me like that I might wonder how *else* you touch a woman," I joke. Over his shoulder, color rises on Callie's cheeks.

Tink goes back to what he was doing, rubbing the surface of the little metal attachment so it blends in better with my dress. I tilt my head down, and it looks like it's just a broach. It's not ornate, but it's the simplicity that lets it match my gown.

"That's the second time in as many minutes that you two have propositioned him. Since when are you swingers?" Xavier interjects.

I scowl at him. "You're just jealous that I never slept with you."

"You know me so well." Xavier says sarcastically. "Perhaps you'll give me a final kiss before we go into battle. Your best friend already refused to do that for me today." My head snaps to Cat, who *refuses* to look at me.

"Please, enough. You're going to make me sick," Essos gags, but he winks at me.

"If you need armor for any reason, double tap that little button twice. It will conform to your body without adding any weight. Only your touch or Essos's will remove it. I tested it myself; the dagger will not penetrate the armor. The only downside is it will only adhere to material and not to skin."

"I'm not letting that woman within ten feet of my wife, let alone close enough for her to be stabbed. Daphne can toss the blade to one of us." Essos pulls me to him, and I want to collapse into his side, exhausted all over again, but now is not the time for that. I want to tell him all the reasons that wouldn't be good enough, but I think for his sake, he needs to keep repeating that I'll stay out of harm's way as if that will make it so.

I pull out of his grip to rush Cat and squeeze her.

"This is not the end," I assure her.

She clenches her teeth, eyes watery and full. Cat only glances at Xavier, regret crossing her face, perhaps for denying him that last kiss. "You need to stay safe. Stay out of it as long as you can. Swear it," she demands.

"I swear it." Our pinkies catch and I hug her for what I tell myself is not the last time.

"I'm staying. Out of sight, but I'm staying all the same," Callie says when Dion offers his hand to her.

Dion gives us all a firm nod, and then he and Cat are gone in the blink of an eye. I take a moment, turning away from the group to regain my composure. The tears I saw in Cat's eyes I'm sure were echoes of the ones brimming my own. I wipe hastily at them before facing the group.

"Let's get this over with."

Ellie is still sitting on the chair we gave her when we arrive in the throne room. The barrier set in the stones around her is still strong, holding her in place. When we all enter, she jumps to her feet, confused by what the presence of the seven of us means. She glares down at my dogs, and they give her a responding growl, except for Dave, who doesn't so much as acknowledge her presence. Tink chose not to come down with us, insisting that he hang back in case anything happened. Callie's absence told me all I needed to know. What they weren't saying was that he's there to get Callie away from Galen if it came to that. I wish we had Lairus and Octavia with us from a power perspective, but I don't know that I can trust them not to turn on us in the heat of battle.

I ignore Ellie, striding hand in hand with Essos to our throne. Kai and Helene flank my side while Xavier and Galen are on Essos's side of the dais. The throne is uncomfortable, just as uncomfortable as it is every other time I've had to be seated here. If we survive this, I'm burning it to the ground.

"What is happening?" Ellie demands, crossing her arms over her chest.

"*Shut up* before I turn you into a garnish," I snap, trying to make myself comfortable.

We don't have to wait long for Posey to show up, thankfully. She makes a big show of it, with wind whipping in the room. I think of what a mistake it was to wear my hair down. It is no doubt tangled in my crown now.

Xavier rests his hand on the pommel of the God Killer dagger we have. It's been fashioned with a new fake gem on top so Posey won't be suspicious. None of us know if the blade will work the same; we assume it still has the potential to kill, but not trap a soul.

Either way, we want it there to show her that we're on an even playing field with her.

"Posey, how nice of you to join us," Essos greets, not getting up from his chair.

"Free her. *Now.*" Posey demands, pointing a finger in Ellie's direction. If I thought she looked bad yesterday, she looks worse today. When she blinks, it's clear one of her eyes won't close completely, and there is a spot on her forehead that makes it look like she's a porcelain doll with a chip on her face.

"I always told you she was bossy, but you never wanted to listen to your baby brother," Galen taunts, glancing at Xavier, who cuts him with a scathing glare.

"Well, if it isn't my very own Benedict Arnold," Posey hisses. "What, did Daphne finally agree to let you between her legs? No pussy, no relationship, is worth the power I have. I gave you *everything*. I could have given you so much more."

"Except, not. Because you promised him the Underworld, and yet here Essos sits." This comes from Helene, who could not look happier to have the upper hand.

"Bitch," Posey snarls. "Free her."

"You mean your *daughter*?" Xavier explodes. "How could you keep a child from me?"

Posey laughs. "What, like, it was hard? I had her before you, while I was planning my next steps. I can't be blamed that you never asked about me."

"Can't you? It doesn't take a fucking genius to figure out that you were the one controlling the council. Is that why I could never vote for my brother to get his soulmate back?"

Posey claps. "Bravo, Xavier. Finally rubbing your two braincells together instead of your testicles. It was the only way to get what I wanted done. Now that you have your answers, free my daughter."

"Free the souls first," I counter. I lift my chin, waiting for her rebuttal.

I'm surprised when she lifts the scepter in her hand and shakes it like it's a dog toy. "This is all you want?"

"I want that and your God Killer blade. I want you to *free the souls*," I demand. My eyes stay trained on the scepter and how carelessly she's waving it about. I doubt it's fragile, but it's not like I want to fuck around and find out at this moment.

She throws it hard at the ground, and while we're all distracted watching the scepter fall, we miss Posey's actual attack. Whoever came with her appears out of the shadows, cloaked somehow. There is no time to question how she's able to glamour her allies, because everything falls apart at once. Two of them break the circle by carving out one of the stones holding Ellie, who grins at me like she's just won the lottery. I know the form of that body that's helping her. Cassius, the god I thought I loved a very long time ago. The god I mourned when I thought Posey had killed him. The god who betrayed us. He gives me a wink before grabbing his accomplice, Lucky, and disappearing from the battle. I shouldn't be surprised they're both cowards.

I'm stepping toward the scepter, hoping to catch it before it hits the ground, but Essos grips my upper arm with a bruising strength, yanking me backward.

The moment feels like it's in slow motion, but I see that it's only us that have slowed, because out of the corner of my eye, Kai is reaching behind his back for his sword as the mele starts.

While the scepter descends to the ground, Posey throws a dagger, and not just any dagger, but the God Killer, at her husband. Xavier doesn't see it because, like me, he's trying to reach for the scepter. There is nothing I can do but watch in horror as it flips through the air toward its intended target. My body might be moving slowly, but my mind is going at a normal speed and all I can consider is how it will destroy Cat if Xavier dies. No amount of trying to force my body to move to block it will let me stop the weapon from its trajectory.

I'm not the only one whose notices because as I'm being tugged backward, Essos is trying to shoulder-check his brother out of the way, and it's nothing but tragic as I feel my eyes widen at what is going to be the end result of Essos pushing his brother out of the way.

It won't be Cat's heartbreak. It will be mine. It takes me back to the moment I had to watch in horror as Cat took a dagger meant for me, only now I have to watch my husband be the one to take the brunt of the impact. Even though he's been shoved, Xavier gets his hand on the scepter, stopping it from hitting the ground.

My scream shatters whatever Posey did to slow us all down. Ellie has made it to Posey's side. Posey gathers Ellie into her arms for a moment, looking her over for damage. I can only watch the blade as it makes contact with my husband. His momentum to save his brother's life sends him out of reach of me, so I do the thing that is within my reach.

If Posey thinks she can take away those I love, I can do the same to her.

Posey watches in horror as Ellie shrivels down until she is a small green plant, growing out of my floor. Even from where I stand, the scent of mint reaches me, but I don't let my vengeance stop there. I speed through the life cycle of the garnish I promised I would turn her into. I watch as Ellie the mint shrivels up then I ground her down into nothing.

Posey's shriek rattles the whole room, knocking candles from the wall. She falls to her knees, the rest of us seemingly forgotten as she grabs at all that is left of her daughter.

This woman has struck at Essos, the person I care most about, and if she thinks that she can do this, harm him, she's wrong. I can't think. I can't look because I know that I'll never be able to unsee my husband with a knife sticking out of his chest. It's a horrible twist the way the Fates play with us. He had to watch me die with that very weapon and now I'll have to see it, forever haunted by this memory.

I make myself look, and I nearly sag with relief. Posey is not a marksman. The hilt protrudes from Essos's chest, closer to his shoulder in almost the same spot I stabbed her. His blue eyes find me before he gives me a slow blink, confirming that he's okay.

Essos grunts when he pulls it out, letting it clatter to the ground. I want to rush toward him and tell him not to do that, especially when the wound releases a horrifying gush of blood. The need to protect him overrides my desire to be by his side.

Around us, the fighting continues and I realize that we're outnumbered three to one. I glimpse numerous nymphs and dryads and other gods fighting. We may be outnumbered, but we're stronger than the average god, and this is like child's play for Bria, Kai, and Galen, who are in their element. Even if Posey stripped Helene and Kai's powers, they're unstoppable with how they fight. There are a few too many familiar faces on Posey's side who are just as skilled, like Renner, the Goddess of Marksmen, and Hadeon, God of Disasters.

From the belt Essos wears, I tug loose the seed of a Redwood and grow it large to protect him while he gets to his feet. I pull the seeds out of my pocket and hurl them in the air, making the seeds grow into weapons that target any enemy that's not a nymph or dryad. Those enemies would just absorb the plants into themselves and use them as fortification or as their own weapon. I want to scream when a nymph jumps in front of a spray and absorbs my weapons with a saucy grin. Her victory is short-lived because Helene spins her sword and slices the nymph's head off with ease.

Dave, Spot, and Shadow have formed themselves into one, and I take a sick delight watching Dave grab for Renner. Shadow growls at him for taking what should have been her snack, but she snatches someone else up instead.

Galen gets punched in the nose, and he only laughs, with blood gushing down his face. He's truly fearsome, snapping necks and ripping spines from Posey's cohorts. He meets my gaze from across the room for a split second and although I've been around him plenty during the last few weeks, there is something about him wearing someone else's blood that makes my blood run cold. I'm frozen to the spot, unable to do anything when he grabs a dagger and launches it in my direction. The breeze created by the small weapon kisses my cheek as it passes my face. The gurgling sound from behind me tells me his aim was true. When I spin, I find a minor deity falling to the ground, holding his throat until he stills, his eyes vacant. His limp hand falls away, exposing the dagger Galen threw.

Knowing that enemies are coming at us from all sides, I run back to my husband and press a hand to his chest. His blood seeps between my fingers too easily, and I have to blink away the tears in my eyes. Essos already looks so pale, his breathing more ragged than I would like. I want to yell and scream that you're not supposed to pull the weapon out, but it's past the point of making a difference.

Essos isn't focused on his own wound. Instead, he presses my gloves into my hands.

"I'll be all right," he swears, but he's breathless when he says it. He takes over pressing on his wound, but I can see it's not enough pressure. I touch his belt, trying to see if there is anything I can use to pack the wound. I may not know much about first aid, but Cat and I binged enough *Grey's Anatomy* that I know Essos needs pressure. My thoughts keep spiraling on how I should know more, and how useless the things I did learn are.

"Put the gloves on," Essos orders and it's weaker than I want his voice to be. It's enough to clear my head, for Essos and for Pom. My hands are shaking as I try to slide them on. Around me, a battle is waging, and all I can hear is Essos's labored breathing and my own shaky breaths. He needs help, better help than I can give him. He needs Callie. Essos presses his hand to my cheek. "You're a badass, and I love you."

I can't read into why he would say that, because I can hear Posey's crying stop behind me.

"I'm going to fucking kill you," Posey howls. She starts to progress toward me, and I throw vines up to grab her, but she's in full control of her powers. The chip on her forehead seems to grow, and I realize that maybe it's not that she's in full control, but that her powers and emotions are too much. The wind whips around the room and the earth trembles.

I shoot vines out from my gloves, poison ivy and creeping Charlie, hoping to grab a hold of her and bind her up with it, but she sends fire burning up the vines and to my hands. I can't get the gloves off fast enough before she burns me. The flames lick at my skin, and once the gloves are off, I see the pinkening of my skin.

I can see how this will play out. She can freeze time at any moment. Like me, she can't think clearly; her grief is overriding her coherent thoughts. It's my only advantage and maybe my only shot at saving my husband. If I can clear the battlefield and make this fight queen versus queen, I think I can do this. This moment, even if we didn't know it, is what Kai and Finn and Essos have been training me for.

Essos gets to his feet, staggering as he does. With one look at me and my stomach, I can see his resolve hardens as he stands up straighter. He has one hand pressed to his wound, and blood is seeping out. I wish he was wearing black because I can see all the blood coating his grey suit.

It's that resolve I see in my husband that solidifies my own. "Posey might be a Fate, but I am the daughter of Titans, and I have so much more to fight for. She's unfocused right now. It's my chance." The words spill out of my mouth as I rationalize to him what I'm about to do.

Once Posey realizes what she can do, she'll kill us all in the blink of an eye. The memory of Titus having his throat slit rises unbidden to my mind.

I can hear Essos breathing heavily me, ready to keep fighting. All around me, the battle continues. There is no reason for me to risk everyone if I can end this now. This is the best way I can save everyone. My hand presses to my stomach, knowing that Pom is my strength. I'm fighting for something better than power. It might be a cliché, but fighting for love makes me stronger. I turn to Essos, locking eyes with him.

"Go to Callie. You need a healer. Essos, I will love you for every eternity. Nothing, no power, can change that," I vow before digging into my deep well of power and forcing everyone out the door. They slide across the room, confused more than anything else, uncertain of who is making this happen. Even Posey hesitates, which I use to my full advantage.

I barely register the surprise on Essos's face before slamming the door between us shut, locking Posey and I in the room together.

Alone.

I double-tap the pendant and watch, mystified, as the armor rolls out. It changes the soft material of my dress into a wearable shield, the pieces sliding and locking as I stare down my opponent. It only covers my torso, which I was warned about, but it leaves the skirt of my dress, meaning that the Power Eater dagger is still hidden from view. Tink promised the shield would protect against the God Killer, but watching extra protection cover the swell of my abdomen sets my mind at ease. The shield also serves as a reminder that the God Killer blade is still in play. Last I saw, Xavier had the one without the stone and Essos pulled the other from his chest. I can't take my eyes off Posey, so for now it's going to have to stay a wild card.

The fighting continues on the other side of the door, but one sound rises above the others. It's the desperate plea from Essos as he pounds on the door, trying to fight his way in. Why isn't he getting help from Callie?

I roll my neck and clench my jaw, hands raised toward Posey.

"Let's finish this, bitch," I snarl.

It's just me and Posey now. I didn't think I could do it again, take another life, but it's amazing what the right motivation can do. I have to put an end to her scheming. The new dagger sits against my leg, and I take the barest second to glance behind me, where the God Killer is just stupidly lying there after being dropped.

I snap my gaze back to Posey, who grins at me, thinking she has the upper hand. She raises her hands, mania in her eyes.

I can hear Helene join Essos in screaming for us to open the door. I don't know what that means for the fighting, but I need to keep my mind on my opponent. It's how I'll survive.

All that training with Kai, Finn, and Essos is going to boil down to keeping Posey down.

"You can't fight Fate, honey," she says. "Just accept the new world order and maybe I'll let your child live."

It was the wrong thing to say because I roar with fury and punch her right in the face, aiming not for her mouth or cheek, but the spot that looks like her skull is coming apart on her forehead. She howls and tries to come at me again, but I have another swing ready and I drive my fist forward. It's so satisfying, the crunch of her nose as my knuckles connect, that I do it again. She screams in anger, blood pouring down her face. I want to do it again and again and again.

"You messed with the wrong family." I reach into my pocket for some of the powdered red algae. I palm it, and when Posey advances on me, I blow it in her face.

She stumbles back, surprised and coughing. In her effort to get more air after breathing in the irritant, she inhales deeper, ensuring more of it is clinging to her lungs. I can see it already starting to work through her system, the veins on her face glowing red briefly before fading back to black as the algae invades.

"What did you do?!" she screams, clawing at her face.

She has one last trick up her sleeve, the God Killer. She summons it to her before her powers are totally gone. I attempt to draw it in my direction, something I should have done earlier, but it doesn't budge from it's path. Instead, I try to dive for it, but I'm too cautious to slide across the floor because of my stomach. It slips through my fingers before landing soundly in her hand. The metal glints in the light, and I fight the urge to take a step back as I scramble to my feet.

"I am going to carve that child from you like a roast turkey, and I'm going to show your husband and his pathetic spoiled family precisely what I'm made of. This child will have the same fate as all the others before it." I go still, one last piece sliding into place, and I want to drop to my knees in fury.

"It was you." I whisper, a hand going to my abdomen. The life within me kicks furiously, a reminder that Pom is still here ready for me to fight. "All the miscarriages. They were you."

"I needed you raw and weak so when Galen came, you were easy prey. But you and Essos never could keep your hands off each other. I shouldn't be surprised that his seed took root in you *again*."

I want to scream and scream for how far her deception and crimes go. "Why? Why, Posey? Why do any of this? Why me?"

Posey grips the dagger tight, finally blinking away the tears from the powder. The veins on her face remain thick and dark, casting her as a ghoulish figure.

"Because I wanted a kingdom. I just chose the wrong king. Nothing I could do would get Essos to stray from you. I thought Xavier would be powerful. He was, after all, King of the Gods! Why wouldn't he be? But he's lazy and left Essos in charge of everything, and once I realized, it was too late, and I was already married. I even put my daughter in his path and he *still chose you.* I would have ruled this realm fairly and been beloved by all, but instead, you and your family made me a laughingstock. You and Helene were too good to talk to me. Your brother too interested in others to even sleep with me."

"Posey, did you ever stop to consider that no one respects you because they can see that you're a fucking sociopath?"

Posey coughs, and I bide my time, talking to her until I can be sure she's totally powerless.

"I am Fate itself. I wield more power than my two sisters combined. You can't stop me. No matter how many twists and turns you take, I will beat you. I am the one who will cut your thread once and for all." She runs at me head on, which I deflect easily, shoving her to the side. She expects this and spins behind me, her fist connecting with my spine. If I were still mortal, I would have had my back broken by the hit. Even without her powers, Posey is strong. The armor Tink made me protects me from the worst of it, but it still causes me to cry out in pain.

We trade blows and I try to get the dagger from her, but she's not attacking me outright with it. I take a blow to my cheek, once, twice, a third punch until I catch her fist in my hand and squeeze. I feel her bones grinding against each other. She pulls out of my grip and I'm caught off guard as she slams her foot into my knee. I scream as my kneecap shatters. I was able to absorb the hit to my back though the armor, but this awkward angle nearly snaps my leg in half. I can hear the choked sounds of Essos screaming my name. He hasn't stopped, but he still needs help. I can't help but think about the gush of blood from when he pulled the dagger free from his chest. I don't know if I can survive this if he doesn't.

"Don't you think your beloved should watch you die again?" Posey grabs my throat, squeezing. "Make him watch. Open the doors."

I don't oblige her demand. Instead, I hold the barrier. I do make the doors transparent so Essos has to watch what comes next. Maybe he will finally go get help if he sees that I'm going to beat her.

I might be in a vulnerable position on my knees before Posey, but I am not the weak one here. I have both hands wrapped around the wrist that holds my neck and am defiantly watching Posey. I can hear the others trying to throw everything they have at the door to get in, but I won't let them. One glance confirms that even Galen is helping try to break the door in. I hold them at the door. Essos was right about my powers. I had cut myself off from their true depth. It feels like my chest cracks open as I dive into what it really means to be the daughter of not one, but two Titans. In a blink-and-you-miss-it moment, my hands flare with a golden light before returning to normal.

Posey raises the God Killer to plunge it into my heart again, and I can feel the tip of the blade against my skin, in the same spot that Galen had stabbed me, but I catch her hand, stopping the progression of the blade before it can sink too deep. I sweep out my leg with as much force as I can, knocking Posey off her feet while gripping the hand that holds the dagger tightly. I barely move my head in time to avoid being gouged in the face by the dagger. I feel the pointed edge slide against the skin of my cheek, right over the last time she cut me with it. I roll my body with hers so I'm straddling her hips as I gather every last bit of my physical strength.

I twist and twist Posey's arm until she releases the blade, not unlike I did the last time we faced off, and I snatch it out of the air before it clatters to the ground.

"You ruined everything!" Posey screams. "*Again!*" The pounding at the door has stopped, I hope because Essos is finally seeking the help he needs because he can see that I will be victorious. Vines snake out from around my wrists to wrap around where the gem is attached to the hilt. I'm surprised at the ease with which I am able to snap the gem free, but I can't question it, not now, not when time is of the essence. Swirling inside are billions of souls siphoned from the Underworld. These people are *my* people. They were ripped from their Afterlives and controlled by this bitch.

Posey is climbing to her feet, watching me. "What are you doing?" Her voice is anguished as she looks on in horror. She starts to cough before dry heaving as black smoke oozes from her mouth. Posey looks torn between being sick and watching what I'm doing.

"Stick around and find out." Before I drop the stone to the floor, I try to shift my weight onto my shattered knee, but can feel that it won't hold me so I have no choice but to raise my bad leg. It's going to hurt, I know it's going to hurt, but I have to do it anyway. Posey realizes what I'm going to do.

"No!" she screams, diving for the stone, but I bring my heel down as hard as I can, shattering it. It's not just my strength that I'm using to break the gem, but the weight of all the grief of the souls in the Underworld whose stories I listened to. I hoarded and held on to their pain, even as it weighed me down, for just this moment. I yowl in pain as it overwhelms me and I think for a moment I might black out from the agony.

The concussive force of the gem breaking sends both of us flying back, me into the door where Essos can only watch what is happening, and Posey into the opposite wall. I have just enough time to drop the barrier so when I hit the doors, I feel them open as the force of my body slams into them. Warm arms fold around me before we hit the floor, skidding back a few more feet until we hit another wall with a thud.

Essos's arms are tight around me, holding me. I can see the rest of our family and friends equally scattered by the force. Xavier rises first, marching into the room toward his wife, who is writhing on the ground, crying in pain.

"Daphne." Essos's voice cuts through my mental fog and he's turning me to get a good look at me.

"I'm okay," I assure him, even as my whole body screams. If it's not the physical pain, it's the magical exhaustion and the emotional torment of knowing what Posey did to us and why.

"You're bleeding. I don't think that qualifies as all right." Essos reaches for my cheek and my chest, where the dagger pierced my flesh. They're not deep and since I won't be able to heal the cuts the way I usually would, I'll probably need stitches. Essos doesn't look as pale as he did before and I hope maybe he was healed, at least a little while I was out. Maybe I made the wound out to be much worse than it actually was.

"I guess Tink should have made this armor cover all the important bits," I quip, gesturing at how the armor had only covered up to the neckline of my dress. You live and you learn.

Essos clenches his jaw. "I guess so." His head lifts to where Xavier holds his wife by the hair, dragging her toward the group of us. Any supporters she had have fled. Essos gets to his feet, staggering for a second before righting himself. We both hit the wall pretty hard, and I look at him with alarm, but he waves me off. Smart man that he is, he doesn't tell me to stay down or he tell me to rest. He just focuses on the issue at hand.

"Is the baby..." He can barely voice his concern, and I nod.

"Probably a little seasick, but our little pomegranate is just fine."

Essos helps me to my feet, resting a hand on the swell of my stomach to feel it for himself. He's favoring the arm the dagger struck near, and I know that he's going to have to be looked over by Callie since that's not going to heal on its own.

"I'd wager she's a little larger than that by now. How did you know that breaking the gem would work?"

"I didn't know. I had no idea if it would work."

Essos gives me a level glare. "Don't *ever* lock me out like that again. We are a *team* and your fights are my fights. I couldn't bear not knowing what was happening. I could just hear your anguish, feel it.

I don't know how, but I just could feel your heart breaking and..." And then he kisses me, cupping my face and pressing his lips to mine greedily

"I know. I'm sorry I put you through that, but I'm not sorry it worked."

"Let's finish this. For real," Essos says, and we turn to where Posey is a huddled mess before Xavier.

I take the moment to check our allies. For the most part, they're unscathed. Galen looks the worst, but I think that's just because the God of War and Suffering was having fun. I don't know what happened on the other side of the door when I locked them all out, but they're all standing and that's what matters. I pull the new dagger from its holster on my thigh and flip it around, enjoying the look of fear in Posey's eyes.

Estelle, Sybil, and Zara transport in beside Xavier.

"Now you show up," Xavier scoffs.

Zara lets go of Sybil and Estelle and approaches. I think she's going to hug me, but instead, she takes the Power Eater dagger from my hand. Her steps are sure as she walks toward Xavier and Posey, and I expect her to hand it to Xavier. He's even holding his hand out for it, but before anyone can stop her, she plunges it into Posey's heart.

"What are you doing!" Helene and I shout, watching as Posey looks at the weapon then at Zara, confused. Xavier looks too shocked to even react. When Posey's eyes gloss over, Zara removes the dagger. Around us, the world starts to shake.

I look to Xavier, who looks just as confused as thunder rumbles above us.

Zara twists to meet my eye. "Trust me." Those are her last words before she plunges the knife, still slick with Posey's blood, into her own heart.

"No!" I scream, rushing to catch her body before it falls. I ignore the pain in my leg, focused only on my friend. Essos is right behind me, catching Zara and helping me ease her to the ground.

I've done her wrong in so many ways, and I'll never get to make it better. I touch her face, tears flowing freely from my eyes as blood bubbles out of her mouth. She goes still in my arms, but consequently, so does the whole world.

I hold onto her, letting the sobs go.

Essos pulls me off Zara, trying to get me to release her body. With tears still flowing freely, I look up at him. His façade cracks when he spies the look on my face. There are so many things I should have done differently, but why she stabbed herself I can't understand.

"You have to let her go, my love."

The world still shakes beneath my feet. "But, Cat. Cat didn't get to say goodbye. She was a much better friend than I ever was." My voice breaks as I look into his eyes. "Why? Why did she do this?"

Essos's fingers dig into my shoulders, trying to pull me back and away. I'm so focused on him that I'm surprised when I feel Zara's body move. My head whips around so fast, I'm afraid I've given myself whiplash. My hopes are dashed when I find it's not Zara, but Galen, pulling her from my arms.

"It's okay," he assures me. I glare at him, furious that he's daring to get this close to me. Galen manages to pull her from my hands, and I realize that I'm covered in a friend's blood *again*. It threatens to break me.

Tink comes sprinting down the stairs into the throne room, with

Callie hot on his heels. I don't look up at them. I keep my focus on Galen and what he's doing. Essos is tense behind me, trying to pull me upright.

"What happened?" Tink demands.

"Look away, Daphne," Galen growls, but I refuse. It's that same stubbornness that forces me to watch him draw the blade from Zara's chest. I never thought about the sound the blade makes when leaving the body. It's sickening, the slurp of the weapon leaving her flesh. I want to vomit, but I reach for Zara instead. With the weapon in Galen's hands, Essos sweeps me back quickly, placing his body between us.

Lightning crackles in Xavier's hands, and Galen spins, holding the knife toward him, but then he surprises all of us by holding both hands up in supplication. He flips the blade and holds the handle to Xavier who takes it, sheathing it.

The earth stops shaking, and we all glance around, unsure. I get to my feet, clinging to Essos. Sybil and Estelle appear, looking grim. Their eyes are red-rimmed and their mouths are turned down. They won't look at anyone but Zara.

"Rise," they intone together. Their voices are flat and, quite frankly, they're terrifying.

But what happens after that stills my heart. Zara gasps in a breath and sits up, her hand going to her chest where the stab wound is knitting itself back together.

I never want to watch one of my friends go through that again. With the death of Posey, I shouldn't have to.

Pushing past Essos, I fall to my knees again and hug her. I don't care about the show I'm putting on. I'm just thankful, so thankful, that Zara is alive and in my arms. Her arms fold around me, and I can feel her head swiveling as she looks around at everyone gathering.

"Why does everyone look grim as fuck?"

I laugh and cry all at once into her hair until Essos physically removes me from her. She gets up and spies the red running down her top. Her fingers graze the puckered white scar that is stark against her dark skin.

"Well, you died, further traumatizing my wife."

She twists to look up at Essos before taking his proffered hand. Zara is unsteady on her feet for a moment, swaying. Essos is quick to reach and catch her.

"Well, that sucks," Zara says unapologetically.

My laugh starts as a snort and then I'm doubled over, laughing at the understatement of the century. Quickly, everyone else follows me into hysterics. Essos clutches his stomach as he soundlessly laughs so hard it's more of a wheeze.

When our laughter starts to die down, starting with the Fates, I can finally manage to stay upright. I wouldn't be able to if Essos wasn't holding me around my back.

"I had a hunch," Galen says, rubbing at some of the drying blood on his face, "that so long as the knife was in your chest, you wouldn't come back."

Zara turns her eyes on him, appraising. "How did you know what I was doing?"

"I'm not as stupid as you like to insinuate, fateling. That blade was meant to collect Posey's powers. They needed to go somewhere. Her death meant we needed another Fate. I like you, Zara, but you're not type to make the suicide play." She frowns at Galen, but he pushes on. "That said, I'm impressed that you didn't even hesitate to do it. I've seen grown men cry when faced with that kind of act."

"I still think you're a snake," Zara tells him without hesitation. She turns to look at her hands, first at her palms and then the backs of them. When she turns her palms to face each other, a web of strings appears.

"That's new," Helene scoffs.

"There is much for us to show you," Sybil tells her with a smile. Both Fates are careful not to look at their slain sister as she lies there, unmoving.

It's Xavier who falls to his knees beside Posey, brushing a blonde strand of hair from her face. He strokes her cheek, looking at her. Angrily, he turns to Zara. "She wasn't supposed to die."

Helene, who is closest to him, places a hand on his shoulder, soothing him. It's Essos, though, who has the power to ease his grief. When my husband tries to take a step toward his brother, Xavier cuts him with a glare that lowers the temperature of the room several degrees.

"There was no other way. Your aim to keep her alive was admirable, but ultimately foolish," Estelle says, finally looking at Posey. I expect there to be something of what Xavier is feeling, a mixture of regret and sadness, but I only see disappointment. I wonder how much of that is true and how much of Posey's death was a set up. Zara is now standing with Sybil and Estelle. It's clear that this plan to kill Posey is one they hatched together outside of our original designs.

"I'm sorry," Xavier whispers to the prone form in his arms. He lowers his head to press his forehead to hers, a sob shaking his chest. Essos gestures to everyone that we should give Xavier his privacy. For as troubled as their relationship was, they were together for centuries. There will be no closure where Posey is involved, no figuring out if there were moments that were real.

When we get upstairs and settled in the living room, I look back toward the stairs to the throne room, wondering if there is something I can do to soothe his pain. Drops of blood on the floor distract me, and I follow it to its source.

Essos has dropped onto a chair, and I see that his breathing is haggard, his shoulder drooped. His eyes are on our family, checking them over for injuries, letting Callie start to tend to them first.

"Essos," I scold, rushing to him as fast as my damaged knee will let me. I choke down my cry of pain as I settle to one knee before him, the other outstretched to the side.

"I'm fine." His words are more a whisper as I reach for his wound.

"Is my big brother being a cry baby? Needs his wife to lick his wounds? This is why wearing black to battle is best. Never let them see you bleed," Galen taunts from across the room. His wife skips over him as she inventories everyone's wounds.

I ignore him and start to peal Essos's jacket off. Essos huffs out a pained breath, trying to grit his teeth. His eyes nearly cross when I pull the jacket off entirely. The white sleeve of his shirt is coated in blood and so is half of his vest. He was struck with the God Killer, so his wound isn't closing. My throat is utterly dry, stopping the desperate plea that has built up in my throat.

"You're such a jackass, and you wonder why people hate you?" Helene snaps at Galen.

I'm trying to blink away the tears, checking Essos's face as my fingers tremble, undoing the buttons on his vest. He's still conscious and with it, and I have to think I'm overreacting because he was standing up just a minute ago. His good hand comes up to cover mine, stilling them.

"Don't." He lets out a heavy breath. He's unable to finish his sentence before he passes out completely. His hand falls from mine limply, and various versions of my future flash through my head, each more untenable than the last.

I scream, pushing up to put pressure on his shoulder. There is a flurry of movement behind me, but I don't pay it any mind. I focus only on Essos, only on not losing him. A pair of strong hands pulls me away from him, and I turn, ready to shred whoever it is. When I find it's Galen touching me, I scream for a whole new reason. Immediately, he lets me go, and Callie shoulders past us to get to Essos.

She's just as gentle, but firmer when she parts his vest. The amount of blood is staggering, and my head feels lighter the longer I look at it. I refuse to let my emotions get the better of me. Essos needs me to be strong right now. He needs me to be here for him and that is exactly what I'm going to do.

"Help me lay him down," Callie orders, and both Kai and Galen jump into action. She watches her husband closely, not trusting him and, frankly, neither do I, but if he will help Essos and save him, then I am here for it.

One clear thought crosses my mind, and I run as fast as my broken knee will take me to Xavier. He's the only other healer we have on hand right now, and as badly as I want to give him space to grieve, I can't. If I do, we might both be grieving and I didn't go through all of that, all of this, to lose my husband.

As I get to the bottom of the stairs, my knee decides it's done with my bullshit and gives out. My momentum is carrying me forward and I let all of my weight crash onto my hands to avoid throwing my body weight on my belly when I fall. My bump still hits the ground, but not as bad as if I hadn't tried to catch myself.

Xavier's red-rimmed eyes meet mine and he reverently lets Posey back down on the ground to help me. We grip each other's forearms as he assists me to my feet and before he can say anything, I cut him off.

"Essos needs you," I plead, proud of myself for keeping my voice from cracking.

"Of course." He says it without inflection and then helps me back up the stairs. We're halfway when he quits trying to help and just scoops me into his arms. Neither one of us can find it in ourselves to crack a joke.

No one turns when we enter the room. Xavier tries to set me down across from Essos but I refuse, pushing off the couch to limp to him. I kneel again at the top of the couch, bracing his head with my hands. I run my thumbs over his forehead. One look at his wound starts the tears again, but I don't realize it until a drop clears some of the blood and grime from his skin.

"You need to stay. We're not done yet. You're my sun. I need you here for Pom, and for the family we're meant to have. Stay with me, please. I can't have gone through all of that just to lose you again," I whisper to him.

Behind me, there are hushed murmurs of what to do. I watch Callie stitch the wound shut and apply a clean dressing before she starts to talk to everyone else again. I hear words like *blood loss* and *fatal*, but I can't listen to them. I can't acknowledge what they're saying.

A hand on my shoulder tries to pull me away. "Daphne, we need to look at your wounds."

"Don't touch me." My voice sounds shrill and I jerk my shoulder out of their grip. I can't even tell who said it; everyone is speaking so quietly, afraid to startle me.

"Daphne," this voice is harder. Galen. "I will drag you out of this room if you make me. Let Callie look at your injuries."

His interference is enough to get me to really look away from my pale, pale husband. "Since when do you care?" I hiss. "Isn't this what you always wanted? My husband dead so you can rule the Underworld all by yourself? Why isn't anyone doing anything? Why aren't you trying to heal him?" I turn my accusatory gaze to Xavier. "*Help him,*" I plead. "Please."

"It's the blade. We can't do anything about it," Xavier explains.

"*Magical.* You can't do anything *magical.* He needs a blood transfusion, or something. It didn't hit his heart. He needs to be okay. He promised me a family. He promised me a football team's worth of kids and a future together. So, fix him." I'm gritting my teeth, and when I look from Callie to Xavier, I repeat myself. "*Fix him.*"

Every word from my mouth breaks, because I know what everyone is thinking is going to happen, but I won't let this be the end of our story. I need them to believe in him because that's what he needs. Essos has to feel how badly we all need him so he can fight because I know my husband won't give up on us without a fight. But everyone has to believe in him just as much.

The muscle in Xavier's jaw ticks and it's so like his brother that I feel like I'm being crushed under a tide of grief that I can't claim yet. Everyone in this room is acting like he's already gone. Galen takes a step toward me, and I pivot, feeling like a cornered feral cat.

"Gods*damn it.*" I clench my fists, honing my anger into something useful, like focus. I look around the room, taking stock of who is here and who isn't.

"Will you let me set your knee?" Callie asks, reaching toward me. There is still blood, my husband's blood, on her hands, and I stumble backward.

"Don't fucking touch me, Callista," I snarl, glancing around the empty places in the room. "Show yourselves, you fucking cowards. You can't claim to be Fate or Titans and then not be here when you're needed. Show yourselves or I'll make what Posey had planned for life look like a children's birthday party. I will salt and burn the Earth and dance in the ashes of humanity. I will let the dead rule and the living cower in fear, and if you don't think I will, you are so very, *very* wrong." My voice shakes with rage as I glance around the room, waiting for Esmaray, Octavia, and Lairus to show up. I can understand why the Fates aren't here, but fuck that. No one will be exempt from my revenge.

The room starts to get darker as shadows creep in, and they're so like Essos's shadows that I glance at him, but he's still unconscious. The realization that I'm causing them almost forces me to fold in half because it's a stark reminder that a part of him continues to live in me, both with the power shared during our wedding and our child.

This can't be the end. *This can't be the end.*

Not when we've just found each other again and were about to find peace.

I can barely see through the tears in my eyes. Silence lingers in the room, waiting to see what happens.

"Well, this is unexpected."

We all turn in the direction of the male voice, currently shrouded in darkness. It's not Lairus, but if whoever it is will help, they will be welcome. The man steps out from the shadows and into the room, and nearly everyone physically recoils.

"Daddy?" Helene asks, thunderstruck.

Titus gives her a pitying smile. "In the flesh. What have we here?"

"I saw you die. I was covered in your blood. I was the only one that mourned you." Helene's voice cracks as her shoulders turn in on themselves.

Kai comes up behind her, wrapping his arms around her waist and holding her to his chest. She has the same look in her eye that I had. She's a cornered animal ready to strike as her hurt turns to anger.

"He's dying," I choke out, limping toward Titus. "It was Titan blood that created the weapon and I'm willing to bet Titan blood will close his wound."

I can't even give a thought to *how* Titus was the one to answer my call. All that matters to me is that he did. I don't need to know where he has been all these months. He just needs to help Essos now.

Titus's gaze flicks from his son to me. I can't imagine how I look, and I don't care. If looking like I'm on the verge of collapse will get him to help Essos, then I will do it. I will do anything. I will trade my life for his if that is what he demands.

"You're going to need more than just *my* blood. It took two Titans to create the weapon, so we would need at least two of us to have a chance at healing that wound. From the looks of it, not only is it deep, but he's lost a lot of blood. Who knows what sort of damage has been inflicted because of the dagger?" he hedges with a sigh. "And honestly, I'm not sure interference is the best course of action. It's best to let these things do what they need to do."

"Don't taunt my daughter," Esmaray warns, materializing in the room. She turns her silver eyes on me. "What do you need?"

"I haven't agreed to anything," Titus points out.

I turn to Xavier and grab the God Killer blade that's sheathed at his side and lift the dagger to point it at Titus. He flinches just that little bit back, but he shifts closer to cover the move.

"How did you survive?" Xavier asks, and I want to pull my hair out and scream that now is not the *time*.

"Yeah, if you thought I was actually going to attend that wedding with Crazy Pants running around with one of those daggers on the loose? You're delusional. I'm the God Supreme. It was a decoy. Smoke and mirrors. Once she froze us, I did not want to be there anymore." He raises his eyebrows at me quickly, like it's something he's proud of.

"Is that why the Fates changed their tune about bringing you back?" Helene's question goes ignored.

"But you're here now? If Daphne gets stabby with that dagger..." Xavier pushes.

"Then I think I'll be less inclined to actually help." Titus's voice is sharp as he looks to Xavier then the blade and then Essos.

"I don't take kindly to being summoned," Octavia's imperious voice calls as she strolls in with Lairus on her arm.

"Oh, good gods," Titus mutters, rolling his eyes and dropping his head back to look up at the ceiling.

On second thought, maybe calling them all here was a mistake, but it's not like I counted on Titus still being *alive*. Octavia stops short when she sees Titus and is actually speechless. When she recovers, she starts in on him immediately.

"You spineless, worthless weasel of a man. I mourned you. I should have known you would fake your death! Posey was never good enough to take you out. You're like a fucking whack-a-mole, just popping up somewhere else after we thought you were gone."

I notice Lairus is burning brighter, and it's almost uncomfortably bright in the room. Esmaray is pointedly not looking at her ex, while Titus and Octavia start to trade verbal blows. At this point, I'm not sure if they're going to fuck or kill someone.

"*Enough!*" I shout, trying to get everyone to focus on why I called them here instead of their stupid Real Housewives of Solarem *bullshit*.

Attention turns to me, but before I can make the same demand I've been making for what seems like the last two hours, a pain sizes my stomach. I drop the blade, doubling over to hold onto myself. Everyone in the room has already given up on Essos, which feels like they've given up on me too. We are the same heart. We've spent thousands of years together. I no longer know where he ends and I begin. Without him, I don't know if I can do this.

I fall to my knees as the wind is knocked out of me. I can only see people's feet as everyone crowds in to touch me.

"Don't touch me." I struggle to stand up, waiting for the feeling to pass or see if there is something else. Is the adrenaline just leaving my system? "Help Es—"

This time I cry out when I feel the pain. I want to let my whole body fold in on itself, but I can't. I need them to help Essos.

Callie squats in front of me, gently placing her hands on my shoulders.

"Hi, sweetie. You need to let me look at you and check on Pom. I *promise* we will take care of Essos, but you know he's going to be upset if you're suffering, and it sounds like you are." Her full lips pull into a tight smile as she tries to convince me that this is what I should do. Her kind brown eyes are full of concern as she waits for me to do something, anything. I give a small nod.

Callie glances over my shoulder at someone, nodding so whoever it is can see, and I'm scooped up again. It's getting old, being manhandled, but I wrap my arms around Tink's neck, wanting to cry from the pain. He starts to take me out of the room.

"No!" I shriek and start to struggle. I need to be here. I need to see color return to Essos's face. I need to see him smile and take a full breath. There is no reason I can't be taken care of here.

"Put her here," Xavier says from out of my sight. Tink changes direction to another sofa. He sets me down and Callie and Xavier start to check me over. They talk through my injuries, and it's Callie who asks about the fight with Posey because Xavier can't bring himself to say her name, though he tries. When I mention the blow to my back, they share a look. I'm tired of all these silent conversations going on.

I have to double-tap the armor that Tink gave me so Callie can place her hands on my stomach. She's silent and I hold my breath, waiting for her to say something or do something. I want to reach out and feel for Pom to see if she's moving around in there. I look up at Xavier with tears in my eyes.

"I want Cat," I plead, needing my friend now more than ever.

Tink slides his hand into mine, giving it a gentle squeeze. "I'll get her," he promises and then he's gone.

Xavier takes my hand, and I can feel it warming. That warmth spreads through my body, focusing on my knee, which is slowly healing while I wait for Callie to say something.

"Pom's okay. I think she's just feeling your stress. I'm not a mortal doctor, and I'm going to get the midwife to come and look at you, but I can feel her heartbeat and it's strong. You need to rest. Let us worry about Essos."

"No," I say through gritted teeth. "You're not making me go anywhere. I'm seeing this through." I look past Callie to the four awkward Titans who look like teenagers squabbling over who kissed whose boyfriend.

"Are you four just going to stand there or are you going to actually do something useful?" Helene snaps. I'm grateful to her for taking charge. She could be by my side, holding my hand, but she's doing what I need, making sure I still have a husband when this day from hell ends.

Esmaray scoops to pick up the blade I dropped. My whole body tenses as she moves to where Essos lies shirtless and too still. Callie actually growls at me until I let myself relax. Xavier is still infusing me with warmth, while Callie stitches the wound on my chest, the one made with the same blade that might take Essos from me.

It is Esmaray who slides through the bindings of his stitches, reopening the wound. Essos writhes, groaning in pain. When I move to try to be by his side, Xavier and Callie both hold me down. I'm left powerless as I watch the woman who purports to be my mother slice her hand, letting herself bleed freely into Essos's wound. She hands off the blade to Lairus, who compiles without comment.

"Shouldn't that be enough?" Octavia asks, looking down at Essos's wound.

Helene gapes at her mother. "I cannot believe you two monsters actually raised me. That is your son, your *child*. He is dying and needs your help. It's time to put on your big girl panties do something good for once." Helene scolds her parents the way one would scold an insolent child.

Always needing to one-up Octavia, Titus takes the blade and in one brutal action cuts his palm before taking Octavia's hand and cutting hers as well. They squeeze their hands over Essos, letting the blood drop together.

Esmaray walks over to me, blocking my view, and I want to scream at her to move, but her uncut hand smooths over my cheek. She brushes a gentle kiss to my brow.

"Call anytime you need something, even if it's something like babysitting. The Fates have amazing things planned for your girl."

She runs her soothing fingers over my forehead, back and forth. It's rhythmic and surprisingly helps to calm me. I wonder for a moment if she did this when I was a child. It's the last thought I have before I drift into oblivion.

38

My focus hasn't left Essos's sleeping form since I woke up. He's still paler than I would like, but I can watch his bare chest rise and fall as I lie beside him. Cat, my rock, is lying on my other side, snoring softly. As badly as I want to get up to pee, I won't disturb her.

I woke briefly when she came in with red eyes and tear-streaked cheeks. Both Essos and I had been carried to our room after I slipped into my own unconsciousness. Cat's form curled around mine, spooning me so I could feel safe as I lay on my side, facing Essos.

We still don't know if my gamble worked. I'm grateful that he doesn't seem to be in pain and I know that I have done everything I can. My fingers travel along his jaw before I let them settle over his heart, my heart. If I could will him to live, I would, but I have to play the waiting game and let the magic work.

When I can't bear it any longer, I turn to jostle Cat so I can get out of bed.

"Need help?" a male whisper asks from across the room. Xavier is sitting slouched in the same chair Cat did when she dished on what has been going on with them. He looks like he's aged ten years since I last saw him.

"If you can think of a way I can do this without waking her, then yes," I whisper back.

"I'm awake," Cat mumbles in the way of a person who may be awake, but very much does not want to be. Xavier's indulgent smile is soft as he gazes at her. His steps are easy as he makes his way to my side of the bed. It's awkward as he tries to lift me, and I accidentally kick Cat in the stomach doing it.

"Sorry!"

"It would have been easier for me to just get up," she says this, of course, once my feet are firmly on the ground and Xavier gets a face full of my tits.

"I rescind my apology. You could have said that instead of waiting until the pregnant woman's bladder was on the verge of exploding."

"You could have *asked*."

I ignore her point and go to the bathroom. After, I take my time surveying my injuries. Anything more than a bruise has been healed, but there was nothing to be done for the cut my chest and cheek. It's unclear who, but someone changed me into clean leggings and an old shirt that doesn't fit at all, but it was–it *is*–Essos's shirt, and it's giving me some emotional armor. My belly protrudes from where the shirt has ridden up. I marvel at the feel of Pom, what I think might be a leg or a fist nudging against my side, a silent reminder that she's still here.

The shower feels wonderful on my weary limbs. Focusing on the hot water means I can try to block out the memories of the day before. It also means that I can cry in peace without worrying about how it looks. No one that is with us would begrudge me my tears, but absent a King of the Dead, I need to be able to rule in his place. If the blood of the Titan's didn't work...

No.

I can't let myself go there. Essos will be here when Pom is born.

He will wake up. His vibrant blue eyes will be full of love and life again. There is no way fate is cruel enough for this to be our end.

Once I'm cried out for the time being, I burrow into Essos's side of closet until I find an oversized T-shirt and a pair of grey sweats. When I emerge, Cat is sitting on the couch beside Xavier. I want to tease them about how close they're sitting, but I can't, not while Essos is lying on the bed, eyes closed.

My feet carry me the short distance from the door to my bed, but it might as well be five hundred miles. Neither of them say anything as I resettle myself under the covers sitting up, so I can smooth the dark hair from his face. It's uncomfortable but I lean down and press a kiss to his brow.

"Come back to me," I demand. When I sit up, I expect his eyes to open as if my will was enough to wake him.

It's not.

"We have to talk, Daphne."

I ignore Xavier in favor of fixing the blanket on Essos's chest. "So, talk."

Cat crawls into bed beside me and hugs me. I pat her arm, acknowledging the comfort.

"Do you want to talk outside?" Xavier suggests.

"No, I want to stay here."

"She can stay," Cat tells him, her tone warning.

Xavier perches on the edge of the bed, careful not to disturb the delicate equilibrium.

"We need to go to Solarem."

I turn to face him, the frown on my face deepening. "You can go, but I want Callie to stay with me if I need a healer for Essos." I know what he's getting at, but I'm not going to play. I'm not interested in seeing anyone else. I want to be here and wait for Essos to wake up.

"We need you to be there to represent the Underworld. For us to get the confidence of the people back, we need to present a united front. Everyone but Callie will be there. We will reintroduce Callie after some time since she's been missing for so long, but right now the people of Solarem need unity and stability from the royal family."

I'm glad to hear this impassioned plea from Xavier. It's the type of leadership the citizens deserve, but I am not here for it, not now.

"Honey," Cat's voice is pitched low, trying not to scare the brittle thing I've become. "We won't leave Essos alone, but you need to do this."

I turn on her, anger roaring through me. "Do not think to tell me what I *need* to do. I know what is demanded of me. I know what it is to wear the crown. But I am his wife first, and he needs me. What if he wakes up and I'm not here? What will he think?" I hate how my voice cracks on that last word.

"He would be grateful to you for doing what needs to be done." Xavier's attempt at softness falls flat.

"Get out. Both of you." My eyes are burning as I face Xavier and Cat. She looks startled, like I've hit her or yelled, but my voice is barely over that of a whisper. I didn't think I had the strength even for that. "Don't make me ask again." I finally meet her gaze, but I can't find it in me to feel bad about the hurt in her eyes.

I think I'm going to need that strength in the coming days. They both comply wordlessly. Cat presses a kiss to my temple before unwinding herself from me and going to Xavier, who helps her off the bed. He opens his mouth to say something more but I glare at him, putting an end to it.

When the door clicks shut, I press my forehead to Essos's before a silly idea enters my mind. I grew up in the mortal realm, with stories told of princesses who wake from enchanted slumbers after true love's kiss.

Could it be that easy? The press of my lips to his? It got me my memories back so maybe there is something to fairytales.

I have nothing left to lose, so I try. Everything in my being calls out to him, and even Pom kicks viciously. Our lips touch, and it's tender and soft, but then I worry that I'm not pouring enough of myself into it, so I press harder, and still, it doesn't work.

I have to choke down an anguished cry when nothing changes.

Xavier is right, and I hate him for it. Essos would want me to carry on the same way he had to after I died. Is this meant to be our lives? Forever passing each other, never to be together again? I dash the tears away with a swipe of my hand. I can't think like that.

When I climb out of bed, I nearly trip over Dave, who whines, crouched on the floor. I pat the bed and he jumps up, immediately taking advantage of this new height to lick away my tears. I rub his face, letting him so that I can cry in peace again. He's the best dog because there is no complaint when I hug him tightly to my chest.

"You need to stay and watch him. Don't let him be alone."

A low whine comes from the back of Dave's throat, but I point at Essos, and he barks at me before circling around on the bed and settling at Essos's hip.

There is no right dress or outfit to wear today. A deep blue off-the-shoulder dress calls to me, and I slip it on, luxuriating in the feel of the fabric along my skin. The skirt is made of a heavier satin, but I like how it flows down my body to the floor. My feet slip into matching blue flats. When I try to pick out jewelry, I'm drawn to Essos's closet.

Being around his clothes is almost too much. The weight of his absence crushes me harder than any weight on earth. I'm about to leave when something gold catches my eye. It's the same sunburst necklace I gave to Essos in another lifetime. It has a crescent moon with flowers twined around it while the rays of the sun are strong on the other half of it. My thumb runs over the worn metal, and I pluck it off the dresser and slide it on. It's simple, but it keeps a piece of him near me. We've traded it back and forth over the years when one of us needed to feel the presence of the other. It's fitting that I take it now when I need to feel like Essos is with me.

Dave lifts his head, watching me move toward the door, giving a low growl of approval. There is no reward I can give this dog that will be sufficient for what he is protecting. I give Dave what I can, a kiss on the top of his head and a scratch behind his ears before I do the same for Essos, sans ear scratches. My lips brush his forehead and then his lips before I take his hand in mine.

Pressing his hand to my bump, I lean down and whisper in his ear. "She needs you. *I* need you." For what is probably the only time, Pom gives an obedient kick to where his hand is. It's unclear if he can feel that, but I know somewhere in my soul, he does.

I don't know what possesses me, but I lean back down to blow gently on his eyelids.

Closing the door between us might be the hardest thing I've had to do, but I need to prepare myself for the possibility that I have to do this all alone.

Everyone looks up at me when I descend the stairs. Their shock must mirror my own because all four Titans remain. Galen shoves his hands in his pockets, looking away from me while Tink approaches, holding out his arm. I slip mine into his, grateful for the support because my knees feel like they're ready to give out at any moment.

Callie clears her throat. "I'll go sit with Essos until you're back."

My head bobs in a nod, but I'm not sure I'm conscious of the effort to do so. "I don't want him alone, *ever*." I'm aware I've just left him alone, now, but he has Dave with him, and Waffles too, no doubt.

"He won't be," Finn assures me.

I reach up and dab at the corner of my eye, catching a tear before it falls.

"We should go," Xavier tells the group. His voice has taken on a deeper quality, like he's trying his hand at being a full leader.

A small, bitter part of me hates him for it. If he had tried sooner, maybe this wouldn't be my life. The tender-sided part of my heart reminds me that if he hadn't, Cat would still be trapped in a vicious cycle of death and rebirth.

I wrap my arms around Tink's middle and he folds his arms around my shoulders before weightlessness descends on us. I try to keep my stomach from turning even as Pom does somersaults in my womb.

When we land, I stagger away from him, grabbing the first steady thing I can find. When I lift my head to see what I've grabbed, I'm surprised to find it's Lairus, and the warmth makes sense. For once, I'm not about to puke.

"Are you well?" he asks, and I pull out of his grip so fast, I nearly stumble.

I right myself, smoothing my hands over the skirt of my dress. "As well as can be expected."

Lairus extends a hand to me, but I pull out of his reach, nearly colliding with Xavier behind me. My brother-in-law's hands steady me.

"To avoid confusion at this time, I ask that the Titans remain behind the scenes until we can get Solarem back on more sure footing," Xavier tells Lairus while sizing him up.

I finally take in my surroundings. We're in the gardens that Posey pulled me to in the backyard of her home with Xavier. Gone is her garish throne. In its place is a small stage with a meager curtain blocking the view of us. Beyond the stage, I can hear the excited but confused chatter of the crowd. Do they know what Posey was doing? That their queen is dead? Are they relieved that all these restrictive measures have been lifted? Do they even understand what was happening behind the scenes?

"You need this."

I turn to find Xavier ready with a tiara featuring the emblem of Solarem. Every spoke on the crown is a building, each taller than the last as they move from the outside in. It's a crown meant for the Queen of Solarem.

"Are you proposing before your brother is even dead?" My words lack the bite I want them to have.

Xavier sighs, like he's tired of my attitude. "No, but we need to present a united front and I thought this would be the best way to do it."

"Are we not already a united front?"

"We are but–"

I shake my head. "There is no but. Do you want me as your queen?"

Xavier's eyes flick over my shoulder. I don't have to wonder who he's looking at. "No, I have plans for someone else."

"Look, I'm not saying announce your new queen in the same breath as you tell everyone Posey is gone, but you need *her* by your side."

"I don't know if she actually even wants me." He sounds so vulnerable, so I hold back the joke I want to make about pineapples. There is something about Cat that has softened this man, and I'm okay with it.

"Neither of you have to decide that now, but the people of Solarem deserve the truth. They have been lied to about Posey and who she is, the same we had been for millennia. This is a time of change, and they're going to need a strong leader. I will help you. I will stand by your side as you help to guide everyone through this, but I have my own realm and my own problems to contend with. Decide now what future you want and figure out how to get there later."

"It doesn't change that I need you out there, ready to be the face of the Underworld. With Essos out of the picture, you need to step up."

My head snaps back and away from him, surprised by the about-face, but his eyes flick over my shoulder to someone else. When I turn, I see Titus watching us from the shadows. Before I hurt someone, I take a deep breath and walk away.

I want to go to Cat, who I see standing nervously off to the side, but Finn stops me by holding his hand out in my direction.

"You know I may not be able to see what you need right now, but I am here. Always," he assures me.

I slide my hand into his before embracing him. "I know. And I'm here for you too, if you ever want to escape Bria and Dion."

"I'll need one of them to bring me by the house."

"Right, no transporting," I say, wincing.

Finn scoffs. "Yes, but no. I have my powers back and so do Helene and Kai. I'm just not confident in that ability right now, so if my mother hens want to baby me for a little longer, then who am I to object?"

I chuckle then kiss his cheek. "We've gotten through a lot together. We can get through this together too," I assure him.

Dion slides over and grabs Finn's hand to lead him off to the side.

Cat is in a tight, pale pink gown. It hugs her every curve before flaring out at the knees for movement. She glances at me nervously, and a part of me dies that I've made her feel like this.

"I'm sorry," I start, holding my hand up to silence her. "I should do better."

Cat pulls me into a bone-crushing hug, unaware of her new strength. "Hon, your husband is in a magical coma. There is no doing better. Having you on two feet is unbelievable. I don't think I would have gotten out of bed, so kudos to you for doing this. Just tell me what you need. I can tell Xavier to shove it."

I force a smile. "I just want to get this over with."

"Say no more." Then my friend turns and actually snaps at the King of the Gods. Like an obedient dog, his head lifts to her. "Let's get this moving." His dark eyes shift to me before he nods.

Helene and Kai both offer me weak smiles, and I nod at them. I appreciate how they're not crowding me. The only ones left backstage are the Titans, and the rulers, each paired off. Only I stand alone. Cat looks back at me, wanting to reach for me but I shake my head. If I'm out there alone, I may be able to handle this. Once someone offers me the comfort I'm missing, the comfort I want to seek in the solace of my husband's arms, I'll lose it.

Xavier is the first one out, with Cat on his arm. I follow behind them, and last come Helene and Kai. The crowd assembled before us looks to encompass all of Solarem. There are people as far as the eye can see, but in the front are friendly faces. Tink offers a wink and

Dion raises a glass in my direction. I try to force a brave smile, but it comes out a grimace. Essos should be here at my side, celebrating this supposed victory, though I don't know if I can call it a victory without him.

"Citizens of Solarem," Xavier begins. A hush falls over the crowd, but not before a few angry words are shared. If Xavier notices, he doesn't say anything. "There's been too much uncertainty for the last several months and we are here to relieve you of any worry."

I don't know how much he plans to tell them, and I don't know how they will react, but I only hope it will help. A hand on the small of my back makes me stiffen, and when Galen steps up beside me, I want to glower. It should be my husband beside me, not my tormenter.

"Just smile," he orders me.

With as wide a step as I can manage, I step away from him, not caring what it looks like to the people below. If he thinks he can touch me again, I will break his arm, and then get the God Kill blade from Xavier and castrate his baby brother. On second thought, I should do that anyway.

"Many of you experienced unknown terror at the hands of the Queen of the Gods," Xavier hesitates, still unable to call her by her name, but he pushes through. "Posey. It was revealed when the veil between our world and the mortals fell that Posey was more than just a Goddess. She was one of the Fates herself."

Murmurs break out in the crowd, and Xavier pauses, waiting for them to die down. Cat slips her hand into his and squeezes. For just a moment, he glances at where they touch before he looks at her, continuing on.

"I was as shocked as many of you that her betrayal ran so deep. To achieve her means, she cast the true Goddess of Motherhood and Fertility aside, dooming her to be caught in an endless cycle of death. Catalina," he gestures her forward and she dutifully steps into the light, "was meant to be the Queen of the Gods. Posey's machinations included manipulating Galen to overthrow Essos, sending the souls of the Underworld back to the mortal realms, and many more plots that we are just beginning to understand.

"Yesterday, unbeknownst to you all, a battle was waged in the home of the King and Queen of the Underworld, which resulted in Posey's defeat and death. There were tragic losses on both sides, more details of which will be forthcoming, but we wanted to be clear on the state of your leadership. Queen Daphne will be leading the Underworld alone, without the aid of King Essos. She will have the full support of the Council and Galen to do what needs to be done."

My head snaps in Xavier's direction.

What the fuck? Is he serious about making it sound like Essos is dead? Is he assuming his brother will never recover? And what is he thinking alluding to Galen's supporting me in this? I don't think it was a mistake or misstatement to make it sound like Galen will be assisting me in running the Underworld. Absolutely fucking not.

"We are coming to you in hopes of providing full transparency to the people of Solarem. We will continue to strive to do better by you. With Catalina by my side as Queen, I am confident that you will be pleased with the changes that we make. Catalina and I will endeavor to be available to you as we try to right the wrongs that have been done to you. We appreciate your patience during this time of transition. In the coming weeks, we will make another announcement regarding open hours of complaint for Catalina and me to hear you."

Xavier does not wait for applause. He just turns and leads us off the stage, and a surge of frustration and anger rides me as his words echo and sink in my mind.

Once we're out of sight of the public I turn to him. "What in the Underworld was that, Xavier? Why did you make it sound like Essos won't–" No, I can't even say the words. "Why did you make it sound like *Galen* was going to help with the Underworld?"

"I need you to realize that you will still need to do your duty even if Essos never wakes up. He was in a position to do nothing after your death because you had already established much of the Underworlds processes. You do not have that luxury because of how thoroughly the system was fucked during the Trials. The sooner you accept that my brother may never open his eyes again, the sooner the Underworld will be able to move on. You have your work cut out for you. If you need to use Galen–who until you drove a blade into his chest–was the heir apparent to the crown, in order to get things done, then I expect you to do so."

Luxury. He thinks it a luxury for me to be by my husband's side as I wait to see if he will ever wake up. Xavier must be out of his mind if he think's I'll ask Galen for *anything.* I'm not thinking, driven only by my rage, when I shove him, hard. It's a testament to how unexpected the act must have been because he stumbles back a step, eyes wide before they harden. I see the monster king that lurks under his skin, the one he keeps tucked away with a mask of laziness. Pushing him made me feel so good that I move to do it again. Xavier easily catches my wrists and walks me backward until my back connects with something firm, and he still presses forward, invading my space.

"Do not think to strike me again. I told Galen to stand beside you and touch you because we need to show the people that their government still works and that we are concerned for them. If there is friction among the ruling class, it will only create more instability, and I won't have that." Xavier doesn't squeeze my wrists; he just holds them, glaring at me.

"Xavier," Cat warns him only once.

He releases me then grabs me around the waist, before weightlessness takes hold of us.

When my feet are on firm ground I push away from Xavier, itching to hit him again. He releases me, striding out of my bedroom door before I can yell at him for grabbing me like that.

Callie looks up from her book. "What was that all about?"

"You don't want to know."

TAYLOR JADE and his mother are the first people I see when I go to the Underworld. It's bittersweet, coming to the place I'm supposed to rule with Essos without him. Instead, I have Xavier and Rafferty with me.

It's been three weeks without my husband and after two, I decided I had to put my crown on and do what Xavier said: I needed to lead. Which is why I'm here now, feeling a million months pregnant, accepting a hug from an effusive fourteen-year-old.

"Thank you, your ladyship," he whispers.

"I think it should be 'Your Majesty,' Tay," his mom corrects, but I wink at her with a smile.

"Of course," I whisper back to him, tears pricking my eyes. At least someone could get a happily ever after. "If I said you didn't have to remember the zombies, would you be okay with that?" I ask.

Taylor seems to think on it, biting his lower lip while his mom rests her hand on his shoulder. I still harbor some anger toward this woman, but I think the zombie apocalypse brought out the worst in people. It's why I've already started a new department whose job is to review those sent to the Deep based on their actions during that period of time on Earth.

"I think zombies are cool, but I know it's upsetting to a lot of people, so I would be okay with it."

It's hard to hold on to hate for a woman who raised such an empathetic child and who did something she thought was right even if it was so, so wrong.

"I'm going to go to the water source," Rafferty tells me. I know I must look bad if even he's treating me with kid gloves. I watch as he disappears into the crowd, headed toward the river that provides water to the Underworld.

However he's treating the water is meant to be targeted. Souls that were absorbed into the dagger and scepter have no memory of anything being different. There's really no need to alter their memories, which means that what Rafferty is doing is going to affect just those who need to have memories removed.

I catch sight of Margarita with her grandson, who grabs Taylor's hand. The two snatch up two balls, tossing them for Spot and Shadow to chase after.

This is the right call. Pom gives a little kick of confirmation.

"Daphne?" Xavier says my name, and I turn to face him. Cat wanted to come with me today, but I told her not to. I want to be able to show her my realm in all its glory, not while people are still picking up the broken pieces of themselves the way I am.

"Yeah?" I ask. I want to cross my arms, but that just pushes my tits together so I have to settle for letting them rest on my stomach.

"I want to apologize to you." Xavier rubs the back of his neck. "I shouldn't have forced your hand and dragged you out of you house when things with Essos were uncertain. I shouldn't have alluded to his death, and I certainly shouldn't have made it seem like Galen would be helping in any capacity. You've done a great job with the Underworld in Essos's absence. I thought I was doing the right thing for you and the Underworld by getting you out and moving and showing you that you had a lot to live for. I was wrong. Cat helped me see that."

I squeeze his arm. "I'm sorry, I shouldn't have hit you."

"I deserved it for one thing or another. I'll just count that toward my karma. After you died, I saw what it did to Essos. He stopped existing, and I didn't want to see that happen to you. He immediately sank into it, and I thought if I kept you from that long enough, then maybe you could avoid it too. But like I said, I was wrong."

"Wow, you said it twice. I should put this down in my calendar as a momentous day," I tease, but I can't even feign a smile for him.

Xavier chuckles then shoves his hands in his pockets as Rafferty returns to us.

"My work here is done. I also finished in the mortal realms with those exceptions you named. If that's all, I'd like to go back to you people forgetting I exist." Rafferty doesn't wait for a thanks or anything, he just leaves.

"Since we're friends again, can I ask you for a favor?" I say, looking up at Xavier.

He tosses his head back and laughs, and for a second it's too painful to be near him. It's so like Essos that I wish Posey had just carved my heart out with that knife.

"What do you want?"

"Can you get Cat and bring her to my parents? I want to check in on them in the mortal realm."

"Which ones?"

I stop short. "What does that mean?"

"I mean, miss boo hoo, I was an orphan who now has not one, not two, but three sets of parents, which set do you want to check on in the mortal realm? Essos had the souls of your mortal birth parents stashed for safekeeping. Ron and Linda, right? They were at your wedding. I was the one that took them to their safehouse after, so I know where they are."

I tap at the corners of my eyes, trying to catch the tears. Hormones are the fucking worst. "I meant my adoptive parents, but can you get Cat and my mortal birth parents and meet me at Phil and Melinda's?"

"I'll meet you there."

He transports away, and I take a second, looking out over the Underworld. It's small, but I can already see the change in people as their memories of what happened with the zombies washes away. By tomorrow, they will all have a freer future ahead of them.

I BEAT XAVIER TO MY PARENTS' house, and it's a good thing. I never expected to have to prepare them to meet souls.

"Look at you," Melinda squeals, hugging me close to her. Someday, I hope to introduce *all* of my parents, but for now, the mortal ones will do. I'm not even sure Esmaray would know what to do with mortals and I'm still undecided about Lairus. It's nice and all that he's claimed to be my father and willingly bled himself for me twice, but something about him doesn't sit right with me.

"Hey, X sent me as reinforcements," Helene calls to me just as I break free from the hug.

My mom's eyes bug out of her head. "Is she also a goddess?" She asks out of the corner of her mouth. "I'm Melinda."

"I'm actually Queen of the Seas and Goddess of Victory. You must be one of Daphne's mothers!" Helene hugs my mom and she has no idea what to do about it. When Helene breaks free, she turns to face me. "This is not your baby shower, by the way. I know we're goddesses and can make everything, but I learned about this thing mortals do where you design your own baby onesie and I thought since you were mortal for a hot minute, maybe you might enjoy that. It might be a surprise down the road, I don't know. Well, aren't you going to invite me in?"

My mom starts to faint, but thankfully my dad is there to catch her. "You know, this whole being the only people that remember anything is, hard," my dad grunts as he picks up my mom. "Where is that husband of yours? He did this last time. I love your mother, but I can't afford to slip a disc."

"My brother is otherwise indisposed. That's why I'm here. Cat suggested that you and Mellie might faint when X showed up with Daphne's birth parents," Helene says, pushing me inside and closing the door behind her. I notice how she mentions she's here to help if my parents faint, but she hasn't exactly offered to help even as my father grunts, trying to get a better grip on my mom.

"Birth parents? Aren't they dead? *I* might faint," my dad says setting my mom on the couch.

"I hope not," Xavier says as he appears with my other parents.

It winds up being the exact distraction I needed, introducing my parents to each other. Both of my moms have a good laugh over how close their names are, saying that it was fate that they both be my mom. My dads talk over the best type of grill and if calories count for gods.

Cat holds my hand when I get too quiet. Eventually, my worry ratches up higher and higher. Today is the first day I've really spent away from Essos and I start to fear that today is the day that Essos wakes and I'm not there. I should have started with baby steps. Some time in the Underworld, some time here, instead of trying to do it all at once.

Will he be afraid? Will he wonder if something happened to me?

Xavier takes the cue and gracefully pulls the day to a close. I want to give him directions on what to do with my birth parents, but my mind is already back home, wondering if Callie would know to get me if Essos did wake.

I say hurried goodbyes before transporting home to find everything exactly as I left it.

Waffles is curled on his pillow beside Essos's head and Dave is belly-up on my side of the bed, knocked out cold.

And Essos slumbers on.

The tears that fall from my eyes are not new ones, they're the same ones I've been crying for myself and for Pom, who might never get to know her father.

39

Pom's movement keeps me up most of the night. Even when I manage to fall asleep, she's right there again, twisting and kicking. Waffles comes over, pressing his front paws to my belly, making little biscuits, and when Pom hits at him, his eyes lift to mine, startled. Without ceremony, the cat drops onto my abdomen, purring louder than I've ever heard him. It seems to settle the baby, so I set aside my Princess Lorelei book and try to sleep again.

I've managed to doze for a few hours when I feel movement around my stomach. Thinking that it's just Waffles again, I give him a light shove, only my hand connects with another hand and not the warm furry body of a cat. My eyes open, my whole body tensing, but I'm not prepared for the brilliant blue eyes I love to be looking down on me.

"You just looked so peaceful. I'm sorry for waking you." His voice is gruff from disuse, but I don't give a care for anything else. I grip his face and pull him to me.

Our mouths meet in a crush of desire. My lips part so our tongues can dance and flick until I feel him wince in pain from my hands gripping his shoulders. I release him immediately, but he doesn't pull away, only presses his advantage. Essos's hand grips first my side, then moves to my tender breast.

"Essos." His name is more a prayer on my lips than anything else as he moves down to my neck. His mouth is hot as he sucks on my skin, sending my back arching into him. Essos rolls onto his back, the same prone position he's been in for a month. He's not letting me go, pulling my body with him.

I hover over him, unsure if this is the right move. Essos sees my trepidation because he props himself up on his elbows with another wince of pain.

"What's wrong, my love?"

"Say my name," I plead, reaching for his cheek.

"Daphne." There is a rough quality to his voice, which rips my heart open.

I reach between us, gripping his cock. This is a bad idea, but I can feel in my bones how badly we both need this. I rise to my knees over him. "Again."

"Daphne." His voice is begging, and I meet his plea with my body. I slide over him, crying out, and then just crying as we move as one. His body trembles below me with release and I follow him over the edge shortly after.

I collapse into a heap beside him, my tears still flowing freely. Essos gathers me to him, kissing the crown my head and then each tear that follows.

"Is everyone still here?" Essos asks, one hand idly stroking my back.

"Here?"

"Yes, as in our house. Where everyone has been staying for the last several months."

I can't talk around the lump in my throat. "Essos, how long do you think it's been?"

"A few hours? A day?"

I burrow into his chest, and he's silent, waiting for me to continue. "It's been thirty-six days." I manage to choke out.

"You're not...serious." He sits up a little more to get a read on my face. "You are serious."

"Of course, I am. Never do that again," I order, nipping at his pec because it's the closest thing.

"Ow. I won't. I promise it wasn't something that was on my bucket list."

Fresh tears spring to my eyes. "No discussion of bucket lists or dying for the King of the Dead. I was thinking about what I was going to do without you. How would I be a mother when half my heart was with the dead? I don't think I could have pulled myself together."

Essos shifts out from under me, so he can sit up. He helps me into a seated position as well so our eyes are level.

"You would have done it because I know that there is nothing you wouldn't do for Pom. It's all moot now. I'm here, I'm not going anywhere. I strangely feel stronger." His hand goes up to where the weapon split his skin. I kiss the jagged scar, the same scar I've kissed every day after kissing him.

"That's probably the blood of the Titans." My explanation is flimsy, but makes the most sense.

"It seems we have much to discuss."

"Much," I agree.

But we don't talk. We nestle back into bed, holding each other. Essos is restless beside me, but knowing that he's awake, that his arms are around me, helps me settle into a peaceful place, letting me find the deep sleep I've been seeking since I nearly lost him.

I ASK everyone to come over the next morning. Callie was the only one who stayed with me, while everyone else moved back to their own homes. She was delighted to check Essos over once she found out he was awake, if only because it means she can get back to her sons. Part of her escape plan was so that the only person who could find where she and her children were tucked away was Essos. Not even she understands where they're hidden.

Essos and I can hear everyone chattering as we go downstairs. Other than the occasional wince, he seems perfectly Essos. I stand to the back when he enters the room, letting his brother and sister smother him with hugs and kisses. Everyone has their turn, telling him everything that he's missed. Noticeably absent are the Fates and his parents. Galen also doesn't show his face, and I'm grateful. With Essos back, I can see the difference in everyone's moods. They're lighter, happier, now that he's awake.

"So, Titus is alive?" Essos asks, rubbing my knee under the table once we're seated.

Helene nods enthusiastically, looking noticeably brighter now that her brother is awake. "And you have Titan blood running through your veins. Your clever wife thought that if the weapon that wounded you was made from Titan blood, maybe Titan blood would heal you."

Xavier also looks lighter, like the tension that's been riding him since the battle with Posey has eased just enough that he can relax. "I'm glad to have you back. Solarem needs us to rule them and rule well. Catalina and I are going to be having a day each week for our citizens to air their grievances. It was all her idea, but we could use you there." Xavier gives Cat a smile.

"All due respect, brother, but no. I have enough to deal with. I can't manage Solarem and the Underworld. My family has to come first." Essos tells this to Xavier, but his eyes are on me.

Helene clears her throat. "Does this mean you and Cat are getting married?"

"No!" Cat practically shouts at her. She clears her throat and then blushes, pushing her food around on her plate. "I mean, no. We discussed that Solarem shouldn't be without a Queen, but our focus is going to be on my training and helping the people of our realm. I'll be queen in my own right, not through marriage."

The dubious look on Xavier's face says otherwise, but he doesn't contradict her.

"We'll get out of your hair. We can deal with the details later," Helene says. She's the first to rise, pressing a kiss to the top of Essos's head.

Everyone departs, even Callie, who steps outside to talk to Tink. I'm grateful she agreed to stay in Solarem until after the baby is born and while we see if Essos has any limitations. Callie won't be staying with us, though. She'll be in Solarem with Tink. As soon as Essos is able, he's going to get Callie to get her sons so she can fulfill her end of the bargain with Galen.

When the house is empty and it's just me and Essos, I wrap my arms around him. I don't regret immediately calling everyone once Essos woke, but now that we're alone, the relief I feel is so complete. For the first time since I was resurrected, there is no threat hanging over our heads. I'm looking forward to enjoying this time together without fear lurking in dark corners.

Essos holds me to him, knowing that we can finally breathe easier until we have Pom in our arms, because she is going to be the biggest adventure we'll have.

Epilogue

Six Months Later

The realization that I'm alone in bed is what pulls me from my sleep. After everything that happened, panic still steals my breath every so often. I glance to Essos's side of the bed, but I'm not left wondering where he is for long.

There is a low coo from across the room. I contemplate lying there and leaving this moment between my husband and daughter, but I want to be with them too badly.

"Is mommy pretending to still be asleep?" Essos stage whispers.

I sit up, admiring them from the bed. Essos is sitting on the couch next to the window with our daughter laying on his thighs. She has her tiny hands wrapped firmly around his index fingers, a bright smile on her face as she waves his hands. Her arms and legs jerk in excitement, another happy baby coo emerging from her tiny chest.

"Can you blame me for wanting to catch some extra z's? Someone was hungry at three a.m. and didn't want to go back to sleep." I toss my covers back so I can sit with them.

"That's your mother's fault."

Essos isn't wrong. The moon shone brightly, and our little girl reached for it until Esmaray came to her. I'm still undecided about how to feel toward her, but she wants to be involved in my daughter's life, and I won't deny my child a doting grandmother.

"You're not wrong," I confirm, settling at his feet. I lean down to inhale the scent of our daughter's dark hair. I look up at Essos and smile at him.

"You can go back to sleep," he offers, managing to wrangle one hand free so he can cup my cheek. I lean into his touch, admiring as my smart daughter sticks her hand in her mouth, suckling on it.

"And miss a single minute of this? A single moment of Penelope's life?" I twist my head to kiss his palm.

Essos gives me a soft smile. "You're going to have to give up some time so she can become a big sister." His mouth twists into a seductive smirk.

"Good gods, sir. She's only three months old. Give me a chance to recover before we try again."

Penelope lets out a shriek of objection, either to a sibling or waiting, I'm not sure.

"How long do you want? Another week? Maybe two?"

"Ah, the negotiator. No, but maybe. I'm just tired." I nuzzle the top of Penelope's head, unable to stop smelling her. No one told me that this is what parenthood would be like, smelling your baby because you can't get over it or smelling them for a dirty diaper. For now, it's the sweeter of the smells.

Essos laughs. "You just have to lie there. I promise I'll do all the work."

I bark out a laugh and Penelope squeals in response. "How romantic. You really know how to make a girl's panties melt."

Essos lifts Penelope, holding her to his chest as he stands. "It was easier when Pom wasn't keeping us up at all hours."

The rush of desire I feel watching my husband cradle our daughter to his bare chest is obscene. He must sense it because I blink and the baby is in her bassinet, still awake, but content to just flail about, and Essos is lifting me from the chair. My legs wrap around his hips and I can feel his desire pressing against my softest parts.

Essos slants his mouth over mine, claiming me. My body melts into him as I wrap my arms around his shoulders, my fingers delving into his hair. He grips my ass, squeezing before he eases us both on the bed.

For a moment, he hovers over me, his eyes searching my face before he breaks into a brilliant smile.

"My whole world is in this room. We never have to leave, honestly. I say forget today and let me make love to you until the stars rise again."

I prop up and capture his mouth with mine. "What are you waiting for?"

I feel his deep rumbling laugh as he reaches under my nightgown for my panties and slides them off. He kisses along my thigh and knee and calf before sitting me up to take off my nightgown. Essos still finds any reason he can to touch me. Even now as he looks down at me, grinning like he won the lottery, his eyes scorch every inch of skin they see, settling between my legs.

He resumes kissing the inside of my knee, then he kisses up and up and up until he reaches the apex of my thighs. His tongue lashes against the sensitive folds and my body bows off the bed. My fingers dig into his hair as I unapologetically roll my hips up. I feel his chuckle against me, and I want to feel it again.

Essos starts touching my entrance, circling slowly in time with his tongue before he dips a finger inside me.

"Fuck," I whimper, rolling my hips again.

Essos flattens his tongue against my clit, using every trick in the book to get me to the brink of orgasm, and then he stops. I nearly cry as he pulls away from me, keeping his fingers inside me.

"Not yet," he growls, using his free hand to pull down his sweatpants. His cock springs free, and I want to close my mouth around him and suck until he's crying for *my* mercy. I reach forward with one hand and glide it along his shaft, relishing as he throbs under my touch.

Essos removes his hand from inside me, and I glower as he presses my thighs wider. He hooks one arm under one of my legs before lying over me, his cock positioned against my pussy. I'm breathing heavily, waiting for him.

"I'm going to fuck you right now. This is not going to be the love-making we usually have. I am going to fuck you into next week and you're begging for an orgasm."

"All talk and no–*Oh.*"

He thrusts into me, and I cry out at the sudden fullness of him. His hand hooks around my shoulder as he slams into me, unrelenting. My hips rise to meet him thrust for thrust, just as desperate for this release. Our mouths are locked together as the heady taste of my arousal links us, our tongues caressing at odds with the movement of our bodies.

Our kiss breaks as my orgasm takes me over all at once, invading my every nerve ending with only Essos. My whole being is devoted completely to this moment, completely to us. My nails dig into his sides, no doubt taking skin with them as I moan. My back arches, pressing into him, our bodies moving together, slick with sweat. His own release thunders through him, and he groans, leaving what is going to be more than a love bite on my shoulder.

He trembles above me before withdrawing and dropping onto the bed beside me. Both of us are panting. Essos's hand draws a line from my mouth down my chest, circling a nipple before dipping back inside me, where I'm sticky with both of us.

I give an involuntary moan at the feel of him against my sensitive nerves. He leans over, pressing a kiss to my lips before withdrawing his hand.

"Would you hate me if I said I wanted another one?"

"Fuck? No. Baby? Maybe."

Essos grin, kissing my lips. "I'll convince you again soon. Who knows? Maybe this one will take."

He gives me a lascivious wink before helping me up. I watch my husband's sculpted bare ass as he struts into the bathroom to start the shower while I check on Penelope. She's happily chewing on one of her fists. Dave is resting beside her bassinet, ready to get us if we're needed.

We manage to keep the shower relatively tame, both with an ear turned to the baby, but Essos still manages to take me again like he's a man who's been starved.

I FIGHT WITH THE BABY, wrestling her into a blue onesie with a tutu. It's the best I'm willing to manage because dealing with multiple layers of clothing on a baby are more than I am capable of. When she's this little, we're enjoying these tasks, even if they're exhausting. I'm also convinced that when she realizes that clothes can be magicked on her, she will learn to magic them *off* her too.

Essos steps out of his dressing room in a white button down and a navy blue suit. I clench my thighs, knowing that we're already running late.

His eyebrows are raised, taking in my state of undress, and likely the way I tried to hide my arousal.

"We don't have time," I hiss, thrusting the baby and her diaper bag at him. It's with practice that I've learned if I need to be presentable, I should be the last person dressed because I will inevitably wind up with spit up or breast milk on me. I sprint into my closet, pulling on my nursing bra and dress. Our lives are a lot less glamorous, but it's everything I wanted.

When I emerge the first time, I have two different shoes on, which my husband sweetly points out as gently as possible. The next time, I'm wearing different earrings, and by the time I have my hair done, I've forgotten my crown.

"It's fine," Essos assures me, placing something on my head that he pulled from somewhere. I don't know why I bothered because as soon as I take Penelope from his arms, her fingers are fisted in my hair.

"Maybe we shouldn't go."

It's not a serious comment, but I'm clutching my baby just a little tighter. It's an important day and I *want* to be there, but everything is safe here. So much has happened within these walls, but I feel a level of control I don't feel elsewhere.

We've entertained people in the house but have seldom left it. If we were smart, we would have spent the night in our apartment in Solarem, but leaving my house with Penelope always felt too big a step. It would have been good practice, but alas, it's too late for that.

"She's your best friend. We *have* to go."

I nod and step into his arms, letting him lead the way. "No, I know. I didn't mean it."

Essos pauses to cup my face, always willing to go that extra mile. "We're going to all be safe. Xavier assured me that he not only has an army of nannies there for Pom, but she will also her own regiment of guards if we need." He presses his lips to my forehead. "She can't get us or Penelope. Posey is dead."

His blue eyes sear his certainty onto my soul, and I nod. "Let's go."

In my mind, it's good we're late. We arrive just in time to take our positions at the front of the Solarem amphitheater. The open-air space is situated right on the water. Xavier looks anxious at the front of the room, wringing his hands like a nervous groom.

That day may come for Cat and Xavier, but it is not today.

Helene is seated on the other side of Essos and she holds out her hands in a give-me action. There is a question in Essos's eyes. He knows I'm not handling today well, or letting other people hold our daughter, but I have to learn, and with him at my side, I can. I nod, and he passes her to Helene, who immediately snuggles her close and inhales her sweet baby scent.

"Nothing smells better than a baby," she whispers, not even caring who hears. She turns to Kai beside her and places Penelope into his hands. My baby is small enough to fit in the palm of this giant's hands.

Essos slides his arm around my shoulders, tugging me against him. "She's okay," he assures me, and I nod.

"I know, but..."

"No buts. You did the hard part, keeping her safe for nine months. Now you can let me and the rest of us take over. Let loose. Enjoy today."

I never get a chance to say anything more because Octavia, Titus, Lairus, and Esmaray sweep down the aisle, taking their positions behind Xavier. I'm surprised to see Zara lead Sybil and Estelle to the dais, opposite the Titans. I glance around at the familiar faces in the crowd. Callie and Tink are seated with Luminara, Rafferty, and Gisella. My heartrate kicks up when I spy Galen, but Essos rubs my shoulder. It's hard not to look everywhere and see a threat, but I'm trying.

"Thanks for saving my seat," Finn jokes, dropping into the empty seat beside me. He agreed to try one of Tink's mechanical eyes. He's still scarred around his eyes, but it looks better, smoother, though still not the same. The other eye is covered by a burgundy eyepatch, which matches his tie and Dion's suit and Bria's dress.

"Always," I assure him as if that had been my intention.

Zara glows as she takes her spot. We've seen so little of her since she took her place among the Fates. On the rare times we've been able to meet, she says it's because she has so much to learn, but I'm doubtful. I expect the Fates will fall into the roles we always thought they had, watchers who don't interfere. It didn't stop Sybil and Estelle from dropping by with food one day to watch the baby for a few hours so Essos and I could get some shuteye.

Cat is the next to stride down the aisle. Her head is held high, her blonde hair hanging in loose waves down her back. She is the radiant queen we all know and expected her to be. Her dress is a soft petal pink, and with a twist of my wrist, an actual cape of petals drapes down her back from her shoulders. When she notices, she twists to give me a wink.

Xavier kept his word, not lying to the people of Solarem. They held a sparsely attended funeral for Posey and told them of the Fates and the Titans. Gisella is hard at work rewriting our history books with the truth, or something close to it.

Octavia is the first to speak, droning on about what it means to serve Solarem and what Cat's role will seek to achieve. Titus follows up with a brief history of Solarem, the old version of it, anyway.

"Do you agree to uphold the laws of Solarem and lead with grace and dignity?" Xavier asks, watching Cat and only Cat.

"I do," she confirms in a booming voice.

The corner of Xavier's mouth ticks up as she lowers herself first to one knee then bends her head forward.

"Do you agree to put the people of Solarem before all other souls?" Pleasure is slipping into his voice, and I can't help but notice how bright his eyes are as he gazes at my friend.

I squeeze Essos's knee and he gives me a small smile. If Xavier will make Cat happy, I'll be happy for them.

"I do," she practically shouts.

Xavier places the crown on her head. "Rise," he orders, and she does. "Turn and face your people."

Cat turns and looks to the crowd, who all hoot and holler at their new queen. There is still some confusion on how they are ruling but not married, but slowly the people are coming to accept and understand that this is her rightful place and Xavier won't push her into anything she doesn't want. Rumor has it, he hasn't been sleeping around since Cat moved into his house.

The crown on her head sparkles, and she slips her hand into Xavier's. There is a hesitation, a moment where he looks at their joined hands and then her lips, and I will him not to kiss her. This moment belongs to Cat, and a kiss, while romantic, will make it about them and not her and her new role. It seems to work because he guides her forward and out of the fray.

As much as I want to wait for everyone else to leave first, Essos and I are a king and queen in our own right. Essos takes a now-sleeping Penelope into his arms before walking out by my side. Helene and Kai follow us as we go to the after-party.

I HIDE as long as I can, fussing over Penelope.

"I promise if she wakes up, I can handle it," Esmaray swears.

My mouth forms a hard line. "But you don't have any actual experience with a baby. And you know we're trying to avoid using our powers with her as much as possible. We want to encourage her to do things for herself."

"Why would you do that? She uses hers on you all the time," Esmaray says with a snort after pulling a blanket over the baby's sleeping form.

Essos looks up from where he's digging in the diaper bag. "I'm sorry, what?"

"Don't tell me you haven't noticed? Oh gods." Esmaray starts laughing to herself.

"Well, spit it out," I order impatiently.

"She's the Goddess of Dreams and Nightmares. She's been forcing dreams on you since you were pregnant." Esmaray continues to laugh. "Go, enjoy the party. I've got her. If she wakes, I'll come to you immediately."

Most infants have their powers announced on their first birthday, it gives them more time to grow into their powers, but I can't remember the last time a tiny godling was born. I have to think that it's because she's a third generation Titan, the first one to be born since Kai isn't the child of a Titan, at least not that we know of. We still haven't been told more about the two Titans who stopped existing.

Of course, Penelope's bright blue eyes open, and she lets out a bloodcurdling scream. We change her, and when that doesn't work, Esmaray excuses herself so I can try to nurse. Once Penelope latches, Essos pushes a hair from my face.

"When I was out for a month, I had a dream about Nelly."

"Nope," I reject the nickname. We've been trying out different nicknames to see if one sticks. Nothing but Pom has stuck so far.

"I had a dream that she was maybe two or three and was chasing a—"

"Butterfly. I think she gave me the same one."

Essos cups her head before pressing a kiss to my temple.

Once she's burped and settled back to sleep, we emerge to find the party in full swing.

Cat runs over and throws her arms around me. "This is terrifying," she whisper-shouts at me.

Essos bites down on his smile when she pulls away to hug him too. "Congratulations," he tells her before gesturing to me that he's going to get a drink.

"This is terrifying," she repeats, glancing around the room. "I don't know what I'm doing and everyone wants something from me, and Xavier's being so *nice*. Like obsessively so. No innuendos, no posturing me for sexual favors. I don't know what to do about it."

I squeeze her hands. "He's just trying to make sure you're comfortable. Let him. You both need time to adjust to these new roles."

"I'm tired of adjusting."

"Well, the good news is, tonight you can just get blitzed and not worry about it. You don't have any responsibilities for the week because, honestly, everyone is going to be celebrating your coronation, so let loose!"

"Only if you do too. Are you pump and dumping?"

"I'm a goddess, no need. Besides, she just fed."

"Ladies," Essos greets, holding up three glasses of champagne. The three of us cheers and drink them down.

I feel lighter as I dance with my best friend and my husband. Esmaray doesn't come to get us, but I do see her around the edges of the party, holding a very awake Penelope. I'm grateful that she stays close as we step outside to play pong and Essos and I make out in a corner like teenagers.

Dawn is starting to break as our small group sits outside. To my chagrin, Essos told Esmaray to take the baby home, but it was the right call. I'm settled on Essos's lap, his hand resting on my hip as I lean into his chest.

"You never mentioned how fucking awesome it is to wear a crown," Cat says. She's also settled herself on Xavier's lap, but he's trying not to touch her, except on one spot. I can see his thumb rubbing circles on a bare spot on her thigh where the slit in her dress is.

"It's even better when you fuck wearing just that. You feel like you're queen of the fucking universe," Helene tells her, wiggling down onto her husband. Both of her brothers groan. I'm glad it's just the six of us and Galen isn't here to spoil the moment.

"Starfish, there is no reason to tell everyone what we're doing when the doors are closed," Kai chides.

"I will kiss and tell everyone my husband has a tremendous dick, and I love riding it like it's a fucking pogo stick."

"That's an image that's going to be burned into my mind until I die," Essos moans, pressing his forehead into my shoulder. I stiffen at the reminder of how I almost lost him. "I'm here, love. I'm not going anywhere," he whispers only for me.

"And on that note, we're going home," Kai announces, picking up his wife. "Congrats again."

Kai hefts Helene over his shoulder in a fireman's carry and slaps her ass. Her giggle is melodical as he strolls to the water's edge.

"Again!" she begs with a laugh before they drop into the water.

"We're going to go home too. I'll see you next week for baby time," I tell Cat as I slide from Essos's lap. I kiss her on both cheeks. "You're going to be great, and I'm always here," I promise.

Essos says his farewells before wrapping me into his arms and taking me to the place where we belong, the place where our whole lives are.

Home.

When we arrive, Esmaray slips away to let us be. We should let Penelope sleep, waking the baby is never a good idea, but I just want to hold my family close. I'm glad when I go to her bassinet to find her awake, smiling up at us.

We change her and scoop her up, bringing her into bed so the three of us can watch the sun rise. We're not alone for long as Dave, Spot, Shadow, and Waffles join us, crowding the space, but my heart is full, and I have everything I need right here.

Essos presses a kiss to my forehead, and I know that we've found the truest form of love.

ACKNOWLEDGMENTS

This book has been a true journey not just for Daphne and Essos, but for me. I've grown as an author and as a woman since Daphne first told me about a colossal fuck up she had made picking the wrong man. I cannot thank you *enough*, dear reader, for following this story all the way to the end.

I have to thank my amazing editors for seeing me through to the end. Tashya and Amanda, you are *seriously* the best editors a girl could ask for including editorial supervisors Lady, Carli, and Ringo. You brought Daphne and Esso's story to life.

To my amazing PA, Tracy, thank you for always being my safe space, my sounding board and an amazing friend.

To Brea and Harper, for managing to calm me from all of my freak outs and assuring me that what I'm feeling is normal and I'm not alone.

Thank you to Danielle for your feedback on the earliest version of this.

Michael, there are no more words for me to use to thank you. You have my eternal gratitude.

An my reader, for being amazing and for showing up. I hope I have done you proud. Thank you for following Daphne and Essos all the way to their conclusion. Thank you for hearing my tale. I love you, dear reader.

About the Author

Nicole Sanchez has been writing stories on any scrap of paper she could get her hands since before middle school. She lives in New Jersey with her high school sweetheart and love of her life along with their two quirky cats. When she isn't writing or wielding the Force, she can be found traveling the world with her husband or training for her next RunDisney Event.

For more books and updates:

Newsletter

Website

Facebook Reader Group

Also by Nicole Sanchez

Love in the Big Apple Series:

Central Park Collision

Las Vegas Luck

Madison Avenue Mediator

Game of Gods Series:

The King's Game

The Queen's Gamble

The Royal Gauntlet

Anthologies:

Billionaires and Babes Charity Anthology

Getting Witchy With It Charity Anthology